Choosing the Highlander

ALSO BY JESSI GAGE

Highland Wishes Series

Wishing For a Highlander

The Wolf and the Highlander

Blue Collar Boyfriends

Reckless

Jade's Spirit

Cole in My Stocking

Choosing the Highlander

A HIGHLAND WISHES NOVEL

Jessi Gage

To my mechanical engineer

Acknowledgements

Thank you, Julie Brannagh and Amy Raby for your brainstorming help, critiques, and company. I look forward to seeing you both each and every week. Thank you, Shane for your love and support. I couldn't do this without you. That goes for you too, Mom. Between babysitting, plotting help, proofreading, laundry, and just listening when I need to talk, you make it possible for me to follow my dream. Thank you, Piper Denna for editing this manuscript and Damonza for the gorgeous cover. You all helped me make this finished product the best it can be.

Chapter 1

CONNIE FOLLOWED HER twin sister around a chunk of rock in the hillside. Above them, the monoliths forked up into the pre-dawn sky, like prongs on the setting of a solitaire ring.

An unbidden image from two nights ago flashed in her memory: a diamond, round in cut and utterly flawless. Its two carats of tasteful brilliance winked at her from a bed of ivory satin, mocking her with the offer of all she had hoped and planned for but that she could not bring herself to accept.

It was the fault of the couple at the next table, the man who had gazed at his date with such fondness Connie's breath had stuck in her throat, the woman whose cheeks flushed every time her companion brushed his knuckles over her temple or kissed the back of her hand. The meal on their table had been incidental. Love had been the main course. Adoration had glowed around them like a halo, invisible yet impossible to miss.

I want that.

The uncharacteristic thought had sent her into an emotional tailspin. Love had not been on her list of considerations when selecting a potential mate. Her parents didn't have love, but they had everything else and they had given Connie and her sister a childhood filled with privilege and opportunity.

Give her a man who worked hard and had a head for business, like her father, a man who held the same core beliefs as she, desired the same lifestyle as she. Above all, she desired a man who would respect her choices and support her goals.

Dependability. Compatibility. Respect. Her parents had taught her these were the foundations of a solid relationship, not the shifting emotional sands of love and affection. Those things were for shortsighted fools.

Oblivious to the couple behind him, Milt had gotten down on one knee after the dessert course. His proposal flowed as effortlessly as ice wine. Of course the words came easily to him. The Chicago District Attorney's office paid top dollar to retain him as Assistant DA. Milt had many talents, producing convincing arguments foremost among them.

Connie had barely heard the proposal. Her eyes kept wandering to the loving couple.

"Wow. This place is gorgeous!" Leslie's wonder yanked Connie back to the present.

Her twin put on a burst of speed as they neared the top of the hill. Her black dress and storm-cloud gray shawl made her look like a haunting spirit as she disappeared around another bend in the trail full of switchbacks.

Connie followed, glad to put Milt's proposal out of mind.

She'd chosen sturdy sandals for the walk but wished she'd slipped into the linen slacks she'd worn on the plane yesterday. Despite their need for a good pressing, they would have offered more protection against the prickly shrubbery than her knee-length denim skirt. By the light of day, her lower legs were bound to look sunburned for all the scratches she'd endured.

Oh well. What was a little pain when Leslie was having the time of her life? It wasn't every day Connie got to enjoy her twin, who spent her days—and her trust fund—traveling to whichever remote region struck her fancy while Connie built her career in the city.

After the proposal, when the urge to flee Chicago—and Milt—had struck, Connie grabbed the postcard Leslie had sent from her latest destination and phoned the hostel where she was staying.

"Of *course*, I'd love to see you, Con!" her sister had crooned over the crackly connection. "Why don't you fly out to Scotland? If you leave now, you can make it in time for the summer solstice sunrise. Doesn't it sound completely romantic? Watching the earliest sunrise of the year from an ancient Druid site? Oh, come on, Con. Come with me. It will be so much fun!"

Getting up before dawn to hike a scrubby hill and watch the sunrise after an international flight was the furthest thing Connie could think of from fun. But it sounded preferable to hiding out in her condo and dodging Milt's calls, so she'd hopped on a plane and met her sister in Inverness yesterday evening. A few hours of sleep and a change of clothes later, and here they were, at Druids Temple, with Inverness—and breakfast—a four-mile bike ride toward the sea.

Cresting the top of the hill, she found Leslie spinning in a circle in the middle of the stone formation. Her sister had her arms spread wide and her face upturned to the velvet-blue sky, which had rolled up its carpet of stars in preparation for the coming day. It was as if she was dancing with the Earth, itself.

For all Connie knew, that could be the truth. Leslie's new passion, Wicca, involved appreciation of the Earth and other natural elements, or so Leslie had told her during the taxi ride from the airport.

Connie had to smile at her sister's exuberance. And she had to admit that the place was, in fact, gorgeous.

The circle of standing stones rose up around them like a ring of witnesses to history. How many centuries had these stones presided over the acres of rolling meadowland below? How many generations of shepherds had guided their goats and sheep under the watchful gaze of these sentinels? How many sunrises, like the one burgeoning below the rosy-orange horizon, had turned these rocks into dynamic time-pieces?

Leslie stopped spinning and faced Connie with a breathtaking smile. Her sister might color her auburn hair black and cover her slender body in dark Goth-style clothes, but she'd never been able to pull off the dispassionate air typical of her cohorts. Which was why Connie suspected the Wicca phase wouldn't last long. Just like the bohemian musician phase, the backpacking through Peru phase, and the sexual adventures in Amsterdam phase that Connie would have preferred never to have heard about.

Whoever Leslie would be tomorrow, Connie was thankful to be with her today. Leslie stretched out her hand, and Connie went to her, taking it. "I'm glad I let you talk me into this."

"Me too." Leslie lowered herself to sit with her legs crossed in the center of the stone circle, still holding Connie's hand.

She had no choice but to kneel at Leslie's side, even though it would have been more dignified to sit on the fallen log she'd spotted outside the circle. At least no one was around to see her flash the countryside before she managed to arrange her skirt. Covered, if not exactly comfortable, she settled against her sister and tried to feel as connected to the beauty all around them as Leslie seemed.

"I've missed you, sis," Leslie said, lacing their fingers together.

No one else held her hand like this. Not even Milt. But she and Leslie had clasped hands like this since childhood. There was a sweet security in it, and it underscored the unique affection they had for each other.

"I've missed you too," she told her twin, meaning it more than she could convey with words. They'd been apart too long. Connie had been working so hard at managing her current project that she'd neglected to connect with Leslie, even by phone, in more than a month.

Leslie's smile turned serious. "Don't get me wrong. I'm not complaining, but, um, I kind of doubt you came all this way just to watch the sunrise with me. What's with the impromptu vacation? Is it Milt? Did you two break up?" Her voice lifted with hope at the end, evidence of Leslie's disapproval of Milt.

Connie gave her a stern look. Then she slumped and rested her head on her sister's shoulder. "No. Worse," she admitted. "He proposed."

Leslie held herself too still. Then she nudged Connie's head off her shoulder. "Who are you, and what have you done with my sister?" Her forehead creased in confusion. "That's what you wanted, isn't it? Milt was your anti-knight-in-shining-armor. He was your ticket to—shoot, what is it you want instead of happiness? Satisfaction, right? Milt was your ticket to the satisfying life you had all engineered to perfection." She rotated her hands like she was solving a Rubik's Cube.

"Don't knock engineering," she chided. It was an old argument between them. Leslie was the artsy type and couldn't understand why Connie would want to work at all, let alone do math all day, when they each had a cushy trust fund at their disposal. Connie couldn't understand how Leslie could be content to live off their parents' money and never make any of her own, how she could flit from place to place calling no address home, how she could go through life without a solid plan.

"I'm not knocking engineering. I'm knocking Milt. Or maybe I'm knocking your whole satisfaction plan." Leslie jostled her with an elbow, taking the edge off the criticism. "I take it you didn't say yes, or you would be celebrating with Milt, not here with me."

"I didn't say yes," Connie confirmed. "I told him I would think about it."

She winced at her cowardice. After witnessing the love flowing between the man and woman at the neighboring table, her answer could only be no. But a no to Milt was a red slash in permanent ink across the plan she had spent the last few years of her life bringing to fruition.

"Think about it?" Leslie said. "Really? Oh, Con. Tell me you're going to say no."

She stared at the brightening horizon. "I should have said no already." She couldn't help noticing Leslie had gone carefully quiet. It was probably taking all her willpower not to gloat. "Go ahead," she sighed. "I believe the saying goes, 'I told you so.'"

"I would never say that. Especially when you look so miserable." Leslie's compassion brought Connie's attention to her radiant face. Everyone told them they looked just the same, but to Connie, her sister would always be the pretty one. It was more than just her hazel eyes, much more expressive than Connie's, and her easy smile. It was who she was. Caring, sweet, free-spirited Leslie. Sometimes, though she would never admit it, Connie wished she were more like her sister, able to embrace the joy of life without analyzing everything to death.

"Oh, Con." Leslie wrapped an arm around her shoulders. "I know you don't think you want happiness and love and all that 'emotional nonsense.' But I've always wanted those things for you. You deserve so much more than a life planned out in boring detail." She sat up suddenly and clapped her hands. "Oh! Oh, this is perfect!"

Just like Leslie to go from serious to excited in a heartbeat.

"What's perfect?"

Her twin bounced where she sat, gripping both of Connie's hands like when they were children and used to spin in circles until they both fell on the grass, dizzy and giggling. "You know how Daddy always says, 'Fate favors the intrepid'?"

"Yeah..." Connie drew out the word. What was Leslie getting at?

"Well, I met a shopkeeper yesterday who asked me what I would wish for on the solstice. *'Zee sunrise is a magical time, mademoiselle.—'*"

"Wait, a French shopkeeper in Inverness?" Connie interrupted.

"I know. Weird. But he had this totally magical vibe to him. I think he might be a warlock," she whispered, wide-eyed. "Anyway." She waved away the man's possibly magical properties while she dug in her backpack. "He told me a wish made from a heart that is pure will sometimes be granted on the solstice, and he gave me this." With a triumphant gleam in her eye, she lifted a necklace from her bag. It was little more than a stone on a braided rawhide rope.

"Did he sell you that? I hope he didn't charge much." It looked like a kindergartener's art project.

"He *gave* it to me," she said with wide eyes, as if this was incredible. "He said it began singing to him the moment I walked into his shop."

Connie rolled her eyes.

"It's a witch's stone," Leslie said, undaunted by her sister's lack of enthusiasm. "The hole through the middle is naturally-occurring, but no one knows the process that forms it. Stones like this are said to have magical properties. Looking through the hole is supposed to allow the owner to see into Faerie." She held the stone up to her eye and looked at Connie through the hole. "Hmm. I don't see anything unusual."

"Of course you don't. They probably manufacture them by the hundreds and sell them to tourists looking to bring home a piece of Scottish history."

"Oh, come on. Let me have my fun." Leslie spread the string like she was about to put it on, but she surprised Connie by draping it over her head instead.

"What are you doing? I don't want this." She tried dodging her sister's hands, but she wasn't quick enough. The stone settled against the sheer fabric of her shirt, cool and heavy.

Leslie shushed her. "It won't bite. I'm going to make a wish for you when the sun comes up. Maybe this will make the magic more powerful."

"Magic? For real?"

"Yes, for real." Leslie stood and spun in a circle with her arms spread. "All of this is magic. Can't you feel it? The stones? The solstice? You and me together after so long." She closed her eyes and inhaled deeply, looking completely at peace.

Connie thought about taking off the ridiculous piece of jewelry and tossing it back at Leslie, but the look on her twin's face stopped her. Indulging Leslie had always been one of Connie's weaknesses. She sighed with resignation.

"Fine. Make your wish. But why don't you make one for yourself? I have everything I want."

That wasn't exactly true. She had a successful career and wonderfully supportive parents. She had a sister she loved more than anything. But she also wanted to be married and have a family of her own. After the other evening with Milt, she realized she needed love to be a part of that, which meant she would have to completely rethink her strategy for finding a partner.

She would start with making a clean break with Milt as soon as she returned home. But that was a problem for another day. Right now, she was enjoying her sister, and she wanted Leslie to have *her* heart's desire.

"The thing I want most is for you to be happy," Leslie said, coming to her and taking her hands.

"I don't need happiness," she argued. "In fact, what I want most in life is to earn my own success. Wishes are for people who would rather get things the easy way than work hard to earn them."

Leslie blew a raspberry at her, making them both laugh. "Phooey on you," she said, echoing one of their mother's favorite comebacks. "Now be quiet while this lazybones makes her wish."

Connie shook her head, mortified that she'd inadvertently insulted her sister. "Oh, hon, I didn't mean it like that." Her energetic sister was at the opposite end of the spectrum from lazy. She might not have a job, but she applied herself to studying art and culture and making friends everywhere she went. She didn't respect Leslie less because of the choices she made. They just made it harder for her to relate to her twin.

Leslie beamed. "I know, silly. It's called sarcasm."

Connie sighed with relief. Her sister was more easy-going than she would ever be. "Gosh, I love you," she said. "All right, make your wish." She owed her sister this indulgence.

Besides, beneath all her protests and eye rolling, she was touched Leslie would use this supposedly magical moment to make a wish on her behalf. It reminded her of when Leslie used to throw pennies in fountains for luck and she would always toss in two, one for each of them.

The sun made a razor-thin neon line on the horizon. It was about to come up.

Leslie let go of Connie's hands. Raising her palms skyward, she looked like a pagan goddess with her long dress flowing around her legs and her ebony hair tangling in the summer wind. Long shadows reached toward her from the stones like supplicant fingers. The neon strip of sunlight swelled into a semicircle.

A frisson of trepidation passed over Connie, gone as soon as she'd felt it.

Strange.

She stood up and hitched her backpack into place to prepare for the hike back to where they'd left their bicycles. "Are you done yet? I seem to remember being promised a hearty Scottish breakfast in exchange for getting up so early." Her stomach grumbled with emptiness. Or was it churning with uneasiness?

Leslie didn't seem to hear her. "I call upon the good spirits," she said in a somber voice so unlike her usual brightness. "I call upon the powers that be. Receive my wish on behalf of my twin. She trusts her mind to find her mate, when it should be her heart to direct her fate. Open her eyes this day. Let her experience love as it is meant to be. Let her feel passion such as she deserves. Shower my womb-mate with your blessings. I know no more deserving soul. Let my wish be cast with the power of the sun on this holy day. So mote it be."

Love. Passion. Trusting one's heart. These were notions Connie outwardly scoffed at. But hearing them voiced by her sister in this beautiful place stirred a warm sadness inside her. It was like a ray of sun touched that most secret place where she guarded the half-formed desires she dared not fully acknowledge. In that secret place, something took root.

Leslie lowered her hands and looked back at Connie. "That felt awesome."

"Sure. Yeah." Connie's throat constricted. She cleared it and forced out, "Thanks for the wish. Ready for breakfast?"

On the heels of the question, a fist tightened inside her, right behind her breastbone—where the witch's stone rested. Dizziness crashed over her.

Impossibly, the standing stones began spinning. The sun flickered between like a headlight through the spokes of a bicycle tire. Roaring filled her ears. She had the strangest sensation that the stone circle was a cog within a vast clock made up of the Scottish countryside.

"What's happening?" She fell to her knees.

"Con?" Leslie's voice echoed faintly, like it came from a great distance. "Where'd you go?"

Connie caught a brief glimpse of Leslie's worried face before her sister's image flickered to nothing. Brilliant light overwhelmed her senses and sent shards of pain through her head.

She clapped her hands over her eyes, but it didn't stop the light from blinding her. How could that be? It was like the light was *inside* her head.

"Leslie? What's happening?" Fear had her in an icy grip.

Surely there was a rational explanation for what she was experiencing. Maybe she was having a stroke. Twenty-eight was rather young for that, but she'd heard of it happening to people in their thirties.

Leslie didn't respond.

The light faded. At first, she thought she'd gone completely blind, but after a moment's adjustment, she realized the flickering of sunlight through the spinning stones had changed to the dim orange glow of a fire. She viewed it through some sort of lattice-work. A bush without leaves.

The dizziness lifted. She found herself on hands and knees on the hard ground. It was night time. The temperature was a far cry from the balmy June morning she had been enjoying with Leslie.

A few moments ago, sweat from the hike had dampened her underarms. Now, that same sweat cooled with alarming speed. She began to shiver.

Sitting back on her haunches, she hugged herself. It felt like the dead of a damp winter. Her breath came too fast as her mind sought to make sense of her surroundings.

"Do ye hear that?"

A man's voice.

"Aye." Another man. "Unless my ears deceive me, we have a lurker beyond yon thicket."

Crisp footsteps approached. Should she run? Should she stand and make herself known? Where the heck had Leslie gone? Fear held her frozen.

"Caution, sir. May be an English spy. We are well into Perthshire by now, after all. I heard Ruthven's men have caught several since harvest."

The other man grunted.

Two dark figures appeared from around the bush. Her eyes had not yet adjusted. The only detail she could make out was that they wore bulky clothes in dark hues.

They came to a stop so close she had to crane her neck to look up at them.

She could see well enough to tell they were both bearded. And frowning.

She stood up on shaking legs. "Hello," she greeted. She attempted a smile past her chattering teeth. "I seem to have become lost."

"*Och*, 'tis but a woman."

"A woman who sounds more English than Scots. And who is oddly dressed."

"You mean partially dressed." One of the men unwound a length of fabric from around his shoulders. He started to hold it out to her.

The other man stopped him by grabbing his arm. "Halt. Might this be one of the witches the bishop has warned about?"

Their brogues were thick, but their words began to register. They were worried about her being an English spy or a witch. Logic suggested these could not be modern-day men. But that was ridiculous. Maybe she'd come across some kind of theater production.

"Mayhap. Best take her to Ruthven to be cert." The men advanced on her.

She edged backward, her breath fogging in front of her. "Look, there seems to have been a misunderstanding. I'm an American. I was just watching the sunrise with my sister. I don't know what happened or how I got here, but I'm not part of…whatever this is. I'll just—uh—be going."

One of the men said, "The sun willna rise for hours. Where is this sister of yours?"

"At Druid's Temple, outside Inverness. You know, the stones on the hill? If you just point me in the right direction, I'll find my way." Uneasiness crept up on her. Her hackles began to rise. Could she be in danger with these men?

One man sucked in a breath. "Inverness? Lass, you're four days' ride from there. Ye be in Perthshire, nay far from Sterling."

Perthshire. Sterling. These names registered vaguely. Sterling, she knew from her travel guide, was the name of the town and the castle where many of Scotland's royalty had preferred to live over the nearby Edinburgh Castle. Perthshire was probably an antiquated name for Perth, which was north of Edinburgh. She and Leslie had been planning to stay in Perth after they left their bed and breakfast in Inverness. From there, they would go on day trips to explore Sterling, Edinburgh, and any other places that struck their fancy.

The man had to be mistaken. Perth was a few hours' drive from Inverness. She couldn't possibly be in Perth. Not looking where she was going, she backed herself up against a hard surface. Her hands sought out what lay behind her. It felt like a wagon wheel.

"She speaks freely of Druids," the other man said. "And look what she wears around her neck. A hag stone."

"She must be a witch. Quickly. Bind her."

They grabbed her.

She screamed.

No one came to her rescue.

Chapter 2

WILHELM DESPISED THE cold. Yet he found the frigid atmosphere of the bailey preferable to the stifling heat and even more stifling company inside the home of the noble who had once tried to murder his mother.

At his back stood Castle Ruthven, the seat of Lord Jacob Ruthven, Baron of Perthshire. To the east and west were the Ruthven family chapel and stables. Straight ahead, to the north, was the seawall beyond which mist rose off the River Almond like icy breath.

He was surrounded by the fortress of his enemy. For only one thing would he consent to set foot in this place: his passion for justice. If he could but remember that, he would survive the evening.

He drew in a breath of air so cold it stung his throat and seared his lungs, steeling himself to reenter the great hall full of pampered nobles. There were seven parliamentarians he must convince to his way of thinking before he could consider this journey a success, and he had spoken to six thus far. Lord Turstan remained. Wilhelm had not been fortunate enough to be seated near the parliamentarian during supper, but he would find him now that the meal had ended.

Footsteps on the stairs behind him made him glance back the way he'd come. He expected to see Terran, his look-alike cousin who had accompanied him to Perth, but to his dismay, 'twas Lord Ruthven himself who approached.

Bugger. He'd hoped to avoid speaking with his host.

"I'd wondered where you'd gone off to." Ruthven clasped his hands in front of his belt as he came grandly down the steps into the bailey.

Jewels sparkled on his fingers, and the expensive dyed wool of his plaid winked indigo in the torchlight. A rabbit-fur cloak swept the stones at his feet. He'd spared no expense in his wardrobe, and he had been just as generous with the feast he had laid out for supper. No amount of grandeur and generosity, however, could hide the glint of malice in Ruthven's gaze. His actions were those of a courteous host, but his tone was one of a man who would just as soon stick a dirk between Wilhelm's ribs as invite him into his home for a meal.

Ruthven came to a halt at Wilhelm's side. "I was beginning to think you had departed before tonight's entertainment."

Would that he could quit himself of Ruthven's presence now that supper had ended, but nay. Not only did propriety demand he remain, but he refused to take leave without first securing Lord Turstan's support.

"If my lord's entertainment is half as fine as his supper, my cousin and I shall be content to remain a while yet." 'Twas a strong temptation to let sarcasm seep into his words, but he refrained. The fact remained that until Wilhelm succeeded his father, Laird Alpin Murray of Dornoch and Baron of Duffus, Ruthven would outrank him.

'Twould not do to provoke the man, especially since Wilhelm's judicial act wasn't the only thing at stake tonight. 'Twas his first gathering representing his aging father. One foot out of place and he risked vital alliances for his clan or stood to make powerful enemies. His father had trusted him to carry the mantle of the Murray. Wilhelm would not disappoint him.

"You honor me with your compliment," Ruthven said as his dinner guests made their way into the bailey. Whatever entertainment Ruthven had planned must be taking place outdoors. Odd, given the season—today was the winter solstice, the darkest day of the year, and oft one of the coldest.

Wilhelm searched among the gathering nobles for Lord Turstan's white hair and heather-gray cap. He'd sought out the parliamentarian toward the start of his journey down the coast. Turstan's home in Inverness had been his and Terran's first destination after departing Dornoch. But the earl hadn't been at home. His master of household had informed them he had left early for tonight's gathering in order to visit kin along the way. Wilhelm had hoped he might meet him on the road, but he'd seen no sign of Turstan's banner.

He didn't ken the parliamentarian well enough to suppose which way he voted on acts regarding education, but Wilhelm hoped to gain his support for the act that if passed would require all lairds in waiting to attend school from the age of nine until qualified for university. Such a law would ensure that dross like Ruthven were at least cured of their ignorance before they came to power. Unfortunately, Wilhelm knew of no possible cure for a depraved heart.

Wilhelm would speak with Turstan during their host's festivities. Then he could find Terran and quit himself of this place. An evening at an inn, and they would be free to return home.

How he missed the rolling hills of Dornoch and the scents of fertile soil and livestock. How he missed his mother and father. He longed to share with them news from his travels along the coast. His father would be pleased at the support Wilhelm had collected.

"Forgive my rudeness for not inquiring earlier." Ruthven interrupted his thoughts. "How fares your mother's health?"

Wilhelm snorted before he could stop himself. Ruthven cared about Gormlaith Murray's health only so far as he hoped to predict when the agreement struck between him and Wilhelm's father might come to an end.

Twenty-six years ago, Ruthven had imprisoned Wilhelm's mother, then a peasant maiden, on false charges. Refusing to win her freedom by marrying the corrupt lord, she had been slated for execution. Upon hearing of this injustice by way of Ruthven's boasting, Wilhelm's father had negotiated for her release.

"'Have your way, an' ye earn naught but a moment's vengeance,' I told the oily bastard." His father never missed an opportunity to relate the tale. *"'But give her to me an' I'll levy to you a tenth share of all I take in from my tenants for the span of her life. Each year she outlives your executioner's blade, you'll profit.' The greedy blight agreed, and to this day, I gladly send the silver. My lady is worth every pound."*

Three days after securing Gormlaith's release, Wilhelm's father took her as his bride. Nine months later, Wilhelm had been born.

"She is hale," Wilhelm said distractedly; he had just spotted Lord Turstan leaving the keep, leaning heavily on his cane.

"That is splendid to hear." Ruthven bared his teeth in an approximation of a smile. "Give her my regard when you return home, will you?"

"If you'll excuse me—" Wilhelm said and took his leave of Ruthven, his eye on Lord Turstan.

Terran appeared at his side as he made his way through the gathering.

"Where have you been?" Wilhelm asked as they picked their way through the growing crowd to the east end of the bailey.

Terran's mouth quirked. "Found a way to pass the time in a private nook off the kitchens. Auld Rat-bum might be a blighter, but he employs his share of bonny maids."

Wilhelm ground his teeth. "You shame our clan by carrying on wi' unwed lasses." Would his cousin never settle down with one woman?

"They arena all unwed." His cousin winked, but sobered at Wilhelm's glare. "*Och,* dinna fash. Tonight was merely a bit of fun. No thinking man would risk bringing a bairn into the home of such a foul fellow."

Wilhelm grunted.

The milling guests parted before them the way the earth made way for the blades of a plow. Wilhelm might be among the lower ranking nobles present, the mere *tainistear* and heir to a rural barony, but he and Terran stood a full head above the other guests and carried themselves like the warriors they were. Most of the other men gave them a wide berth.

The wary respect of the other nobles was a double-edged sword. It served him well on the battlefield but proved a challenge when his aim was cultivating political alliances. Some seemed to question whether he could carry a non-violent thought in his head.

A few paces shy of Lord Turstan, Terran gripped his arm. "Look, cousin." He pointed at the front of the chapel.

Wilhelm followed Terran's gaze. A stake had been erected and slabs of dry wood layered round about. Ruthven's men raced to pile tinder around a second stake.

His feet fused to the ground. *This* was the entertainment Ruthven had planned? Despicable!

"They mean to burn someone tonight," Terran said.

"Two someones."

"Enemies of the church, do you suppose, or enemies of Ruthven?"

Anger was a smoldering flint in his gut as he remembered the fate his mother had nearly suffered. "It doesna matter. If Ruthven's doing the burning, there is sure to be injustice afoot." He met Terran's eyes.

His cousin looked grim. For all his womanizing, he had a thirst for justice as strong as Wilhelm's. "Christ never called for a sinner to be burned alive," Terran said.

"No. He didna." His disciples had once, but Christ hadn't allowed them to do it.

"We must object."

He wished they could. "Nay. I promised my father I wouldna cause trouble."

If they interfered, they would lose more than the support they had gathered on this journey. Ruthven was a favorite of John Ramsay, one of the most influential lords in King James III's court. If Wilhelm angered Ruthven, he could expect to find his act stricken from the next parliament proceedings altogether. Unthinkable.

If Scotia was to survive and thrive alongside England, she needed judicial reform. If Scotia must fight England, she needed warriors who were strong and hale, not disfigured and demoralized by brutal punishments that far exceeded the severity of their crimes. Too many lairds misunderstood the law. That could be helped by passing each noble-born child through school. His act would see that done.

"We must nay offend Ruthven," Wilhelm said with regret. "But I doona wish to witness this spectacle. I havena spoken with Turstan, but an execution is nay the time to do so. Let us take our leave. We shall search for him in the village on the morrow." At worst, they would simply stop in Inverness on their return journey and wait for Turstan to arrive home.

Before they could extract themselves from the gathering, Ruthven mounted the steps of the chapel. He greeted his guests and then locked gazes with Wilhelm. "There are those among us who in their naivety extol the virtues of mercy over just punishment." He puffed his chest, drawing attention to his jewels and gold chains. Fog puffed before his mouth as he broadened his attention to the crowd at large. "'Tis a quaint notion. But one that has no place in modern, thinking society."

"Oily shite," Terran muttered.

Wilhelm agreed. "Come." He shouldered aside a man who had squeezed up front with a well-dressed lady on his arm, no doubt for a better view.

The crowd had grown thick. People grumbled at the disturbance of Wilhelm and Terran pushing their way to the stables, where they could find their horses and depart.

"As God fearing citizens," Ruthven went on, his voice an assault on Wilhelm's ears, "Crown honoring citizens, the vast majority of us understand that we who rule shall be held accountable by God for our failures to enact His justice on the Earth. Who but us will protect the common man from the greed of the thief? Who but us will guard our daughters from the rapist? Who but us will shield our impressionable young from the wiles of witches?"

As if Ruthven wasn't himself a thief and a rapist. Wilhelm knew for a fact he was. And if the man made deals with the devil for all the influence he wielded in Edinburgh, Wilhelm would not be surprised.

They were nearly to the stables when the sound of the chapel's oaken doors swinging open made Wilhelm turn around despite his reluctance to lay eyes on Ruthven's victims.

A robed clergyman and four guards escorted two prisoners to the pyres.

The first prisoner was streaked with dirt and had long, tangled hair falling over his face. He was nude and terribly thin. An urchin, mayhap? He appeared hardly to require one guard, let alone one holding each spindly arm. Poor child. 'Twas doubtful at his tender age he'd done aught to earn a death sentence, let alone one so gruesome. If Wilhelm had hated his host before, his hatred doubled now.

His gaze jumped to the second prisoner and his chest clamped with horror. Hair that gleamed like autumn-gilt leaves framed an oval face with blazing eyes. The prisoner struggled against two guards who worked much harder than the first two. The struggling resulted in brief glimpses of bare breasts and shapely legs between the bodies of the guards.

Beside him, Terran sucked in a breath. "Christ, Will. They're women."

The guards began binding the prisoners to the pyres. Someone had knotted a gag around the mouth of the auburn-haired lass. The cloth cut across cheeks the color of a rosy sunset and had worked its way between lips that refused to be tamed.

Her protests rose on the air, no less scathing for being muffled. If the situation hadn't been so dire, he would have grinned at the lass's spirit.

In contrast, the one Wilhelm had thought an urchin hung unresponsive, with face downturned and hair dangling over small breasts. Now that the guards weren't obscuring his view, he noticed the prisoner's swollen belly. *Och,* a woman with child. She was terribly undernourished. How long had Ruthven kept her locked away?

Ruthven spoke again, but Wilhelm heard naught save the pounding of rage in his ears like war drums and a fierce wind.

It comes upon me again.

Some called it bloodlust, but 'twas nothing so simple as a mindless urge to maim and kill. His mother called it berserker rage. She claimed it came from the fey blood in her family line.

Wilhelm did not doubt the origin lay outside the usual order of things, but he tended to credit his gift to God. He believed himself called as a warrior for justice. Even as a lad, he had devoted himself to protecting the weak and cutting down evil. 'Twas in his blood every bit as deeply as his urge to one day rule his father's barony.

When the holy rage came, strength welled inside him until he felt he could tear down castle walls barehanded. That strength filled him now. He could no more ignore its summons to act than he could cut off his own arm.

He looked to Terran. "They are innocent." He knew this, because his rage wouldn't have come if the women deserved what was about to happen.

"Aye." Terran nodded, resolute. His eyes glowed with rage equal to Wilhelm's. The pair of them had been called the twin blades of Dornoch since they'd matured enough to do battle. They always went together into skirmishes, and they always emerged the other side.

They both knew they were about to destroy any chance Wilhelm ever had of wielding influence in parliament.

"Create a diversion," he told Terran. "I'll stall Ruthven."

For better or worse, they went their separate ways, Terran into the stables and Wilhelm toward the pyres.

Chapter 3

CONNIE WAS LIVING a nightmare. Not dreaming. Living.

An hour ago, she had been anticipating a hearty Scottish breakfast with Leslie. Now, she had been stripped, gagged and bound, and four smelly men were manhandling her onto a stage in a torch-lit courtyard. Despite her ineffective attempts to break free, they were tying her to a stake, of all things, and in front of an apparent audience.

It reminded her of the historic accounts she'd read of the Salem witch-trials when her sister had first embraced Wicca. Connie had a sinking feeling these people wanted to burn her at the stake, a prospect as ridiculous as it was terrifying.

How can this be happening? Where am I? When am I?

Despite oceans of improbability, she seemed to have been transported into the past. By roughly five-hundred years, if her minimal cache of historical knowledge could be trusted. She'd come to this conclusion from her uncomfortable but blessedly warm position across the rump of a horse, where the two men whom she had first encountered had tied her like a sack of supplies. Not only had she overheard them arguing about a James in the context of the crown, but they had also mentioned a Queen Maggie, which must be a nickname for Queen Margaret.

Connie had briefly studied European history while deciding whether to declare her major in engineering or theater. Not having a head for dates, the exact years of the Stuart rulers eluded her, but she recalled that two Queen Margarets had been married to two King Jameses in the late fifteenth century. The only reason she remembered was that she'd gotten the question wrong on an exam.

All other possible explanations for what was happening to her had fallen away one by one as the evidence pointed to a single, reality-altering fact: the world around her wasn't the anomaly—she was.

Leslie, what have you done?

This had to be the result of her sister's wish. Somehow, Connie had been thrust back in time. Whether the cause had been the summer solstice, Druid's Temple, the necklace, her sister's good intentions or some combination thereof, she couldn't deny she'd been touched by magic.

It was too crazy to be believed. Yet here she was, fighting for her life in pre-renaissance Europe.

"Let me go!" she yelled through her gag for the hundredth time. For the hundredth time, she was completely ignored, even by the extravagantly dressed older man who had addressed the crowd in a brogue so thick she could barely make out what he'd said.

She'd tried offering her original captors a bribe since she'd had some Scots currency in her backpack, but they'd merely stolen her bag and handed her over to a robed man in a stone building they called a kirk. She'd tried threatening action by the U.S. Embassy. This earned her a slap by the robed man, who told her she could take her threats with her to the fiery pit of hell. She had tried to fight the men dragging her to the stake, but the only fruits of her labor were a gag and chafed wrists.

She couldn't think of anything more to do, but she couldn't just give up. It wasn't only her life at stake but another woman's too, one who looked to be in much worse shape than she.

The other woman seemed young, maybe still in her teens, and she was dangerously underweight and very pregnant. Connie wished she'd been able to speak with her, but there had been no opportunity before the men had gagged her.

When a robed and hooded man came toward her with a lit torch, the temptation to lose hope made her stomach shrivel. She shook her head. "No, please don't," she said through her gag. "I've done nothing wrong."

The crowd murmured.

The older man who seemed to be in charge nodded at the hooded man.

Oh, God. He was lowering the flame to the tinder at her feet.

She ramped up her struggling. What she wouldn't give for that knight in shining armor she'd always told Leslie didn't exist.

"Halt!" A clear voice rang through the silence as a tall man with impossibly broad shoulders leapt onto the platform.

The hooded man froze. Flames swirled around the tip of his torch inches from the wood. It was so close, she could smell the burning tar and feel its heat on her shins.

"What are the charges against these women, Ruthven?" The man was seriously huge. He topped six feet, and it had to be more than just the leather armor making his shoulders appear so wide. He had blond hair cut in a tidy Roman style, and his eyes were a blue so pale, they seemed to glow with silver light as he prowled toward the man who had addressed the crowd—Ruthven, apparently

The rope was thick and her wrists were bleeding, but hope filled her with the strength to keep testing her bonds.

"The charge is witchcraft," Ruthven replied. "This one requires no trial." He nodded at Connie. "My men witnessed her magic. She brought flame to life in the palm of her hand in an attempt to escape their custody. Furthermore, she was found wearing a hag stone, and in her sack she hides a music box that plays satanic chants. Furthermore, she must be a spy since she carries foreign currency and odd books with renderings of our land's most strategic forts, some shown in ruins! As for the other, she has been tried fairly and condemned to a spirit purging for her sins, not the least of which, as anyone can see, is fornication."

Connie made eye contact with the blue-eyed man. "Help me!" she cried past her gag. "Those things aren't magical! I'm not a spy!"

His furrowed brow showed he couldn't make out her words. "Seems to me, the lass would like to answer the charges. Has she been given this right?"

She shook her head vehemently.

Ruthven sneered and started to argue, but the blue-eyed man shoved past him. Towering over Connie, he held up a knife.

She shook her head harder and yelled, "Don't hurt me! I'm innocent!"

The knife shot toward her face.

She cringed. The gag tightened like someone had grabbed it. A moment later, it fell away. The blue-eyed man had sliced it off her.

She met his eyes, like twin pilot lights glowing with the potential to burn everything in their path. Something strange happened in her chest, a tightening like someone had twisted up her insides. She licked her lips. They were numb from cold and chafing.

"Thank you," she said. Then she glared at Ruthven. "That wasn't magic, you idiot. It was a lighter. Inside the compartment is a flammable fluid that ignites when you make a spark with the wheel. The book is a simple travel guide. I'm not a spy. I'm just on vacation. And if that girl is a witch, I'm Nancy Reagan. I don't care what she's supposed to have done, and I don't care what godforsaken year this is. You can't just burn people!"

Anger filled her limbs with heat until she barely registered the cold.

Ruthven pointed at her and sputtered, "Hear that? With her own mouth, she forsakes God! She's the devil's whore! Burn her!"

The crowd shouted their gleeful approval—blood thirsty barbarians, one and all. The man with the torch lowered it to the kindling around her feet.

"No!" she cried as the fire caught.

The blue-eyed man started kicking away the tinder, but three guards converged on him. He reached over his shoulder like he would grab a weapon, but his hand closed on nothing but air. He growled what must have been a Gaelic curse and took a stance like he intended to fight the guards barehanded while they brandished swords at him.

The man with the torch lit the logs at the other woman's feet.

Enough kindling remained at Connie's feet that smoke billowed around her, black and clotted with ash that singed her nostrils. "Stop!" she tried to say, but racking coughs stole her speech as the smoke stole her view of what was happening with the blue-eyed man. Her feet were hot. From the freezing cold or from the fire, she couldn't tell.

She was going to be burned alive.

"What will you take for her?" the blue-eyed man yelled. "We'll strike a bargain for her life!"

Ruthven's cruel laugh met her ears. "Oh, no. I've let a Murray buy my prisoner once before. This time, I think it shall please me more to let God's justice run its course."

"This is not justice!" the warrior bellowed.

The song of a blade slicing through air cut through the fog of darkness around her. Then fists hitting flesh. The blue-eyed man was fighting for her.

That was so unexpected. So heroic.

Of course, it didn't improve her odds by much, since he was a single man facing so many. Still, as her vision pixelated and she gasped for air, she found herself oddly comforted. If she had to die away from her family and her time, at least someone was upset about the fact.

She only hoped he didn't get too badly hurt for her sake. The thought of punches landing on that clean-shaven jaw stirred a fierce instinct to life in her heart. Pity she wouldn't get to explore the feeling, since her body was growing heavy and tingly, and she was clearly about to pass out.

Memories of Leslie's carefree smile made her descent into unconsciousness rather pleasant. *Sorry, Sis. It was a nice wish, but it didn't quite work out.*

§

"Took you bloody long enough!" Wilhelm shouted as Terran tossed him the double-edged battle axe he'd been forced to place in Ruthven's armory before entering the keep.

Terran leapt from his warhorse to cross swords with one of Ruthven's guards. "You can thank me later for my brilliant diversion."

Terran's diversion had been a cart he must have found behind the stables. Some noble must have been preparing to depart, because the two horses were already tacked and the cart loaded with trunks. Terran had lit the cargo on fire and sent the horses galloping into the bailey. The flaming cart had scattered the crowd most efficiently.

In the confusion, Terran had ridden his warhorse onto the platform, sliced the bonds of the pregnant lass and lifted her onto his saddle. Now the poor girl clutched the gelding's mane, looking bewildered, while the beast pranced and kept an eye on Terran, who jumped down to join Wilhelm in fighting Ruthven's guards. Two more men stood between him and the woman he would rescue or die trying to defend.

He didn't ken how Terran had managed to obtain the weapons they had been required to surrender to Ruthven's house master upon being admitted to the keep—mayhap that maid from earlier had helped. As Wilhelm swung his axe to relieve a guard of his sword hand, he resolved never to scold Terran for his dalliances again.

It had not been his intention to skirmish with Ruthven when he came to Perth—in fact, this was the opposite of what he'd intended—but he couldn't deny the satisfaction that fueled his strength as he cut down his enemy's men in battle. Notably, Ruthven, who was the same age as Wilhelm's father, had retreated into his keep with his guests. The Murray was aging, but even so, he would have fought with his men if his very keep were under siege.

Ruthven's idea of justice was a perversion. Even if Wilhelm brought misery on his clan for opposing the blackhearted baron, he did not regret making this stand. He and Terran were in the right by defending these women.

Mayhap none in attendance here would care, but in the larger scheme of things, all that mattered was that God approved. This Wilhelm knew in his heart, and so he indulged his battle lust.

His fervor might also have somat to do with the bonny lass tied to the stake. He'd been mesmerized as she'd spoken in her defense and in the defense of her fellow prisoner. Even though he'd scarcely understood her queer speech, he'd known she spoke true. Her brave spirit steeled his determination to help her.

She had stirred other things in him as well, softer things that had no place in battle. He would consider those things further when they were well away from Perth.

As he fought, he'd managed to kick most of the wood away from the base of her stake. She was no longer in danger of being singed. But when her coughing came to a shuddering stop, he worried the smoke had overcome her. He must free her soon and get her away to help cleanse her lungs. Failing her was unthinkable. If he must fight a hundred men to get to her, he would emerge victorious.

With Terran's help, he reached the lass and sliced her bonds. She slumped into his arms.

Fear rarely penetrated his battle lust, but he felt fear now, for her. She was too still, too cold, and too pale. He sheathed his axe and ducked through the smoke with her cradled in his arms.

At the mouth of the stable, he found his warhorse, Justice, dancing on a tether. Truly, Terran had moved quickly to ready both their mounts and retrieve their weapons. If Wilhelm hadn't been cert already that he would one day make Terran his second, this night would have confirmed his decision.

But first, he must see them safely from Ruthven's lands. And he must find a way to keep them safe as Ruthven would no doubt seek retribution for this flagrant act of rebellion. That meant no matter how his heart longed for home, he must not return to Dornoch, for that would be the first place Ruthven would look.

Cradling the lass on his lap, he wrapped her in his plaid and took up the reins. As he raced from the bailey, Terran came up alongside him. He held the pregnant lass in front of him in the saddle. The poor thing looked barely alive as her head lolled on his shoulder. Together, they galloped past the seawall and along the River Almond. They must get well away from Perth before they could tend to their charges.

To Wilhelm's great relief, he heard no hoof beats behind them.

"I jammed the stall doors, and set fire to the tack room," Terran said.

Wilhelm grinned. Since the stables were stone, the fire would not easily spread. It would cause confusion and slow Ruthven's pursuit, but wouldn't harm the horses. "Well done, cousin."

"Where will we go? What will become of the women?" Terran kept his eyes straight ahead, but Wilhelm didn't miss the way he clung to the frail female.

They both understood what they'd done. In the eyes of the law, they had obstructed justice and instigated a skirmish. They would be considered fugitives until they could speak in their own defense.

No doubt, Ruthven would bring the case to a noble he had an alliance with, which would put them at a disadvantage unless they found their own magistrate to give a confession to, one who would understand why they'd done what they'd done and rule with leniency.

"We'll hide them," Wilhelm said. "Then we shall send a message to my father. He'll send Kenrick to aid us."

Kenrick was second in authority in Dornoch. He advised Wilhelm's father and had a knowledge of the crown and parliament that had largely inspired Wilhelm's interest. If anyone could steer them clear of consequences, 'twould be Kenrick.

They slowed their horses to veer west. Ruthven would expect them to go north, toward the ferry and toward home, but Wilhelm knew of a place in the northern farmland of Perthshire where they could seek refuge.

Terran gave Wilhelm a worried look. "If he doesna disown you for this spectacle."

His father would never disown him. But he was sure to be furious. "Do you regret it?" he asked, kenning his loyal cousin would bravely face the laird's wrath by his side.

Terran gazed at the woman in his lap. "Nay, cousin."

Wilhelm gripped his charge tightly. Her stillness troubled him. "Neither do I."

Chapter 4

CONNIE HURTLED INTO consciousness with a scream that ravaged her throat. She doubled forward to slap at the flames burning her legs. But there were no flames. There was only darkness and the heavy, hot sensation that her feet had been inserted into an oversized toaster.

Recollection steamrolled her. The fire. The warrior who had tried to buy her then fought for her. Losing consciousness believing she would never see Leslie again.

She clutched at the blankets as she sat up in an unfamiliar bed. Her heart pounded so hard it echoed in her ears. Where was she? Where was the warrior?

He must have succeeded in rescuing her, since she appeared to be alive. She waited to feel rankled that she'd needed rescuing, but she only felt grateful.

It took a moment of blinking into darkness for the gravity of her situation to reassert itself. Heavens. She'd somehow been transported to the distant past. She'd almost been burned to death.

Her hands sought out her singed skin under the blankets. Hot. But not blistered. Her wrists were bandaged. Their aching reminded her of the ropes. A sore spot at the back of her neck marked the place where her skin had broken when her captors ripped Leslie's witch's stone from her. All minor injuries. It could have been a lot worse.

Footsteps sounded nearby. She followed the sound with her gaze and noticed a strip of light on the floor that hadn't been there a moment ago. That must be the door to whatever room she was in. Someone was on the other side.

She became acutely aware of her nakedness beneath the covers. But never mind that. Whatever she'd been through, she must put it behind her and concentrate on getting home. She was a long way from Druid's Temple in 1981, and no knight in shining armor was going to help her get back. In this, she instinctively knew, she was on her own.

She would have to be smart about how she spoke and acted. An American accent and her modern ideas on women's roles weren't going to cut it in fifteenth-century Scotland. Her experience with her captors had proven as much.

She didn't usually approve of dishonesty, but desperate times called for desperate measures. She must pretend to be a well-bred woman in need of escorting to Inverness. From there, she could find her way back to Druid's Temple. Surely the ancient site would be on the hill outside of town, just as it had been—or as it would be—in 1981. If she found those stones, she might be able to find her way home. Unless the key to the magic was the witch's stone…or the summer solstice. Or Leslie.

Gulping down her nerves, she focused on the moment. Since she would never be able to pull off subservience, no matter how well she'd done in acting classes before she had declared her major in engineering, she decided to keep her take-charge attitude. She would just temper it with politeness. She could pretend to be a noblewoman or something. Yes, that should do.

"Who's there?" she called out, attempting an upper-crust British accent. Unfortunately, her smoke ravaged throat didn't cooperate. The words came out in a croak, and a barrage of painful, bronchial coughs followed.

The door flew open, and the blond warrior rushed in.

"Easy, lass." He set down a candelabra and came to the bed. Bending her forward, he supported her with an arm under her breasts. Using his other hand, he rubbed circles on her back.

The coughs kept coming and her throat felt like gravel, but the secure hold the warrior had on her kept her from rattling apart at the seams. Her face heated from the exertion, and she worried she wasn't taking in enough air. She might pass out again.

No. She would have no say in what happened to her if she lost consciousness. She'd surrendered enough control since being dragged into this place and time. Calling on her will, she suppressed the coughing enough to suck in the smallest trickle of air. It couldn't possibly be enough, but it was all she could get.

"That's it. Easy. Slow, shallow breaths. 'Twill take time for your lungs to recover."

The warrior had a soothing burr to match his comforting touch. His voice helped focus her concentration. She kept fighting for each insubstantial breath while he whispered encouragements.

Such a difference in him since she'd last seen him, decked in armor like armadillo skin, teeth bared, eyes throwing off sparks. She'd wondered whether his shoulders truly filled out the protective gear he'd been wearing that night or if like some of her coworkers, male and female alike, his uniform had been designed to exaggerate his size. Now she had her answer.

Gone was his kilt and armor. He now wore a quilted, belted pourpoint of burgundy brocade, the garment that would protect him from the hard joints of his armor. For the college-age guys she'd taken theater classes with, a good pourpoint could make them look like a million bucks. In Wilhelm's case, *he* made the garment look like a million bucks. Buttons stacked one on top of the other fastened it from his throat to where it terminated at mid-thigh. Below the embroidered hem, off-white leggings hugged his well-muscled legs all the way down to shoes of leather that appeared butter-soft. Even with her limited knowledge of historical dress, she understood that peasants of this time wouldn't have access to dyed fabrics and tailored fashions of this quality. She couldn't help being impressed.

It had escaped her attention until just then that the blanket she clutched to her chest didn't cover her back. The warrior's warm hand caressed her skin as his burr caressed her ears.

Someone who spoke and handled her so gently probably didn't intend her harm. Still, she must be careful. He treated her gently now, but how gentle would he be if she asked him the date or if he saw the things in her backpack that had condemned her in the eyes of her accusers?

If she wanted to return home, she couldn't afford mistakes. She couldn't afford to become distracted by the butterflies assaulting her stomach when she met the warrior's gaze.

Attraction wouldn't help toward her goal, so she ignored it. She would be wise to focus on this man's decency, not his rugged good looks. He'd rescued her. That meant he had some sort of morals. Capitalizing on that would be her first order of business.

In her career, she earned the respect and cooperation of her male peers by being all business, and giving no quarter. If she played her cards right, she could do the same here using her adopted persona. She'd have this man tripping over himself to help her in no time.

She opened her mouth to take control of the situation and ask how long she had been unconscious, but at that very moment a slender man dressed all in black except for a white cloth on his head entered the room. Lines around his eyes and mouth suggested he was much older than the warrior, but when he aimed a smile her way, years melted off his face.

"Thank ye, Father Anselm," the warrior said, taking a cup from the older man.

He's a monk. They must be in a monastery.

The warrior brought the cup to her lips.

38

She was so parched she didn't care what was in it. She drank deeply. Cool liquid eased the tightness of her damaged tissues. Water, clean and nourishing. She emptied the cup, sputtering only a little, while the warrior spoke with Father Anselm.

Their exchange was too rapid for her to follow. She picked out a few words, but their Scots dialect was even more mystifying to her than that of the locals she'd interacted with in modern-day Inverness. It was the English language, but accented so differently it might as well have been another tongue.

The words that stood out to her were "other lass" and "bairn," which she thought meant baby.

She gasped, remembering the pregnant woman. "Where is she?" she asked the warrior. "The other woman. Is she all right?" Her voice was croaky, but it would have to do.

"*Whist.* Doona speak." He slowed his speech when addressing her, making him much easier to understand. "Your lungs have been abused and will require rest. 'Tis but a few hours since we arrived. Ye canna tell from this windowless room, but 'tis early morn'. Have ye some spirits and bread?" he asked the monk.

Anselm left, presumably to get something alcoholic for her, which she had no intention of refusing. Hopefully, he would bring some meat as well as the bread the warrior had mentioned. Her stomach felt so hollow it ached. She'd never gotten that breakfast she'd been looking forward to with Leslie, and it felt like a whole day had passed since then, although her sense of timing could be off after losing consciousness.

When the door closed behind Anselm, the warrior returned his attention to her. An angry bruise with a scabbed-over cut marred his cheek. What other injuries had he sustained? Why did it upset her to see him battered?

The bruise didn't detract from his impeccable handsomeness. The light of the candelabra gilded the pleasing angles of his face. His short hair had been combed and his smooth cheeks suggested a recent shave. She could look at this man for hours, study him like a priceless sculpture and envy the artist whose hands had touched him intimately enough to create such rugged beauty.

Connie had chosen to pursue Milt in large part because he was handsome and particular about his appearance. But looking at Milt had never made her insides burn with embers of attraction like they did now, in the presence of this masculine work of art.

So much for ignoring your attraction, Connie girl. Hard to ignore something so visceral.

This warrior carried himself in a way that resonated with her on a base level. He possessed an air of brutal masculinity that no modern-day corporate ladder climber could hope to match. Never in a million years would she have expected to be drawn to a man for his unapologetic maleness and his superiority at something as barbaric as warfare. A man like this had never been part of the plan for her life.

Still wasn't.

And yet, she couldn't look away from him. His eyes glinted like silver, almost like they radiated an unearthly inner light, which must, of course, be a trick of the candles and the man's unusual eye color.

She had the strangest feeling those eyes could see more than she wanted to reveal. For an instant, she welcomed the notion. She wanted to speak the truth and only the truth. It would be liberating.

Then she remembered herself. She couldn't tell him the truth. She would be wise to avoid speaking much at all, let alone asking the biggest question on her mind: the date. He would think she was nuts. Why had she entertained the thought of confessing everything, even for an instant?

His gaze flickered, and his lips quirked, giving her the impression he had just accepted a challenge. When he rose to his full height to tower over her, she missed his nearness. She also steeled herself to take control of the situation before he did, because she didn't like that look in his eye one bit. She'd seen that same look too many times from her coworkers. It often preceded an attempt to distract her from her goal or to railroad her before she could achieve it.

"You never answered my question," she said in a flawless British accent despite the scraping rawness of her throat. "How is the other woman?"

"I'll be the one making queries, lass. And you'll cease this nonsense. You're no' English."

Her heart stumbled around in her chest. He couldn't know that—unless he remembered the way she'd spoken last night. But there had been so much chaos, and she had been panicked. Surely she could convince him there was nothing unusual about her if she committed to the lie.

"How dare you insult me by questioning my nationality?" She kicked at the bedding until she could climb out with a blanket wrapped around her for modesty. Her feet burned and she trembled with weakness, but she stood toe to toe with him.

He was half a foot taller, and he didn't back up a single inch, even though they were practically close enough to waltz.

"Sit down," he commanded.

"I will not. You have no authority over me." The refusal came to her swiftly. Caution kicked into gear a second later. She sucked in a breath. Had she gone too far? Had she dropped the accent? Oh, no. She had. *Great job, Connie girl. Good thing you didn't pursue acting after all.*

The warrior scooped her up so fast she didn't have time to react. The throbbing in her feet instantly eased, and the secure way he held her made her want to curl up against his chest and sob out all her fear and uncertainty. When she was near this warrior her innermost, secret thoughts seemed closer to the surface.

What was happening to her? Men never affected her this way. Even Milt, whom she'd been with for years, hadn't made her skin tingle and her heart leap with giddiness at his touch. He hadn't made her want to confide in him and trust him with her weaknesses.

The warrior laid her gently in the bed and remained over her, feet on the floor, hands planted in the bedding on either side of her shoulders.

Kiss me, she thought ridiculously. Her nipples tightened and her body softened beneath the blankets.

"I shall speak, and you shall listen," the warrior said with authority.

Somehow, she understood this was not a man she could manipulate by pretending to be something she was not. In fact, as she met his gaze, she felt a fool for the charade.

"The young lass is in the next room," he said.

Thank heavens. The pregnant woman hadn't been left behind. Connie determined to concentrate on the poor girl's plight rather than her body's reaction to the warrior's closeness.

"She wasna touched by the fire, but she is in poor condition. I doubt she has the strength to deliver her bairn, but my cousin is determined to see her through it. My guess is it'll be happening any day now."

The poor thing. "Is there anything I can do?"

"Terran and Anselm are doing all that can be done. Your duty here is to rest and heal."

Anselm was the monk. Terran must be the cousin. She began slotting bits of information into categories. The more data she had, the more sound her decisions would be. She added knowledge of Anselm and Terran to her cache along with their location, which was either Perth or not far from Perth, since travel in this time would be limited to walking and riding horses.

"My name is Wilhelm Murray," the warrior said, pronouncing the Germanic name with only the slightest hint of an initial *V*.

That tidbit fell into a slot too: the name of her rescuer…and the first man who had ever made her stomach tighten pleasurably upon entering the room.

"Son of the Murray," he went on. "My father is Laird and Barron of Dornoch. You will be telling me your name when I ask for it, and you willna attempt to lie to me. Understand?"

Being presumed a liar rubbed her the wrong way—even though she had attempted to lie, in a roundabout way, with that British accent. Making matters worse, her body's reactions to him were amplified when he dictated orders to her. Never had she found *that* particular characteristic attractive in a man before. Attempting to boss her around was a sure way for a man to become the recipient of a Dear John letter. Milt had understood that. It was one of the reasons they were so well suited to one another.

"Understand?" he pressed when she flattened her lips instead of responding.

Did the man have a lie detector hidden under his pourpoint? *No, don't think about his clothing or what it might conceal.*

She couldn't tell the truth because he would never believe her. She couldn't lie because she couldn't afford to make an enemy of him, especially when he'd rattled off some impressive sounding credentials—and apparently she wasn't as good an actor as she'd thought, because he'd seen right through her.

Not knowing what else to do, she nodded. Hopefully, he wouldn't ask more than her name.

Wilhelm lifted his chin. All at once, he projected arrogance and pleasure at her capitulation.

The look should have infuriated her. Instead, it made her oddly aware of her nakedness beneath the blankets, and the awareness was far from unpleasant.

He dropped his gaze to her mouth for a split second. "Since you've suffered damage from the smoke, I shall ask naught of you until the morrow—" Oh good, she'd have the night to figure something out. "Naught save that ye listen."

That she could do. The more information she gathered, the better.

"I have gone to considerable trouble to rescue you from Ruthven," he said. She remembered the bearded man with a churning of her stomach. "We both ken ye would have died, so let us not pretend otherwise."

She felt her lips thin. Did he have to remind her of her helplessness? Unfortunately, he was completely right. If not for him, she wouldn't be here right now. She should be thankful to be anywhere, in any time. She was alive, after all. Her mouth softened.

The warrior glanced at it again. "Here is how you shall be thanking me, lass."

She held her breath. Would he command her to sleep with him? She kind of hoped so. She'd tolerated sex with Milt, but had never really enjoyed it, viewing it as a way to show she valued him and to ensure his faithfulness. Wilhelm made her suspect there could be more to sex than a sometimes pleasant but more often awkward rubbing of body parts.

"Who are you, and what have you done with my sister?" Leslie's teasing words from Druid's Temple came back to her. True, her reaction to Wilhelm was extremely out of character. But goodness, she'd been through an ordeal. She had a right to have sex with a stunning warrior if she wanted to. Didn't she?

Her loyalty to Milt flickered faintly at this surprising desire. She hadn't exactly broken up with him. Maybe sex would be a bit much. Still, if Wilhelm demanded it, she just might comply.

"First, you shall regain your strength," he went on. "Then you shall aid in the birthing of the child. When that is done, you shall travel with me and Terran to Inverness, where we shall all three of us give sworn testimony as to your mistreatment by Ruthven and his men."

Mistreatment. What a civil way to put what happened to her. She'd been kidnapped, robbed, assaulted, and nearly murdered. Wait. Had she heard him correctly? "We're going to Inverness?" That's exactly where she needed to go.

"Aye. With luck, our testimony will counter any charges Ruthven sets against my cousin and I and cause the man to have a care next time he takes it into his head to harm innocent women for the amusement of his guests."

That's all? What about a kiss? Or sex?

Wilhelm glowered at her as if he expected her to argue. Apparently, he was finished listing his terms.

"All right." She was happy to do everything he'd asked and oddly disappointed he hadn't asked for more.

She would do what Wilhelm asked. Then they would part ways, he and his cousin Terran to wherever they lived and she to Druid's Temple, and from there hopefully home. The trick would be evading questions on the way.

"That's a good lass." Wilhelm nodded with satisfaction. "Now that that is settled." He cupped her face in a large hand and kissed her.

Chapter 5

MERCIFUL LORD IN heaven. This woman tempts me like no other.

Wilhelm had known her less than a full day. In that time she had attempted to lie to him. She had destroyed any chance of success his judicial act had ever possessed by falling into the hands of his most vicious enemy. And yet, this mating of mouths, of breath, and of wills erased every kernel of annoyance she had caused him.

Unable to keep his distance from her any longer, he'd taken her lips the way he'd longed to since entering the room to find her awake and more lovely than a heather-dressed meadow. He pressed his mouth to hers while she lay beneath him in naught but bed linens, fully expecting her to protest, for surely a lass so bonny and brave must belong to someone.

But she did not protest. Rather, she met him movement for movement as if this kiss had been written in ancient scrolls of prophecy, and they merely carried out the plan.

Her hand shaped to his shoulder, welcoming him closer. Her acceptance of his advance thrilled him to his core.

He was only too happy to heed her summons. A frisson of carnal delight lengthened his cock beneath his plaid as he pressed her more snugly to the bed. She gasped into his mouth, and her legs parted to accommodate his knee.

"Aye," he whispered. "That's a good lass. Open for me now."

How brazen he was! Never before had he grown this heated with a lass. He prized his control as well as he prized his position as heir to his father's seat. But this woman made him lust for indulgences he'd thought himself too disciplined for.

He stroked the corner of her mouth with his thumb, and to his astonishment, she flicked it with her tongue and parted her lips in an invitation he wasted no time accepting. It occurred to him she might think to manipulate him with her affections, but no. He sensed truth in her kiss. And he saw surprise in her eyes suggesting that, like him, she did not normally behave in this manner.

She would have him believe her to be from the south, from England, but he'd recognized the lie in an instant. Not only had he noticed a difference in her speech at the abbey compared to yester eve at Ruthven's, but like his father, he had a knack for distinguishing truth from lies. *Truth sense,* his mother called it. She claimed 'twas a remnant of their fey ancestry like the battle lust, which she insisted made him a berserker like his father. Wilhelm tended to side with his father, who attributed their abilities to good instincts passed from laird to laird.

Whatever the origin of his truth sense, he'd felt it powerfully when she'd been bound upon Ruthven's pyre, proclaiming her innocence. He felt it just as powerfully now, as her body communicated to him more clearly than any words a truth growing between them: they were meant for each other.

Her eyes closed as their kiss deepened, but he kept his open. He would not waste a single moment of appreciating her novel beauty. Her hair ranged in shade from dark honey to red rock, and when her eyes were open, he saw in them every earthy color under the sun, streaks of sea green, palest gold, rich loam, and sky blue. Hazel, the color was called. Too simple a word for the complexity he had never noticed until her. He could watch her for days, nay years, and still long to watch some more.

He didn't even ken her name.

Terran would have no qualms about committing such an intimate act with a near stranger, but Wilhelm was not Terran.

Cursing himself for his lack of control, he lifted his face from hers. Just in time, too, as his father's former schoolmate chose that moment to return with somat for her to eat.

She panted silently and touched trembling fingertips to her lips as he put a respectable distance between them. When she opened her eyes, her gaze lingered on him like a caress before acknowledging the abbot's presence.

Aye. She felt it too, this connection between them.

Anselm deposited a tray on the table next to the candles and slipped out without comment, even though it had to be evident what Wilhelm had been about before he'd come in. He would not be surprised if the abbot chided him later. For now, he was content to give his full attention to his charge.

"Tell me your name," he commanded. He would ken whose lips he'd been sipping at.

Her eyes flashed in that way of hers that told him she didn't make a habit of following orders.

Och, her brazen spirit drew him from the moment he first saw her, when she'd been demanding Ruthven release her despite being bound, gagged, and outnumbered, not to mention completely bare. Such bravery! Such intrepid determination!

"You told me no questions tonight." Her voice scratched like sun dried wool not yet tamed into softness. The damage to her tender throat and lungs made him lust to slay her abusers all over again. Noticeably absent was her feigned English speech.

He suppressed a grin, wondering if she'd done it intentionally. "Simply telling me your name would have required fewer words than the rebuke, my lady, if your throat pains thee."

"It wasn't a rebuke." A look of affront tugged her eyebrows low over those captivating eyes.

How was it her every expression affected his viscera? With each change in her features, his stomach leapt and dove like a hawk in pursuit of prey.

"Only a reminder." The briefest flicker of nervousness belied the stubborn lift of her chin.

The kiss had made her uncertain. Before, she'd approached him as an adversary, though why she should do so, he could not guess. Now, she recognized the connection between them, but, if he guessed correctly, she feared it.

The lass needed time. She needed food and rest. He would ask no more of her for now. Not even her name. It mattered not. His heart knew her regardless of what she called herself.

"Consider me reminded, sweet lady." He inclined his head in farewell. "Good rest to you, then. Until later." He brought the tray to her bed. The monks serving in the kitchen this morning had prepared parritch, buttered bread and ale. The pale color of the drink suggested it was the second brew, from which the monks themselves partook, rather than the stronger first brew they sold to fund their order.

Once Wilhelm cleared his name and could bring her to Dornoch, he would have a feast prepared for her at every meal. He would serve her fine French wine instead of weakened ale. He would dress her in gowns and drape her in gems. His father would marry them. Mayhap by this time next year, he'd have a bairn with her.

If he could clear his name. Otherwise, all his dreaming would be for naught.

"Wait."

Her voice made him pause at the door.

"Thank you," she said. "For—" She cleared her throat. "Rescuing me." The proud lass disliked the fact she'd needed rescuing. "And it's Constance. My name is Constance." Her gaze lowered before rising up to challenge him once more. Rosy color bloomed in her cheeks.

She'd given him a gift. Not just her gratitude and her name, but a wee bit of her trust and formidable will. If he lusted to secure her affections, he sensed he must be tender with her. The realization came as a shock. Never would he have imagined he would crave a willful woman at all, or that he would relish taming such a woman with gentleness.

Like a spirited filly.

"Constance," he repeated, liking the sound of the syllables as well as the meaning, steadfast, permanent. His father's favorite request from the bard came to mind. *My Constant Rose.*

Aye, she would be his steadfast lady, the permanent complement to his life. But only if he could provide her with the security his position as heir to a barony and lairdship offered. As it stood, he would be accountable for killing Ruthven's guards and executioner unless a magistrate ruled his actions had been justified. If he obtained no such ruling, he could lose far more than an act of parliament.

"Rest, now," he told her, and he left to find Terran and check on the other woman. Every step away from Constance pulled taut places low inside him. His very bowels objected to his leaving her.

Och, he had better set things right in Inverness. Because it was just a matter of time before he took what he knew to be his, regardless of the consequences.

§

CONNIE HAD NEVER been more grateful for bland oatmeal. She chewed the mixture, which was like grainy bread moistened with milk, and washed it down with warm beer weak on the hops but strong on the malt. Not a bad meal, all in all. It certainly did the trick of sating her hunger.

Testing her legs, she slipped out of bed to place the tray back on the dresser. Putting weight on her feet made them feel like sausages someone had forgotten to prick before cooking. The pain-pressure made her clench her teeth. She'd lain out in the sun too long one time at Lake Michigan with high school friends. The pain the next day had been similar to what she felt now. Maybe that meant her injuries were on par with a bad sunburn. One could hope, anyway.

A knock sounded at the door.

"Come in." Her voice still rasped, but she could use it without coughing.

The monk Wilhelm had called Father Anselm entered, smiling kindly. "I've brought a salve for your burns," he said, handing her a shallow jar.

The substance inside reminded her of the bacon fat her grandmother used to keep in a can under the kitchen sink.

"How are you feeling?" He spoke slowly enough that she could understand him despite his thick brogue. Did he wear his hair tonsured under that white handkerchief? What was it like to be a monk in Scotland in…whatever year this was?

She had better not ask any questions if she wanted to fly under radar, so to speak.

"Better. Thank you, Father." Instinct had her return to the English accent. For some reason, she only felt comfortable speaking naturally with Wilhelm, and only him because he somehow saw through this precaution.

Anselm seemed to accept her accent, so she carried on with it as she took the jar and unwrapped the linen cover. A round slab of cork served as the jar's cover. There was a date written on the cork. "Fourteen eighty-two," she read, stunned. She'd traveled almost exactly 500 years.

"'Tis still good, I assure you. Five years is naught. That salve lasts for decades."

She stared at the date, doing the math. If the salve was made five years ago, in 1482, that would make it 1487. Judging by the weather, it was wintertime. She wouldn't press her luck by asking the month and day.

Blinking to focus on Father Anselm, she forced a smile. "I'm sure it's perfectly fine. Thank you. For the salve and the meal and, well, everything." She used a fingernail to lift the cork and sniffed the salve. "What is it made of?"

"Mostly beeswax and honey from the abbey's hives." He leaned back on his heels and folded his hands in front. A casual pose, likely meant to put her at ease, along with his gentle manner.

She remained wary, however. Wilhelm treated this man with respect, as if he were in authority. She would follow suit.

"Also alder bark for its soothing properties," he went on, conversationally, "comfrey for reduction of swelling, and root of burdock to speed the healing and prevent infection. I placed a bit of burdock infusion in your ale as well. Did you taste it too strongly?" He wrinkled his nose.

The ale had tasted bitter, but not the way a hoppy brew should. She'd drunk it anyway, figuring Wilhelm wouldn't poison her after going to so much trouble to rescue her. Besides, she'd been hungry enough to eat and drink just about anything.

"It was fine. Thank you." None of the ingredients he'd mentioned sounded familiar in a medicinal context, but she wouldn't risk offending him by asking more questions. As soon as he left, she would put the mixture on a small patch of healthy skin to test it before using it on her burns.

"'Tis an honor to serve a charge of the Murray." Anselm said with a bow of his head. "If all is well, I shall return to my other duties."

"Of course. But please, tell me, how is the other woman?"

A pleat formed between his brows. "I am afraid she is unwell. I have sent for a sister of the faith who performs midwife duties on occasion. But she shall not arrive until tonight at the earliest."

"Is there anything I can do to help?"

"Mayhap the lass would like some company. She sleeps fitfully and suffers from stomach pains when she tries to eat. But use the salve and rest for a while first. Your feet are in wont of mending."

Rest sounded good, but her heart went out to the poor girl. From her condition, it seemed she had been through harder times than Connie. She resolved to check on her first thing after a good, long sleep.

After Anselm left, a test of the salve produced no ill effects, so she liberally applied it to her reddened skin. A cool tingling soothed the burns, and the pleasing, herbal scent relaxed her. Getting up one last time before her nap, she blew out the candles.

Darkness closed around her. As she felt her way back to the bed, a low moan met her ears. It came from somewhere nearby. Oh, no. What if the girl was in labor?

Connie put one foot in front of the other and made her painful way to the door. Cracking it open, she listened. She heard a man's voice. Down the hall a streak of light shone across the floor, showing the door to the room beside hers was open.

"Easy, lass. Breathe through it. Aye. Like that." The voice sounded similar to Wilhelm's when he was being gentle with her. But it wasn't him. Could it be the cousin he'd mentioned?

"*Och,* are you a midwife now?" A feminine voice, soft and thready, but laced with humor.

A soft chuckle. "Nay, but I remember when my youngest brother was born. My da was away, so it was up to me to fetch the midwife and help my mother."

"Mmm—ohhh. 'Tis a queer feeling. Not quite pain, but not nice either. I doona wish for it to grow worse."

"Shhh. Think of somat else. Think of a happy memory."

Whoever the man was, he clearly cared for the girl. Furthermore, it sounded as if he had things under control. Connie didn't know much about giving birth, having never done it before, but she knew labor tended to go on for hours.

The bed beckoned her back. She tucked herself in, hoping for a bit of rest…and that the midwife nun would arrive before the birth. Thoughts of kissing Wilhelm filled her head as she drifted off.

A field of wildflowers spread out before her, and she knew she was dreaming. Rays of pink, lilac, and gold reached skyward from the horizon, heralding sunrise. A figure, slender and still, sat a few paces away. Connie saw only the person's back. Dark waves of hair shifted with a faint breeze.

"Leslie?" she asked.

The figure didn't acknowledge her. All was eerily silent. No birds sang from hidden burns. Grass stalks didn't rustle as she stepped through them toward the other person. She felt no texture of plant life beneath her feet.

Sensation was muted, like the colors of an old photograph.

The figure had hair similar to Leslie's, but absent was the prickle of awareness she always felt when she saw her twin after a time apart. "Hello? Can you hear me?"

The figure turned, revealing an angled jaw and a proud nose. He exuded maleness the way the field exuded tranquility, yet he was beautiful in the way few men were, with the perfectly symmetrical features of a high-fashion model or a European stage actor.

"Greetings, *mademoiselle*." He extended an elegant hand to her. Shirt sleeves of a light, shimmery material floated around an arm somehow both graceful and masculine. "Join me, if you will. I have been waiting for you."

He's French. Hadn't Leslie mentioned a French shopkeeper in Inverness?

"Do you know who I am?" The question leapt from her lips as hope sparked to life in her chest. Could Leslie be trying to contact her right now? It seemed crazy, but then so did time travel.

"But of course. You are the one so blessed." He still held out his hand.

Something about the twinkle in his onyx eyes hinted at trustworthiness.

Leslie claimed she could see auras around people sometimes. If there really were such a thing as auras, this man's would radiate secret knowledge and mischief, but also kindness. A knot of tension in her stomach relaxed as she placed him decisively in the category of people she approved of.

Maybe he knew how she could get home.

She took his hand and let him draw her closer. It was only then she realized she was clothed in the same material as he. On him, it shaped to his body in shimmering trousers and a tunic with billowing sleeves. His cuffs were embroidered with gold. On her, it draped to her calves in a weightless toga with a knot-work belt that reminded her of the Celtic relics she'd seen on the cover of a museum brochure in the bed and breakfast.

"One so blessed," she stated, in no mood for riddles, if that's what this guy had in mind. "Not exactly what I was hoping for. 'One who is but a step away from returning to her own time' would have been my preference." She didn't bother pretending she was English. In the dream, it seemed obvious this man had knowledge of her situation.

A pinch of his lips sufficed as an expression of humor as well as a kissing gesture that didn't quite make a landing on the back of her hand. "Tell me, do you weary of fulfilling the wish of your heart so quickly?"

She sat beside him and hugged her shins, fingering the fabric of her toga. It was softer and thinner than silk. With such insignificant weight, it should have been transparent, but when she looked at it, it shimmered between dove gray and the pale blue of a wintery horizon. *Like Wilhelm's eyes.*

She shoved the warrior from her mind to focus on the here and now. "You mean my sister's wish. Leslie made the wish, not me."

"If you say so."

She snorted. "I know so. *So*. How do I get back?"

"You must choose your way."

She glared at him. Riddles. Figured.

The glare slid off him like eggs off Teflon. Despite her best effort, she found herself taking pleasure in the twinkle in his eye.

"So, I'll have a choice, huh?"

"*Oui*."

"When? How?"

He wagged a finger at her. "Do not be so impatient to leave, *mademoiselle*. How do you know you are not needed?"

She thought about the pregnant girl. "I don't know how to deliver a baby. I can't possibly be of help." She was willing to do what she could, but if the girl's or the baby's chances depended on her, they were all going to be up a creek without a paddle.

The man's only response was to shrug one elegant shoulder.

She tried a different tack. "Have you spoken with Leslie?"

"*Oui*. She paid a visit to my shop."

Connie forgot he was a stranger and hugged his arm in her excitement. "How is she? Is she scared? Will she be able to bring me back? Is there anything I can do to help?"

"You misunderstand, *mademoiselle*. I saw her but the one time, before the solstice. I am sorry. I have not been to Inverness again since then, though I do open my shop from...time to time."

Great. He hadn't spoken with Leslie since her one and only visit to his shop. Wait. He'd just admitted to having a shop in Inverness...and opening it from "time to time." Did that mean she might be able to find him while awake if she went to Inverness?

"Who are you, anyway? How are you in my dream? Or is this just some random concoction of my mind and I completely made you up?"

He laughed the way an aristocrat might, making even that seem elegant. "Oh, my dear, no. Your imagination is far too grounded in sense and logic to create something like me."

Her back straightened. "Hey. I can imagine just fine, thank you." She'd imagined a satisfying future with Milt, rising up to management in her firm, having children one day.

"Ah. But you do not dream from your heart. You make plans. From here." He tapped her temple.

She batted at his finger, failing to make contact—goodness, the man was quick.

"Of course. Why not set goals that make sense?" He made sense and logic sound like bad things. "Why would I hope for things that might change with time, like love? Why would I hope for things I have no power to achieve? Life will be much more stable and rewarding if I plan it logically, set reasonable goals."

She saw now that she needed to make some concession to chemical attraction in her plan. That's where she had gone wrong with Milt. When she returned home, she would simply revise her goals and carry on basing the bulk of her choices on facts and logic, while making allowances for certain physiological and emotional requirements.

The man cocked his head, as if straining to hear something far away.

She listened but heard nothing.

"Ah, but I am being summoned. I must go." He stood from his cross-legged position without pushing off with his hands, all grace and long limbs and strength. Taking her hand, he pulled her up too but didn't let go. "Many mortals place high value on sense and logic. And yet, your world is filled with senseless acts of violence. Should there not also be senseless acts of love?"

A high-pitched moan shattered the dream. She salt bolt upright in bed, heart pounding. The baby was coming.

Chapter 6

THE ABBEY'S KITCHEN faced to the north and was therefore one of the coldest rooms unless the monks were baking their morning bread. As it was mid-afternoon, Wilhelm must perform the chores Anselm had delegated to him without the comfort of warmth.

At the moment, he stood at a basin of frigid water rinsing bricks of cheese from which he'd just pressed out the whey. 'Twas while he rubbed his reddened hands together to warm them that Terran strolled in, tore off a chunk of the most recently rinsed brick, and popped it in his mouth.

Eye twitching, Wilhelm returned the brick to the press to reshape it. "How fares Aifric?" he asked of the lass Terran had taken a liking to.

The twinkle he'd had in his eye when he'd stolen the cheese faded. Terran wiped a hand down his face. His cousin hadn't slept a wink since they'd arrived in the middle of the previous night. Instead of seeing to his own rest, he'd been sitting watch over Aifric. It seemed he'd finally found a woman he might care about as more than a body to warm his bed for a night.

"Spent. Hurting," Terran said. "'Tis killing me. Wish I could take it for her. Anselm's been sitting with her so I could move about some." He stretched his arms overhead, fingertips gripping the wooden beam above. Bracing on the pads of his fingers, he leaned forward with a groan. "*Och,* sore from the skirmish."

Wilhelm nodded. His muscles ached, too, but in a way that was most welcome since they hadn't done much training on their journey. As for Aifric, he was worrit she might not make it through the day, let alone deliver a bairn, but he didn't share his thoughts with Terran.

"I see Anselm put you to work." Terran helped himself to some candied figs that Wilhelm had been grazing on while he did his chores. "I would offer my aid, but I just came for a bite. I doona wish to leave her for long."

Wilhelm wrapped a freshly rinsed brick in cloth for stacking in the cellar, where it would keep for months. "You ought to rest. You'll be no good to her weary. She needs you strong." He reached for another brick.

"Have ye no faith in me, cousin?" He feigned offense. "You've seen me cut down foes on less sleep."

"Aye. I have faith in you. 'Tis why you'll be my second one day." He clapped his cousin on the back. "Will she eat?" He offered Terran the rest of the figs before continuing with the cheese.

"Nay. Canna tolerate aught but sips of tea. Even that, she takes sparingly."

Wilhelm prayed silently for the lass as he finished his task. He prayed for Constance as well. Mayhap she would be awake by now. An hour ago, he'd slipped into her room to assure himself she was sleeping comfortably. 'Twas a good thing she had been or he might have resumed their kiss from earlier.

Soon, he would have her sleeping in his bed. Of this, he was cert.

Terran interrupted his thoughts. "Any more news from Perth?"

Wilhelm shook his head. Ruthven's men hadn't given chase after the skirmish—he'd learned that much from his early morning trip to the village and already shared the information with Terran. It seemed the fire had spread and all Ruthven's resources had been directed toward putting it out. The lack of pursuit, however, didn't mean the baron hadn't named them fugitives. Wilhelm figured 'twas merely a matter of time. Ruthven would never ignore an opportunity to crush a Murray.

"Havena been down to the village again," Wilhelm said. "I'll go before the evening meal and see what I can learn."

"Did you send the letter to your da?"

"Aye." It left in the hands of a young monk who promised to make the journey to Dornoch in three days. Wilhelm had not believed this would be healthy for any horse, but Anselm assured him the lad would change mounts when he reached the monastery in Aviemore. Apparently, the monks had become skilled enough at delivering messages that they often did so for coin to support their orders. Anselm had refused to accept payment from Wilhelm, however.

"Ye asked to meet Kenrick in Inverness?" Terran didn't normally ask so many questions. He must feel uneasy.

Wilhelm stopped what he was doing and gave his cousin his full attention. "Aye. In a week's to ten days' time, like we discussed."

They had decided to ride for Inverness with Constance, as soon as she healed enough to travel, likely in two to three days. Aifric, if she survived the birth, would remain under Anselm's care for her safety.

In Inverness, they would enlist Kenrick's help in finding a magistrate to hear their confession—they had instigated a skirmish, after all—but they'd had good reason for doing so. Ideally, the magistrate would hear their confession and rule their actions justified before Ruthven submitted formal charges against them.

Even better, if the magistrate was a proponent of evidence-based justice, as Wilhelm was—and if he was a man of influence and courage, he might even file charges against Ruthven for abusing his power of local rule. 'Twas the sunniest of possible outcomes and not at all likely, but he'd learned to strive for things that seemed out of reach, for the only true failure was in not making the attempt. He'd described all this in the letter to his father and requested Kenrick meet them in Inverness.

"I'll breathe easier when I lay eyes on the man," Terran said.

"I will as well." Kenrick's experience in advocating would surely aid them in thwarting any petty schemes Ruthven might hatch.

Wilhelm was about to offer Terran some reassurance, but the opportunity was lost when Anselm burst into the kitchen.

"'Tis time." Eyes wide, he nodded toward Terran. "The pains have increased." He turned on his heel and disappeared again.

Terran raced after him.

Anselm's acquaintance from the priory in Perth would not arrive for hours yet. After all the poor lass must have been through as Ruthven's prisoner, Wilhelm hoped for Godspeed in her birthing.

He followed Anselm and Terran. When he arrived at the guest quarters, he found Constance already at Aifric's side. She had attempted to sit with the young lass earlier, he'd learned from Terran, but Anselm had ushered her back to her bed, where she could rest and heal. Now that Aifric's birthing was impending, he approved Constance's participation, especially since she'd been resting now for most of the day.

The young lass sat forward with folded linens behind her. Constance rubbed vigorous circles on her back while murmuring encouragements.

Wilhelm's chest swelled with pride. She would make a fine Lady of Dornoch one day, provided he found a way to rid himself of the Ruthven-sized thorn in his side.

Anselm directed the other monks to supply hot water and extra bedding. He attempted to shoo Terran out of the room, but his cousin was having none of it.

"I stay," he said simply.

Wilhelm, on the other hand, had no reason for being there. Satisfied that Constance seemed up to the task of delivering a bairn, he set off to find more chores that needed tending—the farther from the poor lass's whimpers the better. Mayhap the sheep could use feeding.

Never would his father forgive him if he neglected to earn his keep as a guest of the church. After all that had transpired at Ruthven's, he would be presuming enough on his father's forgiveness without adding unnecessary offenses.

§

THE YOUNG WOMAN—Aifric was her name, Connie had learned—lost consciousness after an afternoon of intense labor. At first Connie thought she'd fallen asleep, and she'd been relieved, because the girl looked beyond exhausted. But when her rounded belly clamped down of its own accord with a powerful contraction and Aifric didn't wake, she became worried.

"What do we do?" she asked Anselm.

Earlier, the monk had brought her clothes and an afternoon meal. He had insisted she remain in bed to rest even though Aifric had sounded distressed. But when the girl's moans had become urgent, she'd offered her help and Anselm had finally accepted. The nun he'd sent for wouldn't be expected until later tonight at the earliest. That left Connie and Wilhelm's cousin Terran, at the helm. Anselm seemed relieved to be demoted to the role of hot water fetcher and provider of supplies.

Connie held one of Aifric's hands. Terran held the other. He looked even more worried than she felt. In her worry over the girl, her own pain had faded to a manageable level. A few hours of sleep had no doubt helped her healing as well.

"When will the midwife be here?" Terran asked.

The man was a strapping warrior, like Wilhelm but with longer and slightly darker hair. His presence seemed to take up most of the tiny room. Anselm had tried several times to get him to leave, but Terran refused.

"Not soon enough," Anselm replied with his face set grimly. "Mayhap you should attempt to wake her," he said to Connie.

She patted Aifric's cheek, terrified of hurting her. She was so frail. It had likely been weeks since she'd eaten. Malnutrition made sharp angles of her cheekbones, and bruise-like shadows made her eyes appear sunken. How had this happened? Where was her family? Why had Ruthven treated her this way?

She didn't have a husband. That much she'd learned from Aifric between contractions. It seemed Terran had more than a polite interest in her. Maybe, if Aifric made it through this ordeal, she and Terran would find happiness together.

Though she would never admit it to anyone, she liked to unwind in the evenings with a romance novel from the library. The busyness of the city and the stress of her job made her crave a small dose of softness in the evenings. Maybe the stress of the past two days had made her cling to the romantic notion of an instant attraction. Or maybe the dream she'd had last night was making her sentimental.

She spoke directly into Aifric's ear while patting her shoulder. "Wake up, hon. We've got to deliver your baby." Still no response. "She won't wake up."

"Keep trying." Anselm looked resigned, like he didn't expect this to go well.

"Wake, love," Terran whispered to Aifric. "A little while longer, and you'll have your bairn in your arms. You can rest then." He kissed her forehead. "I'd give ye my strength if I could, lass. Would that I could." His voice cracked. "Wake now. Please. For me."

Aifric remained motionless except for her chest rising and falling with shallow breaths.

Terran's tenderness with a woman he had only met the night before caused Connie's heart to constrict. It wasn't just Connie's secret romantic inclinations making her see something that wasn't there. Love had bloomed for these two, and it had done so incredibly quickly. Maybe this was what the man in her dream had meant by *senseless acts of love.*

It could happen to you too.

But it wouldn't. This kind of love had never been part of her plans. Too unpredictable. Too abstract. Love wasn't something you could quantify like income and career status. She could never depend on something of indeterminate value.

Maybe sudden devotion wasn't for her, but that didn't mean she was immune to the sweetness of it. She would be damned if she didn't do everything in her power to give these two the happy ending they deserved.

She racked her brain for every bit of information she'd ever learned about giving birth. Everyone knew a woman's cervix had to dilate ten centimeters. Doctors would check by inserting fingers into the birth canal. What they felt for, Connie could guess at; the cervix must feel like a ring, stretched taut with the baby's head creating a hard plane in the center. Once the opening was large enough to accommodate an infant's head, there would be pushing. Someone usually helped guide the baby out. The cord had to be cut. She could do those things. Provided nothing went wrong.

Time to roll up your sleeves and get to work, Con.

She'd never shied from hard work, and wasn't about to start now. She certainly wasn't going to leave Aifric to the ineptness of a monk who stammered every time Connie suggested looking between the girl's legs and a man who was so besotted he couldn't stand to see her in pain.

"I'll check her cervix," Connie said, more to herself than to the men. They both gave her blank stares. "To see if she's close." The explanation didn't seem to help their understanding. She sighed. "I'm going to place my hand at the entrance to her womb and see if she has—" would they know the word dilated? "Stretched enough to allow the baby to pass."

Anselm's face turned red. "I'll just fetch some more hot water."

Terran said, "Do it."

She took a bracing breath and rolled up the sleeves of her borrowed dress so she could dip her hand in a bowl of warm water, the only thing available for washing. Wincing, because she had never viewed another woman so intimately, she lifted the blankets. There was instantly no question that Aifric's cervix had dilated to ten centimeters because a bluish scalp with matted black hair pressed at a perfect tight circle of flesh like a cereal bowl coming through a hole in a sock.

"Oh. Um." She glanced at Terran, her hands trembling. "It's happening. The baby is coming."

Terran was there with her less than a heartbeat later, looking between Aifric's legs. Just then another contraction eased the baby a little further. The child's closed eyes were just visible near the front of Aifric's mound. Instinct told her it wouldn't be long now.

"That's it, lass. Your bairn is coming." Terran cupped his hands like a catcher in a baseball game.

Connie laughed, oddly jubilant at witnessing this miracle. "Wash your hands first."

He blushed and obeyed.

Ten minutes later, Terran delivered a pink, wrinkly little girl. She wasn't moving.

With tears in his eyes, he asked, "Is she...?"

"No," Connie said. "Here. Give her to me."

Terran placed her carefully on the bed between Aifric's legs, where Connie began rubbing the tiny, beautiful thing with a clean blanket. She used quick, firm strokes, remembering that babies needed to cry when they were born. Sure enough, the infant's face got even redder and her little mouth opened. A distinctive newborn cry filled the room.

"There you are, sweetheart," she said to the baby. She wrapped the little girl in the blanket and transferred her to the arms of a shocked looking Terran. "You find something to tie off the cord while I check on mommy."

Giving commands came easily to her thanks to managing projects at her engineering firm. Sometimes confidence could even make up for lack of knowledge, if a gal got lucky. Hopefully, they'd all be lucky today, because unlike at work, she had no idea what to do with a newborn.

Aifric was still breathing, and she didn't seem to be bleeding badly. "I think she's all right," she said to Terran. "Probably just weak from not being able to eat?" She hoped that was all that held Aifric unconscious and that they could get some sustenance into her now that the birth was over.

A throat-clearing sound called her attention to the doorway. Anselm hovered there with a cautious smile on his face. "All is well?"

"Aye," Terran said, grinning like a fool as he looked up from the cord. He had double-knotted a length of twine-like rope around it. While she and Anselm watched, he sliced it clean through with a long-handled knife. "Look at the wee lass." He held her up for Anselm to see. "A bonny sweet thing." Her skin was pink and soft, and her face was scrunched up but somehow more beautiful than anything Connie had ever seen before. She wasn't a chubby baby, but she wasn't skinny either. Her mother had given her a good start, it seemed, despite her own poor health.

"Aye," Anselm agreed. "Would you like to be her da?"

Terran didn't miss a beat. "We'll do it as soon as she can stand at my side for the vows." He turned his attention to Aifric, who stirred and moaned, oblivious to the men. She was probably in a lot of pain and exhausted. Connie didn't blame her one bit for losing consciousness.

Terran tried to show her the baby, but she didn't open her eyes. "Bring her mead," he told Anselm.

"No," Connie said. "Water or tea, but nothing alcoholic while she's breast feeding. And something to eat. Maybe she'll be able to keep it down now that she's delivered the baby." After Anselm left, she told Terran, "Let's see if we can get her to nurse."

She lowered the neckline of Aifric's nightgown, and directed Terran to put the baby at one swollen breast. Nature took its course, and the baby attempted to suck. But the breast was too firm. The tiny mouth couldn't seem to latch on.

Connie did what felt natural. She grabbed Aifric's breast none too gently and compressed just behind the nipple. This did the trick. The baby girl sucked the entire areola into her mouth and began nursing. Connie let go, and the baby continued without difficulty.

How amazing! The little thing was born with an instinct to survive, and her mother, even while malnourished, was able to not only give birth to her but also provide sustenance.

Wonder expanded in her chest as she watched Terran bring one of Aifric's hands up to rest on the baby. He whispered sweetly. To mother or baby, Connie wasn't sure. She stood and tiptoed out of the room, leaving the little family to their privacy and hoping Aifric would recover and be all right.

When she returned to her room, weary and hungry, it was to find Wilhelm pouring steaming water into a ewer. "Take off your clothes," he said. "I intend to bathe you."

Chapter 7

SHOCK AND LUST held Connie paralyzed in the doorway.

Wilhelm had traded his pourpoint and hose for a linen shirt and simple trousers. Both garments looked like they could use a washing, as did the man himself. Grime and sweat streaked his face. Between that and his faint odor of earth and hard-working man, her heart thumped extra hard, pumping blood spiked with attraction.

The son of a baron and laird, he would be considered nobility. But he had clearly worked hard today, not demanding service, but serving instead. And now, he wanted to serve her.

For a heart-stopping moment, she wanted to let him. Heck, she wanted to let him do more than bathe her. *I'll undress if you do first.* It was on the tip of her tongue. But no. She was not about to undress in front of a man she hardly knew.

It must be her exposure to the love between Terran and Aifric making her desire a connection with this warrior from the past. No doubt an intimate interlude with Wilhelm would prove exceptional, but short-term flings weren't her style.

In one day, two tops, Wilhelm would be a memory, nothing more. Her dream had given her hope that this shopkeeper Leslie had spoken with might actually exist. She needed to find him. Or at the very least return to Druid's Temple so she could make her way back to the present day.

"No, thank you," she made herself say. She kept her voice low so no one overheard her Midwestern-American accent. "I can wash myself. I wouldn't say no to something to eat, though, if you have anything handy."

She winced, realizing she'd just treated Wilhelm like wait staff at a hotel. It had to be the stress of the day. It wasn't easy seeing someone suffer, especially when they'd already been through so much.

Poor Aifric. Thank heaven the baby appeared healthy. That had been far from a guarantee considering the young mother's condition.

Wilhelm watched her with intense blue eyes while he untied the laces of his shirt. The linen parted, revealing nothing underneath but fair, firm skin.

Connie gulped.

"You mistake my meaning. 'Twas no' meant to be a request." He let the shirt slip down his arms. It fell to the floor, but her gaze remained glued on Wilhelm.

He. Was. Magnificent.

His skin was paler than the linen he'd just shed. Creamy and smooth, his muscular chest and torso made her want to lap him up like the most decadent white chocolate. And maybe even take a nibble.

His shoulders were so thick with muscle she would be hard pressed to get a good grip if she wanted to give him a massage, and she *did* want to give him a massage. She'd never wanted that with any other man, but at the moment, she desired nothing more than to dig her fingers into Wilhelm's flesh and ease his aches after his hard day of work.

She would begin at those massive shoulders and work her way down his muscled torso. Back, front, all of him would receive the attention of her kneading fingers. Maybe even her tongue. Yes, that would be the perfect tool for tracing the enticing line that bisected his pectorals and ridged abdominals and disappeared past the waist of his trousers.

"I shall bring you supper soon," he said, yanking her gaze back up to his face.

Goodness, she'd lost herself so thoroughly in the fantasy she could practically taste the salt of his skin. Were her cheeks as red as they felt?

"But first, I. Intend. To. Bathe. You."

Power and intent radiated from him like heat off the hood of a race car. Places low inside her clenched as for the first time in her life a man issued her an order and she *wanted* to obey.

But obeying Wilhelm would lead her to places she did not want to go, no matter what kind of fantasies he inspired.

"I hardly think that's proper," she said, lifting her chin. "Thank you for the water, but I. Intend. To. Bathe. Myself." She echoed the command in his voice, a tactic that usually made men think twice about how they spoke to her.

Wilhelm only grinned. His eyes hooded.

The look caused a pulse deep between her legs. No man had ever looked at her that way before. Nor had her body ever reacted so obviously to any man before.

She couldn't allow the novelty to distract her. She must keep her distance from Wilhelm but she must also take care not to offend him. His cooperation was vital to her returning home. Maybe she should be more respectful when addressing him. He probably didn't have many women challenge his authority.

"Think you I would trespass on your person in any way while we take shelter in a holy place?"

"Trespass on my person?" Was he saying he wasn't going to do more than actually bathe her?

"Aye, lass. Trespass. Take liberties. Touch you with unseemly intent. Ye ken my meaning."

She nodded, her mouth gone dry at the thought of Wilhelm taking and touching and doing whatever the heck he pleased with her. "Y-you said you *won't*, um, trespass on my person?"

"You have my word I shall not defile you in any way. Now undress for me, lass."

She believed he was a man of his word. His promising not to molest her should be a comfort. Instead, it caused a bitter pill of disappointment that she swallowed down along with her temptation to capitulate.

Did he really not want to "trespass on her person" because they were in a holy place or was that just an excuse? Did he not find her pretty enough or feminine enough? Was she too bitchy? Few men had shown more than a perfunctory interest in her sexually. This had never really bothered her before, but at the moment, the words Wilhelm likely meant as a comfort left her feeling rejected.

Never mind. It shouldn't matter. *He* shouldn't matter.

Crossing her arms over her chest, she countered with, "I don't show my body to just any man." Truth. She had always been selective. In her twenty-eight years, she'd taken only three lovers, all of them chosen carefully and compatible with whatever life goals she'd had at the time.

"I am not just any man," he said simply, and everything about him from his posture to his actions backed up his claim.

He wasn't just any man. He was regal and impressive, strong and genuine. He valued honesty and fairness. He moved in political circles. He was special. And alluring in the extreme.

If she didn't have her sights set on Inverness and finding her way back to Leslie, she would consider trespassing on *his* person, holy place or not. If he weren't part of a world five hundred years in her past, he would be just the kind of man she might select for herself.

"Nevertheless," she said, making her voice firm. "I would prefer to wash myself."

He took the final step to close the distance between them and cupped her face in his hand. His touch was warm, and it weakened her resolve.

"You may leave your small clothes on, if you wish, and I will wash only what skin you choose to show me. But I long to bathe all of you, lass. You've still the stench of smoke to you, and you've Aifric's blood on your hands. I'm fair proud of you for your hard work today and your bravery yester eve. You have earned a thorough bath. You have earned my service.

"There is no fireplace to warm you, and no hipbath for you to sink into and thus preserve your modesty. These things you deserve and much, much more. Would that I could give them to you here, but I cannot. Will you trust my word, lass, that I intend nothing untoward?"

His words sank in slowly, like the soothing heat from his hand. His pride in her meant more than it should. His humility in wanting to serve her meant even more, especially since she suspected he'd worked all day while she'd been resting and sitting with Aifric, being next to useless. She didn't know much about him, but she suspected from his usually tidy appearance he liked to be clean and put together. He was putting off his ablutions to take care of her.

"I suppose a bath would be welcome." Maybe bathing a near stranger was customary in this time. Maybe it was considered an honor to be tended by a member of the nobility. Deciding to treat the situation thusly and to trust Wilhelm's sincerity, she uncrossed her arms and let them fall to her sides, an invitation.

"That's my lass."

His lass? Why did that make her stomach do a roll?

He curled a strong finger in the ties lacing up the front of her overdress. The sleeveless straps kept slipping down over the threadbare linen of her borrowed shift, as if it had been fitted for someone broader through the shoulders than she. After loosening the ties, he brushed his knuckles up her arms, carefully avoiding the outside of her breasts on his way to those straps.

How could a simple touch make tingles race up and down her entire body? It was like Wilhelm's fingers closed a circuit when they came into contact with her and she sparked to life in new and interesting ways.

Down went the straps. The overdress puddled at her feet, and even that sliding of fabric on fabric resonated in barely-there pops of sensation all over.

Her eyes fluttered closed. She had thought herself moderately worldly, but this chaste touching was better than any sex she'd ever had. She wanted to stand there and revel in this feeling forever.

The shift Anselm had brought her that morning had a large opening for the collar. It took but a brush of Wilhelm's hands over her shoulders to send it rippling down to meet the dress on the floor.

She was naked from the waist up. Below, she wore only the undergarment that had been provided with her dress and shift. Made of undyed linen, the garment cinched at the waist and below each knee with ribbons. They made her feel like she had a parachute around each of her thighs, but it was better than—what was the saying?—going commando.

Cool air brought goosebumps out on her skin. Or was it Wilhelm's heated gaze? Either way, the sensation spread to her nipples, making them tighten. A moan escaped her.

"Are you in pain, lass?" He whispered it near her ear. His breath was hot, as were the shivers that raced up and down her body.

She should be cold, but Wilhelm radiated warmth, and he stood close. Very close. He smelled of fields, livestock, and sweat, all things she had never associated with sexiness, until now.

She wanted him to touch her. His palm to her upper arm. His lips to her jaw. His forehead to hers. Anything. "Pain? Hmm?"

"Your feet." His breath on the side of her neck did more to arouse her than anything Milt had ever done to her. "They were fair burned yester eve. Anselm told me he brought you a salve."

Oh. The fire. Heavens. She'd nearly been burned alive. It still seemed so surreal, but it had happened. The lingering discomfort in her feet proved it.

Now she burned in a different way. She burned for more of Wilhelm.

She suspected he was willing to give her more. But he wouldn't. He would remain true to his word. No sex in the monastery. His promise allowed her to enjoy this, enjoy him. It was just a bath.

"Yes. The salve. He brought it." She was babbling. She made herself shut up.

Just then, she heard voices beyond the closed door.

She made an *X* with her arms to hide her breasts.

"Easy, lass." His grip on her shoulders grounded her.

If anyone came in, he would shield her body with his. She knew this instinctively, and the knowledge pleased her. Still, knowing they could be interrupted ruined the relaxation she'd begun to give in to.

Glancing at the closed door, she said, "There's no lock. Someone could come in."

"Aye. They could. But they willna. Terran is busy with Aifric. Anselm kens I'm tending to you. He also kens I would sooner fall on my sword than compromise your virtue."

She blinked. Her virtue? Was he merely being chivalrous or did he actually think she was a virgin?

He turned his back to her and bent over the ewer. His sculpted shoulders moved, muscles sliding under skin, as the sounds of water being wrung out met her ears. He had dimples near his shoulder blades that she had a sudden urge to explore with her tongue.

But she wouldn't do any exploring. She reminded herself this man would be long dead by the time she returned home.

A lump formed in her throat.

Wilhelm faced her with a soapy rag in his hands and heat in his gaze. His irises were a blue so pale they seemed to glow like diamonds in the candle light. As he stalked toward her, she couldn't look away from those captivating eyes.

Her anxiety slipped away, and she lowered her arms to her sides.

He froze. His gaze fell to her breasts and lingered there. "You are fine, woman," he said. The husky notes in his voice spoke of lust and hunger.

Pride warmed her from her toes to the top of her head. He found her attractive. It shouldn't matter, but it did. Oh, it did.

He might be nothing but a memory in a few days, a man long dead. But he was alive now. *Very* alive, as evidenced by his tented trousers.

Never before had a man's erection made her feel powerful and beautiful. Always before, she'd reacted with mild curiosity when faced with the biological phenomenon. She'd accepted it as a fact of life, and when she felt like it, she would treat her lover to a few moments of pleasure, taking some for herself in the process.

With Wilhelm, she found herself salivating at the way his trousers became taut over the head of his erection. She could only guess at his size and shape, but even the suggestion of his form pulled delicious threads of arousal through her until her whole body felt like a sexual instrument.

Her breasts ached for touch. Her abdomen tightened with anticipation. Her sex quested for filling with tiny, needy pulses. Everything felt connected. All her parts sought fulfillment together. Remarkable. Beautiful.

She had never wanted like this before.

Wilhelm came close enough that only a whisper separated his chest from her breasts.

Even this closeness caused her pleasure. A frisson of awareness lifted every fine hair on her body. She breathed his name. "Wilhelm."

"Aye, lass." His voice was low and intimate. "I feel it as well."

Did every cell in his body reach for her the way hers did for him? If he felt as wonderful in her presence as she did in his, he hid it well. His face remained passive, and his eyes looked only where they needed to as he washed her, beginning with her neck and working his patient way down to each individual fingertip. His gentle rubbing left cool tingles on the surface of her skin and trails of fire beneath, but he never touched her in any way that suggested this was anything but a bath.

With a force of will Connie had never called on before, she held back her urge to moan as his large hands returned to her neck and spread slick and strong over her collar bones and below. He spent no more time on her breasts than on any other part of her. She should be grateful he was holding to his word, but instead she experienced a pang of disappointment.

When he reached the waistband of her undergarment, she bit her lip.

He touched the ribbon.

She should tell him to stop.

He tugged, loosening the waist. Sliding his soapy hand inside, he lathered her curls. Only his hand touched her, but she felt enveloped by him. He seemed above and below her, in front and behind.

His tall body blocked her field of vision and his shoulders bowed around her. She longed to have those shoulders above her while she lay beneath him, to have blankets capturing their heat, turning them from two to one.

His hot breath ghosted over her face, and desire pounded in her blood, a thrilling, terrifying rush.

What was happening to her? She'd never had thoughts like this for any other man.

It's all physical, Connie girl. It's simple biology. Don't make more of it than what it is: attraction. Chemistry.

But she'd dated attractive men before and never reacted to them like this. What if she never met another man she reacted to like this? Now that she knew this kind of chemistry was possible, how could she not include it in her plans? She would have to add chemical attraction to her list of qualities for a prospective spouse, but the likelihood of finding a man who met all her other qualifications and did this to her physically seemed unlikely.

She held her breath, waiting for Wilhelm to break his word and touch between her legs. *Please, break your word.*

But he didn't. He only rinsed the washrag and wiped the soap away before retying her ribbon. With the rag newly-soaped, he knelt to wash her legs one at a time.

"So smooth," he said, fingers slicking her shin and calf. She'd never once given thought to the skin behind her knee before, not until he stimulated it with his electric touch. "Do you nay grow hair here?"

"I shave it off."

His eyebrows went up, but he said no more.

She decided to attempt conversation. That would keep her from fantasizing about him trespassing on her person.

"Why Wilhelm?" she asked.

He stopped his washing. "Why me?" He cocked an eyebrow in confusion.

"I mean, why did your parents give you a German name? Are you of German descent?" She would believe it given his light coloring.

"Ah." He nodded his understanding. "No. We are Scots through and through. My father chose my name for its similarity to Anselm's. When they were lads, they attended university together and became fast friends. Anselm's name means 'protected by God' or more literally, 'God-helmet.' My father named me after Anselm but altered it to mean 'strong-helmet.' Wil-helm."

She could listen to him talk for days. His brogue was thick but understandable, sexy in the extreme. Even sexier was the intentionality of his speech. He struck her as a man who thought before he spoke.

His father had gone to university. Did that mean Wilhelm had too? She had never given much thought to advanced education in medieval times, but here was an apparently well-educated warrior, a man as smart as he was strong.

"It's a nice name," she said.

His only response was a brief glance and maybe, unless it was a trick of the candle light, a flush of extra color across his cheekbones.

"Why Constance?" he asked as he lavished sudsy attention on her other foot.

She smiled at the playful rise of his eyebrows as he mimicked her question. "My mother says it's a family name, but I'm the only Constance I know in our family. Maybe it dates back to previous generations."

He didn't ask about her nationality. Instead, he finished washing her in silence. After wringing out the washrag one last time, he slipped into his shirt and left without a word.

Feeling suddenly very alone, she dressed by the light of the candelabra.

A few minutes later, a knock sounded at the door. Heart lifting, she rushed to open it, but found only Anselm with a tray.

"Your supper," he said.

"Thank you." She took the tray and watched him retreat down the hall. She had hoped it would be Wilhelm, come to kiss her again. Or perhaps to spend the night.

As she closed the door, that lonely feeling returned. It was longing, she realized. She longed to be with Wilhelm.

Eating her oatmeal, this time served with cooked carrots and some kind of leafy herb, it occurred to her he hadn't interviewed her as he'd warned the day before. He had given her a reprieve.

She ought to prepare what she would tell him about herself when he finally did ask, but all she could think about was his hands on her and his fingers massaging away the smoky evidence of her near death experience. His shimmering eyes, his strong jaw, his undeniably masculine scent.

Heavens. She was in a world of trouble.

Chapter 8

WILHELM SPENT A fitful night attempting and failing to ignore the most painful arousal he had ever experienced. Bathing Constance had been his personal heaven. And his worst hell. Because no matter how he lusted to take her, he could not. Not until he knew he could give her the life she deserved.

That was why she must come with him and Terran to Inverness. Her testimony would help justify their slaying of Ruthven's guards. Personal testimony was always given more weight than written, and he didn't ken yet whether Constance could write. He suspected she could. The lass struck him as highly educated.

There was just one thing that must be done before they set out, and that involved his cousin and Aifric. Wilhelm finished his morning grooming and wended his way to a part of the abbey that had become familiar to him. 'Twas an otherwise unoccupied wing where Anselm had set aside neighboring rooms for the women.

"Good morn," he said, easing open the door to Aifric's room. It was dark inside, as were all the rooms along this interior corridor, but his candles provided light to guide his steps.

It came as no surprise when the light fell on Terran, sound asleep in the bed. 'Twas improper for him to be here, but neither he nor Anselm had seen fit to chastise him. They both recognized the miracle of Terran finally finding a woman he wished to claim.

Terran had the bairn swaddled between his arm and side. Aifric lay on the other side of the wee bundle, her hand resting on her child. Terran's head was bowed so that even in his sleep he pressed his forehead to his beloved's. A bonny family they made.

Aifric stirred and opened her eyes. She started when she saw Wilhelm, as though embarrassed to be found in such a compromising position.

"Easy, lass. No one here judges you."

At his words, her creased brow smoothed only to crease again when she strained to sit upright in the bed. Wilhelm moved swiftly to help her. "Allow me," he said with a hand at her back. She weighed next to nothing.

He knew naught of Aifric, save her parents were cottars on Ruthven's land and she had been imprisoned at the baron's order. Wilhelm's father had never enacted his right to punish sins such as fornication so severely, but not all lairds were as merciful as his father. Fortunately, neither were all lairds as vile as Ruthven.

Kenning the black-hearted baron and what he was capable of, Wilhelm suspected he had been the one to get the bairn on the poor lass. And he doubted Aifric had done aught to encourage his attentions. Why else would Ruthven trouble himself with the affairs of his cottars if not to destroy all evidence of his indiscretion? Likely, Terran suspected the same, but they had refrained from speaking of it.

"How do you fare?" he asked as he rumpled a blanket to support her back.

"Not too poorly," she said in her soft voice. "Anice is taking milk, and she slept the whole night."

"Anice. Lovely name."

Aifric smiled. "Terran helped me choose it." Though purple shadows cradled her eyes, happiness shone there bright as day.

Wilhelm glanced at his cousin. "Did *he* sleep the whole night?"

She breathed a laugh. "No. Every time I woke, 'twas to find him watching over us." She bit her lip and cast a fond look at Terran. 'Twas clear the affection between them went both ways.

He hated to drag Terran to Inverness and away from his new charges. It occurred to him that he might make the journey with only Constance for company, but no. Terran would never hear of it. His duty was to protect the future laird of the Murray.

Heavy hearted, he said, "Would that I could give him more time to rest, but we must be off as soon as possible. I'll return him to you safely, lass. I vow it."

Aifric nodded. Her chin dimpled as she struggled not to show her sadness.

"The time will fly. You'll see." He grabbed Terran's foot and shook it.

His cousin moaned. "Too early. Go away."

"Have ye forgotten what today is?" Wilhelm said.

Terran's brows pressed together. His eyes popped open. A grin spread across his face as he looked first to Wilhelm then to Aifric. "Nay," he said simply, and he sat up to lay the tenderest of kisses upon Aifric's lips. "Today we will be wed."

"Aye," Aifric whispered. All traces of sadness vanished from her as she beheld her groom.

They pressed their foreheads together again, as they had been in slumber. Terran held the bairn secure in one arm, a natural father. The sight warmed Wilhelm's heart and multiplied his longing for the woman in the next room. He lusted to lay eyes on her, but he must see to Terran first. The man was hopeless in his grooming. 'Twould take at least an hour to make him presentable.

"Come, cousin. Let us prepare you for your bride."

While Terran and Aifric said their temporary goodbyes, Anselm carried a laden breakfast tray into the room. "I thought the women could break their fast together. Wake Mistress Constance, would you?" He set the tray down and began pouring the tea.

It seemed he would have the pleasure of laying eyes on Constance after all. He went to her room and rapped on the door.

There was no response.

The lass must be sleeping soundly. Since there were no bars on the doors in the abbey, he pushed it open and stuck his head in.

"Constance," he said. "Are you awake, lass?"

She didn't answer.

He had left the candles in Aifric's room and couldn't see much in the dim light from the corridor. Remembering where the bed was, he went to it in the dark, thinking to touch her bonny hair and mayhap wake her with a kiss on her cheek.

He found the edge of the bed and felt for her warm form. All he found were cold blankets. She was gone.

His heart lunged into his throat. "Anselm!"

The abbot came running.

"She's gone. Have ye seen her?"

Anselm shook his head. "Nay. I'll ask the others." He turned and hurried toward the refectory.

Wilhelm ran in the other direction, toward the nearest door to the grounds. *Curse you, man, why did you nay sleep in front of her door to prevent her from fleeing!*

What a fool he'd been! He still hadn't discovered where she hailed from. Her origins seemed less and less important the more he imagined her as a permanent fixture in his life. But now, thanks to his oversight, he might never see her again. If she'd run away in the night, he hadn't the faintest notion where he ought to begin searching.

He burst through the door to the cloister and pushed his legs to carry him as fast as they could toward the stables. If a horse and saddle were missing, he would mount up and ride after her. She was still healing from injuries and had no business taking to the wilderness alone. She had no business fleeing from him. Did she not ken by now she was safer by his side than any other place on God's green Earth?

"Where's the fire?" someone called from the direction of the garden.

He stopped his mad dash and turned to find the speaker. The small plot within the cloister was used mostly for herbs. It lay largely fallow for winter, but the monks had dedicated a few rows to winter vegetables. Yesterday, Wilhelm had helped them transfer young kale and radish plants from the glasshouse. There amidst the fresh green leaves knelt Constance. She'd wrapped herself in a blanket from her bed.

Relief sang through him.

"What are ye doing, lass?" His voice cracked unbecomingly. He cleared his throat and willed his racing heart to slow. "When I didna find you in your bed, I feared you'd gone."

She stood from where she'd been kneeling. He glimpsed her lower legs and bare feet as she let down the hem of her shift. He lusted to wash her again to free her creamy skin of the black specks of earth.

"I didn't mean to worry you. I woke early and wanted to watch the sun rise." She glanced toward the east with a pensive expression. Hugging herself, she stared out over the meadow where the monks grazed their sheep. Her breath fogged in front of her. "I noticed the garden and it seemed like a peaceful spot. I've always liked growing things."

He didn't ken what to make of her tone. Was it sadness he heard in her voice? Why should she be sad when she had been so near to death and had been saved?

She had a new beginning. She should be joyful.

Careful of the plants, he strode to her. He was about to tell her to go inside and get warm, but a heaviness to her manner stayed his tongue.

"Lass?"

He held out a hand to her, inviting her into his arms, but she didn't heed the invitation. Instead, she hugged herself tighter.

After the trust she'd shown him yester eve, her rejection stung.

"My parents never kept a garden. All our food was prepared by our chef." She scoffed a bitter laugh. "I had never even been to a grocery store before until I went to college. Once I bought my condo, I was finally able to have my own garden. There was a grassy, fenced-in area, and I took a great deal of enjoyment in removing the sod from a sunny corner and planting some annuals."

He didn't ken what a condo was, but she didn't give him time to ponder it. "I love salad, so I started about twenty tomato plants from seeds." She smiled wistfully as she went on, leaving him perplexed as to what a *tow-may-tow* was. "I planted them in little cardboard cups with such care and wrapped them in cellophane to keep them moist. I set them on a sunny windowsill every morning and made sure they were warm every night. Seeing their tiny little delicate stems sprout up made me so happy. I would come home from work excited to see how much they'd grown. They would twist and lean toward the sun like little reaching hands."

She sighed, a heavy sound.

His heart melted for her, though why she was so distraught he couldn't guess.

"When they were about six inches tall, I moved them outside to the little patch I'd cultivated. I planted them one weekend and put a tent of plastic over them to protect them.

"That Monday, when I got home from work, I went out to check on them, and they were gone. All gone."

He felt her despair, wondering at it. She was speaking about plants. And this story had the feel of an event long past. Why she told him these things, he couldn't guess, but he sensed truth in her words, a truth that ran as deep as mineral veins in the earth.

"There were little footprints all around and ragged tears in the plastic. Mice, an exterminator told me. Apparently, they crave the water in the plants. I hadn't known. I could have put netting around them to keep rodents out, but I never dreamed my plants would get eaten."

She laughed bitterly and finally looked at him. "It was an unforeseen complication, and it ruined my plans to have garden fresh tomatoes that summer. I cried for hours over those plants. All the work I'd put into them, all my excitement, and a bunch of rodents just took them away from me. Every last plant. Gone."

Why was she telling him this?

"I've been here going on three days now. I might never get home. But I haven't shed a single tear. Why?" She looked utterly at a loss.

Despite her earlier rejection, he still longed to hold her, but her manner gave him pause. She had a look about her like she'd found herself adrift at sea and was searching desperately for land.

What or whom had taken her from her home? Clearly, she had not left of her own accord. He would press her for answers once they began their journey.

"Why should I cry over tomato plants, but not over this, this—" She made a sweeping motion to indicate the countryside. "Just, all of this? I'm so far from home, from everything I've worked so hard for. I'm completely lost. Why aren't I more upset?"

She seemed plenty upset as she turned pleading eyes his way.

Whatever burden she shouldered, he couldn't permit her to bear it alone a moment longer. Whether she wanted his comfort or not, he pressed it upon her, touching her shoulders with both hands and drawing her into his embrace.

She came willingly and rested her cheek on his chest.

A feeling of completion and satisfaction filled him.

Slowly, tentatively, her arms encircled his waist. Aye. Whatever was between them was special. By coming to him, she showed him she felt it too.

"I doona pretend to understand all of what ye said, lass, but mayhap when the mice ate those plants, the loss was so poignant because you were left with naught in return. But being taken from your home, you have been given much in return."

She lifted her chin to meet his gaze. Questions swam in her gaze.

"Your life," he said. "You nearly lost it, but 'twas given back to you. A second chance at life is a grand gift indeed. And you've been given the opportunity to aid Aifric. She and her bairn fare well. I've no doubt you had a hand in that."

She graced him with a wee, thoughtful smile. "Yes," she said. "That could be."

You have me, as well, he wanted to say, but what came out instead was, "Dinnae fash. I vow to you, if I am free to do so, I will return you to your home once my name is cleared and I am free to do so." He planned to be wed to her by then and take her home so he could meet her kin and she could bid them a proper farewell. Surely her home couldn't be terribly far. Mayhap Holland or from across the Northern Sea.

He suspected now was not the time to trouble her with the details. He sought merely to comfort her and assure her that her concerns were important to him.

A pleat appeared between her eyebrows. Not the reaction he'd hoped for.

"Once your name is cleared," she said, her voice flat. "You mean, you're in trouble for rescuing me and Aifric? I thought this trip to Inverness was to bring justice down on Ruthven, but there's more to it, isn't there? You're in trouble. You and Terran. Because of me."

"*Whist.* I'll no have you fashin' about me and Terran. You're safe, aye? That is what we must hold fast to." He intended to keep her safe for all time. "Now that that's settled, we have much to do. It is my hope we may ride out at midday. You feel well enough?" He wouldn't insist on leaving so soon if she needed more time to heal.

"Today is fine." She nodded, almost distractedly and pulled free from his embrace.

He released her reluctantly. "Go inside and warm yourself by the fire in the kitchens. Then find Aifric. She'll want a lady to attend her this morn."

A genuine if weary smile brightened her countenance. "I hear there's going to be a wedding."

"Aye." And another soon after, if he had his way.

Chapter 9

CONNIE'S THOUGHTS WERE a jumble as she made her way through the monastery. They had been a jumble for hours. Ever since Wilhelm had bathed her, if she was honest. Unable to sleep a wink all night, she had risen with the bells calling the monks to their early-morning prayers and snuck outside. After being cooped up in either her windowless room or Aifric's for two days, the fresh, cold air had helped her think.

By the light of the coming dawn, she'd walked the rows of the garden, one after the other. With every step over the hard-packed soil, the reality of her situation sank in. She might never get home. She might never see Leslie again.

What was Leslie doing right now? Did it even make sense that there might be another "right now"? How could Connie be present in 1487 when the year of her birth wouldn't happen for roughly five hundred years?

The concept would boggle the mind quite enough if she had been a typical single birth, but she and Leslie had come into the world just minutes apart. Being a twin made this whole time-travel thing even more disturbing.

She'd never given much thought to the nature of time, but had always taken its linearity for granted. Time marched forward, never backward. Certainly time wouldn't jump around at random. Such a notion would have struck her as not only impossible but ridiculous.

Her presupposition had not mattered one wit. Magic had made a mockery of her logical approach to life by shoving her into a scenario she never could have prepared herself for.

She should be beyond distraught. She should seek a way home with single-minded purpose.

She should *not* be giddy over a wedding between two individuals whom she had just met. She should *definitely* not be craving the companionship of a man who would be long dead by the time her present happened.

She must remain focused on her goal: returning home. It would be unwise to let her emotions grow for the people here in the past.

Entering the kitchen, she snatched up a bread roll and nibbled it while making her way to Aifric's door. She was spared the need to knock since the door was wide open. Inside, Terran and Aifric were conversing and laughing while Anice napped beside her mommy on the bed. The dark shadows under Aifric's eyes were fading, and the light in her eyes gave her a fresh glow of health. She was still pitifully underweight, but she would recover. Terran would make sure of it, Connie knew.

She hadn't a clue what they were saying in their rapid Scot's dialect, but it didn't matter. Their being together this morning was a crime against matrimony.

"What are you doing in here?" she asked Terran in her faux-British accent.

He eyed her coolly. "*I* am having a lovely morning with my soon-to-be bride." He slouched back in his chair, arms folded over his chest.

"Out." She folded her arms to match his posture. "It's bad luck to see your bride before the wedding. Besides, I need time to get her ready." There weren't many beauty supplies at her disposal, but someone—probably Anselm—had left a hair brush and a folded garment on the chest at the foot of the bed.

"I donna put stock in luck, good or bad." He propped an ankle on his knee, the picture of immovable man.

It was remarkable how much Terran resembled Wilhelm, both in appearance and stubbornness. She'd learned they were a year apart in age and related through their fathers, who were brothers. If she hadn't been told otherwise, she might have assumed them to be twins—fraternal, because of the small differences, like the color of their hair and the shapes of their noses. Wilhelm's nose was more refined and his hair a fairer shade of blond. Further differentiating the two men, Wilhelm kept his hair cropped closely to his head in that Roman style that looked so handsome around a face that might have been sculpted by a master. Terran's face was much the same, but his posture was often sullen in comparison to the disciplined set of Wilhelm's shoulders and the aristocratic angle of his chin.

Wilhelm's air of authority threw her for a loop, because she'd never met another man whose self-assurance she found enticing rather than repulsive. Stubbornness, though, she could handle.

She strode to the bed with a smile for Aifric. "Fine," she said with a glance Terran's way. "Aifric, lift up the blankets, darling, so I can change your bloody rags and check on your healing. How is the bleeding, by the way? Slowing at all?"

Terran planted both feet on the floor. "I'll go and see if I might find some food." He raced for the door as Connie threw off Aifric's blankets.

As his footsteps faded down the hall, Connie shared a conspiratorial grin with the new mother.

"He hates the sight of blood," Aifric said.

"I suspect it's only the sight of your blood," Connie replied. Terran was a warrior like Wilhelm. Blood would not be off-putting to him if it belonged to a foe. But judging from his quick departure after Anice's birth, when Connie had begun muddling her way through birth-canal damage control, she'd guessed he wouldn't want to stick around to see bloody bedding changed. Besides, with his hair flat on one side and his beard coming in, he looked like he could use a little freshening up, too.

Connie helped Aifric with her necessities and washing. While the young mother was out of bed, Connie replaced the folded-up blankets where Aifric typically sat with the fresh ones Anselm had brought.

Before long, Anice woke. While Aifric nursed her, Connie brushed Aifric's hair. She had never been overly interested in hair styles, but she did know a few tricks thanks to Leslie's obsession with fashion. While she worked on a series of symmetrical buns along Aifric's nape, they talked. At first, they discussed Anice and what a good baby she was, but the topic soon turned to more serious things.

"We almost died together, you and I," Aifric said. "Mayhap that is why I feel so connected to you."

Between her soft voice, the nursing baby, and the task of styling the younger woman's hair, Connie took note of a previously untapped longing for this type of charming domesticity. There was a peace in this moment she hadn't felt since she and Leslie were young. Their childhood had ended so quickly. Before Connie knew it, she was enrolled in college and Leslie had become addicted to globetrotting.

Why hadn't she insisted on spending more time with her sister? Connie's laser beam focus on her career had left little room for building memories. She had met many goals and received many accolades. She had found success and was on track to find even more. Faced now with the possibility of never seeing her twin again, all her professional accomplishments felt less significant than the dust under her feet.

"When Sir Ruthven called for my execution, I knew 'twas the end for me," Aifric went on.

Connie focused on the young woman. She would have plenty of time to go over the what-might-have-been's later. Today was about Aifric.

"I thought so, too," Connie admitted, holding to the British accent. "It was terrifying."

"But you didn't just stand there and accept it. You fought the guards. You proclaimed your innocence. I was not so brave."

"Pfft. You were in no condition to fight. I'd only recently been captured, and I hadn't been hurt badly. I wouldn't call it bravery. Mostly, it felt like panic."

"Looked like bravery to me." Aifric reached up to pat Connie's hands, stilling her work for a moment.

A lump stuck in her throat.

Aifric saved her from having to reply. "I thought I would never meet her." She bent her neck to kiss Anice's forehead while she shifted the baby to her other breast.

The movement caused Connie to drop a lock of hair, but she didn't mind. She was working slowly on purpose. Life was too short to squander these simple moments. Seeing Anice come into the world was one of the most beautiful things Connie had ever witnessed. That and Terran's sudden fierce devotion to both mother and child.

Had Aifric been a modern-day woman pregnant without a husband, the likelihood of a near stranger insisting upon marrying her immediately would have been laughable. Maybe young men so willing to take on the responsibility of an instant family existed, but if so, Connie had yet to hear of one.

Of course, the couple's newfound infatuation with each other would fade and they would settle into more of a partnership than a romantic affair, but that was the way of marriages. At least that was what Connie had observed with her friends and family, especially her parents.

The point was that even once the romance ended, Aifric and Anice would be safe with Terran. He was strong, and it seemed he—or at least Wilhelm—was well-to-do. Terran would provide for his wife and daughter their whole lives, and Aifric would no doubt contribute in the way of women in this time. They would be family, stronger for their togetherness, like a tightly-twisted rope.

"Well, you did get to meet her," Connie said. "And what a precious little thing she is."

"Aye. I feel as though I've been given a second chance. Instead of losing everything, I have gained a daughter and a husband. And a friend." She said the last tentatively, almost as a question.

Well, gosh, that was sweet. Connie might not be sentimental, but she wasn't made of stone. "Of course you've gained a friend."

"And mayhap a sister." Her voice brightened. "I see the way Wilhelm looks at you. I ken they're but cousins, but Terran says they've always been more like brothers. I doona believe Terran is the only one with marriage on his mind."

She might as well have slapped Connie for the shock her statement delivered. "I beg your pardon?" She'd almost gaped and uttered a very American "What!" but she'd recovered herself in time to keep up her role.

"Surely, you've noticed. Has Wilhelm nay spoken to you about his intentions?"

"Intentions? His only intention is that we travel to Inverness to clear his name after the—er—unpleasantness in Perth."

Connie mentally reviewed every interaction between her and Wilhelm. True, there seemed to be something between them, but Aifric made their attraction seem like something far more serious than Connie was prepared for.

It might be nice to explore this thing between her and Wilhelm, but she couldn't indulge that fantasy. She had to get home. As much as she liked him, they would say their goodbyes in

Inverness. She would sever their acquaintance quickly and neatly, and Wilhelm would get on with his life.

But what Wilhelm had told her in the garden worried her. It seemed he was a wanted man. The trip to Inverness wasn't to bring justice against Ruthven, as she'd assumed, but rather to clear his and Terran's names.

Anger pulsed through her at the thought of her heroic rescuer standing accused of wrongdoing. It was the height of unfairness and more proof that she had to escape this time as soon as possible.

Things didn't work the way they did in modern America. Ruthven, it seemed, would get away with the attempted murder of two innocent women. Meanwhile, Wilhelm, a man who gave every appearance of being a force for good in Scotland, was supposed to give testimony to explain why he'd saved her and Aifric?

It was so backwards.

And it made her uneasy. Wilhelm told her not to "fash" about him and Terran, but that was one order she couldn't obey. The thought of him being punished for his good deed infuriated her. She wouldn't allow it.

It seemed this trip to Inverness was much more important than she'd realized. As she finished with Aifric's hair, she determined to fix things for Wilhelm. Maybe it was idealistic of her, but she also wanted to make Ruthven pay for what he'd done. If the law wouldn't hold him accountable, someone should.

There was no mirror to show Aifric what her hair looked like, but Connie found the effect pleasing. "I've swept it into three small buns. Here." She took one of the girl's hands and guided it to feel what she'd done. The three knots looked a bit like roses with little bits of hair sticking out here and there like leaves. "If only I had some ribbon or pretty pins to embellish it with. Oh!" She had an idea.

Rucking up her dress, she untied the ribbons securing the legs of her undergarment and pulled them out. With frayed ends and a snag here and there, they had seen better days, but they were better than nothing.

"Here we go." She wove one of the ribbons through Aifric's hair. The other, she tied gently around Anice's head.

Aifric touched the hairdo again. "It feels divine. My thanks. Terran will love it."

Connie chuckled. "That man would love you bald."

Aifric blushed.

"Come on. Let's get you dressed for your big day. I hope you'll let me be your bride's maid."

By the time she had Aifric fastened into her borrowed gown, she was practically vibrating with eagerness to lay eyes on Wilhelm again. Surely this only was because she'd set goals for the near future, and he was key to achieving them, not because she had been intrigued by a young mother's romantic supposition.

Chapter 10

AFTER SATISFYING HIMSELF that Constance was safe inside the monastery, Wilhelm went in search of Terran.

"There you are." A male voice stopped him on his way to the guest quarters.

'Twas Elias, the young monk he had sent to the village to purchase gifts for his cousin and Aifric. He was a burly youth with tonsured head. His mouth was set in a grim line. Mayhap like Wilhelm, the lad despised the cold.

"Just arrived back, aye? Did ye fetch the gifts?"

Elias handed him a parcel. "The book of Ruth for the lass and a fine shaving kit for your cousin. I saw him in the refectory when I arrived."

"Very well. Thank you, Elias." Having already paid the lad for taking on the errand, he turned his feet toward the refectory, where the monks dined.

"Wait. There's somat you should hear. Gossip in the village." Elias's entreaty stopped him.

"What have ye heard?"

Elias wrung his hands. "That the baron's departed for parts north. He's rumored to have a capias with him for you and your cousin, signed by the Bishop of Perthshire."

Ice cold dread slammed into him. If the rumor was true, it meant Ruthven had wasted no time filing charges against him and Terran.

Wilhelm had hoped to find a magistrate to hear their side before formal charges were filed. It seemed this was no longer possible. They were wanted men. This made traveling to Inverness much more dangerous since a capias would allow Ruthven to arrest them on sight.

If Ruthven was heading north, he must mean to find them in Dornoch. Wilhelm hoped the letter he'd written to his father would arrive well in advance of Ruthven. The black-hearted baron was not a guest one liked to receive without preparation.

"My thanks, Elias." He made haste for the refectory. Terran must hear of this immediately.

In contrast to the black-robed monks with their white head cloths, Terran's burgundy wool and fair hair were easy to spot. Also a head taller than the few men bent over their meals, he stood out for his size.

Wilhelm tapped his shoulder in greeting since the monks observed silence in the refectory unless the Scriptures were being read, as was custom for the midday and evening meals. A jerk of his thumb in the direction of the guest room they shared indicated Terran should follow him there.

His cousin understood and rose with his trencher, still heaped with eggs and strawberry preserves. Together, they made their quiet way to their quarters.

While Constance and Aifric had been put in rooms far away from the abbey's residents due to their gender and Aifric's condition, he and Terran had been given the state room kept for high ranking guests. He'd tried convincing Anselm to put the women in that room since 'twas the finest, but Anselm insisted the old dorter chambers given to the women were a better choice because they abutted the infirmary, where supplies for Aifric would be close at hand. Wilhelm hadn't failed to notice that wing also happened to be closest to the abbey's burial yard. Thank the

Lord they hadn't required use of that particular portion of Anselm's domain.

"Sit," he commanded Terran once they entered their room. He motioned toward the weapons chest at the foot of the bed they would have shared if Terran had seen fit to leave Aifric's side at night, which he hadn't. "I wish to tidy your appearance."

"What are ye planning to do to me?" Terran eyed him warily as he partook of his meal.

Wilhelm opened his shaving kit for the second time that morning. "You need a shave. I plan to comb your hair as well. There isna time to wash it, but I'll tame it with some oil."

Terran harrumphed and submitted to Wilhelm's care.

While Wilhelm shaved his cousin, he inquired after Aifric and told him how he'd found Constance in the cloister. He didn't mention the *tow-ma-tow* plants they'd spoken of, only that she seemed hale and well rested.

He didn't look forward to telling Terran that their plan to ride as a threesome to Inverness had suddenly changed. Best to have it over and done with.

"I leave with Constance after the midday meal." He braced himself for argument.

"I've been thinking," Terran replied, tilting his chin for the blade. "Why not return home first? Inverness isna far from Dornoch. We could take Aifric. I'll see her and the bairn safe to our kin. That way, we could speak to Kenrick directly and ride with him to find a magistrate to hear our case. We could even ride out under the banner of the Murray. Make an impression when we arrive."

Wilhelm understood Terran's reluctance to be separated from his bride. Fortunately for his cousin, he would have opportunity to remain with Aifric and Anice. But Wilhelm suspected Terran would not like the reason.

"You misunderstand, cousin."

He plopped a damp rag in Terran's hands so he could wipe his face. Meanwhile, Wilhelm picked up a comb and began the arduous task of detangling the lad's lion's mane. "I said *I* would ride for Inverness. Not *we*. And I'll no' be stopping in Dornoch first."

Terran had been dodging the pulling of the comb, but at this, he ignored Wilhelm's grooming and growled, "Listen here. You'll not be riding anywhere without my protection. We travel together. Always."

Wilhelm gripped a hank of Terran's hair with command. "*You* listen." He worked the comb's teeth in short strokes. "I told you the gossip in the village, aye?" Yesterday, he'd gone with two of Anselm's monks for supplies to aid in Anice's birth. Since the abbey wasn't far from Perth, rumors about Ruthven's gathering had naturally been plentiful. The rescue of the women didn't feature prominently, but news of the fire did.

"Aye." Terran huffed with mirth. "If Ruthven hadn't retreated into his keep, he might have commanded his men to put the fire out before it spread to the kirk. Bloody coward. Serves him right the fire spread as wide as it did."

Wilhelm agreed. The damage would have been easily contained if Ruthven had taken up command of his men and brought order into the panic. But all that was beside the point. Terran must hear what Wilhelm had learned this morning from Elias. "There is more, brother."

Terran stilled at the affectionate term Wilhelm reserved for nights before battle.

"It seems Ruthven has a capias signed by the Bishop of Perthshire," he said.

Terran was quiet for a moment. Then he cursed, and it wasn't because the comb had caught. In fact, Wilhelm had removed the worst of the tangles. He was now combing simply to have somat to do with his hands.

Terran's concern was not misplaced. When the church became involved in the affairs of nobles, no good ever came of it.

Wilhelm put down the comb and removed the cork from a bottle of grooming oil. Rubbing a drop between his palms, he said, "You and I both ken the sensible charges would be instigating and arson. We would appear before the Earl of Perthshire, admit to such, give our reasons, and face losing some of Dornoch's holdings if we come out on the losing end. But if Ruthven sought a capias from the bishop, it must mean the charges are serious enough to warrant a bishop's ruling. Mayhap the fire did more damage than we've heard. Mayhap Ruthven claims we attempted to burn down his kirk or harm his priest in the skirmish."

A stream of curses erupted from Terran, who leapt up and stalked back and forth across the room. "First thing a warrior learns is to ne'er lay hands on one ordained by the church. We didna touch that poor excuse for a priest. We wouldna have, even if he'd put himself in the path of our swords."

Terran spoke true. They'd slain the guards and the executioner, but they hadn't touched the priest, who had fled into the kirk while Ruthven had disappeared into the keep.

"*We* didna touch him, but the fire might have. I canna imagine any other reason for the bishop's involvement."

"I hope the bastard burned to a cinder," Terran spat. "I hope the fire killed him. Pity it didn't kill Ruthven." Not an ounce of mercy in Terran for those who didn't deserve any.

Wilhelm heartily approved the sentiment. But he must keep them focused on the matter at hand. "Regardless of the charges, Ruthven has ridden north with his capias. He must intend to find us in Dornoch."

Terran snorted. "Our kin would never fulfill the capias, even if we were there. Your father will most likely tear it to bits the moment Ruthven rides away."

"Mayhap, especially after reading my letter." Which would his father receive first, Wilhelm's letter recounting the rescue and requesting Kenrick's aid or Ruthven's capias? Wilhelm's messenger had a day's head start if Ruthven had left Perth this morn'.

"Even if my father ignores the capias, the charges will remain," Wilhelm reminded his cousin. "We would eventually have to face Ruthven's bishop. Our only hope is to meet the baron action for action. 'Tis more imperative than ever we find a magistrate who will hear our confession and rule justly. Our only defense is an official ruling that can be pitted against the capias in court. Kenrick will aid us.

"Until then, 'tis vital we avoid Ruthven. That is the reason we must separate. Ruthven canna be in two places. If the worst happens and one of us is arrested, the other can still meet with Kenrick and find a magistrate to reduce the charges." That wasn't the only reason Wilhelm wanted to leave Terran behind, but he didn't want to burden the lad with the more important reason on his wedding day.

Hands on hips, Terran faced him. The grooming had taken. He looked like a man a lass would be proud to wed, except for his scowl. "You put too much faith in finding a fair magistrate, cousin. 'Twould be better to simply track Ruthven and slay the bastard. If we leave now, we can catch him before he reaches Dornoch."

That would be Wilhelm's preference as well, but killing Ruthven would ruin his chances at sitting in parliament one day. Terran knew it as well as he did. His cousin did not intend to cut Ruthven down in truth. 'Twas merely a fantasy.

"Aye," Wilhelm agreed in jest. "Come, let's saddle the horses. What will ye tell your bride? You'll wed her when we return, if we escape judgment as murderers?"

Terran snorted and continued his pacing. "Speaking of the women, you claim your Constance will give testimony to aid you, but are you cert she willna attempt to sully your name? Or harm you on the road?"

A growl rose in his throat. He did not appreciate Terran suggesting Constance was capable of treachery.

Terran held up a hand. "Your truth sense told you she considers herself innocent of the crimes Ruthven charged her with, but beyond that, you ken naught of her. You canna be cert her testimony will help our cause. Somat about her is off, Will. Taking her with you could do more harm than good. If we must be separated, you ought to leave both the lasses with me."

"Constance comes with me," he said simply.

Terran rolled his eyes. "You havena pressed her for answers as yet, have you? What assurance do you have she'll not attempt to harm you?"

"I shall obtain answers on the journey," he said shortly. He wouldn't explain to Terran his assessment that fully kenning Constance would require gentleness. Or that he longed to win her heart. "You forget I am a fine warrior. Think you I'd allow a woman to harm me?"

Terran threw his hands up in the air. "That's bloody grand, Will, so long as ye doona require rest on the road. What will you do if she slits your throat in your sleep?"

Anger heated Wilhelm's neck. "Enough. You speak of the woman who helped Aifric give birth. Your soon-to-be wife and daughter you trusted to her, but you willna trust her with me?"

"I was there when she tended Aifric and Anice. If you have your way, I willna be there to defend you—as I vowed to your da I would—should she attempt to harm you."

"She willna."

"You canna predict such." Terran's cheeks took on a ruddy hue. Anger riled them both, but they kept their argument quiet. It would not do to raise voices in an abbey.

"I can," Wilhelm insisted.

"No. You canna. You desire her. I see that. Think you I doona understand desire?" He smirked.

Aye, Terran understood desire, all right. He had understood it and paid it more heed than he ought since he was but a lad.

"A bonny one she is, cousin, but she has secrets in her eyes. I doona trust her to ride alone with you to Inverness. If you insist on taking her, I must go with you. One of us must watch the woman at all times."

"No." Frustration banded his lungs, because there was no ideal scenario. "I need you safe. Canna you see? Ruthven has many allies, more than we do. If we're arrested together, we'll have no hope of refuting his charges."

"Then we refuse to be taken." Bloodlust shone from Terran's eyes.

Wilhelm sighed. He must make his cousin understand. "Listen, brother. My parents have only me. Your brothers are fine men, but if I canna lead the Murray, I wouldna trust the lairdship to any but you. If I am arrested, you must flee with your bride and find another way to clear our names. If a way canna be found, then you must remain hidden until Ruthven forgets his grudge."

There. He'd said it without saying it. Terran would understand his meaning, that he feared losing his life to this plot of Ruthven's. The only way he could bear such a fate would be if he knew Terran was safe and would eventually return to their home to take up the mantle of laird.

Terran's eyes widened. They hadn't spoken of such things before, but Wilhelm and his father had. "Christ, Will. It willna come to that, surely. Ruthven canna end you over this." He spoke the words with confidence, but uncertainty showed in his eyes.

"He might."

Terran wiped a hand down his face.

"I need you safe," Wilhelm impressed upon his cousin and truest friend.

"I understand," Terran said solemnly. "But that leaves the question of your Constance. I doona trust her."

"*I* do."

"I would say you are a fool to do so, but I have never known you to be foolish."

He strode to the cupboard and removed the one object that condemned Constance of being precisely what Ruthven had claimed, a witch, a spy or both. Wilhelm knew in his heart of hearts his Constance was neither, and he suspected Terran knew it too, but the traveling sack dangling from Terran's hand contained items that some men would consider evidence enough to return her to Ruthven.

Terran tossed the sack at Wilhelm's feet. "Has she answered for this?" He'd found Ruthven's guards pawing through it in the stables. Apparently, they'd lifted it from the priest's quarters after he'd convicted her of her so-called crimes. Terran had taken it in the confusion caused by the fire.

True to Ruthven's claims, its contents were queer. Though Wilhelm hadn't had time to search her possessions thoroughly, he'd found the fire stick Ruthven had mentioned and had noted some strange materials, including a book too neatly-written to have been penned by a man's hand, even a skilled scribe. The images within were perfect renderings, as if a magic mirror had somehow transferred them to the oddly-white pages. Would that he had found the time to study these and her other items more closely, but he had been far too busy.

"I havena spoken with her about it as yet." Between her healing and Aifric's birthing, there hadn't seemed a good time. Though mayhap 'twas more a matter of cowardice than timing. If Wilhelm confronted her, he risked her rebuilding the walls he'd only just convinced her to let down.

By going slow and easy with her, he had gained her trust enough that she spoke naturally with him, whereas she still pretended to be English with everyone else. He'd succeeded in luring her into his embrace in the garden. She had sought comfort in his arms, if only for a moment.

She would explain the contents of the sack, but he did not wish to demand an explanation. He wished for her to offer it to him because he had fully earned her faith, a goal he intended to accomplish during the four-day journey to Inverness.

"Yet you claim to trust her?" Terran's expression said it all. He thought Wilhelm was blinded by his affection for the woman. The supposition was not unwarranted. If their roles had been reversed, Wilhelm would feel the same.

But Terran didn't see how she was when they were alone together. He only saw her steely bravery and the stubborn lift of her chin. Wilhelm had seen a vulnerable side of her. He had seen sweetness in her gaze when she looked on him. Constance would not intentionally cause him harm. Of this, he was cert. But who she was and where she had come from he still did not ken. Terran was right to be cautious.

"I trust her in this. And I ask that you trust me. The items she carries are queer, but they doona cause me alarm. Remain here with Aifric for a fortnight. If I havena returned or sent a message by then, take her and the bairn far away. Wait a time, then send a message to our kin to learn of Ruthven's movements. I will do all I can to clear both our names, but should I fail in whole or in part, you must return to Dornoch only when ye deem it safe." He gave Terran a look of significance.

His cousin's grave expression told Wilhelm he understood that could mean waiting a very long time, mayhap even until Ruthven's death.

The baron was the same age as Wilhelm's father, so it did not please Wilhelm to think of his passing, but kenning what he did of the man, any grievances Ruthven held would not be released while he lived. If Wilhelm could not clear their names, at least his cousin would be safe once their accuser died, or more accurately, when Ruthven's political alliances dissolved upon his death and powerful men like the bishop no longer had motive to honor them.

Terran ground his teeth. "I gain a wife and daughter this day. But you ask me to risk losing my cousin and closest friend. I will never forgive you if we part ways here and I ne'er see you again."

Wilhelm grasped his shoulder. "All this is merely precaution. I intend to return. I have my own woman to wed, after all. Think you I lust for the executioner's blade when I have such a bonny mystery to sink my teeth into?"

Terran grinned, but his serious eyes proved he understood the uncertainty they faced. "Aye, teeth and other things."

Any other day, Wilhelm would have scolded his cousin for suggesting such impropriety. Today, Wilhelm only shook his head and laughed with him. It might be the last time, after all.

"Let us hope she doesna sink a blade into you first, aye?" Terran clapped Wilhelm's back and strode for the door. They had a wedding to attend.

Chapter 11

THE CHAPEL WAS the size of the living room in Connie's condo. At the front, a stone alcove housed a shrine of some saint or other. Similar alcoves along the sides framed busts of other figures she might recognize if she had studied religious history. Three rows of stone benches served as pews, but their little group didn't use them. Rather, they all stood around Anselm at the front.

Terran supported Aifric on his arm, the pair facing Anselm. Hovering a few steps away were Elias, one of Anselm's young monks, and Sister Bethany, the nun Anselm had sent for. Connie learned she had arrived late at night and after a brief examination had pronounced Anice healthy and Aifric underfed but healing well.

Connie stood two steps behind Aifric, rocking sweet Anice. Beside her Wilhelm held himself at military ease. He took up so much space that when she rocked his way with Anice, her shoulder brushed his elbow. She could have taken a step sideways to gain some personal space, but she didn't. Neither did he.

With his straight back, lifted chin, and clasped hands, he projected strength and power. She could certainly picture him as the laird he would one day be. His only movement was the occasional glance her way, accompanied by a twitch at the corner of his mouth. That momentary softening of his expression made her stomach flutter. The sensation, though pleasant, caused her distress.

She had never felt attraction like this for a man before. The temptation to explore it rode her hard, especially after her talk with Aifric.

Once she left the monastery with Wilhelm, it would take them several days on horseback to reach Inverness. They would be alone on the road—and at night when they stopped to rest. Opportunity to indulge her desires would abound. But opportunity did not demand action.

What kind of person would she be if she allowed Wilhelm closer only to leave him at the first chance? She would be as heartless as the men she avoided at all costs, the ones who took a new woman home every night, never committing, never sparing a thought for anything but physical satisfaction.

If two people agreed their relationship would be casual, more power to them. But something about the intensity in Wilhelm's eyes when he looked at her told her he didn't feel casual about her in the least. She'd suspected he had feelings for her, but after talking with Aifric this morning, she couldn't help entertaining the possibility that this handsome, intelligent man had more than a fling on his mind.

While such a possibility was flattering, she must not encourage him. If she did, he would assume her feelings were more than physical. Which of course they weren't. She couldn't afford emotional attachments here when she intended to leave soon. It wouldn't be fair to either of them.

Anselm's brogue filled the chapel as he began the wedding ceremony. After a brief greeting, he began speaking in another language. It took Connie a minute to recognize it as Latin. Once she identified the language, she was able to interpret the majority of what he said, thanks to her boarding school education. That had been years ago, though, and she was rusty.

She could pick out enough words to know he was reciting from memory the Bible passage where the woman is said to have been made by God from a rib in the man's side. She'd heard this bit at weddings before and it always offended her. It made it seem as if women were inherently dependent on men, even from the very beginning of their existence. What nonsense. She refrained from rolling her eyes, but a huff of annoyance managed to escape her.

Wilhelm noticed. "'Tis Latin," he told her. He must have thought her annoyance was due to not understanding because he began interpreting for her in whispers that felt more intimate than they should.

Latin had been long enough ago that she found his interpretation helpful as Anselm continued. The current passage was from the New Testament. She knew because Wilhelm told her so. The section described several attributes of love, including patience, kindness, and selflessness. She enjoyed the novelty of hearing a wedding ceremony in this formal, precise language. Even more, she enjoyed Wilhelm's closeness and attention.

His brogue wove a spell of romance around her. Anice was a warm, trusting weight in her arms. She found herself closing her eyes and finding great beauty in the moment.

"*Entreat me nay to leave you,*" Wilhelm translated. "*Or to turn back from following after you. Where you go, I will go. And where you lodge, I will lodge. Your clan shall be my clan, and your God my God. Where you die, I will die and there be buried. The Lord so do to me and more also if aught but death parts you and me.* That is from the book of Ruth," he said. "'Tis one of my favorite passages in all of Scripture."

She caught his eye and found him looking solemnly at her.

Her heart squeezed. Forcing her gaze from Wilhelm's, she focused on the passage.

"It's lovely," she whispered truthfully.

In fact, she'd never heard it before, at a wedding or anywhere else. It fit the situation perfectly. Aifric was leaving behind all she had known, not out of choice, but because if she returned home,

Ruthven might hear of it and attempt to execute her again. Connie had gathered as much in overhearing conversation between the men the last two days.

She had also learned that Wilhelm and Terran were essentially fugitives of the law after rescuing her and Aifric. Their staying at a monastery was no accident. They were giving her and Aifric time to heal, yes, but also taking refuge while they planned their next step. Knowing Wilhelm was in trouble because of her made her appreciate what he and Terran had done that much more.

It also redoubled her determination to give testimony to clear their names. Maybe that task was one of those gifts of purpose Wilhelm had mentioned in the garden. She might be thousands of miles and hundreds of years away from home, but she had something important to do. That fact made her being here bearable, more than bearable, if she was honest with herself.

She wasn't too proud to shed a few tears as Anselm led the bride and groom through the vows. She didn't even mind the obey part. It seemed to fit the era. Aifric would want to obey her husband. He would want to provide for her. They were both products of their time, and Connie was beginning to see that if it made them happy, there was nothing wrong with that.

As the vows came to an end, deep happiness swelled in her chest. Aifric and Terran were practically strangers to her, but their union felt like a family celebration. Aifric's eyes shone with love when she gazed up at Terran. His eyes hooded with affection when he leaned in to kiss her, sealing their vows.

Anselm intoned a prayer, reverting again to Latin. Then Elias led them into a modest dining hall with a single long table running the length of the room. Several cooked birds dotted the top of the table, likely pheasants or some other small game. Two wooden bowls of steaming root vegetables occupied the center. Near the archway to the kitchen, a monk filled cups from a barrel. The drink looked like the weak beer she'd drunk at every meal she'd been served at the monastery.

They ate together, she beside Aifric and across the table from Wilhelm. She couldn't take her eyes off of him, mainly because he seemed never to run out of amusing stories to tell about Terran, during which Aifric would laughed demurely behind her hand on cue.

Connie had a feeling her eyes would have been glued to Wilhelm even if he hadn't been commanding attention with his stories. His very presence seemed to draw her notice regardless of where they were or who was with them. He was like a powerful magnet and she an object composed of ferrous metals.

As the meal wound down, Wilhelm and Terran fell into quiet conversation. Aifric invited Connie to the far end of the room, where a monk had just added new bricks of peat to the fire. Afric lowered herself to the floor and began to nurse Anice.

"Can I fetch you a blanket to sit on?" Connie asked in her British accent.

It didn't seem right that a woman who had given birth a day ago should have to sit on a stone hearth, but Sister Bethany, whose wrinkled face and general lack of teeth pointed to her advanced age, occupied the only chair at this end of the room. Until a few moments ago, the nun had been rocking near the fire. Now the rocker was still and Sister Bethany had her chin tucked to her chest, where her muffled snores reminded Connie of a purring cat.

Aifric waved aside Connie's concern. "I'll be all right."

Her cheeks glowed with happiness. The shadows under her eyes were fading, and her bleeding was slowing. Before the ceremony, sister Bethany had given Aifric some dark liquid from a vial. Shortly after, Aifric's color had returned to normal. Connie was beginning to see hints of who this vibrant young girl had been before Ruthven's abuse, and who she would be again with Terran at her side.

Connie knelt beside her, getting as comfortable as she could on the floor. The rushes didn't provide much cushioning, but at least they smelled clean. She was learning that the monks worked hard at keeping their space spotless and well ordered. If it upset their routine to have guests, they didn't show it. Several of them silently cleared the table, leaving their guests to their respective conversations. It reminded her of being a guest at a bed and breakfast, only her hosts here were far less chatty.

The delicious meal filled her pleasantly, and the fire warmed her. Her burns were almost completely healed, and her wrists had scabbed over. If not for the fact she didn't belong here, she might actually feel content. Chicago's rat race was a world away.

She wasn't the only one who had vastly improved in the last couple of days. "Congratulations on your nuptials," Connie said to Aifric. "You look quite happy."

"Thank you." Aifric blushed. "You look happy as well." She grinned conspiratorially then lifted her chin in Wilhelm's direction.

Connie felt her cheeks heat. "He's nice," she admitted. "But he's not for me."

Aifric gave her an incredulous look that reminded Connie that for everything the young woman had been through, she was still a teenager. "Not for you? Are you mad?" She gaped at Connie as if she were drowning and had just turned down a life preserver.

"Not mad, no." She forced a smile and a casual shrug even though it grated to deny she wanted Wilhelm. The wanting was completely carnal, though, and she wasn't about to have a conversation about lust versus love with Aifric. "He simply doesn't fit with what I want out of life. I didn't choose him. I know it's hard to understand," she said at the girl's expression of disbelief. "But choice is important to me."

Aifric frowned. After a moment, she regained her composure, showing she might be from a poor cottar's family, but she had been raised to hold her own in polite company. "When I was a young lass, I dreamt of my wedding day." She smiled into the fire and absently kissed Anice's head. "I created an image in my mind of my future husband, painting each stroke with care from his toes all the way up to his head. I decided what qualities I would prize in him and which ones he might have that I would seek to change." She huffed and met Connie's eyes, looking abashed. "Silly of me, aye? You must think me very immature."

If those sentiments were immature, then Connie would have to think of herself as such because she'd done the exact same thing. Milt had been the closest she'd found to her picture-perfect man. "Not at all. I suspect many girls do just the same."

"I suppose." Aifric faced the fire again. "But the reality is that we canna choose. At least, not usually. I always thought it the greatest of privileges to be given a choice in the matter. But now I ken the truth of it."

"What's that?"

Aifric leveled a gaze at her. "'Tis much better to be chosen than to do the choosing, especially if the man is a fine one."

Maybe in this time, that was true. But Connie was a modern day woman with a modern outlook. She had always lived her life believing she deserved to make her own choices. What good was choice if one couldn't wield it to control the most important aspects of life, like career, lifestyle, and marriage?

Aifric's gaze darted over Connie's shoulder.

Connie turned to find Wilhelm striding their way. When he reached them, he squatted down and laid a hand on her shoulder. His touch felt natural and comfortable. They could never be lovers, but she would enjoy his friendship while she had it.

"Time to say your farewells, lass," he said to her. To Aifric, he said, "Take care of him, aye?" and he inclined his head toward where Terran spoke with Anselm.

"I will," Aifric promised.

Wilhelm kissed her forehead. He kissed the top of Anice's head next. Connie couldn't help wishing he would bestow a kiss on her head too. Or on her mouth. But she shouldn't think about him that way when they were about to leave for Inverness and their separate futures.

Wilhelm left, and she took in the sweet image of mother and infant before her. A sharp pain accompanied the thought that this really was goodbye. She would never see this sweet young woman again. She wouldn't get to see Anice grow. Overcome, she pulled Aifric, baby and all, into her arms. "I will miss you."

Aifric hugged her with surprising strength. She would be fine. Terran and Wilhelm would take care of her. They were family. They belonged together.

She kissed Aifric's temple and gave her the goodbye she wished she had been able to give Leslie. But then, she would find her way back to Leslie, making the point moot.

"He will be laird one day," Aifric said. "He may not always have the ability to choose. If you doona have him, another will, and soon."

The warning hit Connie like a wrecking ball. Imagining Wilhelm standing before a religious official with another woman at his side caused an ache in her stomach.

"Remember what would have become of us without our men," Aifric said. "I have vowed to take care of mine. Will you do the same?"

She should have said, "He's not mine," but what came out instead was, "I will."

Whatever she felt for Wilhelm, whatever happened after Inverness, she would do everything she could to clear his name. That was how she would care for him. He'd risked much to save her life. She would repay that kindness if it was the last thing she did.

Chapter 12

"HERE WE ARE." Anselm used a cast iron pull to open the door to a room he called the buttery.

Inside, shelves lined the walls. Sacks, buckets, and crates crammed the small space. She couldn't even begin to guess at what filled them all, but she got the feeling this space was akin to a modern-day pantry.

Anselm shuffled to a shelf that held folded fabrics, all darkly colored. He lifted a few items and thrust them into her arms. "Try these on."

At the top of the pile were a pair of thickly felted boots. They fell to the floor with a muted thud as she shook out the next item, a brown cloak with a hood. She wrapped it around her shoulders and fastened it then slipped her stocking feet into the boots. They were warm and heavy enough to protect her feet over rough terrain.

"Night boots," Anselm said. "We keep them on hand lest we freeze our toes off during the midnight prayers."

"Thank you," she told Anselm, using the British accent she was beginning to feel at home with. "I wish I had something to offer in exchange. You've been so generous."

She was going to miss him and the monastery. He'd been so kind and thorough in his care. At least when she returned home, she would have the memories.

Anselm waved away her thanks. "'Tis the brothers' honor to offer aid where needed. God bless you, my lady."

She had never been religious, but she accepted his blessing gratefully. She would need all the help she could get if she were going to find her way back to the present day. She'd spent the morning trying and failing to isolate the precise factors required for the magic to occur. Had it been Leslie's wish, the solstice, Druid's Temple, the witch's stone or some combination? Possibly, the magic could be attributed to none of those things. She wouldn't put it past the shopkeeper in her dream to have worked the magic himself for whatever reason. What if there was nothing she could do to reverse what had happened?

She had to find the shopkeeper. He seemed like the key to all this. But if she couldn't find his shop in Inverness, it left her with few options. It wasn't as if she could go door to door asking if anyone knew a witch she could consult. She'd nearly been burned at the stake for supposedly being a witch. That had to mean witches weren't popular among the general population.

Uncertainty and helplessness swirled around her. If she let them, they would drag her down in a whirlpool of doubt. This she couldn't afford. She must be strong for Wilhelm and then for herself. First she would clear his name. Then she *would* find her way back.

Anselm loaded her arms with supplies, including a basket of cracker-like wafers, a wheel of cheese, a jar of fig jam, and a bag of oats he told her could be used to make parritch. When Anselm led her from the buttery, Terran met them and relieved her of her burden.

"I'll take her to the stables, Father," he said.

This was it. She was leaving. "Goodbye, Father," she said, her heart heavy.

"Farewell, mistress Constance. Godspeed on your journey."

When she was alone with Terran, she asked after Aifric.

He led her through the kitchens to the outdoors, holding the door for her. A cold drizzle made her glad for her cloak.

"She is resting," he said, setting a slow pace as they followed the path to a big stone barn. "Your feet? Are they improved?"

"Yes, thank you." Her toes were toasty warm in the boots Anselm had given her, but in a good way, not a burned way. "Congratulations on your marriage."

Tiny raindrops made his thick mane of golden hair sparkle. He was handsome, but not quite as handsome as Wilhelm. He nodded, unsmiling.

Terran almost always had either a smile or a smirk on his face. "Is something wrong?" she asked.

He stopped midway down the trail.

To be polite, she stopped too. Up ahead, Wilhelm placed the bridle on a stunning horse. If she had to guess at the breed, she would say it was an Andalusian based on the grayish-white coloring and the sturdy neck and hindquarters. The dark gray mane and tail matched the horse's muzzle.

A horse that fine must belong to Wilhelm. He would look amazing sitting atop that shiny black saddle.

Terran stared at his cousin, a look of dismay on his face.

Why had he stopped?

"Terran?" she asked. "What's wrong?"

"He has a gift, you know." He inclined his head her way but kept his eyes on Wilhelm.

"I'm sure he has many." Had she said that out loud?

Terran's eyes crinkled at the corners for a brief second. But his overall tone was unusually serious as he said, "He can sense truth."

She didn't say anything. To say she'd noticed would be too much like admitting she had attempted to lie to him and been caught in the act. Did Terran know she wasn't really English? But of course he did. He and Wilhelm were confidantes. That didn't keep her from maintaining the accent, however. She only felt comfortable dropping it around Wilhelm.

"I know," she said at last, because he seemed to be waiting for a response.

He cut his gaze to her. Normally, Terran provided the easygoing counterpart to Wilhelm's formal bearing. There was nothing easygoing about him now.

If she were a lesser woman, she might be cowed by his stormy look.

"I have a gift as well, lass."

Here it came. He was going to tell her to drop the act. He was going to ask her where she'd come from and who she was. She'd avoided the questions long enough.

"Oh?" She braced herself.

"I can sense loyalty." His gaze bored into hers.

He made her want to squirm, but she resisted.

"My loyalty is to him. My future laird. I am sworn to protect him and bring him home to his mother and father, my aunt and uncle. Yet he has asked me to remain behind while he goes to Inverness. You ken as much."

She nodded. "It must be difficult, wanting to be two places." She knew that feeling well.

Part of her enjoyed this time in the past. She didn't have to constantly assert herself or risk being passed over for management of a new project. There was no pollution, at least not out here in the country. There was no traffic, no constant noise. When night fell, the darkness was complete in a way that made her feel at peace. The rat race of the city felt a million miles away.

Being here, with Wilhelm, was refreshing. But she would begin to miss Chicago. Once the sense of being on vacation vanished, she would want to return to her job and her busy life. Already she missed having resources and control over what happened to her.

"Aye. 'Tis." he said simply. His nostrils flared, and his gaze intensified. "Your loyalty is not to him. Let us not pretend otherwise."

She reeled back as if he'd slapped her. "Excuse me?"

"He is taken with you. Mayhap this prevents him from using caution. Mayhap he gives you his trust too easily. This is not commonly his way." A hint of worry softened his eyes.

"I would never hurt him. He saved my life. I'm going to Inverness to help clear his name. And yours," she pointed out. How dare this man question her loyalty?

He dares because he loves his cousin, whispered her conscience. *And he's right.*

Her first loyalty was to herself. She would help Wilhelm, yes, but her foremost goal was to return to Chicago and Leslie and a job she was darn good at, even if it wasn't exactly heaven on Earth. She had to break up with Milt. Her father had a retirement party in a few weeks. She'd been helping her mother plan it. Of course her loyalty was to her home and family. She wouldn't let this near-stranger make her feel guilty about the fact.

"Nevertheless, your loyalty is not to him. If I didna ken better, I might suspect you of casting a spell over him."

She gasped.

"I said, if I didna ken better. You're no witch. I doona abide such nonsense. But you're also no' English. Ye sound English, but Will says your speech is different when you are alone with him."

She opened her mouth to argue, but he silenced her with a cutting motion of his hand.

"*Whist.* I'll no' have ye taking umbrage with me for acting on Will's behalf. He'll be taking you to Inverness, and that's that. I say this to you, though. If you raise a hand to him or bring any ill fate down on his head, I will hunt you down and repay you in kind."

Her heart missed a beat. Before coming to the past, no man had ever threatened her with violence. For all Terran's joviality, underneath, he was a warrior. That was the side he showed her now. If provoked, he could be a dangerous man. She suspected that went for Wilhelm too. She must not underestimate him simply because she found him attractive.

"I said I would never hurt him," she said, relieved her voice didn't betray her sudden intimidation.

"See that you hold to that, lass, and we shall get along fine when we meet again."

They wouldn't meet again. She would be long gone by the time Wilhelm rode home to Dornoch and reunited with Terran and Aifric.

Pasting a smile on his face, he continued down the path. "Hail, Will!" he called, voice upbeat, as if he hadn't just scared the bejeezus out of her. "That the pony you found in the village?" When he reached the barn, he tied the cargo Anselm had given her onto the back of the gray horse's saddle.

"Aye. A beauty, he is. A fine gelding for a fine lady." The horse was for her? Wow. Thanks to riding lessons all through high school, Connie knew her horses, and this was, as Wilhelm had said, a fine one. He must have cost a pretty penny.

She couldn't wait to ride him.

"Come, Constance. 'Tis time we mount up. If we make haste, I ken of a place to lodge tonight out of the rain." Wilhelm linked his hands at the gelding's side to help her.

She'd been away from him for an hour as Anselm helped her prepare for their journey. Laying eyes on him again was like the sun coming out after months of winter. He'd had the kilt on for the wedding. Since then, he'd fastened on his armor and wrapped a blanket-sized length of kilt around his armor and head for warmth. A war helm hid his blond hair. He was clean shaven, and his blue eyes filled her with warmth as he looked expectantly at her.

Heavens. I'm about to ride across historical Scotland with an actual Highland warrior.

She put her foot in his hands, the first step in her journey home.

§

Connie hadn't been on a horse in years, but her muscles remembered what to do. It took a few minutes, but eventually, her spine began working in concert with the gelding's energetic walk, and she felt one with the animal.

Wilhelm rode ahead of her on a black gelding that looked like a cross between a draft horse and a solid riding breed. A warhorse, he called it, by the name of Justice. If her horse had a name, Wilhelm hadn't gotten it from the seller. She would have to think of something to call it, but she would need to get to know him a little first.

Patting the horse's neck, she spoke quietly to him. Riding hunt seat had been a passion of hers when she'd been a teenager. Her parents had bought her a Thoroughbred named Monica's Journey, and Connie had won many ribbons jumping the mare in shows. The time for such entertainments had passed, though, once Connie graduated from boarding school. She had done the sensible thing and arranged for the horse's sale before leaving for college. She missed Monica, but her life didn't have room for frivolities like riding and showing.

She focused on the horse beneath her because thinking about Terran's warning made her tremble inside. His words reminded her that even though she sometimes felt like she was on vacation, her presence in the past wasn't a game. If she said or did the wrong thing, it could mean the difference between life and death. Hers or Wilhelm's.

She'd meant what she'd told Terran. She would do everything in her power to help Wilhelm. But Terran had been right. Her first priority was returning home. What if she had to choose between helping Wilhelm or helping herself?

No. She wouldn't go there. There were other, more likely problems for her to deal with, like what she would say when

Wilhelm finally asked her all the questions she'd been anticipating since waking up in the monastery.

While he seemed to have thawed toward her since their initial meeting, he would still expect her to tell him who she was and where she was from. If he didn't like her answers, he was capable of overpowering her, of hurting her if he wanted to. She didn't think he would, but then, she wouldn't have thought Terran would threaten her, either.

Atop his warhorse, Wilhelm seemed more imposing than ever. Straight backed and armed with a double-headed axe in a sling between his shoulder blades, not to mention the Highland broadsword at his hip, he was the quintessential Scottish warrior. If she were a villager and he a knight riding through with a cadre of men, she would be terrified.

Maybe a small part of her *was* terrified, but not of the warrior in Wilhelm. His kindness and softness frightened her more. Why, she couldn't figure out, and decided to put it from her mind.

Wilhelm rounded a copse of trees. She followed and found him angling his warhorse toward an open vista. She did the same and found herself looking out over miles of farmland. They'd been riding ever so gradually uphill, and here at the top of a ridge, they had a perfect view of their starting point.

"It's the monastery," she said.

The collection of stone and wood buildings huddled in the rain on the edge of a sodden grazing pasture. Black patches of wooded areas wound between flat green fields. Beyond was the village where Wilhelm had gotten her horse. Past the village a body of water shimmered in distant sunlight like a spill of molten aluminum.

"Loch Tay." Wilhelm's voice was close and deep. He'd nudged his horse alongside hers. Justice was a good hand taller than her horse. This resulted in her thigh nestling just under Wilhelm's as the horses nearly touched, probably enjoying each other's warmth. She wouldn't mind enjoying Wilhelm's warmth, but there was no time for cuddling—thank goodness. They had an afternoon of riding ahead of them.

Besides the horses' heavy breathing, the only other sound was the patter of rain on their tack and cloaks. Wait, no. There was another sound, a dull roar.

"That rushing you hear is the Falls of Moness." Wilhelm lifted his chin toward a wall of tall, leafless birches.

Now that she concentrated, she recognized the sound of a waterfall. She couldn't see it, but clearly, it wasn't far beyond those trees.

"'Tis said Queen Joan stopped there with her son, the soon-to-be-crowned king, after her husband's assassination. She was wounded in the coup in Perth and fled to the north to hide. Later, she appeared in Edinburgh, healed and with a healthy James the second in tow. But rumor has it the lad had been injured and was treated by a monk they met at the falls when they stopped to drink."

"Maybe a monk from Anselm's monastery," she mused.

"Mayhap. Would have been more than forty years ago, before Anselm's tenure."

Who needed a travel guide when she had a real-live Highlander to show her around?

"Fascinating," she said, feeling lighter than she had since her talk with Terran.

Wilhelm glanced her way with a hint of smile. "Aye," he said, and she had the impression he wasn't talking about Queen Joan's flight from Perth. He clucked, and his horse returned to the path.

Her cheeks heated as her horse followed automatically. This man made her feel like a school girl with a crush. Even when she'd been a school girl, she hadn't had crushes this potent.

Ah. That explained the fear. *Having a crush on a man gives him power over you, Connie girl. Rein in your emotions or the next few days are going to leave a mark.*

"You know a lot about this area," she said, giving him an opening to boast. She needed him to reveal some kind of personality deficiency quick before she fell any deeper in lust.

He only grunted. It could have been assent or disagreement.

She wouldn't give up that easily. She'd find another way to get him to expose some critical failing that would kill her attraction to him.

They rode in silence while she thought about that night at Ruthven's home. It hadn't escaped her attention that it had been a castle. Ruthven was well-to-do. And Wilhelm had been present, apparently by invitation. Why? If Wilhelm was the moral, kind man she thought he might be, what was he doing at the house of a cruel man like Ruthven?

"Is Ruthven an acquaintance of yours?" She had to raise her voice to be heard over the rush of the falls.

He nodded and glanced at her over his shoulder. "And my father's before me." His dark expression reinforced her suspicion that he and Ruthven might be acquaintances but they were not friends.

The path was wide enough that she could ride alongside him, so she clucked to get her mount to speed up until it was neck and neck with Wilhelm's horse.

"You are competent in the saddle," he commented, mild surprise on his face.

"Yes," she said simply. "But I want to hear more about how you know Ruthven. Who is he? And what were all those well-dressed people doing at his home?"

With a shiver that had nothing to do with the cold, she remembered the eager anticipation on the faces in the crowd.

Those people might have looked civilized, but they'd wanted to see her burn.

"I will tell you, if you will tell me where you learned such horsemanship."

"Agreed."

He grinned as though he'd won a concession. But he hadn't, really. She could tell him about the riding instructor her parents had hired without admitting where—or when—she was from.

"Well?" she demanded. "Out with it."

Wilhelm chuckled. The sound turned her insides to jelly. Despite her best effort, she liked amusing him. She liked *him*.

"Ruthven is a baron, like my father, but that is where the comparison ends." His voice darkened. "Ruthven's a corrupt deceiver of men who seeks naught but his own gain. My preference would be ne'er to deal with the likes of him, but he has alliances my father canna match. Being so near to Edinburgh, Ruthven travels in circles I canna hope to touch until I attain a seat in parliament. As that is a long way off, I must occasionally seek supporters under the noses of my enemies. That is why I was present at Castle Ruthven."

Wilhelm was a politician? He wanted to be in parliament? She hadn't even known Scotland had a parliament in the fifteenth century. It had to be a young system. Goodness, might Wilhelm have a hand in shaping the very political climate of Scotland? Her heart thumped hard at the thought.

"I thought you were going to be laird one day. Why do you want a seat in parliament? Do you hope for power? Riches?"

Wilhelm laughed. "Nay, lass. Such goals would be sooner reached by serving my clan as laird alone and cultivating alliances and resources from Dornoch. 'Twill be the more rigorous path, dividing my time between clan and country, but improvements willna come without good, moral men supporting the crown."

"Improvements for your clan?"

"Aye," he said with a shrug. "But for all of Scotia as well. If our nation is to survive and thrive alongside England, she needs reform."

Darn the man for sounding both logical and compassionate. She could find no fault with him, and that was saying something because she could always find fault with someone if she set her mind to it.

"For example," he went on, "the judicial act my father and I hope to bring before the spring assembly would require all children of the nobility to obtain education from the age of nine until qualified for university. If such a law had been in place when Ruthven was young, he might be less ignorant. One can hope, at any rate." He smirked her way.

Great. He had a sense of humor too.

"Such an act would vastly decrease the injustices plaguing our judicial system," he went on. "What nearly happened to you would become rarer and rarer."

"Uh huh," she said. She'd lost the ability to think clearly, because in the past five minutes, her world had turned upside down.

Milt had fit most of Connie's requirements for what her prospective life partner should be like. Most, but not all. He'd been kind, motivated, attractive, sensible, and successful as a lawyer in the Chicago District Attorney's office. He'd had a promising legal career ahead of him.

But Connie had always imagined that if she married, she would like her husband to have political aspirations. She'd grown up watching her mother organize fund raisers as a hobby. She'd shaken hands with the senators and congressmen her father supported. Participating in the political engine, even in her small supportive role, excited her. She'd always imagined finding some way to continue those endeavors while having her engineering career.

Passion for policy and public service had been on her list. It was the one area in which she'd found Milt lacking. Whenever she had discussed policy with him, he would steer the conversation back to law. When she suggested doing something about ineffectual laws, he would insist that wasn't the point. The point to Milt always seemed to be manipulating translations of the law to suit his client's purpose, not changing laws themselves, not benefiting society at large.

As she rode across the Scottish countryside with Wilhelm, she realized that aside from being born more than five hundred years before her, he was pretty much her perfect man.

Chapter 13

THE RAIN CONTINUED throughout the afternoon and into the evening, but Wilhelm had sunshine in his heart as he conversed with his intrepid lady. Though she avoided divulging her clan name and her nationality, she told him stories of her youth. She had belonged to a wealthy family, of that he was cert, since she had been given access to tutors and riding instructors. Her parents had clearly given her the best life had to offer.

At least a dozen times, he'd come close to asking those necessary questions that had been plaguing his mind. He must ask them before they reached Inverness, but each time he came close, he curbed the impulse.

She was talking with him. She was laughing with him. Doorways of trust were opening between them. Pressing her would undo that progress.

Besides, he noticed a change in her since leaving the abbey. Before, when she looked at him, her eyes held friendliness and caution, also an unmistakable interest, fragile as a new sprout.

More and more, the caution seemed to be leaving her. That sprout of interest seemed to be growing. Once, he had made her laugh and glanced over to find a secret smile on her lips and her eyelids lowered. Another time, after he told her about his valiant father and beloved mother, her eyes were large and liquid and filled with soft wonder, as if she'd never known a man to openly admire his parents before.

Each new expression of hers filled him with more and more affection. He would be daft to put an end to their easy conversation by becoming the inquisitor again. He wanted nothing more than to nurture her interest in him and welcome its blooming with open arms.

Gentleness with her. Going slowly had worked so far. He had four days of riding and three nights of camping to earn her trust enough that he could show her the sack he'd brought with him, the one that belonged to her.

He would coax answers from her little by little, proving each step of the way that nothing she told him would change how he acted toward her. Wherever she was from, whatever trouble she was in—for he was certain she had trouble nipping at her heels—he would not only help, but he would deal with it as with his own trouble.

She was already his. She just didn't ken it yet. She would. By the time they reached Inverness, his intentions would be clear.

The rain stopped around the time the sun began setting, but the clouds remained. There was so little light after darkness fell, he considered stopping and camping beneath the trees, but if they pressed on two more hours, they would find shelter, complete with a fireplace and a bed for Constance. He, of course, would take the floor.

"How do you fare?" he asked her. "Are ye warm enough?"

"I'm fine," she said.

"A little farther and I'll see you warmed and fed."

The sounds of hooves on frozen ground accompanied their climb to a share lodge he had used years ago, when traveling to and from university. In remote areas, if one knew where to look, shelters waited for a traveler's use. Manners dictated that a person leave somat of value to other travelers, such as some freshly-chopped wood, ration of preserves, or a skin of wine. He and Terran, on their journey to gather support for his judicial act, had ridden mostly through populated areas where lodging was easy to come by, but on occasion, they had used share lodges. One evening, they'd lodged with a young couple and their children on their way to a physician for their sick bairn. While Wilhelm enjoyed meeting other travelers, he hoped this night to find their lodging unoccupied.

Finally, the log building came into view. No path led to it, but markings on rocks and trees pointed the way. 'Twas a single room structure, scarcely large enough to accommodate a fireplace and pallet. Behind, he knew he would find a lean-to where they could store their belongings and mayhap find some hay or grain for the horses.

With relief, he noted the barred window at the top of the door was dark, and the clearing was silent. Solitude with his lady would be his at last.

He brought Justice to a halt and dismounted. The warhorse was well trained and would remain where Wilhelm dropped his reins until he returned. "Good lad." He praised Justice before taking the reins of Constance's mount. Not kenning if the gelding would ground tie, he led horse and rider to the rear of the share lodge.

To his dismay, Constance dismounted before he could offer his aid. Her feet hit the ground with barely a sound. If the day's ride had caused her discomfort, she didn't show it.

"Go inside," he told her. "Rest while I tend the horses."

"I'll do no such thing." She immediately lifted the stirrup and began unfastening the girth.

He ought to scold her for disobeying, but he found himself grinning instead. "You are a disagreeable woman, my Constant Rose."

"Constant Rose?" Humor laced her speech. "That's some epithet. Maybe I should think of one for you."

He chuckled as he untied the heavy saddle bags and lifted them down before his lady could do it. "To you I will answer no matter what name ye call me by."

"You must not find me too disagreeable, then."

'Twas too dark to see her smile, but he heard it. Even better, by jesting with him, she declared her desire for him. Though he still sensed hesitancy in her, she seemed to grow bolder every hour. Aye, she was slowly accepting what existed between them.

"Speaking of names, have ye thought of one for this lad?" He reached for the saddle and blanket, but Constance beat him to it, hefting them off the gelding and setting them on a log someone had arranged under the lean-to for the purpose.

She straightened and buried her fists in her back, likely working out the aches from riding. Her eyes reflected the meager light as she looked at him. Another of those secret smiles played at her lips. "I was thinking about Honesty."

Silence filled the air. He'd named his warhorse Justice because acting honorably and justly was of utmost importance to him. He held truth and honesty in high esteem as well, because without them, justice would be impossible. Was honesty important to Constance? He wouldn't have thought so since she had already attempted to lie to him.

Mayhap her horse's new name was a sort of peace offering. Mayhap she invited his questions.

"'Tis a fine name."

Working together, they cared for the horses and stowed their supplies for the night. It didn't take long for him to start a fire in the small indoor hearth and for Constance to follow his instructions for preparing parritch.

The interior of the share lodge glowed with the fire's light and soon filled with enough warmth they could remove their outer layers. Peat smoke and the grainy scent of their meal infused the air as they seated themselves on the dirt floor and partook of their late supper.

He'd brought several skins of a spiced wine made by Anselm's monks, one of which he would leave for a future traveler. When the pot of parritch had cooled enough to wipe it clean, he poured half a skin of the wine inside and replaced it over the fire. The heady aroma of cloves and alcohol wove a spell of peace around him as it heated, and he found he enjoyed the tight quarters of a share lodge much more when his company was so lovely. Not that he minded Terran for a bedmate, but not even kenning he would sleep on the floor tonight could dull his excitement at occupying the same intimate space as Constance.

Terran had cautioned him she might intend him harm and act upon such intent while he slept, but Terran forgot what a light sleeper he was. Wilhelm doubted Constance bore him any ill will. Even if she did and stole close enough to harm him in the night, he would wake. He would then relish reversing the advantage and pinning her beneath him to deliver punishment of a sensual sort.

So far, he had acted a gentleman with her, but should she prove to be a viper, he would show her that he, too, could strike. He would reward any treachery she might attempt with an assault of passion. He would subdue her with kisses and caresses until she learned beyond any doubt they were not—and never would be—enemies.

His cock stirred at these thoughts and lifted his plaid in a telling fashion. Clearing his throat, he got up to pour the wine into their bowls lest Constance notice his state.

"You told me about your intentions for an act of parliament," she said when he handed her a steaming bowl.

When he sat again, she scooted close to his side, cupping the bowl between her hands. Leaning against the sleeping pallet, she stretched her stocking feet toward the fire and sipped the wine. A hum of approval accompanied the momentary closing of her eyes.

A pang of desire shot through him.

Would that he could be the cause of her bliss, instead of a sip of hot drink. He sipped from his own bowl to ease the tightening in his chest and the renewed stirring of his cock.

"You believe every child of the nobility should obtain an education," she went on. "And yet you called it a judicial act. Why not call it an education act?"

Wilhelm did not oft speak to women about his political aspirations because he had learned they did not typically take interest in the topic. Constance was different. She'd listened to his ramblings on the matter and had understood enough to ask an astute question. His esteem for her grew. So did his determination to make her his. A woman like Constance could not only serve him as lover and friend, but as adviser as well. Such a treasure she was!

"The proposal is named for its intended result," he said, proud to share his ideas with her. "Education for the children of nobles is merely a beginning. The result is that in time, those children will rise to hold positions of power. They will become lairds and earls and stewards of their holdings. They will rule in disputes from large to small, and their judgments will be more consistent and more fair if they have all been educated in the same manner. Stability for our people will come only once a foundation of education is made available to all who may one day rule. You see? Education begets a stronger foundation for justice. That is why I call it a judicial act."

Constance blinked several times then took a long draught of wine.

"Easy, lass. The monks may serve weak ale, but their wine is strong."

When she lowered her bowl, her cheeks were flushed with the most delicate shade of rose. How bonny she was with her coppery hair and her eyes of every color. She bit her lip and released it.

"You have a passion for justice," she said. "Is that why you named your horse as you did?"

"Aye." Her ability to draw such conclusions pleased him. "Tell me," he said putting his arm along the pallet, circling her shoulders but not touching her. "What prompted the choice of Honesty?"

Constance smiled demurely and leaned into him, inviting him to embrace her fully with his outstretched arm. When he did so, her lashes lowered then lifted, revealing those stunning eyes. *Och,* the firelight made the various hues dance with each shift of her gaze.

"Well," she said with a mischievous quirk to her mouth. "Where I come from, there is a musician—a bard—named Billy Joel. He sings a ballad by that title. It's one of my favorite songs."

So, she'd named the horse after a song sung by another man. This unsettled him.

By the twinkle in her eye, that had been her intention.

Playfulness aside, he sensed she was not telling him the whole truth, ironic, given the subject of their discussion. "Is that the only reason you named him Honesty?" He rubbed his thumb over her upper arm, a teasing touch, a testing touch.

"No." She rested her head in the crook of his shoulder, indicating his touch had been well received. "I thought it might be nice for Justice to have a companion named Honesty."

His heart melted for her.

"And," she said softly. "I have decided to tell you only the truth from now on. No more lies. But." She sat straighter and gave him a look of warning. "If you ask me something I don't want to answer, I'll say so."

He coaxed her back into the space between his arm and his side. "So I shall have honesty, but not totality."

"Correct."

"I suppose I shall have to accept your terms." Their banter was light, but he understood it for the delicate dance it was. As he'd suspected earlier, she was inviting him to question her. But there were things she did not feel safe divulging. So be it.

In time, she would come to understand that she could trust him with all of her. Every last secret would be his to protect. Every problem she faced would be his to solve. Until then, he would ask of her only what she could give.

He fingered her hair. It shone with health and was soft as rabbit fur. "Will you tell me this? What is your full name? Who is your father?" Who must he inform of his intention to wed her?

She leaned into his petting like a contented feline, but her voice was steel when she said, "I'm not ready to tell you that."

That gave him pause. Why would she not wish him to ken the name of her father? Was it someone he'd dealt with? An enemy? Not Ruthven, since she hadn't known the man's name until Wilhelm had told it to her.

He tried a different tack. "Very well, lass. Will you answer this? Where is your clan, your home?" It couldn't be far, because they understood each other. Were she from as far away as France or the Slavic lands, she would not speak English. Nor would she be familiar enough with the patterns of speech in England to speak it so convincingly. He'd only detected the lie in her dialect due to his truth sense.

"I don't want to tell you," she replied, eyes narrowing as if she expected him to argue and was preparing for verbal combat.

"Very well," he said, continuing his stroking. *Gentle with her. Easy with her.*

When training a young horse, one didn't toss a saddle on its back immediately. The trick was to determine what each young horse would accept and then gradually introduce new things while providing rewards.

Constance was not an animal, but her skittishness reminded him of some of the fillies he'd observed at the stables. She was equally spirited and willful. Just as the most spirited and willful young horses grew into the most prized mares, this fascinating lady would be well worth his patience in earning her trust.

He ran his hand down her head in long, slow passes, combing with his fingers. When he met with a tangle, he worked it carefully. He refrained from asking more questions. He was rewarding her for accepting his touch and for holding to her word. She might not have answered his queries, but she hadn't attempted to lie. This was progress.

She propped her chin on his chest to gaze up at him. The wariness was still there, but it had eased somewhat. "Very well? You'll accept my non-answer?"

"Of course. I agreed to your terms, and I am a man of my word."

Her slow smile took his breath away. Her eyebrows remained slanted, mayhap with caution, but clearly with gratitude. He'd not seen such softness from her before. Not even when he'd had her nearly naked so he could bathe her. The fact that he had put that beatific expression on her face made his chest swell with pride.

"Shall I make another attempt? Will you answer this? Wherever your home might be, do you wish to return?"

She went very still. "I do," she said. Her brows slanted even more. Her expression was one of apology.

"Then we have a problem." He continued stroking.

"Yes." Her agreement came as a surprise. So did the way she leaned into him and licked her lush lips.

Their faces were close. Close enough that he could kiss her with naught but a dip of his head. He was considering doing just that when she surprised him again by climbing upon his lap and squeezing him between her thighs.

She clasped his face, thumbs grazing his cheeks. "But it's a problem for another day." She sealed her mouth over his, and the distance between them shrank to insignificance.

Chapter 14

KISSING WILHELM WAS more than a physical connection between lips and tongues. More than a clutching of arms and a melding of stomachs. More, so much more, than a simple expression of mutual affection.

This kiss, like their first, was need expressed through motion. It was the potential energy of desire turned into kinetic passion. Together, they closed a circuit. Sensation was amplified until the heat from their joined mouths spread like wildfire through her whole body.

This is what it's supposed to be like. This is the part that's always been missing. Fire. Excitement.

Wilhelm crushed her in his arms. Having her breasts mashed up against his hard chest should have been uncomfortable. Instead, the pressure soothed something deep inside her that verged on aching.

One powerful hand squeezed her hip, keeping her pinned in such a way that she couldn't miss the physical effect of his growing interest. As his arousal lengthened and hardened, it provided friction in just the right spot at the apex of her thighs. Shards of pleasure sang through her nervous system. The only other times she'd felt such jolts of sensation had been when she would touch herself to urge her body on when the few lovers she'd taken would do their thing on top of her.

But tonight, she wasn't touching herself. Neither was Wilhelm. Well, not with his hands. It was as if the arousal she felt for him had primed her for pleasure and the coming together of their bodies set off a chain reaction of sensations. She'd never experienced anything like this before.

Is this why Leslie dives into relationships head first? Is it simply easier for her to feel aroused than it is for me?

Connie might have been more interested in the physical aspect of relationships if she reacted to other men the way she reacted to Wilhelm.

She hardly recognized the crazed creature she'd become. She should be embarrassed about writhing on the lap of her traveling companion, biting at his lips, and moaning into his mouth. But she wasn't. She couldn't be. Not when he pushed back at her with tiny lifts of his pelvis. Not when his heavy breathing matched hers. Not when he cupped her head with one huge hand to keep her where he wanted her so he could thrust his tongue even deeper.

Oh, yes. He's burning too.

The thought drove her to clutch him tighter, to give him more of herself. She wanted to give him all of herself.

Crazed with need, she scrabbled at the buttons at his throat. The pourpoint had dozens of them staked one on top of the other. "Want you," she muttered between kisses, despairing at the time it was going to take to expose his chest.

She changed tactics. Below his groin, the pourpoint parted to allow for the movement of his legs. Reaching into the gap, she found his linen shirt underneath. Grabbing onto the fabric, she rucked it up, pulling it from where his great kilt wrapped around his waist. All she managed to do was create a pouch of fabric. The shirt kept coming, like a handkerchief out of a clown's pocket.

A whine of frustration burst from her. She needed to feel his skin so badly she was near tears.

Wilhelm stilled her hands and leaned back from their kiss.

Reality crashed over her. She met his eyes, seeing herself from his perspective. He must think her completely uncouth.

Respectable women in this time probably didn't throw themselves at men and claw at their clothing.

"I—I'm sorry," she said, her cheeks flaming. "I don't know what came over me." Continuing down this path would be unwise. They both knew she intended to return home. Surely, that's why he'd stopped her. Either that or because of her unwillingness to answer his questions.

She couldn't meet his eyes as she waited for his rejection.

But his crooked finger under her chin didn't feel like rejection. "Look at me," he commanded.

She hated how automatically she obeyed. No. She hated him for wielding such power over her that she actually enjoyed obeying him.

As quickly as her anger flared, it fizzled at the sight of his flushed cheeks and heavy-lidded eyes. He'd wanted her to look because he'd wanted her to know the need wasn't one-sided. He looked as desperate for her as she was for him.

She hadn't realized she'd clenched her fists at her sides until he took her hands and one by one replaced them around his waist, encouraging her to hold onto him.

"Lass," he said, cupping her face. His hands were warm and callused and so big they seemed to swallow her up. His hoarse voice held her every bit as captive as his gentle grip.

She swallowed thickly, wishing he would fall on her like a beast and make love to her so she could take the memory of him back to Chicago. But she knew better. He was about to set a boundary. How would she survive without his touch? Without his kiss?

"My desire for you overcomes my good intentions," he said.

She could relate. "I understand." She pulled her arms from around his waist and tried to climb off his lap.

"Nay, lass." He gripped her roughly and held tight, banding an arm around her lower back. He was still hard beneath her, and judging by the way he held her, he didn't mind her knowing.

He wasn't alone in his arousal. Her body was alight with it too. Her breasts felt wonderfully swollen, and the linen of her undergarment stuck to her inner thighs with wetness. She'd never wanted like this before. She'd never actually *craved* sex before.

"I want you, *mo luaidh*. I want you with everything I am." He cupped her head again and brought her close so he could kiss her temple.

The feel of his lips on that tender skin made her shiver. His scent made her feel drunk. "But," she whispered, bracing herself for whatever he said next.

I canna lie with a woman who willna tell me her full name, she imagined him saying.

"I shouldna touch you in such a way until I can call you my wife."

She blinked. "Wife." An image of saying vows before Anselm as she stood hand-in-hand with Wilhelm bloomed in her mind. Then she came to her senses. "We can't get married. I'm from— I'm from far away. I need to go home."

"'Tis a problem for another day," he said with a grin, echoing what she'd said before she'd accosted him. His hands roamed her back, stroking her, showing her he truly did want her, but not all of her, not unless she married him, apparently.

"But—then—" She couldn't tell him that if he was waiting for marriage, they'd never become intimate. She wasn't about to marry a man from the past, no matter how wonderful he was. He belonged here. His clan and country needed him. She belonged in 1981.

"I'll have you, lass. And I'll give you all of myself in return. But not as long as my future is uncertain."

146

That was the sweetest, sexiest thing she'd ever heard. It was also highly disappointing since she was worked up *now*.

"Dinnae fash, lass." He stroked his thumb over her frown. "'Tis only precaution. When this business is behind us, I'll be courting you in earnest. But for now, we must both of us exhibit patience."

He thought she was worried about them clearing his name. She *was* worried about that since he'd gotten into this mess by saving her life. But she was more worried about whether she would make it home. Wasn't she?

It must be her lingering arousal clouding her mind. She couldn't decide which she wanted more. The uncertainty should be enough to kill her arousal. But it wasn't.

Wilhelm brushed his knuckles over her cheek, and she leaned into his petting. It felt so good, being touched this gently, having a man she liked and respected so much declare his intention to court her, even if it couldn't possibly lead anywhere. It would be wrong to encourage him when she intended to leave.

On the other hand, it could take weeks or even months to find the shopkeeper she'd dreamt about. All she knew about the dark-haired man was what he'd told her in the dream: "*I have not been to Inverness again since then, though I do open my shop from...time to time.*"

Her entire plan for returning home hinged on finding this guy, and she didn't even know whether he was real. He'd said she didn't have enough imagination to create something like him, but it *had* been a dream. It could be nothing more than wishful thinking making her suspect the shopkeeper was real and could help reunite her with Leslie. She had no proof.

What if she never found him? What if she did but he couldn't or wouldn't help?

Would it be so awful to spend time with Wilhelm while she searched? Dornoch wasn't far from Inverness, after all. But to spend time with him the way she wanted to—between the sheets— it seemed she would have to marry him.

She enjoyed Wilhelm's company. They had amazing chemistry. But even if she weren't planning on going home, it was too soon to talk of marriage.

Besides, she could never marry someone she had to hide things from. Marriage partners were just that: partners. They helped each other, shared everything with each other. The most essential part of who she was, a twentieth-century professional woman, was something she could never explain to Wilhelm. He might recognize the truth in her words, but there was no way he could possibly believe what had happened to her. He would think her crazy, babbling about time-travel and a future world with cars and telephones and sky-scrapers.

She should climb off his lap and keep her distance from him, but she couldn't bring herself to break their contact. "Wilhelm." She breathed his name, at a loss how to respond to his attempt to comfort her.

"I like the sound of my name on your lips, lass, but this—" He touched between her brows. "This, I doona like. Why do ye fash? Tell me, my Constant Rose."

She couldn't help smiling at his nickname for her. He'd given her another name, too, a Gaelic one, by the sound of it. "What does it mean, that other word you called me? *Moe-loo-ee*?"

He huffed a chuckle at her pronunciation. "*Mo-luaidh,* my dear one." He lowered his face to hers until their foreheads pressed together.

The gesture was so tender it brought tears to her eyes. If she blinked, they would fall. Stubbornly, she forced her eyes to stay open until the urge to cry passed.

"I can't be your dear one," she said.

"Because," he prompted.

"Because I need to go home."

"Aye. You'll come home with me, to Dornoch." His voice was steel while his caresses remained gentle.

"Dornoch is your home. Not mine."

"It can be ours. All you have to do is trust me. Trust *in* me, *mo luaidh.*"

Her body had relaxed under his petting, but at this, she sat up. "I don't want Dornoch. I want Chicago. I want to go home, and I resent you minimizing my desires in favor of your own."

At last, he'd given her a reason to resist him. She leapt at the chance. Who knew when or if he would ever present her another opportunity to push him away?

Anger at his presumption replaced her yearning for his touch. She scrambled off his lap. Her body wanted his, but where it counted, on the inside, they were not compatible. He was just like any other chauvinist. He put his ambitions above hers and expected that if she married him, naturally, she would give up her own life to become part of his. He wanted her, but he didn't care about her goals and desires.

A small part of her recognized she was grasping at straws of offense, but she didn't turn back from this course. She couldn't, because being with Wilhelm ran in direct opposition to her goal of returning to 1981.

She should be relieved. She now had the freedom to leave Wilhelm without guilt when the time came. But it wasn't relief she felt as she stood with her back to him in the small cabin. Weariness tugged at her eyelids, both physical and emotional. Her legs and bottom were sore from the ride, but more, her heart felt bruised. She felt more alone than she had since those men had tied her up and called her a witch.

The fire had faded to glowing embers, and the small room grew colder by the minute.

A pair of strong arms encircled her waist. Wilhelm rested his chin on her shoulder. Rasped the stubble of his day-old beard along her cheek.

Biting her lip, she shrugged him off.

"I have upset you."

She wheeled on him, annoyed when he stood his ground rather than take a step back as most men would have. She had to look up at him. "Of course you upset me. You just implied that I should go with you to Dornoch and forget all about my sister, my parents, my job, my *life*. You suggest marriage, but you don't even care that I'm lost and alone and I might never find my way home." Her voice broke.

Those tears she'd been fighting returned with a vengeance. This time, they wouldn't be held back.

She swatted at them and gave Wilhelm her back again. "Just leave me alone. I want to go to bed."

"Very well." He sighed close behind her but didn't touch her again. "Take the bed. I'll use the floor, but first, I'll check on the horses."

His shoes scuffed in the dirt as he went to the door.

Disappointment steamrolled her. Which was ridiculous. She should be glad he was taking the hint and backing off. She wouldn't have to fight her attraction to him anymore. This was a good thing.

Too bad it didn't feel like a good thing. As she waited for the sound of the door closing, her heart sank into her stomach. She wrapped her arms around her middle to ease the overwhelming sense of loss.

Why wasn't the door closing?

"You have my apology, lass." Wilhelm's voice was quiet. Cold air from outside chilled her ankles. "You also have my ire."

She turned, confused. *His* ire?

"You heard me," he said, as if he'd understood her unspoken question. A muscle ticked in his jaw. His eyes absorbed the meager firelight and reflected it back until they glowed silvery-white, like twin moons. How dare he look so stunning when she was trying to be mad at him?

She squared her shoulders. "What do you have to be angry about?"

"Plenty. You tell me naught of your home, of your sister, your parents, your...job, whatever that might be. I ken naught of a *Shick-ah-go*. I canna so much as picture where you hail from because ye give me nothing. Nothing. Yet you expect me to understand your desire to return?"

Her mouth fell open. She shook her head, ready to argue, but he made that same cutting motion Terran had made earlier.

"*Whist.* I am not finished. What I do ken—and I ken it well—is that we have somat strong and true between us. I lust to taste you, explore you, to make you mine. *That* is what I ken. *Shick-ah-go* means naught to me. But you." That muscle in his jaw relaxed. "You mean everything to me."

His words took her breath away. But he couldn't possibly mean them.

"No," she made herself say. "I can't mean everything to you. Your clan is important to you. Scotland is important to you. As they should be. You are a man with many responsibilities. You'd be a fool to let a woman mean everything to you." She'd been a fool to let him mean so much to her.

"Nay, lass. A fool is one who imposes limits on somat as limitless as love." He shut the door, leaving her alone inside the cabin.

She hugged herself until the fire went out. Then she climbed into bed, wondering why she missed Wilhelm so much when he'd just called her a fool.

Chapter 15

CONNIE'S BOTTOM HURT. She might not be a stranger to riding horseback, but it had been years, and her body wasn't accustomed to sitting on a hard saddle for hours on end. She could handle the ache in her inner thighs, which was no worse than her discomfort after a good aerobics session. But her pelvic bones throbbed with the abuse they'd taken as her unpracticed body found its seat again.

The scenery made up for her bodily woes. Though the sunlight came in dribs and drabs through the white-gray cloud cover, the Highland landscape offered layer upon layer of beauty. Currently, they rode over a marshy plain of brilliant yellow-green. The black waters of a creek cut a lively path alongside their trail. Beyond the creek leafless trees with bark the color of pomegranates fanned upward like artfully arranged reeds in a flower arrangement. Further in the distance, blue hills rose into snow-dusted mountains.

Wilhelm lived in a remarkable place. If it was this colorful on an overcast day in winter, what might it look like beneath a clear June sky?

Her eyes returned to her traveling companion as he rode ahead of her. From his helm to his armor-covered shoes to the way he sat his warhorse like he'd been born in the saddle, his visage inspired her even more than the scenery. Except every time she looked his way, she remembered his words from last night with a jolt.

You mean everything to me. Closely followed by his accusation that she was a fool for placing limits on love.

At first, she'd resented his censure. She was *smart* to place limits on love, darn it. She refused to place more importance on an emotion than on something more tangible, like success. She refused to offer her heart up on a platter to any man who showed an interest, like Leslie did routinely.

But as sleepless minutes had turned to an hour and then some, she'd wondered if there might be wisdom in what he'd said. She'd also wondered what he would do if she invited him up on the pillow-thin, straw-stuffed mattress. It didn't seem right that her rescuer and now her guide should sleep on the cold dirt floor while she enjoyed the relative comfort of a primitive bed. But she hadn't worked up the courage before sleep finally claimed her.

Maybe she would tonight. Because Wilhelm meant a lot to her, as well. Maybe not everything. She could never let any man mean that much, let alone a man she couldn't have a future with. But he meant *something*. Maybe they could enjoy some closeness without losing their heads to desire.

As the day wore on, the throbbing in her bottom bloomed into numbness. It was like her body had accepted the discomfort and figured, *To hell with it. It's part of me now.*

There was a freedom in the acceptance. Her muscles released tension and her mind relaxed. All the familiar sensations of moving in concert with a horse played through her bones and ligaments like a symphony.

There was beauty in this kind of pain. Her body was becoming stronger for it. By the time they reached Inverness, her seat bones would no longer hurt. Her muscles would gain conditioning. The human body was an amazing thing. Sitting behind a desk in the city had made her forget. When she returned, she would join a gym or maybe even take riding lessons again.

Her spirits had lifted significantly by the time Wilhelm called back to her, "Time to rest the horses." He stopped Justice on a gentle downward slope. In the distance, the tree line opened up to a wide river or maybe a loch. They could water the horses and fill their water skins. Maybe she could even wash herself.

Wilhelm dismounted with grace, his feet barely making a sound upon hitting the ground. He was like a bird landing from a flight. Riding was as natural for him as driving a car was for her. Would riding become second nature if she remained here? She might find out if she couldn't locate that Frenchman in Inverness.

"How do you fare, lass?" Wilhelm asked as he ground-tied his horse and came her way.

"Fine, thank you." Every ounce of her defensiveness from last night had crumbled away as she'd relived Wilhelm's round-about proposal during their ride. That's what it had been, after all. He'd essentially declared his intention to marry her with the peat fire warming their skin and spiced wine heating their bellies.

And she'd rebuffed him without any finesse whatsoever.

Her predicament wasn't his fault. He couldn't possibly understand why they couldn't have a future together. Yet she'd hauled off and given him a verbal lashing for failing to consider all the things she'd neglected to tell him.

When she put her longing for home aside, Wilhelm's attention flattered her. He was right about there being something special between them. To feel for someone and have that person return those feelings—that was rare enough in itself to be special. But for those feelings to lodge in her heart with such strength and for her to have crossed not just an ocean but half a century of time to experience them? If she'd ever had opportunity to apply the word *miraculous* to anything in her life, it was this.

Maybe there's meaning in it, said a tiny voice in her head that sounded an awfully lot like Leslie. *Maybe this journey is teaching you something.*

If that was the case, she wanted to be receptive. Maybe by accepting the learning, like her body accepted the retraining of its muscles, she would grow stronger. Maybe if she accepted what was happening to her, it would hasten her return home, like Ebenezer Scrooge in *A Christmas Carol*. She would only wake up from this craziness once she internalized the lesson fate was trying to teach her. And she *did* want to wake up, no matter how hard it would be to shake off this beautiful dream.

When Wilhelm presented an upturned palm—an invitation to help her down—she accepted, turning to dismount with her back to the horse as opposed to holding onto the saddle, which was the traditional way to dismount. This put her facing Wilhelm and his intense eyes as she slid down, down, down off Honesty into his waiting arms.

"Chicago is a large city near the center of the North American continent," she said. She had to give him something to make up for last night. "It's across the Atlantic Ocean, and the journey takes weeks if not months by ship." At least it would in this time. She wouldn't mention she had made the trip in less than one day.

His gaze shifted between her eyes then lowered to her mouth. The corner of his mouth lifted, and he pressed his lips to hers in a gentle kiss.

"My thanks, dear lady. You have given me a kernel of truth." He brushed her cheek with his thumb, making her bite back a sigh. "I ken 'twas not easy for you."

"You're welcome."

"'Tis Vinland you speak of?"

She stared at him, drawing a blank.

"Across the sea? This land of yours. Vinland, aye?"

"Ah." She remembered her history lessons now. Leif Erikson had dubbed the Canadian coast such upon landing there in 1000 AD. "Yes. I do think it's called that by some," she hedged. She wouldn't give him any clues that she was from another time by telling him that Europeans would come to call it "The New World" within the next fifty years. Goodness. Christopher Columbus hadn't even set sail yet on his famous voyage of 1492.

This time and place felt so real she kept forgetting she didn't belong here. Wilhelm felt so real she kept forgetting he wasn't hers.

His eyes warmed. "'Tis a good start," he said, and he moved away to tend his horse.

She barked a laugh, unable to help herself. "Quite confident, aren't you?"

"Aye," was all he said as he lifted a hoof to scrape the dirt from it with a rock. The gleam in his eye as he glanced her way made her laugh again.

Damn the man for his charm when they couldn't be intimate. Shaking her head, she said, "I'm taking Honesty to the water. Please give me a few minutes before you come down so I can wash."

She led her horse to the water's edge then along the bank until trees blocked her view of Wilhelm and Justice. About a quarter mile wide and as still as a mirror, the body of water had to be a loch. Beyond stood more of those reddish trees she'd noticed before and more black-blue mountains with snow on top like confectioner's sugar.

Honesty stepped into the water up to his knees and dunked his muzzle in for a long drink, which forced Connie to let go of the reins or risk getting her boots wet. They were made of thick wool that would soak in the water like a sponge and never dry in this weather. She should have anticipated his eagerness to drink and used her shoulder to keep him from going in too far.

For a minute, she watched the horse nervously and cooed to him. The last thing she needed was Honesty running off and losing travel time to chase him. It seemed she was worried for nothing. When Honesty finished drinking, he sploshed out of the water and stood patiently on the shore, neck low and ears splayed. Resting.

"Good boy," she told him. Content he wasn't making plans to abandon her, she rucked up her skirt and shift and slipped out of her undergarment. Though she'd found them awkward at first, she was getting used to their bulk. In fact, being exposed to the elements like this, she downright appreciated the extra layer. They kept her a lot warmer than modern underwear would have.

With her undergarment fanned out on the rocky shore and her boots set neatly beside, she gathered up her skirts and ventured into the water up to her shins.

"Christ on a crutch, that's cold!" Every part of her body set to shaking uncontrollably, but if she wanted to freshen up, she would have to tolerate the discomfort for a minute. Making quick work of it, she brought cupped water up between her legs and cleaned away the stickiness remaining from her interlude with Wilhelm in the cabin last night. She'd been so ready for him, so needy. But her desires, it seemed, were to go unmet. His too.

"Probably for the best," she said partly to Honesty, partly to herself. She turned to climb out of the water and found Honesty standing stiffly with his ears snapped forward. Sometimes this posture meant excitement, but she recognized fear in the whites of his eyes.

She froze with her feet still in the water and followed his line of sight. Two gray wolves stood motionless at the tree line about thirty feet away. Their yellow eyes bored into her and Honesty.

Fear made a fist in her stomach, but she stepped slowly toward Honesty. "Easy, buddy. They're just curious." She hoped. "Ignore them, and they'll go away."

She took her eyes off the wolves to reach for Honesty's reins. With no more warning than the flattening of his ears, he bolted off into the trees, spraying her with tiny rocks and dirt. "No! Honesty!"

She whipped her head back toward the tree line where the wolves were. They were no longer stationary. They were trotting. Straight at her.

One of them watched Honesty tear into the forest, but it returned its gaze to her. Oh. Shit.

"Wilhelm!"

Chapter 16

Every day with Constance was like leading a skirmish. Sometimes he must sneak in quietly to gain the advantage. Sometimes he must ride in strong with swords drawn. Sometimes, like today, he found it most beneficial to wait her out.

The lass put him through his paces, 'twas cert. If she were any other person he might become annoyed, but with her—*och,* he reveled in her changing moods. Whether she lowered her eyelids to hide her ardor or ire rose in her cheeks with hues to rival the red in her hair, she always pleased him. She always intrigued him.

There is more to her than she would have me learn. She seeks to hide more than just her ardor.

Something about this *Shick-ah-go* of Vinland wanted meat on its bones. His truth sense told him that she had given him a wee dose of truth, but 'twas not truth in its entirety. Discovering each and every one of her secrets would be his pleasure. Whether it took the rest of their journey to Inverness or the rest of his life, he had already committed himself to the cause.

Done watering the ferns, he gathered up Justice's reins and prepared to walk him to the loch for a drink. Hopefully Constance had finished washing. He adored looking on her bare form, but part of the fun was convincing her to reveal herself to him. Not wishing to take liberties, not even with his eyes, he called ahead, but a commotion of hooves on rock made him halt.

Honesty galloped up the slope and came to a skidding stop in front of him. Justice flattened his ears in affront.

Honesty's eyes rolled to show their whites. Even though he'd come to a stop, he danced with agitation.

Constance's voice rose on the air. "Wilhelm!"

He dropped Justice's reins and raced to the loch.

"Wilhelm! Wolves! Get back, you!" That last had obviously been directed at the wolves. The edge of panic in her voice meant they were closing in on her. Lord help them.

He pushed his legs faster. Midstride, he drew his double-edged axe. Rounding the trees, he took in the situation.

Two wolves advanced on Constance, teeth bared. Their coats lacked luster and hollows showed at their hips. Their hunger would make them vicious. It also explained why they were targeting people—they were desperate.

"Behind me!" he yelled as he neared his lady.

She wasted no time obeying, scurrying backward with skirts gathered to aid her haste. The wise woman didn't turn and give the wolves her back. Her bravery never ceased to amaze him.

He lusted to send her back to the horses. Atop Honesty, no wolf would be able to reach her. But he was no more inclined to trust her safety to spooked horses than to wolves. She would be safest here with him. No wild beast would touch her with him in front of her. He'd slay a thousand wolves to keep her safe.

Whirling his axe, he pressed forward. "Think you to make a meal of her, aye? I wouldna recommend it. Tough as tanned hide, my lady."

Constance clucked her tongue. "Honestly, Wilhelm."

He grinned at her chiding as he took two more steps forward.

The wolf on the right had a yellowish gray coat. It held its ground, but the other, slightly smaller wolf, retreated a step. A decisive show of strength would likely frighten the pair off. If need be, he'd fight the yellow one. The other wouldn't pose a problem.

"Besides, you'll have to get through me to take a bite of her."

"Please be careful, please be careful, please be careful." Constance's murmuring filled him with pride. She cared for him. He wouldn't fail her.

Wilhelm made the first move. He lunged to put himself nose to nose with the yellow wolf and carved his axe through the air. Wisely, the dominant beast scurried out of the way. Due to Wilhelm's position, it had to move backward, away from Constance.

"Off with you, now. You've no business attacking men or women." He sliced his axe through the air again for emphasis.

The meeker wolf stopped its growling and tucked its tail, but the yellow wolf kept up its vocal threat. It wouldn't relent unless he proved his superiority. So be it.

Wilhelm charged, axe whistling toward the beast's shoulder.

"Wilhelm! Look out!"

Somat collided with his side, knocking him to the ground. Pain shot up his arm. A third wolf!

The beast had come out of nowhere and struck at his elbow, exactly where the joint in his armor left him vulnerable. Were it not for his pourpoint, those wicked teeth might have sunk to the bone. As it was, discomfort flared at the wolf's vise-like clamp, but it gave him an advantage. If he could roll the beast beneath him and get his axe into position, he could use its own body for leverage and slit the thing's throat.

Before he could get a leg over the wolf to pin it, Constance rushed in.

What was she doing? She would get herself killed! "No! Back with you!"

Unsurprisingly, his lady didn't listen.

Screaming like a Valkyrie, she stretched a length of linen over the wolf's head as if she meant to smother it. To his utter shock, she began pummeling it. "Let go, you son of a bitch! Let go of him! I'll kill you!"

Her punches jarred the wolf's teeth in his flesh, but the pain only lasted a moment. The wolf released him with a snarl and aimed that vicious mouth at Constance. The growl of the yellow wolf grew closer.

If Wilhelm didn't act swiftly, they would attack as a pack.

He launched to his feet and scooped Constance behind him. Wielding his axe one-handed, he drew his broadsword with the other and passed it to her. 'Twas not a weapon he would trust in the hands of just any woman, but since *his* woman seemed disinclined to stand by and let him perform the rescue by himself, she had better have more than a piece of linen to defend herself.

The meek wolf trotted in circles, indecisive. But the other two still bared their teeth. Their ears flattened to their heads. Good. They'd drawn first blood. He would draw the last.

As the two larger wolves sprang forward in unison, battle lust struck him like lightning. The urge to protect his lady surged through his limbs. As always when he faced worthy foes, time seemed to slow. Every move his enemy made announced itself in advance.

He swung his blade with precision. With a single arc, his axe disabled the yellow wolf with a neck wound and lodged in the ribcage of the surprise attacker.

Both wolves fell. Because they were animals and not men who should face justice for attacking a woman, he ended their lives with swift mercy.

The meek wolf ran into the forest. It would not attack men again.

Flush with the thrill of victory, he turned to Constance and yanked her to him by her hip. The blade of his axe clinked with the broadsword in her hand, the tip of which rested in the sand.

She gasped. Her lips parted, and those eyes of every color widened. Her cape hung crookedly, and a lock of her hair formed a ragged loop as it came partly undone from its binding. Even disheveled and pale with fright, she was the bonniest sight he'd ever gazed upon.

The sword fell from her grasp and hit the ground with a slap.

He let the axe join it so he could wrap both his arms around her. Tight. Tighter. *His.*

He took her mouth while the battle lust still rode him. Lips and tongue more bold than was proper, he plundered the wet, welcoming heat of her.

A groan rumbled in his chest.

She answered with a whimper and matched his fervor, throwing her arms around his neck and crushing herself to him from thigh to chest.

A feeling of completion overwhelmed him. He lusted to lay her down on the beach and take her roughly and thoroughly. But where there were three hungry wolves, there might be more.

Tearing his mouth from hers, he growled, "We should make haste."

She nodded, cheeks flushed. Her gaze jumped all around, avoiding his.

He grasped her chin. "Look at me, my Constant Rose."

She did and swallowed hard.

"Why do you fash, lass?"

Pinning her shoulders back, she lifted her chin from his hold. "Just, you know, not used to wolf attacks." A bushel full of words containing but a grain of truth.

He did not press her. Instead, he sheathed his weapons, took her hand, and led her in silence back to the horses.

He didn't require his truth sense to ken it had upset her greatly to see him threatened. While fighting that third wolf, she had acted as a woman determined to protect what was hers.

Taking vows was merely a formality. They were as good as wed. Whatever he must do to make her his in the eyes of the crown, he would do, but they already belonged to each other. 'Twas as certain as rain in springtime.

As soon as they neared the horses, Constance tried to tug her hand away.

He didn't let her go. Not only did he intend to assure himself the horses had calmed before trusting them near his lady, but he loathed the thought of losing contact with her. She might have been gravely injured or worse this day. Her touch assured him that she was alive and hale.

"Wait," he said, pulling her close and wrapping an arm around her.

Honesty bobbed his head, agitated. His ears moved to and fro, searching for the sounds of predators. In contrast, Justice's ears pricked forward at their approach. He knew his master well enough to interpret his lack of haste to mean he'd dealt with the threat.

"Easy, lads," he cooed. "The beasties are gone." Rather than go to his horse first, he left Constance with Justice and took Honesty's reins with a firm hand. "You'll be all right then, aye, lad? Easy. Easy."

The gelding lowered its head, seemingly reassured. Still, Wilhelm wouldn't trust him to carry his lady just yet.

He peered back at Constance, keeping his movements slow. "Are you fit to ride? I'll be taking Honesty for this stretch. You'll have Justice."

"No," Constance said. Her face was still pale, but she kept her voice low, no doubt following his cues to keep the horses calm. "I'm not fit to ride. Not until I look at that arm of yours."

She began plundering his saddle bag. "Do you have bandages in here? I suppose a first-aid kit is too much to hope for. No hydrogen peroxide in the fifteenth century. No *Neosporin* or *Band-Aids*. Not even *Bag Balm*, for crying out loud. None of it's even been invented yet."

Her pitch rose as she rattled off word after word he didn't recognize. The curious tirade terminated on a hiccup.

He left Honesty to go to her. His lady's emotional state was far more important than that of a horse. Clearly, the encounter with the wolves had greatly upset her.

She waved him away. "No. No. Never mind me. Forget everything I just said."

Her eyes went wide—almost frightened—as she returned to her search. But what did she have to be frightened of now that the wolves were gone?

"Stupid," she muttered to herself, resuming her search through Justice's saddle bag. She kept her eyes on the bag, but she couldn't hide her welling tears from him.

"Lass? What fashes you? We are safe now, you and I. And I vow to keep you safe. For all time, lass. You may trust me on that." 'Twas a vow from the depths of his heart.

She froze with her hands deep in Justice's saddle bag. After a long moment she lifted out somat large and brown and said, "You shouldn't make promises you can't keep."

In her fist, she held her travelling sack. In her gaze was confusion and, worse, mistrust.

Chapter 17

OCH, WILHELM HAD forgotten all about the sack when he'd insisted Constance ride Justice. He'd planned to tell her about it gently before showing it to her. Her finding it like this couldn't be worse for the fragile trust growing between them.

"You've had it the whole time." She spoke as if her lips had gone numb. Her gaze was sharp as a brooch pin. Those eyes of every color accused him of keeping this from her to hurt her rather than to protect her.

"Not me. Terran." He took a tentative step toward her. Then another. "He found Ruthven's men pawing through it before he set the fire, and he took it. I did not intend for you to find it thusly."

Clutching the sack to her chest, she backed away from him. "Of course you didn't. You were holding onto it, waiting for the moment it would benefit you in some way. You'll never stop with the questions, will you? And now you have something to hold over me. Right here. Proof that there's something wrong about me, that I don't belong here."

Her chest rose and fell too quickly. Her pitch rose again until her voice trembled with unshed tears. He was learning this behavior indicated a crisis of emotion.

He reached out a hand, hoping she would trust him and take it. "Easy, lass. I am not your enemy. Never will I hurt you. Never."

She ignored his offered hand, his offered comfort. "Surely, you've seen inside. Terran too. Oh. Of course." Her gaze went distant, as if she'd forgotten he was there. She might have been talking to herself. "This explains why he threatened me. No wonder he questions my loyalty."

"Terran threatened you? When?" He took another step closer.

His rising agitation robbed his movements of subtlety. How dare his cousin treat Constance harshly? He would have words with him when they met again.

Constance retreated another step, quicker this time to match his increasing pace. "And you. You've been so nice to me, but it's all to get me to let my guard down, isn't it? I should have known. No one is nice just to be nice. Everyone wants something. What do you want, Wilhelm? What do you want from me?" Her back hit the peeling bark of a birch tree. The sack dangled from the fingers of her right hand.

He wasted no time capturing her shoulders. The firm touch was not only to soothe her but to soothe himself as well. Now that he had her stationary, he could explain.

Her captivating eyes grew wide with fear. She mistook his intent. "What are you going to do with me?" Her voice was steady.

He admired that about her. No matter how frightened she was, it never showed in her voice. But this questioning his honor after all they'd been through would not do. It would not do at all.

"I was considering kissing you," he said. 'Twas the truth.

She blinked.

"Mayhap even ravishing you here against this tree. Taking you again and again until you ken beyond all doubt I'll never keep secrets to use against you."

Overcome with need for her now that he had her in his arms, he lowered his mouth to her neck. He held himself back from kissing her there, but only just. He would be certain she was not afraid of him before he acted on the lust he couldn't help but feel whenever he was this near her.

"Wilhelm." His name might have been a warning. Or it might have been a plea.

"That linen you used to blind the wolf." He nuzzled the silky skin below her ear. "That wouldn't happen to have been your undergarment, would it?" With his lips alone he nipped her lobe. She tasted like a sweet orchard breeze in summer time. He dropped his hands to her waist.

"Wilhelm." There was no mistaking that one word for what it was: an invitation.

"Tell me you trust me, lass."

She said nothing.

He drew back to meet her gaze. "Tell me."

"How can I?" She twitched the sack. "Why did you keep this from me?"

Anger he could have dealt with, but the hurt in her eyes made him feel helpless. All he had with which to combat the suspicion in her gaze was the truth.

"Caution, at first," he said. "To bring it to you in the abbey would have been an unnecessary risk. Anselm might have seen it. Besides, I didna ken you so well then. Then the bairn came, and there was much to do. Then enough time had passed and you'd captured my heart so thoroughly I didna ken how to broach the subject." While he made his confession, he cupped her jaw and stroked her cheeks with his thumbs. So soft, her skin. So creamy and warm.

Forgetting what he'd been talking about, he made another sort of confession. "To think I might have lost you today. I doona ken whether to praise you for your bravery or chide you for your foolhardiness. Never make me fash like that again."

She blew out a breath. Her lips flattened then softened as the fight went out of her. "Then you'd better stay away from wolves," she said, and he understood he was forgiven.

He could hold back no longer. With a growl, he descended on her, hungry as any starved beast, but not for food.

§

HOW COULD A single kiss erase every last hint of Connie's anxiety? Well, maybe "single kiss" was selling it short. This desperate clinging of mouths and groping of hands was more like a hot and heavy make-out session, only that term made it sound paltry, like that time she'd made out with Kenny Garretson in the music room after Mrs. Bemis's cello class. Except, this was not an exploration undertaken out of boredom and opportunity. This make-out session was honest and full of adult passion. It was driven by mutual need and welcomed with mutual longing.

It was an apology from Wilhelm, she imagined, for the betrayal she'd experienced over the discovery of her backpack. It was a promise from her not to doubt him again—how could she have doubted him even for a second when he'd saved her life not once but twice? It was a return to normalcy after the horror of a wolf attack.

Wolves! They'd been attacked by wolves!

She could hardly fathom it. A week ago, she'd been driving her Mercedes through the concrete jungle of Chicago. The most trying aspect of her commute was stopping for jaywalkers and weaving around cabs and busses. Now, to make a trip that would take less than three hours by car, she was riding a horse over the course of several days, battling winter elements and wild animals.

She sobbed into Wilhelm's mouth as the reality of her situation reasserted itself.

"I have you, love. I have you."

"Wilhelm."

Saying his name did something to her. She had the absurd feeling that every time she spoke it aloud it strengthened her connection to him. This should make her never want to say it again. Why would she build connections of any sort in the past when she intended to return to the present? But she *would* say it again. And again and again. She loved saying it.

"Lass," he murmured, rolling his hips forward and taking her mouth again, this time with an urgency similar to when he'd kissed her near the loch.

His armor covered him to mid-thigh. She was glad for it because it had saved him from what might have been a terrible injury today, but she wished it gone at the moment so she could feel his arousal.

"Wilhelm," she gasped when he trailed kisses across her jaw and down her neck.

"Aye. Say my name, lass." His strong hands clawed at her skirts, dragging them up.

Yes. Yes! He was going to give her what she'd been wanting from him for days, and he was going to do it right up against a tree, like a man possessed with lust. For her!

An encounter outdoors had always been one of her fantasies. Of course, she'd never seriously considered it, not back home, anyway. But the rules here were different. They were surrounded by forest. The only witnesses would be the trees and rocks and their horses.

A thrill of anticipation shot through her like lightning. Come what may, she needed this, needed him. But a niggling of concern lodged itself in her consciousness. There were reasons they shouldn't. Many. But she couldn't seem to remember them. Maybe if he stopped nibbling her neck.

"Wait." Gasping for breath, she put a palm on his chest. Ah, yes. She remembered. "Your arm." She'd seen pain register on his face when the wolf had attacked. He might be hurt. "And what if the wolves come back? What if there are more?" Also, he'd told her he didn't want to become intimate with her until they were married—which wasn't going to happen, so...no sex with the tempting Highlander.

She screamed with frustration inside her own head.

Wilhelm had rucked her skirts up to her knees. He stilled his movements with fists full of fabric at her hips. Cold air found its way beneath her dress to chill her heated private parts. She was going to miss the warmth of that underwear. Maybe she could find it and see about mending it when they stopped for the night. She was going to need it around Wilhelm, because the feeling of being bare *down there* shot her level of friskiness through the roof.

Oh, heck. Who was she kidding? It was Wilhelm who made her frisky.

Wilhelm pressed his forehead to hers. "Forgive me. I forgot myself." He smoothed her dress back into place. When he met her gaze, his cheeks were flushed and his eyes were silvery bright. While she watched, the fierce light seemed to bank itself and his irises returned to the blue of a winter sky, their normal color, though the word *normal* fell far short of describing something so beautiful. It had to be her imagination making her romanticize the emotions she read in his gaze. Surely his eyes didn't actually glow.

"There's nothing to forgive," she assured him.

When he tried to back away from her she grabbed his wrists and pulled his arms around her waist again, like he'd done with her the night before. Stickiness on his right hand made her look down. Blood. It had come from inside his sleeve.

Goodness. The wolf had broken his skin. Worry tightened her throat.

"How badly are you hurt?"

"Dinnae fash. 'Tis but a scratch."

She snorted. Scratches didn't bleed enough to create a slick of blood several inches from the wound.

"Come on. Let's take a look." She flicked his armor with a finger. "Get all this off. I might have some supplies to fix you up if it really is 'just a scratch.'" She thought of the first-aid kit in her backpack, hoping it was still there and that his injury wouldn't require stitches.

While Wilhelm removed his armor and went to work on the buttons of his pourpoint, she crouched with her back to him to look through her backpack. Wilhelm and Terran had most likely seen the contents, but it seemed foolish to flaunt them, especially when she had no intention of explaining them to anyone in this time.

On initial inspection, everything she'd packed for her morning hike with Leslie seemed to be there, though the upside-down tourist book and the rumpled silk scarf proved the contents had been rifled through. But never mind that. With a rush of gratitude, she lifted out the first-aid kit and opened it on her lap.

A glance over her shoulder showed Wilhelm still working his way down the buttons. While he disrobed, she discreetly removed the *Johnson & Johnson* packaging from several sterile pads and added a giant glob of antibiotic ointment to a self-adhesive bandage. After tucking an Ace bandage with its metal fasteners and a small glass bottle of hydrogen peroxide into a pocket in her dress, she carefully packed everything else away and returned to her wounded warrior.

He was sitting with his back to their tree, torso bare. His muscular chest gleamed with traces of sweat. The way he sat was incredibly masculine, knees spread and pointed to the sky, forearms resting on said knees.

She'd always heard Scotsmen wore nothing under their kilts, but Wilhelm had a baggy kind of undergarment covering his loins and hose that attached to them with ties. She knew this because she could see it all plainly.

His posture was so very *male*. So very alluring. Heat rushed to her cheeks.

Wilhelm must have noticed, because he grinned knowingly and said, "I doubt I shall ever look upon a birch again without my staff stirring. Were it summertime, you'd ken for yourself how you affect me. I only wear all the layers because I despise the cold."

Heavens. He bantered with her as if they were lovers. The familiarity of it flooded her with tender feelings. Even Milt had always held himself somewhat in reserve with her. There had been comfort in the formality of their relationship. Comfort, but not much happiness.

As she often did when faced with her own feelings, she turned her laser focus to the task at hand. Clearing her throat, she knelt beside Wilhelm. "I'm more interested in your arm than your tree at the moment. Give it here."

He barked a laugh, and she realized what she'd just said.

"I mean *the* tree. Our tree. Oh, you know what I meant." She reached for his wounded arm.

He chuckled silently while she inspected it. Her cheeks flamed hotter than ever.

Her embarrassment was nothing compared to the pain he had to be in. A deep puncture wound in his bulging forearm muscle welled with blood. Smaller puncture wounds showed where other teeth had bruised him near the bony portion of his elbow. The main wound had to have been from a canine tooth.

She hissed as she inspected it. "Does it hurt?" Dumb question. Of course it hurt.

"Aye." He said it softly, not making her feel dumb in the least. "My thanks, lass."

She glanced up to find his eyes crinkled with fondness. Her heart fluttered pleasantly even as the depth of affection she felt for this man terrified her. "Thank me when I'm done," she said, keeping her voice all business. "This will hurt. I need to clean it."

"Go on with it, then." He tilted his head back against the tree and closed his eyes.

She pulled the hydrogen peroxide from her pocket and unscrewed the lid. To distract him from the pain when she poured the liquid over the wound, she asked "Is there a plan for if the wolves come back?"

He groaned deep in his throat as the liquid foamed and did its work, but he didn't move his arm an inch. "Saint's teeth. What is that?"

"A cleaning agent. It should keep you from getting an infection. The wolves. What will we do if they come back?"

"Ride away," he said through gritted teeth. A waggle of his brows told her he was making a joke.

"Brilliant plan." She dried the wound and wiped off the excess blood. "Wish I had thought of that down by the water." They both knew she'd had no chance at gaining the saddle atop a spooked horse. Connie suspected if the wolves came back, Wilhelm would fight them again. He'd fight to protect her as many times as it took.

That shouldn't make her feel as good as it did, her being an independent woman and all. She fought her own battles, and usually won. But this was another world compared to where she was from. It might come in handy to have a "native" looking out for her while she searched for a way home.

Wilhelm smirked as she placed the self-adhesive bandage over the wound and smoothed its edges to seal the antibiotic ointment inside. Well, his mouth was smirking. His eyes dropped to her chest and darkened with hunger.

The dress the monks had given her had a modest neckline that hit near her collar bones, but when she leaned forward, it sagged just enough that he was probably getting an eyeful. She decided to let him look if it would help keep his mind off his injury.

He'd seen it all before anyway when he'd bathed her. She couldn't hold back the memory of that tender washing. It made her bite her lip as she wrapped the Ace bandage around the wound to offer it some extra protection.

"You are lovely when the color rises in your cheeks."

Damn the man for noticing every time she had illicit thoughts about him. "Only then?"

"Especially then."

She didn't want to explain the metal fastener for the bandage, so she slipped it into her pocket and simply tucked in the tail to fasten it. To keep Wilhelm's mind off the stretchy synthetic material, she decided to encourage his flirting. "Have I told you how incredible I find your eyes? I know it has to be a trick of the light and their unique coloring, but sometimes I could swear they glow."

"My mother says the same, only she claims my eyes are because I have the soul of a berserker."

Finished wrapping his injury, she stood and offered him a hand up. "A berserker?"

He accepted her help. Once standing, he leaned against the tree and drew her to stand chest to chest with him. His scent of clean musk and leather filled her with the desire to wrap herself around him more securely than any bandage.

He touched her hair, stroked it behind her ear and ran his fingers through it. The rush of adrenaline from the attack followed by history's best make-out session had left her feeling wrung out. They might be set upon by wolves at any moment, but as she rested her cheek on Wilhelm's chest, she longed to stay like this just a bit longer.

She'd never been within nuzzling distance of a chest like Wilhelm's before. With skin the color of Ivory soap and muscles to put any buff beefcake to shame, his chest was simply irresistible. A light dusting of blond hair fanned over his pecs and tickled at her cheek. A little searching with her tongue and she could probably find his nipple. It would be hard in this cold weather.

Don't do it, Connie girl. You'd be starting something you can't finish.

She couldn't act on it, but the lust was there, and it was powerful. Add to their physical attraction the qualities of the man himself—his mind, his passion for justice and truth—and it was like he'd been engineered for her and her alone.

His voice close and quiet, he said, "A berserker is a warrior possessed with purpose. Some say he is gifted by the gods or imbued with magic. Fate favors him and propels him toward victory."

"Magic, huh?" She closed her eyes and relaxed into Wilhelm's petting. Her mind was only half on the conversation. The other half was reeling at the realization that she was becoming dangerously attached to him. Every hour she spent in this time would make their eventual parting more painful.

But she wasn't leaving yet. She'd be a fool not to enjoy him while she could, come what may.

"You strike me as far too practical to believe in magic," she slurred, body and mind reveling in the moment.

"You are correct. I do not abide such nonsense. I fight well because I train hard. I train hard so I may defend those I love." He tilted up her chin to give her a significant look.

He was telling her he loved her.

She'd known that already, but the words gave her a thrill. Then the rest of what he'd said sank in. "You don't believe in magic?"

"No," he stated with the finality of a door closing.

Her heart dropped. The wintry air seeped through her clothes and chilled her to the bone. If Wilhelm didn't believe in magic, she could never tell him the truth about where she'd come from. He would think her insane.

Suddenly feeling very alone, she stepped away from him. "Better get dressed," she said, turning to Justice. "You'll catch a cold with all that skin exposed." After pulling on her backpack, she placed her foot in the stirrup and mounted, refusing to watch the play of muscles under his skin as he slipped his arms into his shirt and pourpoint.

Leaving Wilhelm to dress himself, she aimed her temporary mount toward the beach. Intimacy with Wilhelm was out of the question, which meant she had better keep her distance from him. And she'd better keep her old-fashioned undergarments on around him. She only hoped they weren't too badly torn.

Chapter 18

SOMAT ABOUT THE sight of Constance on the back of his warhorse stirred Wilhelm's pride and lust in equal measure. Never had he allowed another to ride the gelding he'd trained with since he was a lad, not even Terran. Yet somehow it seemed right she should share his trusted mount. It seemed right she should share everything he owned.

Normally, he would loathe a wintertime journey; the cold, ever his nemesis, would occupy his attention the entire way. But not this time. Having Constance with him filled him with warmth and appreciation for these rugged lands. He saw them as if for the first time, wondering how similar or different Scotia was from her homeland.

Red willow bushes, black firs, and white birches lined the southern branch of the River Spey, which they would follow all the way to the MacPherson lands. There, they would turn due north and ride straight to Inverness.

During the afternoon, the gray-white clouds rolled back to reveal a sky as blue as the silks his father liked to buy for his mother on special occasions. Yellow moss and green and purple plants splashed color along the sides of the muddied trail, but the best hues of all were those winking at him from Constance's hair as she rode several paces ahead. He had never seen her in sunshine before. It was like seeing *her* for the first time.

In sunlight, her hair shone with copper and gold, lending a blond caste to her auburn locks, whereas in darkness, it teased the eye with the same burgundy as his clan's tartan. Yet again, in the mist, it appeared a dun as soft and sleek as the coat of a doe. Just like her eyes, her hair didn't ken which color to be, but every shade intrigued him.

What would her eyes look like in golden daylight? When the trail widened, he urged Honesty alongside Justice so he could look his fill.

She didn't protest his presence as he came within knee-bumping distance of her, but nor did she acknowledge him, except by a straightening of her posture and a lifting of her chin. This was not a surprise, merely a challenge he intended to overcome.

His lady had withdrawn again. Back at the loch, she'd reveled in his petting and soft words, his tame kitten. Then she'd becoming the elusive tigress, almost without warning.

'Twas the mention of magic that put a swift end to her affections, or more specifically, his admitting that he did not believe in such nonsense. Interesting, since he'd sensed the truth of her denial when Ruthven had accused her of being a witch.

Not that it mattered much to him. Witch or no, she was his now, and he knew in his heart of hearts she wouldn't hurt a fly, unless mayhap that fly was pestering a person she loved. Then, *och,* that fly would be better off facing a horde of ants than the wrath of his intrepid lady.

This was not the first time she had withdrawn from him after accepting some affection. Yesterday, declaring his intent to wed her had caused a similar reaction. Through her silences, he learned more about her than she revealed with her words. Soon, he would have the puzzle of her solved.

Unfortunately, he had the feeling he was running out of time. Each time she withdrew, he felt the unmistakable truth of it. She was not playing coy, his lady. For reasons she refused to confide in him, she honestly believed they could not make a life together.

He would put an end to this notion.

He wanted her with a ferocity he'd never before experienced. She wanted him just as badly. That too was a truth that shivered all around her every time she turned her gaze his way.

"Let us rehearse what we will say once Kenrick finds us a magistrate," he said, kenning she would talk with him if the topic was somat other than the barriers to their love.

She looked at him then, and her eyes caught the sun like raw gold in a blue-green pool. Truly, she had eyes of every color. Never had he seen beauty like her eyes, not in any living or manmade thing.

"I thought we were going to give testimony to clear your name. I was planning on telling the truth: That bastard Ruthven ordered me burned at the stake without justification and without giving me a chance to speak for myself. Worse, he ordered Aifric's execution, claiming she had fornicated." She scoffed. "We both know Ruthven is Anice's biological father."

His heart skipped a beat at the victory of luring her into conversation, but anger welled in his chest at her confirmation of what he and Terran had feared. "She confided this to you?"

"No." Her voice softened, and her shoulders relaxed. The lass adored the pair of them, Aifric and Anice. "But I gathered as much from some of the things she did tell me. Did you know Ruthven himself came to take her away from her parents when her pregnancy began showing and the gossip started? He came alone at night and threatened her parents with harm if they breathed a word of it to anyone."

He grunted. This did not surprise him.

"He put her in his dungeon, and she remained there until that night. No daylight, no bed. Only bread and water to eat for months. Makes me sick. I want that man to suffer everything he put her through and then some."

Wilhelm sighed, his heart heavy. He wanted that as well. But... "The truth is always a good place to begin. However, we must remember that Ruthven's influence spreads far and wide. 'Tis no' certain we'll find a magistrate the baron hasna tainted. We would be wise to take this into consideration and adjust our testimony to bring minimum offense. The goal is, as you said, to clear my name and Terran's of the charges—likely obstructing justice and seeking to harm a member of the clergy. Our testimony must speak to those issues while avoiding open opposition to Ruthven himself."

Constance's tongue poked at the inside of her cheek while her eyes bored into the space in front of her. The woman was stewing.

"You doona agree, I surmise."

"No. I *doona,*" she said. "I thought you cared about justice. If anyone deserves to meet the business end of the law, it's that…that…"

"Wretch, toad boil, pig's arse?"

A flicker of a smile curved her lips, but they remained pursed.

Quietly, he admitted, "I would relish the chance to skewer that fiend on the very law he manipulates for his own advantage. But I canna bring justice against men like Ruthven and incite the kind of change I wish, the kind that shall make Scotia a more just place for all."

"Why can't you? For that matter, why can't you skewer him on your sword? If anyone deserves it, that man does."

"Respectable men of parliament meet their enemies pen for pen instead of sword for sword. They battle within the bounds of the law, as proscribed by the crown. As in warfare where one man might have an advantage of size or strength, certain political foes have influential allies. Ruthven happens to have many. It would take an outlaw to put him in his place, and I am not an outlaw." He winced. "At least, I shall no' be much longer if all goes well in Inverness."

She was quiet for a while. At last, she said, "I think you're more of an outlaw than you give yourself credit for." Her eyes twinkled when she looked his way. "You went outside of the law to recue me and Aifric, and you did it in front of a whole gaggle of powerful men. You were very courageous and honorable to do that."

She eviscerated him with her praise.

"Mayhap. I have no regrets, lass, but by opposing Ruthven so publicly, I forfeited the right to bring my father's judicial act before parliament. I may very well have forfeited my inheritance as well. Morally, Ruthven was in the wrong, but the crown is on his side because of the purses he has lined and the alliances he has struck."

Constance's jaw tightened. "That's not justice. You shouldn't stand for it."

"I have no choice."

"I disagree." Her voice trembled with conviction. His truth sense flared. Her bravery and thirst for justice knew no end. How he wanted this woman!

"You are a disagreeable woman, my Constant Rose."

She would not look at him again, even though his teasing had been meant to bring out another of her rare smiles. Instead, she looked straight ahead, her attention focused inward.

What manner of trouble follows you, lass? Why will you not trust me with it? He wanted to ask. He wanted to learn everything about her. He wanted to *know* her intimately, not just her mind but her body as well. His reasons for waiting to bed her fell away with every step toward Inverness.

Uncertainty awaited them. He would do all in his power to reclaim his freedom, but should he fail, he faced separation from his beloved lady, either due to imprisonment or death.

Should the accusations against him stand, he had wished to spare her the dishonor of being wed to a criminal, but he'd failed to ask himself what would become of her then. If he did not take her as his bride, another man would, either a man from Scotia or from her homeland, to which she was so eager to return. This knowledge would destroy him, unless he could be sure her husband would be a good and decent man and one who was worthy of her.

The only way to ensure that to his satisfaction would be to claim her now. Decisively. Permanently, in the way of his ancestors in the absence of an officiator or chieftain. Then, if a magistrate's judgment went against him, he could rest in the knowledge his mother and father would care for her.

If he lost his life as a result of rescuing her and Aifric, he would go kenning his parents would look after her as their own daughter. They would see her wed to an honorable member of their clan, mayhap even a man she could someday trust with her secrets and would take her to her clan so she could slay whatever demons chased her if need be. If he could not be that man, he wanted her to have every opportunity to find him.

Wilhelm refused to trust her safety to chance. If he failed to bind her to him on this journey, he would possibly be doing just that.

Yesterday, it had seemed chivalrous to wait to claim her. Today, it seemed like foolishness to let another night pass without showing her the full measure of what he felt for her.

§

SOMETIMES IN WINTER, the wind would scrape across Lake Michigan and come up against the city like a shotgun blast of numbing air. Though there wouldn't be any precipitation, Connie would feel the frozen moisture in the atmosphere like needles stabbing every inch of her exposed skin.

The trick to staying warm in the wind tunnels formed by Chicago's downtown was not to leave any skin exposed. This was her strategy tonight since the sun had taken with it what little warmth she'd enjoyed that day when it dipped below the horizon.

The cloak Anselm had given her wasn't very thick, but it was made of wool. This made it surprisingly good at trapping in her body heat. It was also large enough she could wrap it around herself and her backpack and still have enough left over to tuck it securely beneath one arm. Thanks to the thinness of the fabric, she could hold the reins through the cloak, keeping her hands from freezing. Between the cloak and her dress, which was also made of wool, she found the cold more than manageable. Her undergarments would have helped, too, but they were currently in her backpack. The voluminous drawers had survived the wolf attack but would need mending before she could wear them again.

Last night had been so dark she hadn't been able to see where her horse was going. Tonight, the moon illuminated their path. Even though it waned, it provided plenty of light. And the stars—goodness, the stars! She couldn't stop gazing at them. They looked so fat and bright, and there were so many of them they made the sky look like an inverted colander. The night sky back home didn't hold a candle to this beauty, not even at her parents' estate well outside the city.

"Lovely, aye?" Wilhelm had slowed Justice until she and Honesty came up alongside. She'd ridden his warhorse for most of the afternoon, but after they'd stopped for a meal and to rest the horses, she'd gotten back on Honesty, whom Wilhelm had declared calm enough for her to ride. He lifted his chin to look up at the bright canopy.

"It's amazing," she said. "Are we stopping for the night?"

"Soon." They were in an open area of rolling hills matted with brown grass and scrubby growth. Here and there were copses of trees that might offer them some protection from the wind.

"I don't suppose there are any share lodges out here." She peered into night and searched for any structures that might be manmade, but saw nothing resembling shelter for anything larger than a rabbit or fox.

"Not that I ken."

"So, we're just going to sleep out in the open?"

The moonlight made his skin look like marble. When he grinned, creases formed in his cheeks, framing his mouth and reminding her how wonderful it felt to kiss him.

"Think you I would let my lady freeze in the night?"

"I'm yours now, am I?" She worked to fill the words with sarcasm, but it was an effort. They came out breathier than she'd intended.

He looked at her with lowered eyelids. "You are my lady inasmuch as I am your man."

She wanted to find his possessiveness objectionable, but the reciprocity made that impossible. *I want you to be mine,* he was saying, *and in exchange, I will give you myself.*

"Come." He clucked to Justice and led the way between some hills. "I'll find a dell worthy of a queen."

She snorted and followed. His gentle humor helped ease her anxiety over Inverness.

Instead of worrying about finding her way home, she found herself more concerned for Wilhelm. Before, when he would talk about finding a magistrate to clear his name, he made giving testimony sound like a formality. She'd thought once a magistrate heard the truth about Ruthven, he would wave his lordly scepter and declare Wilhelm justified in his somewhat violent rescuing of her and Aifric. But today, Wilhelm admitted he couldn't predict the outcome so neatly. There was risk involved that he hadn't made her aware of before.

Wilhelm didn't act overly concerned, but she had a feeling that was for her benefit. Things could go badly for him in Inverness. He hadn't gone into detail, but Connie suspected he faced possible imprisonment...or worse. But he was choosing to go anyway because it was the right thing to do. Which of course only made her admire him more.

Just what I need. More reasons to be attracted to him.

Wilhelm simply couldn't be found guilty of the crimes he was accused of. Scotland needed him. He was quite obviously a rising political star who could potentially bring necessary reform not only to his country but Europe as a whole.

If she had never come here, he would still be on track with his political goals. She had derailed them and possibly cost him his freedom or life.

Unacceptable.

"Oh, Con." Leslie's voice piped up in her mind. Her twin's imagined tone conveyed her utter disappointment that Connie was missing the bigger picture. *"Scotland needs him? Is that the real reason you can't bear the thought of him being punished?"*

She'd told Wilhelm she would not lie to him, but here she was lying to herself.

Leaving Wilhelm to return to the present day would tear her heart out, but doing so would be her choice. She could live with any choice *she* made as long as the motivation was good and the logic was sound. But the thought of him being forcibly taken from her flipped some switch in her heart. A light came on and shone directly on a truth that had been building every minute she spent with him.

I love him.

Scotland does need him. But I need him too.

That was why she couldn't tolerate the thought of him losing his freedom or his life. That was why she would fight for him. If necessary, she would beg, cheat, and steal for him.

But would she stay in the past for him?

"Here," Wilhelm said, halting Justice near a copse of trees with thickets of whitish wildflowers growing all around. He dismounted and strode to her with unmistakable heat in his eyes. "We will lie down here, and we will lie together for warmth." He offered his hands to help her down.

She wanted this man with a need so potent it choked her. She dismounted into his arms, letting her body slide against his. Where she would spend her future was a problem for another day.

Chapter 19

WAS THIS REALLY only Connie's second night with Wilhelm on the road? How was it she already took comfort in a routine they'd only established the night before? She didn't miss her nightly news date with Dan Rather or curling up with a romance novel before lights-out. Something about undertaking tasks to ensure one's basic survival satisfied her like no amount of passive enjoyment ever had.

Words weren't needed as she and Wilhelm cared for the horses and prepared their camp. Wilhelm placed a brick of peat on a rocky patch of ground and built a cone of kindling around it. She fed the horses with grain from their saddle bags and prepared the parritch mixture that would soak up heated water and provide them a nutritious, if not exactly delicious, dinner. They did not communicate with words as they worked, but the glances they shared spoke volumes.

Wilhelm would look her way every so often with his moon-bright eyes that he did not believe were magical in any way.

She would catch herself smiling in return and biting her lower lip like a silly romance heroine.

Wilhelm would turn his attention back to his task, a satisfied grin on his face.

Her heart would swell with affection. Her body would soften with arousal.

This went on until Wilhelm broke the silence with, "Pass me your lighter, if you please, lass."

She was in the middle of stowing their saddle bags under a fragrant bush with tiny white flowers, wondering at what kind of shrub this was to bloom in winter. Wilhelm's words jerked her attention away from the plant. "What did you say?"

"'Tis what you call it, no? A lighter? The fire stick in your traveling sack."

Her heart pounded as the arousal in her veins turned to anxiety. How did Wilhelm know the modern word for one of her belongings? How could she have settled so deeply into routine with him that she forgot about the multitude of secrets she must keep from him?

He left the cone of tinder and rushed to her. Worry furrowed his brow, but his voice was gentle when he said, "You referred to it by that name at Ruthven's."

His hands found her shoulders, soothing her with their calming weight.

"He accused you of using magic to bring fire to life in the palm of your hand." He smiled crookedly. "You called him an idiot—a sentiment with which I wholeheartedly agree—and you denied creating fire with magic. You said it was merely a lighter with a spark wheel and fluid inside.

"When Terran showed me your sack, I remembered your description and couldna help myself. I tried it." He tilted his head as he grinned, an admission that he'd been snooping. "I'd recognized the truth in your words, that night, but 'twas with no small amount of relief I used the lighter and saw for myself 'twas naught magical about it. 'Tis simply an ingenious device made of materials not common here in Scotia. To think your people have access to instant fire using somat a tenth the size of a tinder box."

His gaze was soft on her. He didn't have a single confrontational molecule in his body at the moment. He told her with everything he was that he hadn't intended to spook her, he didn't want to interrogate her.

It should feel like a violation, him going through her things so thoroughly. But she understood why he'd done it. She would have done the same in his place. In fact, the idea of a fifteenth-century Scot playing with her Bic lighter brought a smile to her lips.

I guess I didn't need to keep the first-aid kit hidden from him.

"If you like it, it's yours," she said, fetching it from her bag. "But use it sparingly. Once the fluid runs out, it won't work anymore."

She placed it in his hand, relieved he didn't seem to think she was a witch or that the things in her bag were magical. Like her, he wasn't one to sensationalize circumstances or to misinterpret facts based on suspicion. He preferred logic to assumption.

Scotland needed more men like him. And fewer like Ruthven.

He wrapped both his hands around hers and the lighter. "My thanks, lass."

To her, the lighter was a small thing—it had cost her less than fifty cents—but the intensity of his gaze showed that he was deeply touched.

"What shall I give you in return, I wonder?" Curling one arm around her, he insinuated his large body against hers and dropped his gaze to her lips.

She couldn't help licking them. They felt so much plumper when he looked at her that way, like he wanted to devour her. "You already gave me a horse," she made herself say. "And you saved my life today. Those things are much more valuable than a lighter."

"Mmmm." He purred. Purred!

For the second time that day, she mentally cursed his armor and pourpoint because they kept her from feeling the vibration in her own chest.

"What you're saying, then, is that *you* owe *me*, aye?"

One-handed, he lifted the swath of his great kilt over his head and draped it around her like a sash, using it to cinch her hips tight to his.

Last night in the share lodge, she'd watched Wilhelm take off his great kilt. She'd been surprised to see it was one long piece of tightly-woven fabric. He'd wrapped himself in it three times for warmth before lying down for the night and had enough left over to bunch up for a pillow. Today, he'd used the wool as a cloak and hood to keep him dry and warm. At the moment, he used it to capture her against him so firmly her breasts mashed up against his armor.

"It would seem so." She pitched her voice so Wilhelm would have no doubt she welcomed whatever naughty plans he might have for her tonight.

They would have to be his plans, though, because she didn't want to challenge his physical boundaries. She wasn't his wife, after all. Sex was probably out of the question. But he clearly had something pleasurable in mind. Maybe more of his kisses. Maybe falling asleep in each other's arms.

Dizzy with the possibilities, she walked her fingers up his chest, once again wishing his armor gone. "How would you like me to repay you, good sir?"

Goodness. Had she actually just said that? Flirting was a skill she had never possessed or cared to possess. *You have more of Leslie in you than you thought, Connie girl.*

"Allow me to think on it," he said. There was no mistaking the suggestive notes in his voice.

He grinned then backed away from her, dragging the wool across her bottom as he went. When the fabric fell away, a shiver passed over every inch of her skin, and it wasn't from the cold.

Wilhelm tucked the loose length of wool into his belt and stooped to light the fire with her gift. What a sight he made! An impeccably groomed Highland warrior using a Bic to start a campfire.

She chuckled to herself and felt happier and more carefree than she had since she was a teenager. Odd, since they faced so much uncertainty in just a few days' time.

Wilhelm set the pot of water she'd collected amidst the growing flames. When he glanced up at her, orange light made wicked angles of his face. With his eyelids lowered, he looked her up and down, leaving no question he was "thinking on it" and "it" would likely involve something that made them both happy.

As she joined him near the fire to help prepare their dinner, she suspected that whatever he asked of her tonight, she would do without question or hesitation. What a very long way she was from 1981.

§

WILHELM COULD COUNT on one hand the number of times he'd spilled his seed. The first time had been in his sleep after a dream about a milk maid at his family's dairy. He'd been fourteen and newly interested in the fairer sex. Three times had resulted from lapses in the discipline he prided himself in and had all been by his own hand without desire for any specific woman. The fifth had occurred only days ago.

The night he'd bathed Constance at the abbey, he'd returned to his room alone and given in to his lust for her. After the blissful moments of self-indulgence, the bell summoning the monks to their morning prayers sounded. Kneeling by his cot, he joined them in spirit, but summoning words of contrition had proven difficult.

While the fire faded, Wilhelm removed his armor and pourpoint for sleeping. Constance watched him with hunger in her eyes. This pleased him. *Och, she* pleased him.

All his life, Wilhelm had striven to abide by the Scriptures. He'd read every page of the holy writings his father had collected with Anselm's help, but his favorite passages were those that spoke of God's justice. From an early age, he'd felt deep in his bones that he would be an agent of God's justice on Earth. He'd accepted this as his calling.

With the same certainty, he understood that Constance was a gift from God. He was called to be her husband.

Furthermore, when he thought about Inverness, a sense of foreboding stole over him. In matters of importance, he always trusted his instincts. This day, his instincts were telling him he must make Constance his before arriving at their destination. 'Twas a truth in golden script emblazoned on his very heart.

In days of old, a man called to battle would take a bride in the hours before he must leave with his fellows. He would bed his beloved, surrounded by flowers, and speak vows to her with the solemn promise to repeat those vows upon his return from the skirmish. A man who returned from battle and did not keep his promise would be exiled. The practice was called "wedding by bedding."

Clans accepted and honored this arrangement, treating the couple as handfasted until an officiator could draw up a marriage contract. 'Twas even considered good luck to the warrior. A man with a new wife to return to would surely fight to the best of his ability.

Tonight, he intended to wed and bed his Constant Rose. 'Twas for her protection and his peace of mind. 'Twas also to sate his loins because he was growing weary of battling his body's craving for her.

"Take off your dress," he told his beloved.

"Won't we be colder without our clothes on? It's not like last night when we were indoors out of the weather."

"Tonight, we lie down together. Inside my plaid. The fewer clothes we have on, the better we'll share our warmth."

'Twas the truth. 'Twas also convenient, because the time was most assuredly right to claim what was his. He wouldn't wait another day, not another hour.

Her eyes widened. "Of course. All right. I'll just…" Her words trailed off as she stood and began unbuttoning her bodice. The lass was nervous.

He was as well. But he would lead her in this. His father had prepared him for the marriage bed. He knew what to expect. He knew how to bring his lady pleasure.

Once she was in naught but her shift and he in his shirt, he spread his plaid lengthwise over the saddle blankets near the smoldering fire. "Lie down just here," he commanded, motioning toward the very edge of the plaid farthest from the saddle blankets.

While she obeyed, he used his dirk to slice off several sheaves of winter heather from the nearby bushes and placed them on the fire. The flames leapt to new life. The blaze wouldn't last long, but 'twould provide a last bit of heat as well as a heady perfume to accompany their lovemaking.

'Twas tradition to incorporate flowers when wedding by bedding. Wilhelm would see this done right. Constance deserved no less.

"Like this?" she asked, a doubtful slant to her brows.

"Aye." He would lie atop her and roll them up in the wool, leaving just enough room inside for movement.

Her brows relaxed. She propped herself up on her elbows. This made her breasts push against her shift. 'Twas too dark to make out much detail, but he would learn the shape and feel of those glorious mounds soon, more intimately than he'd done when he'd bathed her.

Had she recovered the undergarments she'd used to thwart that wolf? He hoped not. Once he joined her and rubbed his hand up her silky thigh, he longed to find her bare, hot, and wet, as his father had told him a woman would be when ready to be taken.

He knelt beside her. Beneath his shirt was naught but his already thickening manhood. "Are you ready for me, my Constant Rose?"

Her eyes widened. "Ready for what, exactly?"

The cold made his skin pebble. Hers too. Closer now, he noticed the points of her nipples. Saint's teeth, he wanted to touch them. Taste them.

"I'm about to give you my pledge," he said, moving to straddle her with one knee on either side of her hips. Bending over her, he made a cage of his arms and legs. "Hold onto me. I shall roll us together."

Her arms came tentatively around his waist. "Your pledge?" She made it easy for him as he scooped her to his chest and rolled them toward the fire, wrapping them in his plaid as they went.

"Aye, lass," he said when they came to a halt on their padded bed.

No chill would find them here within layers of wool and sharing their heat in each other's arms.

"You are under no obligation to return it, you ken. But I shall pledge myself to you in such a way that you shall be protected by the Murray clan should aught ill come to me in Inverness."

Her hands tightened on him.

Already, the cold was leaving his skin. They lay on their sides facing each other, their legs tangled. She was so warm and soft against him he felt he would melt against her. But her forehead creased with worry.

"Please, don't worry about me. I'll be—" She came to a halt mid-thought and bit her lip. "Heavens. I won't be fine. Not at all. If something happens to you, I won't be fine." Her eyes grew shiny.

"You will. My father and mother will look after you."

She began to protest.

"*Whist,* lass. They will. I ken you have secrets. You've kept them from me. You will likely keep them from my parents as well."

He stroked her hair to ensure she felt no ill will from him as he stated this truth.

"'Tis my hope you will one day trust me, but if I am not able to be at your side to earn your trust day by day, as I pledge this night to always be, I would ken you are at least protected."

She pursed her lips, her lovely, kissable lips, in dismay. It seemed she didn't like to depend on another. Mayhap where she hailed from, she was a leader of women. He would not be surprised if she'd been a leader of men as well. She had the strength of spirit to lead an army, his lady.

Mayhap she was the chatelaine of some holding, responsible for the running of the house. Mayhap she instructed at university, for her learnedness showed in everything she did. Unfortunately, that learning had not been sufficient to keep her out of trouble. If she was not protected and protected well, Ruthven would find her and attempt to complete her execution. Or if not Ruthven, some other ignorant lob.

"This is a foreign land for you, love. For all your wits and bravery, ye canna be left on your own. You need protection. You need a friend to help you carry your burdens. I would be that friend. I would go with you to your home, wherever 'tis. I doona care how far. But ken you this, 'twill be for a visit and naught more, because you *are* mine."

She stiffened.

He didn't relent. "I would meet your father and your mother or whomever I must ask for your hand. I would remain with you there until you've had time to say your goodbyes. Do you understand, lass? I have not the patience nor the time to court you properly, but you and I both ken we are already as good as wed."

"Wilhelm." She softened at this. Her fingers curled in his shirt, knuckles pressing his side.

"You and I both ken it," he stated again.

When she didn't disagree, his heart leapt.

"But I doona ken whether I will have the freedom to do these things, love. Do you understand what I'm saying? I shall bind you to me tonight in an ancient tradition. 'Wedding by bedding,' 'tis called."

He smiled apologetically, kenning the phrase lacked grace.

"My clan will accept us as handfasted. You will be one of the Murray, and they will see to your health and happiness in my absence, should we become separated."

A lump formed in his throat at the thought of separation from Constance.

Throughout his speech, her eyes swam with somat he dared to think might be wonder, but at his mention of taking her home, the fragile hope in her eyes dimmed. "Wilhelm," she said, and the sound was beyond sad.

"What is it, lass? You can tell me anything. You can tell me everything." He kissed her worrit brow. Then he bestowed a light kiss on her lips.

She sighed and closed her eyes. When she opened them, she had a look of despair about her that sent his heart to beating like a drum against his ribs.

A shaky breath came from her parted lips. She smelled of cloves from the spiced wine they'd shared.

"When I was tied to that stake, I said I wasn't a witch. You remember?"

"Aye." He kissed the corner of her mouth.

She must feel his staff against her stomach. She must feel the need pulling taught every muscle in his body. Did she need him as well? How he longed to touch her intimately and find out.

"That was the truth," she said.

"I ken it, lass." Another kiss.

"But it wasn't the whole truth."

He studied her.

"I—I came here by magic, Wilhelm. I didn't mean to. Oh, heavens, I can't believe I'm going to tell you this. But you have to know. You have to know why we can't be married. You have to know why we can't sleep together. I mean we can *sleep*, but we can't have sex." She gasped as if this statement pained her.

"Go on, *mo luaidh.*" He recognized the truth of her words, as she must ken he would. Unease stirred behind his breastbone.

"You're going to think I'm completely crazy, but I can't keep pretending. Not with you." She cupped his face with both her hands. "I'm from the future, Wilhelm. From five-hundred years in the future. I was born in 1953. Only days ago for me, it was the year 1981. I was visiting Scotland with my sister. By the time my feet touched Scottish soil, you would have been dead for centuries."

She firmed her jaw and lifted her chin, seeming to brace herself for his disbelief. At the same time, her lower lip trembled. She was so bonny, such a mesmerizing combination of bravery and vulnerability.

At her admission, truth shot him through like a whole quiver of arrows. This time she told him the whole truth, and 'twas so bizarre no wonder she'd kept it to herself.

This explained everything.

She'd said she was from Vinland, but she was nothing like the Inuit peoples described by explorers. Her speech was understandable, but queer. He'd never heard anything like it before. The items in her travelling sack were queerer still, especially the documents describing Scotia not only in word but in impossibly realistic renderings.

He blinked, letting this new knowledge alter all he had assumed about her.

"Go on," she said. "Say it. 'You're quite mad, my Constant Rose.'" She imitated his English, making him smile despite the shock of what she'd just confessed.

"Why would I say such a thing, love?"

"Because you don't believe in magic. I just told you I came here by magic, and you'll know I believe this to be true. Therefore, you must think I've lost my mind." She wouldn't quite look at him. Her gaze travelled all around his face but never landed.

"Look at me," he commanded.

She obeyed. His formidable lady did not obey just any man. That she listened to him made his chest burn with affection for her. Truly, unequivocally, she was his.

"I doona think you wode, if that's what ye fear."

She bit her lip. Her brow furrowed.

He kissed both, brow first, then her mouth.

"You don't?"

"No."

"But—"

"I said I doona believe in magic," he interrupted. "But, lass, I never said I doona believe in miracles."

Chapter 20

CONNIE'S HEART DID a free fall. One of the architects she worked with liked to jump out of planes. For fun. She would tell Connie how exhilarating it was when the yank of the opening parachute turned the primal terror to overwhelming relief. Connie couldn't imagine finding pleasure in such helplessness. Until now.

Confessing her true origins to Wilhelm had been her last-ditch effort at stopping her free fall. She yearned so badly for him in every way from intellectual to emotional to physical, but if she gave in, she knew—she just knew—her determination to return home would lose purchase.

The truth will push him away, she'd thought even as she'd clung to him in their cozy bedroll that smelled of Wilhelm, smoky peat, and toasted flowers. She'd pulled the cord.

But no chute opened.

Instead of arresting her free fall with shock and disapproval, Wilhelm had tightened his arms around her and kissed her tenderly. He'd uttered words of reassurance that soothed her soul every bit as thoroughly as his touch aroused her body.

I never said I doona believe in miracles.

With a single sentence, he'd declared his support and strengthened the bond of love between them. Now, there was nothing left to hold her back as she hurtled toward a destination that was going to take her breath away when she reached it.

But it's not going to be the end of me. Maybe a new beginning?

She couldn't believe she was considering such a thing: a new beginning with Wilhelm. Marriage. A lifetime in the past.

Leslie would clap her hands in glee if she could eavesdrop on Connie's thoughts. Her twin had wanted her to find love. But would she have still wanted it if she'd known they might never see each other again?

Panic seeped into their intimate cocoon, but before it could take hold, Wilhelm distracted her with a brush of his hand over her temple. "When you say you wish to return home, what ye mean is your future time, aye? Not a place I can take you by horse or by ship?" He stroked her hair. The comfort of his touch spread through her body.

"Yes," she said. "I don't belong here. This is all a big mistake." Her reserve parachute. Even as she made one last-ditch effort to talk them both out of a future together, she hoped the gravity of their connection would win out.

The fire was fading again, but they still had enough light that she could see Wilhelm's silvery eyes fixed on her. They studied her thoughtfully.

"I disagree, lass."

"Who's being disagreeable now?" She attempted a joke, but her mouth twisted with sadness.

Giving in to Wilhelm would mean turning her back on her past and accepting a new present. With him. Was she brave enough to do that? To dive headlong into a life she hadn't planned out in exacting detail?

Wilhelm did not crack a smile. Rather, his jaw set with determination. "I shall always disagree, lass, if you attempt to convince me we are not meant for each other. My very marrow recognizes you as bone of my bone. Each beat of my heart acknowledges you as blood of my blood. I pursue justice with a certainty that runs truer and deeper than the currents of my humors.

There is no accepting or rejecting this calling. 'Tis part of me. In the same way, I ken that you are mine, and I am yours."

He'd just compared his feelings for her with his passion for justice. This humbled her and weakened her resolve. Her heart would have to be made out of stone for such passionate words not to penetrate.

"Wilhelm," she squeezed out past lungs locked up with affection.

"I love you, lass. Whether you're here with me or away in a future where I canna reach you, I will always love you."

She closed her eyes against a wave of pain through her middle. The thought of leaving him to go home caused her actual, physical pain.

He didn't give her an opportunity to respond. "There will never be another woman for me. With everything I am, I commit myself to you wholly and without reservation. Without condition, lass."

He ran his hand down her side, over her hip, along the length of her outer thigh. His fingertips tickled the back of her knee, but rather than making her laugh, the light touch made her womb clench.

"I expect naught in return, not even a promise that you'll take vows with me should I be free to court you properly in a few days' time, though you may be assured I will do all in my power to convince you."

She longed for him to rub his hand back up and bring her shift with it. The clothing between them was an affront to her. Despite her need, his words caused her distress.

She had never taken her parents' wealth for granted. She had never been, would never be, a freeloader. As justice was important to Wilhelm, fairness and equality were important to her, and what he suggested did not favor them equally.

"I don't accept that. I won't accept a promise that I'm not willing to return."

"Then return it, lass." He leaned over her, supporting his weight on his elbows. Crooking one leg over both of hers, he pinned her. If Milt had held her like this, she would have felt crowded and pushed him off, but Wilhelm doing so filled her with a sense of safety. Lips ghosting over hers, he said, "You are the wife of my heart. I ken you feel it. 'Tis more than lust between us. 'Tis more than I ever thought I could feel for another."

She bit her lip. She wanted him more than she could fathom, but factoring even more prominently in her decision was the fact that he wanted her. He loved her. If she left him, she would break his heart. What did it mean that the greater portion of her concern was for him rather than herself?

Heavens. My mind is made up. I'm staying. I'm staying.

She closed her eyes as agony ripped through her soul. She wouldn't indulge it though. There would be time for that later. Tonight was for Wilhelm.

Heaven help me. I've made my choice.

It might be selfish, considering her loved ones back home would never know what happened to her. It might be premature, considering she'd known Wilhelm less than a week. But there was no denying the truth of her feelings.

Someone check the temperature in hell, because Constance Emmaline Thurston just made a decision based on emotion.

She anchored her gaze on Wilhelm's, willing the panic of her free fall to turn into exhilaration. Nope. It still felt like panic. Her exhale came out choppy.

Wilhelm's lips compressed in a way she hadn't seen before. A pleat formed between his eyebrows. Could he see she'd come to a decision? Could he guess how badly she was hurting, how badly she needed him to take away the pain?

"Lass," he said, and sympathy shone from his gorgeous eyes. Yes, he understood. He returned to stroking her hair, this time with both hands. Somehow, in this position, the action seemed more intimate. He encompassed her head with each stroke. His breath fanned over her lips. His chest compressed her breasts. He was all around her.

She wanted him inside her.

"Tell me, my iron beauty, my Constant Rose, why this touch melts you so."

A tear trickled from each of her eyes. "It's not just the way you touch me. It's you. All of you." She sniffed as she struggled to put what she felt into words. "I thought I wanted success out of life, and success must be defined before it can be achieved. But I defined it all wrong. I left out the most important thing."

"Aye? What might that be?"

She thought about her answer. "Sharing," she said, testing the concept.

Yes. That was the word. That's what she hadn't considered with Milt. She'd wanted to include a man in her future, but she hadn't wanted to *share* her future, as in allow another input into her future or to alter her plans to accommodate another. She'd wanted to retain control and compromise only where it suited her.

His hands stilled, cupping her head. "Sharing?"

She nodded. "I wanted my life to be this certain way, this perfect way. A man only figured into that if his goals were the same as mine. But with you—" She experienced an urge to hide her face from him, but fought it. Holding his gaze, she said, "With you, I actually think your satisfaction is more important to me than my own. I want you to have everything you've worked so hard to achieve. I want you to look back on your life when it's over and think, yes, it was good. I want—heavens, I want your life to be good because I'm in it."

As she spoke the words, a wonderfully unsteady heat spread through her core. There it was, the exhilaration. Panic still rode underneath, but in a way that heightened the thrill of giving in to her emotions. Never in a million years would she have thought letting go of control would feel this freeing. A smile pulled at her cheeks as happiness filled her from head to toe.

"The thing I want most is for you to be happy." Leslie had spoken those words just before articulating her wish.

I'm happy, sis. I'm truly happy.

Wilhelm's Adam's apple moved. His thumbs rubbed her hair. "You are speaking of love."

"I suppose I am."

"Then all will be well for us, for wherever, *when*-ever we are, we shall always be together. Hear me? My greatest success shall be a lifetime of lending you my strength, my protection, and my love."

"Is that a proposal?"

"Nay, lass. 'Tis a vow."

§

WILHELM MARVELED AT the woman in his arms. Her beauty ran deeper than the contours of her features and hues of her hair. Her appeal lay in more than the softness of her curves and the clean, peachy scent of her skin. It shone in eyes that adored him and in a bravery of spirit that had led her to give him her trust and finally confess her secrets.

Even before she'd told him the incredible story of her origin, he'd felt that her coming to him had been divinely orchestrated. Now he knew for cert. He would cherish this gift always, and he would do all he could to be a gift to her as well.

He had to clear his throat before he spoke again. "Tomorrow, I would like you to tell me about your family and your future Vinland. But tonight, lass, what I would like—what I lust for with all I am—is for you to kindly relieve me of my virtue."

No truer words had he ever spoken.

Holding her like this, so close to the position of lovemaking, and having her pour out her heart to him had his staff hard as steel. If he didn't sink within her soon, he might die of wanting.

She had been lightly stroking his sides. The stroking stopped. "Your virtue?"

"Aye." The way Terran had carried on with the lasses made Wilhelm look upon tupping as a frivolity a disciplined man would do well to avoid, like too much drink or too strong a thirst for violence. By keeping his mind on his studies and duties, he'd incurred Terran's jesting. *Are ye in training to be a monk, Will? If ye doona use your prick, it'll shrivel up and fall off, Will.* Och, *Will, if you doona want that bonny creature, I'll be happy to put the roses in her cheeks.*

Thanks to his parents and the fond looks and stolen kisses they would share, he knew there was more to tupping than the mere "scratching of an itch," as Terran would oft call it. But he'd had difficulty imagining himself so taken with a woman he would spend hours with her in the marriage bed when he could be doing somat productive. Now, 'twas difficult for him to imagine wanting to be anywhere other than united in pleasure with his Constant Rose.

She placed a hand along his cheek. Her thumb traced the smooth skin above where his beard was coming in. "Darling," she said, her voice whisper soft, "it will be my honor."

He expelled a breath he hadn't realized he'd been holding and raised her shift with a questing hand on her thigh.

"No undergarments?" Not that he was complaining.

She chuckled. "I need to mend them."

"Mmmm. I doona mind if you take your time about it." He moved atop her, sprinkling her skin with kisses.

With a sigh that sounded like, "Yes," she opened her legs so he could settle in her intimate cradle. A shock of lust hit him like a mace when she raked her fingers up his buttocks, raising his shirt as he'd raised her shift. No passive kitten, his lady. In their bed, she would be a tigress.

"Fine, lass. You're fine." He delved into her mouth with deep kisses, reveling in the sensation of being skin to skin with her below the waist. In a proper bed, they would have room to strip each other and admire each other's bodies, but snug in his plaid, they had limited freedom of movement. 'Twould be enough. He would make certain of it.

With his cock nestled sweetly against her silky stomach and his mouth feasting at hers, he let his hands learn all the shapes of her—the angles of her collarbones, the plump roundness of her breasts, the succulent heart shape of her bottom.

Skimming his knuckles downward from her navel, he said, "If I keep going, will I find you wet for me?" Never before had he spoken such bold words. Never before had he been consumed with lust, love or anything else a tenth as powerful as this.

She nibbled his lower lip. "Why don't you keep going and find out for yourself?"

A growl rumbled from his chest. "Is that a challenge?"

"An invitation." From the feel of her mouth on his, he knew she was smiling.

"Then I heed it," he murmured, trailing kisses across her cheek to the warm place just below her ear. He tasted her salt, her sweetness.

Turning his wrist, he pushed his fingers down through her curls, down to explore her tender folds, down further to see what lay in their heated depths. When his fingers sank into a pool of slick moisture, he hissed, "Saints above."

He sucked in a breath to steady himself lest he give in to the fullness of his pleasure too soon.

"Like what you feel?"

"*Och,* lass. You ken I do." With difficulty, he found his control and ordered his thoughts. Thanks to Terran, his father, and countless married members of his clan, he possessed no shortage of knowledge on how to please a woman. He lacked expertise, but judging from the eagerness of Constance's kisses, he did not think she minded.

Her slickness made it easy for him to glide over her petals and find his target, her pearl of pleasure.

Her body jerked and she whimpered.

Immediately, he eased his touch. Drawing gentle circles, he memorized her, and from the breathy moans rising in the night, his touch had the intended effect.

She murmured wee assurances like, "Oh, yes" and "please" between kisses, but it didn't take his lady long to seek more than a passive role. Reaching between them, she took hold of his staff.

With a nip to her earlobe, he said, "Doona take me in hand, lass, or 'twill be the end before we've begun."

In this, she did not obey. "Don't take your time with me. I need you now." She wriggled upward and guided him to where he played in her wetness.

She deserved more tenderness from him, more patience, but he had none left. Breath heavy in his lungs, he eased forward, joining them.

Constance grabbed his buttocks and urged him deeper.

The heat, the sharp pleasure, the need, it all drove him on. With great effort, he restrained himself, taking her easy and slow. But he could not gentle the long, low groan that forced itself from his lungs as he claimed her for his own.

Constance threw her head back and moaned, a sound as helpless as he'd ever heard from his lady. Pride replenished his breath. The determination to please her restored his control.

Nature's instinct took over. He moved with a deliberate pace, and his lady rose to meet him. She kneaded his hips and then locked her arms around his back. Their bodies fused from lips to groin, and the building pleasure robbed him of gentleness.

"Need you, lass," he breathed as his thrusts gained in power. An urge akin to his battle lust filled him until he couldn't hold back, not with her, not any longer.

"Need you, too. Give me everything. Please."

In her eyes was a depth of craving that spoke to his soul. That look told him he didn't have to hold back. His lady was brave and strong and possessed a power of her own. She'd been built to receive the totality of his passion.

Her soul called to his. Mayhap their connection had called her through time itself, for no other woman that had ever or would ever walk the Earth could be his match in every way as this woman was.

Love swelled in his heart as sensation expanded into every part of his being. He gave her everything, and she welcomed it all.

Chapter 21

CONNIE WOKE TO the gray light of a winter dawn and the memory of what she'd done last night. Sex. With Wilhelm. And not just any sex. The best sex of her life.

She'd never known it could be *that* amazing. Their first round of "wedding by bedding" had catapulted her into an orgasm that explained the phrase, "Earth shattering." She'd heard people describe sex that way and had wondered if she was missing something. Oh, she'd had orgasms before, but the ordeal of striving for one almost seemed to cancel out the miniscule moment of bliss.

Now she knew she had, in fact, been missing something. That something was a Highland warrior whose mind, heart, and body all called to her in a way that made what affection she'd had for former lovers seem silly in comparison.

She'd been missing Wilhelm.

For their second round, they had taken their time. Despite the tight quarters of their makeshift sleeping bag, she'd managed to pull off his shirt so she could skim her hands over his delectable abdominals. He'd wrangled her shift over her head and rewarded her for the twinge she'd gotten in her shoulder by feasting on her breasts for long, rapturous minutes.

Connie had learned the skin on the insides of her elbows, when licked, aroused her to an insane degree. She'd shown Wilhelm that a scraping of teeth over his nipple could be pleasurable when done firmly enough not to tickle. Discovering the right amount of pressure to apply had resulted in his boyish wiggling and much mutual laughter.

When they made love again, it was with a tenderness that had slammed the door on the regret still lurking in her mind after choosing to stay with Wilhelm.

If Leslie knew how happy she was, how much she loved this incredible man, she would forgive Connie for the choice.

If only Connie could somehow tell her twin that her wish had come true.

I've found love, Leslie, and it's so much better than I ever thought it could be.

Unfortunately, the happiness she'd found didn't cancel out her heartache. Last night, she'd put off the grief of leaving everything she knew and everyone she loved behind. Now, it was morning. As she stared up at the pewter sky, the weight of what she'd done pressed down on her, crushing the breath from her lungs.

After "relieving Wilhelm of his virtue"—twice—Connie had passed out in the crook of his arm. Judging by the crick in her neck, she hadn't moved since. Her handfasted husband—or her fiancé, as she thought of him in modern-day terminology—snored quietly, face turned toward her. Unshaven since they'd left the monastery and with his hair mussed from last night's activity, he looked every bit the rugged Highland warrior she knew him to be.

Under normal circumstances, she might enjoy cuddling beside him as they began a new day together, but this morning she needed time alone. Moving at a snail's pace so she didn't wake him, she disentangled her legs from his and began scooting out of their warm cocoon.

His arm tightened around her. "Good, morn,' my Constant Rose," he said with a sleepy smile.

Her heart skipped a beat. Heavens, she loved this man.

"Good morning." Feeling a little shy, she used her rumpled shift to cover her breasts. "Go back to sleep. I'm just going to freshen up."

"Truth," he said, smile fading, "but only by half." The muscles in his abdomen bunched as he sat up. "Tell me the rest, love. Or have you nay learned by now that I am willing and able to share your burdens?" He cupped her face in his hands and kissed her forehead. "I see the sadness in your eyes. It slays me. Let me soothe it for you." He kissed her lips softly, so softly.

His tenderness drew forth the heartbreak she'd hoped to hide. A sob ripped up and out of her. There was no stopping it under the onslaught of his concern.

In a flash, his arms went around her. "I've got you, lass," he said over her ear. "I've got you."

In the shelter of his embrace, the tears came. She hated crying in front of someone else. Always had. She wanted to push Wilhelm away and find a private place to mourn all she'd lost, but she couldn't. First, his grip communicated he did not intend to let her go. Second, she needed him. She needed this.

To need another was a revelation.

"Are these for your sister?" he asked, rubbing his thumb through her tear tracks.

She nodded. She'd given up her entire life for this man. Hiding from him would defeat the purpose. Goodness, she hardly recognized the woman leaning into a man's touch, letting him comfort her rather than calling on her own strength to overcome her troubles. Had giving in to love weakened her?

No. She couldn't believe that. Being with Wilhelm made her feel strong and valued. The tears were because she'd had to choose between him and everything else. They didn't mean she regretted the choice, only that she had to let the pain have its way with her.

"Tell me about her." The way he bowed his head to meet her gaze melted her heart.

"Her name is Leslie. She's my twin, and I—I don't think I'll ever see her again." Shuddering, she wept for Leslie and for herself, for the separation they would both feel like a lost limb. Wilhelm held her through it, moving her onto his lap and wrapping them both in his kilt. Where the cold air touched her skin, it pebbled, but where her body rested against Wilhelm's she was warm. So warm.

"Would that our places could be reversed," he said. "I could have come to your time and you could still have Leslie and your place in the world that ye ken so well."

She sniffed. "I'd still be sad." She wiped away the wetness on her face. "Because then you'd be missing your home and your family." Lifting her chin, she added, "Besides, Scotland needs you a lot more than Chicago needs me. I'm convinced of that. If I weren't, I wouldn't have committed myself to you last night. It's part of who you are, and part of why I've fallen so completely for you. Now—" She cleared her throat and slipped her arms into her shift. Wilhelm helped her pull it over her head. "Let's get the horses ready. We've got to clear your name so you can bring me to my new home and marry me officially."

She started to rise, but he held her fast. "You are remarkable, woman."

His praise helped her muster up a smile. "Yes, well, there's no sense in putting off Inverness." Determined to use the ride today to strategize, she got up and dressed. She was engaged to be married now, and she refused to sit on the sidelines while her future husband faced his day of judgment.

§

WILHELM GRINNED TO himself as his bonny new handfasted bride shifted once more in the saddle. He held her in his arms as she sat before him. At his insistence, they'd loaded Honesty with their cargo and his heavy armor so they could ride together. Justice wouldn't mind carrying two riders; however, Wilhelm would mind greatly not having his Constant Rose in his arms today.

"Riding a horse after a night of 'wedding by bedding' should be considered cruel and unusual punishment," she grumbled.

"Do you regret what we've done, love?" he asked with a kiss to her shoulder. He had them both wrapped in his plaid, and Constance wore her cloak hood up. Despite the drizzle, they remained warm and dry as they rode.

"No," she said quietly. A single-word response that carried a world of meaning.

Neither did he have regrets.

A man gave away his virginity but once. 'Twas right he should give his to Constance. She would be the only woman he would bed for his entire life. No other had ever called to him the way she did. No other ever would.

The need to protect this treasure redoubled his determination to clear himself and Terran of Ruthven's exaggerated charges. Once this task was behind him, he would devote himself to compensating Constance for all she had lost in order to become his.

Squeezing her tight to him, he said, "Tell me about your family. Your Vinland. Tell me what you ken of Scotia. What is the world like in your time?"

"Is that all you want to know?"

They laughed together.

"I'm not sure where to begin," she said, her fingers entwined with his. "Some things are the same. The world's continents are largely the same, though map-making has improved by leaps and bounds. Many of the countries you're familiar with still exist, but some are known by different names.

"Scotland is still Scotland. It's known for being an important place for commerce and industrialization in Europe. But its history has not been easy...or bloodless.

"I'm not sure how much I should tell you. What if your knowing things affects the future? A man like you—you're well positioned to be a force for change in Scotland. What if things I tell you—or even just my being here, alters events and changes the world I know—or knew?"

Saints above, she could be right. "Mayhap, if events are altered, they will be altered for the better."

Connie hummed thoughtfully. "Possibly. Conversely, though, events could be altered for the worse. Or people who should exist might not come to be. I mean, what if my parents never meet or don't get married and Leslie and I are never born? Would I simply disappear? Cease to exist? I could be here with you one minute and then just—poof—gone the next."

Fear slithered low in his viscera. He tightened his arms around her. "*Och,* lass, 'tis too terrible to contemplate."

At her mention of Scotia featuring prominently in commerce and somat she called *in-dust-reel-zay-shun* he'd felt proud. But she'd also suggested the future for his countrymen would be bloody and difficult. This worried him. Hadn't this land already seen enough warfare? To him, it seemed long past time for peace.

He wanted to learn all she knew of his Scotia, but what if she was right? What if the mere fact of his knowing such things changed the world so she never came into it? He couldn't risk losing her.

"Tell me naught of Scotia. Much as I long to ken what the future holds, I willna risk you."

She lifted one of his hands to her lips and kissed his knuckles. Her lips were soft, her breath a warm caress. "Maybe that's for the best. I never want to leave your side."

He heard the truth in her words and felt steadier for it. He only hoped they were not forced apart by events in the more immediate future. Talking with her helped him not to fash over Inverness, but they would arrive there in two days, and uncertainty lurked despite his best efforts not to indulge it.

"I'll tell you about my country, instead" she said. "The United States of America. It shouldn't do much harm since it doesn't even exist yet, but still, we should probably keep this information just between ourselves."

"You have my vow I willna breathe a word to anyone." He huffed a mirthless laugh. "They wouldna believe me if I did."

He listened with rapt attention as she described a government with three branches. In this, her land was like his, except the branches of her government were executive, legislative, and judicial rather than the crown, privy council, and parliament. She told him of wars her country had fought, some with European allies, some pitting countryman against countryman for the prize of human rights.

At his request, she explained industrialization. Her descriptions of steel production, manufacturing, and the construction of towers tall enough to scrape the sky fascinated him. He was even more intrigued when she confessed her part in this process. She designed "systems" that brought clean water to these buildings and shunted the dirtied water away.

"Like the Roman aqueducts," he said, as they rode along the River Spey.

"Yes," she agreed. "Only on a much larger scale."

He felt his eyebrows rise in disbelief. "Have ye heard of the aqueducts, lass?" 'Twas difficult to imagine structures larger than those in the south. "Some of the passageways are large as castles. Some run for leagues under the ground."

"Don't become distracted by the word 'larger,'" she said, sounding like an instructor at university. "Think in terms of units of water moved. The aqueducts are made mostly of stone, which is heavy, brittle and prone to erosion. What if you could use a stronger, lighter material that resists erosion? You could move more water at a faster rate with less wear and tear on the system, and the channels could be much smaller. You could even hide them completely underground or in the walls of buildings, because the likelihood of needing to repair them would be greatly reduced compared to stone water ways.

"Now, think about not just a city using a system like this, but an entire continent. In my time, most families, even very poor families, enjoy indoor plumbing. In fact, most people take it for granted. They never see the results of what I do, and that's part of the goal, to provide the client hot and cold water in such a way that they rarely have to think about it."

His mind spun with the marvel of clean water being available to so many. People in her United States of America didn't draw from wells or toss the contents of chamber pots into the gutters. Their water and waste came and went through narrow canals she called "pipes."

Questions spun in his mind as he longed to understand this marvel, but one question came to the fore. "*Och,* lass, did you say *hot* water?"

"Yes. Water is heated in a boiler on the premises. When a handle is turned, the hot water flows from the boiler. It can be used by itself or mixed with the ground-temperature water to become any temperature the user desires." She sighed. "I took a hot bath at the bed and breakfast in Inverness after getting off the plane to meet Leslie. If I'd known it would be my last, I would have taken my time instead of rushing through it." She turned to grace him with a smile, but he saw the sadness in her eyes.

He couldn't give her back her sister, but he vowed in his heart to give her as many hot baths as he could manage.

"Well," she said as she pulled herself up straight. "I think it's time for a little pick-me-up. Would you like to listen to some modern popular music?"

"Do you intend to sing for me? I should like to hear that."

She laughed. "I'm not much of a singer. Do you remember that bard I told you about, Billy Joel?"

He remembered with a pang of jealousy. "You named the horse I gave you for one of his songs."

She half turned, revealing a mischievous twinkle in her eye. "I suspect once you hear the song, you'll agree it's worthy of your wonderful gift."

He harrumphed. "Since you willna sing for me, how am I to hear it?"

"Like this."

She handed him a wafer of some odd, gray fabric that reminded him of the head of a mushroom. But the wafer did not appear edible. It was connected to a thin black cord that disappeared inside her cloak.

"Here. Put this up to your ear." She demonstrated with an identical object. The two fabric wafers were joined together at the place where the cords made a *Y*-shape and became one.

"What are these?" he asked, testing his wafer with gentle squeezes. It felt as if the soft surface protected somat firm underneath. A coin, mayhap.

She slipped a wee box from her cloak. "This device is called a Walkman. It delivers sound to the headphones through this port." She pointed to where the cord connected to the box. "The sounds come from a medium called 'magnetic tape.' Music or stories or, well, pretty much anything you can hear, can be recorded on the tape and played back when this button is pressed."

She depressed a segment of the box. A brief clucking sound came from it, like a hen maid calling her chickens to feed. A faint noise came from the wafers.

"Put it up to your ear and see for yourself." She demonstrated with her wafer, pressing it to her ear. She began humming a tune.

Curious about her *Walk-man*, he did as she bade.

A fullness of music he'd not experienced since vespers at Oxford invaded his senses. Only this was not a chorus of voices chanting in Latin. At first, he heard only jangling noise thumping in a nonsensical burst. Then a voice soared to the fore and brought sense to the chaos. The voice sang, *"Ho-nes-ty,"* in a litany rivaling the passion of the most devout balladeer.

Transfixed, Wilhelm didn't notice he'd drawn Justice to a halt until Honesty came up alongside. Both horses twitched their ears, no doubt wondering at the unfamiliar sound.

The more he listened, the more he recognized the complex blend of melody and harmony and the better he could pick out tunes played by individual instruments. However, he couldn't name the instruments, having never before heard music of this ilk.

A touch on his cheek brought his attention to the face of his beloved. Her liquid eyes reflected the emotion swelling in his heart. She reached up a hand and pressed her wafer to his other ear, and the music became his whole world.

After a short while, the song reached a crescendo then gentled to a soft series of chords before coming to an end.

"Did you like it?" Constance took the wafers and snapped them to a shiny half-circle of metal.

"May I hear it again?"

She laughed. "Here. Headphones." She twisted in the saddle and arranged the half-circle over his head.

To aid her, he leaned to the side. The metal held the wafers over his ears with a wee bit of pressure. The *Y* of the cord rested on his chest.

"Like the lighter, my Walkman won't work for long." Constance's voice found its way around the wafers. "I have a spare set of batteries, but once they're used up, this will be nothing but a useless hunk of plastic." She wiggled the *walk-man*.

She was telling him this miracle of music could not be enjoyed for long without more *batteries* from her time.

"Of course. I understand, lass." He removed the *head-fones*.

"No!" She stopped him. "I want you to listen as much as you can. I just wanted to warn you this pleasure will be fleeting."

His heart contracted with sweet joy. His lady wished to give him this gift, as she'd given him her lighter. He could not deny wishing to accept it, but he would not steal from her the last moments of music from her time.

"We shall listen together." Recalling her fiddling with the *head-fones*, he disconnected the wafers and held one out to her.

"We'll listen together," she agreed with a smile that slayed him. A cluck of her *walk-man* and the music resumed.

He gave Justice the command to move. While they made their way to Newtonshire, where he intended to present her with a bit of luxury if his old friend was biddable, they listened to her favorite bard. No longer would he feel jealousy at the mention of this "Billy Joel." Truly, the bard was a talent worthy of bestowing a name on a fine mount.

Chapter 22

DARK FELL, AND with it, the misty rain turned to needles of ice. Connie turned her face up to it now and then to catch some moisture on her tongue, but she was glad to have her cloak and Wilhelm's kilt providing cover.

"Is there any chance of finding a dry place to camp tonight?" she asked. The prospect of being wrapped up tight with Wilhelm again excited her, but after shielding them from the rain all day, his kilt was soaked. It would be like lying down in a sodden sleeping bag. She supposed there was no help for it. It wasn't like they would happen across a Ritz Carlton here in the fifteenth-century Highlands.

"I believe I can find us a wee bit of shelter."

"A share lodge?" She tried not to sound too hopeful, but Wilhelm's chuckle meant he'd caught her fantasizing about lying down on a bed tonight.

"Nay, lass. We ought to arrive at our destination within the hour. Have ye grown weary of telling me stories? I should like to hear of the medicines you mentioned. Have you required any for an illness? How effective are they?"

They'd been talking throughout the day's ride. Well, mostly, she'd been talking, and Wilhelm had listened and asked questions. He seemed to find her modern world fascinating, especially anything having to do with infrastructure and manufacturing. Certain inventions excited him as well. They'd talked for over an hour about the telephone, switchboards, and operators. He'd marveled at the fact she'd spoken with Leslie on the phone only last week, when they'd been separated by half a world. He'd uttered his preferred exclamation, "Saints above," when she'd told him how she'd gotten on an airplane and flown across the ocean in the course of a night to join her sister on vacation.

Her throat was becoming raw from talking so much, but worse, the more she described the world she knew, the deeper it sank in that she wasn't going back. Her family, her career, her condo, her American freedoms…all gone.

While grief ravaged her soul, she told Wilhelm about antibiotics and life-saving surgeries, cancer treatments and artificial limbs for wounded soldiers, all things she'd read about in *Time Magazine* or heard about on the news. At the other end of the health-care spectrum were things she considered simple, like vitamins, cold medicines, and aspirin.

She would never take another aspirin.

With a start, she realized she hadn't taken her birth control pill since meeting Wilhelm. The last time she'd seen her clamshell case was when she'd set it on the nightstand at the bed and breakfast. She'd intended to take a pill after returning from the hike with Leslie and the promised breakfast that never came to be.

After some mental calculation, she concluded she could very well become pregnant after their handfasting last night. Anxiety churned in her stomach, but only because she hadn't planned for a pregnancy. There was another feeling too, one even stronger than her anxiety. Excitement.

The Connie of a week ago would have been horrified at her lack of attention to the rather important detail of contraception. The Connie who was beginning to believe in magic and had become engaged to a man after knowing him only a few days, that Connie wanted a child with this amazing man. Preferably more than one.

Her life was going to look nothing like she'd imagined. Try as she might, she could hardly picture her future. Would Wilhelm's family accept her? In what capacity would she work to contribute to their clan? She envisioned supporting Wilhelm in his political ambitions, but what would that look like? Would she act like a secretary to him? A sounding board? Heavens, she knew nothing about late-medieval politics. She couldn't possibly offer advice.

"You are quiet, lass. What fashes you?"

"Fash," she repeated. A word for worry. She was getting used to Wilhelm's dialect. Would she begin to speak with a Scottish accent? Would she learn words and phrases in Gaelic?

The foreignness of this historic world roused a sharp panic in her chest. She gasped for air, and a sob cut from her throat.

Wilhelm was there, holding her, shushing her soothingly. He brought Justice to a halt. "Easy, lass. Easy. I've got you."

"It's so different here." In talking about her past, she'd painted a portrait of a place she loved to which she would never return. "I'm lost. I'm so lost." She gripped his forearms as tears came. "Damn it. Not again." She swatted at them as they fell.

"*Whist.*"

Another foreign word, but one she associated with Wilhelm's comfort.

He rocked her gently. "Never fear to show me your heart, love. Your pain is my pain. Aye? I've got you. I've got you."

"I don't know anything here. I don't know what life is going to be like. I've committed to staying here, but I have no idea what it will entail. I'm afraid. I have no point of reference."

He whispered harsh words to her in Gaelic. Somehow, even though she didn't understand the words, they soothed her. His harshness was for her, not against her. He cared that she was hurting.

"*Mo luaidh, mo luaidh, mo luaidh.*" Those words, she understood. "I shall be your point of reference. You may hang all your understanding on this: I love you, and nothing will ever change that. This shall be the constant in your life, in our life together."

His words pulled more tears from her. She couldn't tell if they were happy or sad tears. Likely, a combination of both. He held her while she cried herself out.

His reassurance helped. It did. But she couldn't help worrying what the future would hold. All she knew was that there was no going back.

Connie's father was an exceptional businessman. He had some favorite sayings that he liked to share with anyone who would listen. Among them were "Fortune favors the bold" and "Drink the whole cup." Leslie would roll her eyes when he spouted such things, but Connie had taken her father's messages to heart. He'd carved out his own success. He'd done it on his terms and on his own merits. She wanted that kind of success as well, the kind that came from refusing to compromise, from living boldly, from drinking the whole cup.

For the most part, she'd lived her life that way. While Leslie waffled over major decisions, Connie tended to act quickly and decisively. She'd taken only a semester to choose engineering over theater, and despite the emotional toll of giving up something she loved, she'd never looked back. Engineering had simply made more sense. It was the choice more likely to guarantee success.

After putting in her three years in a starting engineering position, she'd set her sights on an associate position and pursued it with every ounce of determination she possessed. As a result, she'd become the first female associate the firm had ever hired.

Looking back, she could see that her relationship with Milt had been an aberration. Several times, he'd dropped hints that he would like to see their relationship progress. Her reluctance to move boldly into matrimony with him should have been an obvious sign they weren't as compatible as she had wished.

Some part of her had known he wasn't right for her, but she'd kept trying to shoehorn Milt into her life. Adored by her family, driven to succeed, considerate of her goals, he'd seemed like the sensible, logical choice. But her heart, it seemed, didn't care one whit about sense and logic.

Forgive me, Milt, for not giving you your freedom sooner.

She'd never "drunk the whole cup" with Milt. She'd always held something of herself in reserve with him. The first time she'd given her whole heart and truly "drunk the whole cup" was last night with Wilhelm.

This is my life now. He will be my husband soon. I've chosen this, and I have no regrets.

Not even knowing everything her choice had cost her. Not even if she was pregnant with his child so soon.

She blew out a breath that fogged in the damp air. "I'm all right. I'm better now."

He didn't relax his hold. "'Tis understandable, lass, to grieve what you've lost. 'Twill take time, aye?"

She hoped they had time. Considering she was engaged to a wanted man with a determined enemy, time was not a guarantee. She'd been too busy processing her situation today and sharing a bit of her home with Wilhelm to strategize about Inverness.

A new worry presented itself as she thought ahead to meeting the judges and lawmakers of his time and giving testimony to clear her fiancé's name. "Wilhelm?"

"Aye, love?" He urged Justice to continue on at an ambling walk. Quiet steps behind them meant Honesty was obediently following.

"Who am I supposed to be when we arrive in Inverness?"

He went still at her back. "Our union will be binding, if that's what you're asking. You need no' fear your acceptance with the Murray. Or that I would deny you your contract. I shall present you as my wife to all we meet." His arms tightened around her.

She patted his hands, careful not to disturb the reins. "I'm not worried about you backing out on me, my honest man. But I do have questions. We invoked an old custom last night, yes? One reserved for warriors going into battle. It's true you're headed into uncertainty in Inverness, but it's not technically battle. And we had no witnesses. Will our arrangement be recognized beyond the local level of your clan?"

"What makes you fash about such things?"

"Ruthven," she stated. "He's a weasel. And he hates you." At least she'd gathered as much from what she'd managed to observe the night she'd met Wilhelm. "You jumped up on the platform and asked him how much he would take for me." She'd been too terrified to find it insulting at the time, and now that she knew Wilhelm, she was flattered he'd offered to purchase her freedom without knowing a single thing about her. "He refused. He said something about letting a Murray buy a prisoner from him before and that this time, he'd find it more enjoyable to watch justice run its course."

The memory of that vile man taking pleasure in her suffering sat in her stomach like a cold stone.

"I wasna about to let his so-called justice run its course." His gravelly words carried the weight of his conviction.

"I know. You didn't even know me then, but you were willing to risk everything to save me. You *did* risk everything to save me. You might have been killed." She felt sick at the thought.

"No. Terran and I are fine warriors. I'd already noticed Ruthven's preparations that night were designed to impress his social peers rather than to protect his guests and his household. Many of his usual guards had been dismissed for the night so as not to sully the gathering with their rough appearances."

"You still would have fought for me, even if his security had been top notch." She knew this was true because she knew her man.

He responded by leaning forward to press his cheek to hers over her shoulder. "What point are ye making, lass?"

"The last time anyone of note saw me, I was a prisoner about to be executed. You can introduce me as your wife all you want, but outside of your clan we have no legal association. I have no legitimacy. I'm nobody here. Literally nobody. I have no record of birth, no family to report me missing or to throw their weight around to ensure my wellbeing. It will be a miracle if anyone takes my testimony seriously. And I can pretty much guarantee Ruthven will exploit my lack of connections.

"Being handfasted is wonderful if we're simply going to Dornoch with the intention of making everything legal as soon as possible. But instead, we're heading into a politically charged situation. 'Battle' is probably an apt term, but it'll be a battle of pens instead of swords. Unfortunately, we're going in essentially unarmed. I won't have any legal ability to argue on your behalf. Technically, I don't even exist."

"*Och,* lass. You've got a mind on you. I hadn't considered the farther-reaching implications of taking you into Inverness without being properly wed. My only concern was binding you to me for your safety and my peace of mind. But if Ruthven finds us before Kenrick arrives, it leaves you completely at Ruthven's mercy.

"Our saving grace is that Ruthven willna ken we're travelling to Inverness. No one save Terran and Anselm kens our whereabouts—and my father, if he's received the letter I sent from the abbey. So long as we avoid Ruthven and his bishop, all should be well. Still, I wonder..." His voice trailed off.

She'd hoped she might be worrying for nothing, but Wilhelm's response suggested she'd found a chink in their armor. Was he thinking the same thing as she? That they should make their "wedding by bedding" more legitimate before reaching Inverness?

From seeing Terran and Aifric through their nuptials, she gathered that would entail an officiator drawing up a contract. Was such a thing even possible? With no knowledge of this fifteenth-century landscape, she had no idea whether they might find an officiator between here and Inverness.

Wait. Her travel guide. That would at least provide a starting point. Surely it would show larger towns that would be likely to exist in this time. Her fingers itched to look at the enclosed map and read about Scotland, not from the perspective of a twentieth-century tourist but as a fifteenth-century woman who needed a better understanding of her new country.

Last night, she thought she'd drunk the whole cup with Wilhelm, but she hadn't. Not really. If Wilhelm was thrown in prison, or condemned to worse for the supposed crime of rescuing her, she wanted the legal ability to fight for his life.

If she was pregnant with his child, she wanted his son or daughter to have every privilege that came with their father's name. Her first child would be in line for a noble title. She refused to gamble such security on the plan of remaining hidden from Ruthven. That man was a weasel through and through. Those black eyes hid a calculating mind and a seething hatred for her would-be husband.

She turned in the saddle to meet Wilhelm's gaze. "I don't want to meet a magistrate as a handfasted couple. I want to be Wilhelm and Constance Murray." Saying their names together like that made her heart smile. It felt *right.*

He swept the hood of her cloak off her head and planted a kiss on the back of her neck. With a growl, he grasped her chin and leaned in to take her lips with bruising force. When he was done kissing her senseless, he said, "Think you to command me, *mo luaidh?*"

Even in the meager light of the starless night, his eyes struck her as brighter than they should be. She might have been frightened if she couldn't see clear as day that the tension in him was due not to anger but love. Her desire to strengthen their bond for all to see roused his passion. Seeing him this way heightened her passion as well.

Nuzzling under his chin, she said, "Of course not, darling. Simply suggesting how you might please me."

"Mmmmm." He slid the hand on her waist lower, fingers pressing her mound, dipping even lower. Even through her clothing his touch was electric. "Shall I suggest, then, how you might please me in return?"

"By all means." Her voice went all breathy.

They were projecting their desire to each other with all the subtlety of neon signs. If only they could happen across a share lodge or some other warm, dry place where they might act on that desire in comfort.

Get used to it, Connie girl. You're going to have to learn how to be content with less.

It would be an adjustment, but Wilhelm was worth it.

Using the hand still on her chin, he angled her head. Thinking he was positioning her for another kiss, she closed her eyes.

"Look," he said. "Just there."

She opened her eyes, annoyed his mouth wasn't on hers.

He pointed toward the treetops, where she noticed a light glowing in the distance. It reminded her of a lighthouse, but it couldn't be since they were nowhere near the ocean.

"What is it?" she asked.

"The peel tower of Newtonshire. I have an acquaintance there. He happens to be a clergyman."

Leave it to Wilhelm to have a trick up his sleeve. "That's a happy coincidence."

"I chose this route for the room I happen to ken is kept ready for guests inside. It contains a grand, soft bed." He purred the words, his breath hot on her neck.

Her whole body vibrated with anticipation, but she made her voice firm. "Well, I hope you plan on making an honest woman of me before taking me to that bed."

"By all means."

Chapter 23

EWAN MACPHERSON WAS the largest man Connie had ever met. Looming over her, and standing more than a head taller than Wilhelm, he had to be six-foot-eight at least. Taken off guard by his size, she fell back on habit when Wilhelm introduced them at the tower's portcullis, and offered him her hand as if to shake.

Ewan stared at it then looked to Wilhelm in confusion. Heavy browed and bearded, the man had a forbidding appearance, but when his eyes widened and his cheeks reddened, he took on the mien of a bashful boy.

Wilhelm saved her from further awkwardness by reaching over her arm to take her hand in his. Entwining their fingers, he lowered their hands.

"What say you, man?" he said to Ewan. "Feel like performing a wedding tonight?"

If Ewan had been blushing before, his cheeks were practically glowing now. "Ye want me to marry you? Now?"

Ewan led them into a parlor with weapons on the walls and a handful of wooden chairs around a cold hearth. The phrase, "Needs a woman's touch," came to mind.

After the men lit a fire, Wilhelm told Ewan about the rescue at Ruthven's and about their stay at the monastery.

"We're traveling to Inverness to find a magistrate who might rule on the charges. If matters go against me and Terran, I would ken Constance is well positioned to be taken in by the Murray and protected from Ruthven's nonsense."

Ewan took everything in with a passive expression. Occasionally, he glanced her way. Wilhelm never mentioned where she'd come from or why she'd been slated for execution, and their host didn't ask for details.

Pushing out his lower lip, he shrugged and said, "Arright. I'll do the contract for you."

Lighting the way with a lantern, Ewan showed them up several flights of stairs. The tower reminded her of a row house, but standing by itself, with no other castle-row-houses on either side. It soared an impressive six stories but had a footprint no larger than a few hundred square feet.

"The light at the top is tended by Ewan," Wilhelm explained. "He keeps it burning low from dusk 'til dawn. When he needs to relay a message from another tower, he burns it high and cranks a shield to and fro to create a code. Anything of note, lately?" He directed the question toward Ewan.

"The usual. Grants are skirmishing. Tryin' to bring in the MacPees. Da' says signal them to take a long leap off a short pier."

"MacPees is Ewan's way of referring to his own clan," Wilhelm said. "His father is laird and not one to go lightly into battle."

"'Specially at the call of Reggie Grant. The man takes offense at the least provocation." Ewan shook his head. "Here we are." He heaved open the door of a room off the fourth-floor landing. "No' much, but there's a bed. Linens are clean."

Peeking around Ewan, she noted the room contained exactly one piece of furniture, a four-poster bed neatly made with blankets the sandy color of undyed linen. A shuttered window on one wall and an empty fireplace on another provided the only other points of visual interest. The rough plank floor had not a speck of dust, and the fireplace had been swept spotlessly clean of ashes.

"At university, Ewan was always the tidiest of us lads. Weren't you, man?" Wilhelm elbowed Ewan.

"Not so much tidy as the rest of you were all slovenly."

Connie caught Wilhelm's eye. "You? A slob? I never would have guessed." She remembered to use the British accent she'd adopted.

Wilhelm acknowledged the change in her voice with a wink before lifting his chin in a show of affront. "Away from home, I didna have a chambermatron to keep my rooms orderly."

Ewan snorted. "I'll dig up an ewer for you. Got a leg of lamb stewing in the kitchen. Should feed us all. Fancy a meal first, or do ye want to get right to it?"

"We'll join you for supper first," Wilhelm said. "But we'll provide our own food. We won't presume upon your hospitality."

"Nonsense. I might not be a monk, but I remember how to treat a guest." He left, presumably to get supper ready.

She and Wilhelm tended the horses and brought their supplies to their room. While they worked, Wilhelm told her about their host and his two brothers, all of whom Wilhelm had known at university. His running monologue helped keep her mind off her niggling worries.

Inverness loomed in the near future. Neither of them could predict what would happen. They could only do their best to clear Wilhelm's name and restore him to his rightful place as heir to his father's barony and lairdship. But even once they dealt with the problem of Ruthven, there was still the prospect of her living out the rest of her life in the fifteenth century. In the last few days, her life had drastically changed. She'd chosen to accept that change, embrace it even, but that didn't remove the pain and fear.

"Ewan was closest to me in age," Wilhelm said as she measured out their dinner parritch plus an extra helping to share with their host.

She let his words soothe her, and found additional comfort in the routine of preparing their camp together, this time in a warm, dry room instead of out in the wintery wilderness.

"Since we both shared an aptitude for studying the Scriptures, we got on well. Now he tends the tower for his clan. I hear he serves as enforcer for his father as well, but I suspect he'd rather not. Given his way, Ewan prefers peace to warfare."

Connie decided she liked the peace-loving, youngest MacPherson brother. Sitting down with him to a meal at the butcher block in the kitchen reinforced her approval. While they ate, he and Wilhelm reminisced with all the enthusiasm expected of schoolmates who had shared trials and triumphs. Though Wilhelm did most of the talking, Ewan had a knack for conveying a lot of information with an economy of words.

He insisted on sharing his leg of lamb with them. In exchange, they shared their parritch and gave Ewan the last of their spiced wine as thanks for his hospitality. Wilhelm must have wanted her to get to know Ewan a little on her own, because he suggested she help their host clean up in the kitchen while he tended some chores.

The kitchen took up the back half of the tower's first floor and smelled of stewed meat, flour, and hops. While Ewan washed the stewing pot and swept out the fire pit, she wiped down surfaces and cleaned utensils. Though this kitchen had none of the modern conveniences she was used to, she felt oddly at home in it.

By observing Ewan, who struck her as a more than competent housekeeper, she learned how to take care of a late-medieval kitchen. He oiled the butcher block to keep it from cracking, wiped moisture from the inside of the walls to prevent mold, and closed the flue to keep the outside air from finding its way in.

"So, Ewan," she said to break the silence. "I hear you're a clergyman. Do you preach sermons for your clan?"

"No," he answered.

"Do you hear confessions?"

"No."

"Then what do you do as a clergyman?"

"Bury the dead." He jabbed his thumb toward the tower's back door. "Kirk's down the hill a ways. No one ever comes 'cept for salt n' earth ceremonies. Da's got a priest at the keep who does all that other whatnot."

"Do you get lonely out here?" She'd gathered over dinner that this signal tower was half a day's ride from the nearest village on MacPherson land.

"No."

She twitched her lips in amusement, wondering what Wilhelm was up to sticking her with Ewan for the last hour. Wiping her hands on a rag, she said, "Well, I think I'll go find my groom. Are we going to the kirk for the nuptials?"

Ewan's eyes went wide. "Er, wait. I—er—have somat to show you."

She smelled a rat. Wilhelm must have asked Ewan to keep her occupied.

Willing to play along, she followed him to the parlor, where she was pleasantly surprised to find a roaring fire in the hearth that hadn't been in use when they'd arrived. Someone had hung a large pot over the fire. Maybe Wilhelm had put the spiced wine on to warm, though the pot seemed too big for the liter or so of drink they had left.

"Wait here," Ewan told her.

She heard his heavy footfalls on the stairs as he climbed to a higher floor. He returned a few minutes later with several wooden objects cupped in his massive hands.

"Sit," he said, indicating the hearth with a jerk of his chin.

Shrugging, she sat with her back to the fire.

Ewan joined her and placed one of the small objects on her palm. It was a miniature wolf about the size of a chess piece.

Whoever had done the carving had paid incredible attention to detail. One front leg was shown lifted in mid step. The tail cocked to one side while the figure's head curved to the other. How the artist had managed to convey a sense of playfulness in the wolf's eyes, she couldn't guess. She could imagine a real wolf looking just like this as it weaved through the trees with its pack mates.

With a shudder, she remembered the wolf attack from the day before.

"Very realistic," she said, handing it back. "Did you do this?"

Ewan nodded, blushing. He handed her another.

"Showing off his carvings, aye?"

Wilhelm came into the room. He'd removed his pourpoint and had his shirtsleeves rolled up. He wore a pair of breeches instead of his kilt, which he'd changed out of when they'd arrived since it had been soaking wet. A sheen of sweat on his face told her he had, in fact, been up to something as she'd suspected.

"She tell you we were set on by wolves on our second day?"

"That why you have a wrap?"

Wilhelm glanced at his arm as if he'd forgotten about the injury. "*Och,* merely a scratch." Taking the chair nearest the fire, he said, "Ewan used to do figures at school, too, but they werena so fine as this." He took the piece Connie handed him. "You could sell these, man. They're lovely."

"I was thinking about it. I hate parting with them though." Holding out his cupped hands, he let them admire the rest.

Connie examined each figure, passing them to Wilhelm one at a time. They were all wolves carved in positions of action. Play poses, running, leaping over a log, digging, curling up in a den, a group of pups playing. "Truly beautiful," Connie said. "Why wolves?"

"I like wolves," he said. "Guess you're ready, then?" he asked Wilhelm.

"As long as my bride hasn't changed her mind." He extended his hand to Connie.

This was it. Once she signed papers to marry Wilhelm, she would be permanently closing the door on the possibility of returning home.

Allowing herself one last mental check, she imagined running into Leslie's arms, reuniting with her sister. It would be such a relief to hold her twin again, to stroke her hair and reassure her she was all right. But the imaginary reunion had the feel of a visit, not a homecoming.

Yes. She'd made the right choice. Even when she gave her emotions free reign to imagine being with Leslie again, it was with the understanding she would return to Wilhelm. She would always long to return to Wilhelm.

She took his hand and let him draw her into his embrace. "I'm ready."

Peace filled her heart as Ewan led the way up the stairs to a room with a desk near the top of the tower. He sat and began writing on a piece of off-white paper flecked with grains of brown. He used a feather quill that had seen better days.

She would need to learn how to write with a quill. No typewriters in this time. No correction fluid. No copy machines for making duplicates. If she assisted Wilhelm in his career, she would have to learn the implements of a fifteenth-century secretary. How were addresses written? How did the post work? Was such a service even in existence yet? Who would teach her these things?

She bit her lip as nerves made her stomach churn.

Wilhelm touched her lower back. "Lass?"

She looked up to find him bending his head to her in that way that made her feel incredibly feminine and special. A glance at Ewan showed him hunched over his quill and paper, deep in concentration. She whispered an admission she had never made to another person: "I don't want to be a failure."

Wilhelm's eyes went liquid with gentleness. "We will both fail on occasion." The scratching of Ewan's quill went on without pause as Wilhelm whispered to her. "But we shall do our best to help each other succeed. Always, lass."

"Yes." The churning gave way to a blooming warmth in her chest.

If there had ever been a man she wanted to help succeed, it was this man. And to know he wanted her to succeed as well struck her as something women in this time wouldn't necessarily expect. Somehow, this warrior from the past made her feel more appreciated than most of the men she'd worked alongside in 1981 Chicago.

In his normal speaking voice, Wilhelm said, "This is where Ewan documents the messages he's sent and works out any code before stoking the signal fire. He's penning our contract now. It'll be a simple one since you have no one present to negotiate the contract or bestow a dowry. Much like the contract Anselm drew up for Terran and Aifric."

She blinked in surprise. "Oh. I hadn't thought of that. You're getting a bum deal, aren't you? I have nothing of value to give you. You could get so much more if you married a fellow noble."

It hadn't occurred to her until then that his family might not be pleased to welcome her into their midst. How would she feel if Leslie came home suddenly married to a husband who had nothing to his name? She'd be furious with the man for taking advantage of her sister.

Connie was likely to be viewed as a gold digger.

"*Whist.* You've given me somat of unspeakable value. Your trust. Your heart. Your body." His words were fierce yet private in their softness. "I've been presented noble lasses, and have found each one lacking."

Jealousy gnawed at her at the thought of his being presented with other marriage candidates. But he'd been a virgin. She let that fact soothe her.

"Never doubt that I choose you," he said. "No matter what, I choose you."

Her chest constricted with a surge of love that overshadowed all her niggling insecurities.

"'Tis much better to be chosen than to do the choosing."

Aifric's words reverberated in her memory. The girl was young, but she possessed the wisdom of someone who had been through hard times and understood that the good times should never be taken for granted.

"I'm ready," Ewan said. "Will, give me your full name."

"Wilhelm Amittai Murray."

He had to spell his middle name for Ewan. While the other man wrote the letters, he said to her, "'Tis a Biblical name meaning truth." A curve of one corner of his mouth acknowledged the secret they shared: his truth sense.

"And your name," Ewan said, looking up at her.

"Constance Emmaline Thurston."

Wilhelm went stock still beside her. "What did ye say, lass?"

She repeated her name, confused as to why it should upset him in any way. "Is something wrong?"

"Nay, lass. 'Tis likely a coincidence, but your surname is the same as the last parliamentarian I'd hoped to discuss my judicial act with."

"Hm. Interesting."

"Do you have Scots ancestors?" he asked her while Ewan wrote out her name.

She'd noticed Ewan didn't ask her to spell her name like he'd asked Wilhelm. Wondering why, she answered Wilhelm distractedly, "It's possible, but my family hasn't kept the most thorough records."

She squinted at Ewan's writing. His penmanship was a tiny scrawl that would have been difficult to read even if it hadn't been upside-down from her perspective.

"There's an *S* after the *N*," she said, noticing he'd botched her first name. "And a *C-E* after the second *N*." He'd left out her middle name all together. He'd spelled Thurston wrong, too, making it *T-U-R-S-T-A-N*.

Before she could correct Ewan any more, Wilhelm said, "The important name is mine. If your father were present, his name would be carefully transcribed as well."

"That's completely archaic. Not to mention sexist." She folded her arms. "Doesn't my name matter?"

Wilhelm reeled back as if her protest took him off guard. "Of course it does, lass." Recovering, he pried her arms away from her chest and held both her hands. "I love your name as I love everything about you. But the contract goes directly to the public record in Edinburgh, where it shall be filed according to the spelling of *my* name. If your father were present, Ewan would make a second copy to be filed with your clan's records, but as no one is here to sign on your behalf, only one contract is needed."

"I remember my history," she argued. "Women here can own property and run businesses. Not every woman is expected to be tied to a man. What of those women? When they marry, are their names horribly misspelled?"

Wilhelm glanced at Ewan.

"You want me to rewrite the thing?" Ewan frowned. He wasn't the fastest at writing. In fact, he seemed to have broken a sweat from the effort.

"Mayhap 'tis for the best," Wilhelm said, giving Ewan an apologetic look.

"Oh, for goodness sake. You don't have to treat me like a petulant child who won't be satisfied until she gets her way. Don't rewrite it," she told Ewan, feeling guilty that she'd essentially insulted him when he was doing them this favor. "Please accept my apology. Both of you. If you say it's a minor detail, I trust you. I shouldn't have taken offense."

She couldn't fly off the handle every time she encountered a cultural difference.

"Apology accepted, lass," Wilhelm said, dragging her into his arms. He kissed her temple and whispered. "You make me so proud, *mo luaidh*."

Ewan cleared his throat and said, "Yeah. Arright, then. Sign here, Will."

Her almost-husband bent over the desk, dipped the quill, and signed his name where Ewan pointed. He had a flowing script dominated by the mountain-like peaks and valleys formed by the capital letters in his name, *W, A,* and *M*.

"Now you," Ewan said.

Wilhelm handed her the quill, and she began to sign her name as she always did, pleased at least her signature would reflect the correct spelling. She'd never written with a quill before, though. It wasn't as easy as using a pen. The ink made blots in places, and in others it didn't quite make a solid line. In the end, her signature wasn't any more legible than Ewan's transcription of her name.

Wrinkling her nose, she decided not to grumble about how the contract appeared. According to the men, she would never see it again, anyway. Besides, this would be the last time she signed her name thusly. From now on, when she had occasion to sign her full name, it would include a proudly-scribed Murray at the end.

Heavens. I'm a married woman now.

Her heart smiled. So did her husband. How handsome he was when he was pleased! It made her want to please him always.

Leslie's joyous laugher rang in her imagination as Connie shared the moment with her twin the only way she could.

Look at him, Les. He's mine. I can't believe he's mine.

She felt Leslie's imagined approval shine around her like a summer sunrise.

Ewan added his signature to the contract and returned the quill to the inkpot. She noted the date, written out as 26th day of

December. She'd known the year, 1487, and that it was wintertime, but she hadn't known the exact date. It seemed Wilhelm had lost his virginity on Christmas and she'd gained a husband on Boxing Day. What a wonderful present!

"I'll send this off to Edie with my next round of letters," Ewan said, standing and rubbing his ink-stained fingers on his kilt. "What are you waiting for, man? Kiss your wife."

Wilhelm crushed her to his chest. His mouth descended on hers. Happiness filled her from head to toe.

How she loved this man! How she wanted to grant him every access to her. Body, mind, and soul. She would hold nothing back. If she gave him enough of herself, maybe it would ease the cracking pain of all she was saying goodbye to by legally binding herself to the past.

No. Not the past. Her present.

From now on, this is where I am. This is where I live. Wilhelm is the man I love.

She fell deeper into the kiss, grasping at Wilhelm's shoulders. His tongue warred with hers, but it was a passionate sparring, not a battle with an intended loser. Victory belonged to both of them.

Wilhelm broke away with blazing eyes. They truly glowed. It was subtle enough that she could tell herself it was just the angle of his face in relation to the candles, but that explanation was wearing thin.

Could she really believe Wilhelm held magic inside of him? Could she believe in something science couldn't explain?

Con, you've traveled through time, for Pete's sake. Imagining Leslie's exasperation made her smile. Her twin would always be with her. *When are you going to accept the fact that magic exists?*

It *was* magic, she admitted to herself. And for some reason, she brought it out in him.

"Come," Wilhelm said. "I have need of you, *mo luaidh*."

His tone of command made her shiver in a decidedly carnal way. No other man could dictate desires to her and create within her an urge to satisfy them. No other man made her feel like a soft, beautiful woman. Only him. Her husband.

Ewan cleared his throat, and the sound was like a needle scratching a record. She and Wilhelm looked to him as one. "Erm, Will, I doona permit tupping in the tower. I am clergy, after all."

Her husband glared at Ewan, who began silently shaking a moment before breaking out in thunderous laughter.

"Jesting, man. Jesting. Go enjoy your bride." He lumbered around the desk and clapped Wilhelm's shoulder.

Connie couldn't help her giggles as Wilhelm mock-punched Ewan in the stomach.

It was far from the wedding she'd imagined for herself, but she would certainly never forget it.

Chapter 24

"HONESTLY, WILHELM. WHERE'S the fire?"

Constance had said the phrase at the abbey, as well, when he'd dashed out of doors to search for her, having found her bed empty. He gathered it meant she didn't approve of his haste.

But he had good reason for haste, and 'twas not merely because he couldn't wait to bed her. He continued jogging down the stairs to their guest room, leading her by her hand. Outside the door, he said, "Close your eyes."

She did not choose to obey.

He grinned at the challenge she presented.

"Why?" She dragged out the word, narrowing her eyes.

"I have a surprise for you. Now, listen to your husband and close. Your. Eyes." With each word, he drew her closer until their bodies were pressed together.

She huffed a put-out sigh but did as he commanded, lips pinched in a smile she tried to stifle.

He opened the door and led her in, loving the feel of both her hands in his, loving the trust she showed him even more. "Keep them closed."

"For how long?"

"Until I give the word."

"I repeat, dear husband. How. Long?"

He kissed her eyelids, one at a time. "'Tis a good surprise," he promised. "Verra good. Now do as I say." He patted her bottom, eliciting a jump from her. Then he left for the downstairs parlor.

Returning, he found her standing facing the door with arms folded over her chest. Her eyes were still closed.

"That better be you," she said.

"Who else would it be?"

"Ewan, come to show me more of his wolf figures." Her bonny lips quirked, telling him her ire was in jest.

"He willna bother us tonight. Likely he'll remain at the top of the tower on watch." While he spoke, he poured the pail of boiling water into the hipbath he'd dragged from Ewan's living quarters.

"What on Earth are you doing? Is that water I hear? Why is our room so hot?"

The guest room wasn't large. She likely felt the heat rising from the bath and saw the glow from the fireplace from behind her closed eyes.

"Patience, love." He fetched the full pot over the fire in their room and added that to the bath. Testing the water, he found it decadently warm, almost too warm for comfort.

"You're lucky I'm smitten." Her grumbling made him grin some more.

He circled her and began undoing her dress, which forced her to drop her arms.

"I'm going to open my eyes," she warned.

"Not yet."

She harrumphed. "This better be good."

"You'll find I am a man of my word." Sliding her dress and shift down, he exposed her breasts. "Saints above, these are perfect."

"Wilhelm Murray, if you think you can ogle me and not let me look my fill of you, you have another think coming." She opened her eyes, and they blazed with indignation. Then they widened with pleasure when she saw the steaming bath. "Is that for me?"

"Hm. I was thinking of using it for myself, but I suppose you may go first."

She swatted at him playfully than elbowed him out of the way to get to the bath. Testing the water, she moaned—just from the touch of the heat on her hand. The sound of pleasure made his cock twitch. Aye, he would make certain she had frequent hot baths.

Made of hammered copper, the hipbath was one of the few luxuries Ewan kept at the tower. Sized for a man, the basin allowed Constance to sink in up to her ribs, an action she did slowly and with much sighing. When she'd fully seated herself, her breasts floated just on the surface, peach nipples playing a coy game of hide and seek.

'Twould take a miracle to bathe her and not expire from lust. Mayhap he should bathe her with his eyes closed. Steeling himself for the task, he dipped the ewer his co-conspirator had found and shielded her eyes with one hand while he wetted her hair.

"Have I told you lately how much I love you?" Her voice slurred with relaxation as she allowed him to cradle her head with his other hand.

"Aye. But I'll never tire of hearing it."

Recalling baths his mother had given him when he was a boy, he took his time lathering her hair, working his fingers over her scalp. Was it as soothing for her as he remembered?

How intimate this was, tending to his *wife*. She would be his to tend for all time. Provided all went well in Inverness. Since a good outcome was far from guaranteed, he guarded his happiness.

It was imperative they steer clear of Ruthven until he'd found a magistrate to hear their testimony. By now his father would have received the letter he'd sent from the abbey. With luck, Kenrick would be packing for Inverness and planning to leave on the morrow. Remaining out of sight in Inverness wouldn't be difficult. He didn't have many acquaintances there. So long as he didn't kick his name about, they should avoid notice.

"Penny for your thoughts." Constance had tipped her head to gaze up at him. Her eyes of every color sparkled like fine whisky.

Och, what was he doing fashing about Inverness when he had a bonny wife to bed?

He glided his fingers along her silky-wet skin to cup her jaw. She let him caress her throat, her most vulnerable place. From there, he explored her slender collar bones then the smooth slope of her chest that led to those decadent buoyant breasts. Between the trust she showed him and the delights of her nude form, his cock throbbed for attention.

"I was thinking about Inverness," he admitted. "But I believe I have somat better to think about."

"Mmmmm. I agree. In fact, I'll bet I can find a way to stop you thinking altogether." She grasped his hands a moment before his splayed fingers would have reached her nipples. Tugging him around the basin, she said, "There's room for two in here, but I'm afraid you'll have to tolerate me sitting on your lap." She flicked at the trews he'd changed into since his plaid had been sodden upon their arrival. "And you might want to take these off."

"Think you to command me?" He hardly recognized his husky voice. This woman brought out animalistic need in him.

"Only suggesting how you might make your wife happy, my darling."

He shed his shirt and trews faster than ever before. "My father tells me a happy wife makes for a happy husband. Mayhap, we'll put that to the test."

"Yes, please."

He stepped into the hipbath and her waiting arms, and as she'd predicted, it didn't take long for him to cede thought to instinct.

§

CONNIE RECLINED ON Wilhelm's chest in the most decadent hot bath she'd ever taken. It wasn't the most comfortable or the most fragrant or even the most relaxing bath she'd had, but it was decadent because Wilhelm had obviously gone to a lot of trouble to create this experience for her. She showed her appreciation by enjoying his gift to the full—and making sure he did too.

Feeling like an infatuated teenager, she stroked her fingers over his face. He hadn't shaved since they'd left the abbey, and his whiskers scraped at her in a delicious reminder of his masculinity—as if the erection prodding at her hip or the hunger in his gaze weren't proof enough.

She appreciated the play of muscles in his cheek when his jaw tensed and the way his eyes fluttered closed when she nuzzled the spot below his ear. His scent of leather, soap, and hard-working man filled her lungs.

She ran her hands over the wet, bulging muscles of his arms and shoulders and trusted his long quadriceps to hold her up. Brushing her knuckles over his firm pectorals and abdominals made him suck in a breath. The sight and feel of those muscles contracting made her sex pulse with need.

His arms held her securely to him, sideways so they could gaze at each other—and so he could palm her breast and sweetly tease her nipple with one rubbing thumb.

Being this close to someone so powerful and beautiful was like being allowed into the tiger's enclosure at the zoo and having a big cat curl up with her and revel in her petting. Her tame warrior.

After observing him at the monastery and here at Ewan's tower, she understood that he used the strength of his sculpted body to serve others. Of all she had come to learn about him, this generosity of spirit was what enticed her most. He wanted to make a difference in the world. And he showed every promise of being able to do just that. As long as they could put that slime-ball Ruthven in his place.

She would work on that problem later. For now, she had an honest to goodness Highland warrior prepared to bring her pleasure. Never before had she anticipated sex with such eagerness. Only with Wilhelm.

The bath made it difficult to feel her own wetness, but there was no mistaking the swelling and throbbing low in her body. Biology was amazing. Her body recognized her mate and prepared the way for their coupling. Even if she were to fight this attraction with her intellect, her body would still belong to Wilhelm.

"It seems we have a little problem," she said.

"Mmmmm. What might that be, love?"

"I want you inside of me, but I don't think we can realistically do that in this glorious bath you've drawn me."

A harsh breath fanned over her lips, evidence she'd shocked and aroused him. Delightful, having power over the most powerful man she'd ever known.

"We could make an attempt all the same," he purred.

"It seems I've married an optimist."

"You doona trust I can accomplish what I set my mind to?"

"Maybe I need to see in order to believe." This had been generally true, until recently. If anyone could stretch her faith, it seemed it was Wilhelm.

He angled her head so he peered directly into her eyes. "Then watch this," he said, and he took her mouth with a savage kiss.

Lifting her while keeping their mouths joined, he got up on his knees. Even with his injured arm, he gave no sign of struggling with her weight.

Instinctively, she wrapped her legs around him, locking her ankles over his buttocks. In this position, the water's surface flirted with her intimate region and the edge of the tub nudged her bottom, adding to her arousal.

Wilhelm supported her with strong hands spanning her cheeks. The muscles in his arms and chest bulged as he positioned her for penetration. "I havena tested you, lass. Will I find your body welcoming, I wonder?"

Retreating the tiniest increment, he brought a whimper of frustration from her, but he wasn't abandoning their game. Instead, he rocked against her with his cock trapped between them. Erotic shocks radiated outward from her clit.

She bit her lip, breasts heaving against his chest with her desire. She didn't know her own body well enough to be able to answer. With other lovers, she'd required plentiful foreplay. But the way Wilhelm's intimate caresses ignited her nerve endings suggested she was ready after no more than a half hour of cuddling.

"Go slow," she said, needing him inside her but anxious about whether she was lubricated enough. She'd never done this in water before. The newness combined with her uncertainty gave her an unexpected thrill.

With no more than a slight adjustment, he was back at her entrance.

"I'll hold you." His voice was rough as sandpaper. "You take me as ye will."

His arms caged her, their strength making her feel protected. His white-hot gaze filled her with a sense of being cherished. Needed.

A tilt of her pelvis brought him inside of her the merest fraction of an inch. No bite of pain accompanied the smooth glide. She bit her lip as pleasure sang through her.

No one else had ever triggered such strong arousal. If she'd needed reassurance this man was meant exclusively for her, this was it. Biology didn't lie.

Slowly, inch by inch, she sank down and welcomed her husband into her body, holding his gaze all the while. There was power in this moment. She'd never been one to put stock in spirituality, but recent events had taught her to believe in the unexplainable. The feeling of being bonded transcended emotion. It was a truth under her skin.

"Lass." A harsh sigh. Wilhelm's jaw clenched as if he were in pain, but she knew she wasn't hurting him. It was pleasure bringing him to this edge, this place between helplessness and ecstasy.

Pride and wonder spurred her to tighten her grip on him. Arms, legs, sex. Everything clenched to hold onto this love.

"I need more," he bit out. Planting one foot, he stood smoothly. Swift steps brought their dripping bodies to the bed, where he laid atop her keeping them joined the whole time.

Fusing his mouth with hers, he lifted her bottom with one hand and drove deeper. Pleasure surged as he set a slow, powerful rhythm and rode it unwaveringly until she cried out with release. He followed soon after, but was apparently not done with her.

Good. She wasn't done with him either. Never would be.

While her heart rate returned to normal, he raised up on his arms and took his time observing her damp skin.

"All mine," he said, and he began running his hands all over her. "You'll not leave this bed until I've imprinted myself on you. You'll be feeling me tomorrow, *mo luaidh.*"

"I'll be feeling you for always."

"Aye."

Wilhelm made love to her a second time. True to his word, he'd made sure she could still feel him even as they lay tangled together afterward. The sensation wasn't exactly soreness, but that of being well used—in the best possible way. Maybe he'd left more than sensations behind. Maybe he'd left a trace of himself that would grow inside her and strengthen their bond even more.

As the fire faded, Wilhelm drifted to sleep. Taking pride in the smile she'd put on his face, she lit a candle from the last of the peat flames in the hearth and pulled her travel guide from her backpack.

Before arriving at the peel tower, she'd considered consulting the book to learn whether there might be a large town nearby where an officiator could be found. That point was moot now, but the little book still called to her—probably because it was the only source of information she had about Scotland. Instead of being an outdated reference, though, as books in the library often were when she had something to research, it was a predated reference. Still, she couldn't help thinking she might find something useful in its pages.

Snuggled in the blankets beside her sleeping husband, she began her reading with the section on Dornoch. She would learn everything she could about Wilhelm's home and the surrounding territory. Knowledge was power. She refused to go to Inverness powerless to help clear her husband's name.

Chapter 25

WILHELM'S BRIDE HAD done the lion's share of the talking yesterday, so while they rode he shared stories about his family. As they made their way north at a brisk walk and oft at a canter, when the road allowed, he described his parents, Alpin and Gormlaith. He told her of Dornoch and the farming his clan was known for since Dornoch was home to some of the most fertile soil in all Scotia.

The story of when Terran released a dozen new lambs into the keep had Constance laughing so hard she emitted a distinctively porcine snort. Endearing herself to him even more, she made light of the unladylike chortle rather than exhibit shame.

Recovering herself, she beamed at him, his rosy-cheeked bride. By all that was holy, he loved her.

Her eyes twinkled in the weak sunlight of the morning. They rode their own horses today, needing to travel swiftly if they were to make Inverness by nightfall. "Gosh, I haven't laughed that hard since—" Her good humor came to an abrupt halt.

He lusted to have her in his arms. Contenting himself with bringing Justice alongside her, he guessed, "Your sister?"

She nodded.

He gave her the time to have what thoughts she would. Time would ease the pain she must be feeling, but 'twould never completely heal. He'd lost a sister as well.

"When I was a boy of twelve, I watched helplessly while my sister died of fever. Marianne. She was seven. She, Terran, and I were thick as thieves."

Constance reached across the space between them to hold his hand. "I'm sorry."

"Death is part of life. Unfortunately, kenning that does not a thing to ease the pain when it strikes close to the heart."

He squeezed her hand. How much more devastating would it be to lose a sister one had shared a womb with, especially after living well into adulthood together?

"Leslie was the one who sent me here," Constance said, releasing his hand. She stared ahead as though looking into the past.

He held his breath, desperate to hear more but hesitant to speak. He sensed she needed to set her own pace in recounting the magic that brought her to him.

"She didn't mean to." She smiled to herself, and the affection in it warmed his heart. "It was dawn on summer solstice. I'd just arrived in Scotland the evening before. I was exhausted—I'd slept on the plane, but still, something about air travel does that to you. Makes you so weary." She shook her head. "Traveling through time was less draining, if you can believe it." She bit her lip, as if nervous about putting such things into words.

"Go on, lass. 'Tis only you and me here."

"And the horses."

"They willna tell."

She looked at him for the first time in several minutes. A thrill of connection tugged on his viscera. This woman was part of him now. She was his to care for. His to cherish. He would protect her secrets with his life.

The worry smoothed from her face. "In the future, people love visiting ancient sites. I don't know if it's that way here, but in my time, there's something so whimsical and exciting about seeing a castle up close and getting to go inside. And the stone formations—they're even older than the castles and ruins tourists pay to see. Maybe it's a desire to connect with humanity's past. Or the fantasy of wondering why our ancestors constructed such places.

"You see, my country isn't very old. The land existed, of course, but Europeans didn't come to it until…well, at the moment, right now, the only people there are the natives, and to my knowledge, they didn't build castles. I think there are some examples of stone formations in North America, but I've never been to one. They're certainly not as prominent as the ones in Europe."

He longed to ask more about her country and when Europeans would begin traveling there, but he made himself hold his tongue. She was telling him of her last moments in the future. This story was precious to her, and therefore it was precious to him. Her choosing to share it honored him greatly.

"I was looking forward to seeing the ruins of structures built so long ago. Leslie had been here—in Scotland—for several weeks already. The novelty of the historic feel had long worn off for her. But she was positively giddy over going to Druid's Temple on the morning of the solstice and not because it's one of the oldest stone circles in Europe."

She sighed. "Leslie is—well, I suppose in this day she would be called a witch."

Shock made his hands tense on the reins.

"She isn't one," she hurried to add. "I mean, it's different in my time. What Leslie's doing—exploring Wicca—it's a fad, a trend that will fade. She's just like that—you know, an explorer. She tries different fads and ingratiates herself with others who share the same inclinations. She's a free spirit. I don't think she's ever actually done anything magical. In my time, at least for Leslie, it was more about appreciating the Earth and nature, in using herbs for health and living naturally. In loving others. There was no malice in it."

Her tone leaned towards defensiveness, as if she expected him to condemn her sister, when in fact, the "free spirit" she described reminded him of his mother. Gormlaith loved nature. She spent more time outdoors than in, tending her gardens, walking the hills, riding her beloved mare, and visiting with the villagers. She often delivered fresh herbs and tea mixes to the sick among their clan. Constance would like her, Wilhelm suspected. He had no doubt his mother would welcome Constance and love her like a daughter.

"I find naught offensive about what ye describe, lass. I am not one of those men quick to condemn a woman of witchcraft simply because she finds pleasure in the bounties of the Earth. I believe God gave us the Earth and is pleased when we enjoy it."

She released a pent-up breath. "You're so level-headed. I wasn't sure what you'd think of Leslie if I told you about the Wicca, but I'm relieved you aren't flinging Scripture at me."

"Of course not. I would have liked to meet your sister."

"I would have liked that too."

They rode for a while in silence before she picked up her story. "Leslie had been to a shop in Inverness," she said, and the words held a weight he'd not noticed in the rest of her tale. "She told me about the shopkeeper while we waited for the sunrise that morning. He was French, she said, and she sensed something magical about him. He gave her this necklace with a stone on it. Leslie called it a witch's stone."

Ah. At the gathering, Ruthven had accused Constance of wearing a hag stone. Legend warned that to some, such stones could be lucky. To others, they would bring curses. Like Constance, Wilhelm didn't put much stock in magic, but he did not deny that forces of good and evil worked among mortals for their own purposes. He didn't doubt that this "witch's stone" had played a part in the magic Constance had experienced. It certainly would have played a part in her arrest. Any woman caught wearing a hag stone would be presumed a witch and treated accordingly.

Could Constance have been spared her ill treatment at Ruthven's hands if her sister had never visited that shop? Mayhap. But mayhap she never would have come here at all without it.

"He said if she made a wish at sunrise on the solstice, fate might grant it." Constance continued her story. "There was some business about a pure heart." She made a scoffing noise, but there was humor in it. "I've never really believed in spells and wishes and magic. But I'm starting to. I think."

Her story fascinated him near to the point of speechlessness. To think, his wife's presence in his life came down to a wish made by her twin, a hag stone, and a solstice. Which of the factors were vital? All of them? Or mayhap none? Mayhap fate would have brought Constance to him without the help of her sister and the objects of lore. He would like to think that their souls had called to each other through time and that no matter the trappings, they would have found each other eventually.

But what if he'd come within a hair's breadth of never meeting her?

He forced a casual tone. "Hard no' to believe in magic when you've been subject to it, aye?"

"Exactly. At a certain point, it becomes more logical to accept it than to continue denying the possibility of its existence."

"You mentioned your sister made a wish," he said, hoping she would tell him what the wish had been. Had Leslie hoped for her sister's wealth, good health, or long life?

"Leslie wished that I would know love. She wanted me to be happy." Her eyes shiny, she held his gaze. "I think her wish came true."

§

CONNIE HAD EXPECTED Inverness to have changed a lot in five hundred years, but she hadn't expected not to recognize a single feature. When Wilhelm announced well after dark that they'd arrived in the city, she blinked and tried to match the sights around her to what she'd seen briefly before the hike with Leslie.

True, she'd spent precious little time in the city. The cab Leslie had taken to meet her at the airport had shuttled her quickly to their bed and breakfast, and they'd biked out of the city nearly as quickly the morning of their hike. Logic suggested she might recognize something, a land feature, a prominent old structure, but no. Nothing registered as *same*.

Gone were the twin towers of St. Andrew's Cathedral on the western bank of the River Ness, spotlights highlighting their cubical shape. Missing on the other side of the river was the sandstone Inverness Castle. Absent were the modern buildings dotted among the older stone row houses and the spires of churches that had made the skyline so wonderfully eclectic.

Even the River Ness seemed different. The absence of city lights reflecting off its inky surface made it difficult to decipher water from shore. The result was an unsettling sensation that the river sent black tendrils into the city, between the buildings and into the streets.

As they rode, she kept searching for some familiar landmark. As far as she could tell, the only architectural feature of note was a single stone tower with a thatched roof to the north. As she and Wilhelm made their way to the town center, the tower grew closer.

"Is that where we're going?" she asked. She kept her voice quiet. It seemed the right thing to do. Every so often, she would spot a horse and cart on the side of the street or a person coming or going from one of the buildings, but the streets were largely free from traffic.

"That is the citadel," Wilhelm said. "We are looking for an inn I've been to before that is near the tower. We'll meet my father's second there. Kenrick. He'll advise us." His confident voice carried in the night.

The medieval city was oddly quiet compared to a modern city. There were so few sounds to compete with the human voice, only hoof beats and the creaking of boats docked in the river. As the streets grew broader and the light from inhabited dwellings more frequent, the noise multiplied. Fiddle music tempted her to tap her fingers on the reins, and the murmur of conversation bubbled from inside a place that must have been a tavern.

Honesty plodded along, his neck low and sweaty. The horses had walked far today. She and Wilhelm had pushed them, eager to get to Inverness. The horses, Wilhelm had assured her, would be pampered in the next few days. He planned to buy them private stalls and daily attention from a stable boy during their stay.

Connie patted Honesty. "A little farther and you'll have a nice rest." To Wilhelm she said, "I'll be relieved when this is all behind us."

"Aye, lass. So shall I. So shall I."

With the citadel looming to their right, Wilhelm led the way under a stone arch and into a courtyard formed by the walls of three separate buildings. One was a wooden structure attached to the citadel, like an addition built on as the need for more space arose. From so close to the tower, she could make out spikes jutting from its second story, as if daring intruders to attempt to scale the wall.

Another side of the courtyard was made up of a three-story building she assumed was the inn. The open windows of the lower level let out the sounds of raucous banter and sent light angling over the cobblestones.

The third wall of the courtyard was a bare two-stories of brick, probably the rear of a row of shops that fronted a neighboring street. An alley between the inn and the bare wall was strewn with straw. Maybe they would find the inn's stables through there.

By daylight, the little courtyard might be quaint, but by night, the jagged shadows left her feeling uneasy.

Wilhelm drew Justice to a stop. "Here we are." He dismounted and helped her down in the way that had become automatic for them. He held her like that for a minute, his armor a shield in front of her, Honesty a wall of safety behind her.

He cupped her head and spoke low into her ear. "Wait here with the horses. I doona like the sound of the party inside. I'll rent our room and hire a stable boy, then meet you here and bring you in a back way."

"Be careful." The warning came naturally. A wife's worrying instinct, perhaps?

He positioned her between Justice and Honesty, effectively hiding her from anyone who might happen by on the street. With a soft kiss on her lips, he left her to go inside.

The laughter from the inn's lower floor swelled when he opened the door. In the relative quiet once the door closed, a voice came from the direction of the bare wall.

"Good evening, *Madame*."

She started. Peeking around Justice, she saw she'd been mistaken. It wasn't a bare wall. Rather, there was a lone door, maybe the back entrance to one of the shops. She must have missed the door when it had been closed, but now that it stood open, spilling light into the courtyard, she saw it clear as day.

A man stood on the threshold, keeping the door open with one arm, a man she hadn't been certain was real—until now. Leslie's shopkeeper.

Chapter 26

"IT'S YOU," CONNIE stated, forgetting her faux British accent.

The intimate feel of the square allowed for a conversational volume. Since there didn't appear many places for a person to hide themselves, the risk of someone eavesdropping and catching her foreign dialect was minimal. Still, she would be more careful.

"*Oui,*" the shopkeeper replied, a twinkle in his onyx eyes. "I am me. This much I know to be true." He was dressed slightly more pedestrian than the last time she'd seen him. Instead of ethereal silk, he wore black, high-waisted trousers and a shirt with a flouncy jabot and cuffs.

His presence unnerved her. It also reassured her. She stepped out from between the horses. "Is this where your shop is located, then?"

"One of the locales, *oui.*"

"Why—" She licked her lips. "Why are you here? Now, I mean? Is everything all right with Leslie?"

"An astute query, *Madame.* As far as I know, your dear sister is safe. It is you I have come to see tonight. Come in, *s'il vous plaît.* I've prepared tea for you. You must be famished after your journey." He motioned into his shop.

She glanced toward the inn. "Wilhelm will be out any minute. He would miss me. I'll come by after we've settled the horses." She wouldn't leave her husband wondering where she'd gone.

His expression grew tense. "I'm afraid that will not do. It must be now. This very minute."

"I can't. I won't give him cause to worry. He has enough on his mind."

"This is more true than you know. It pleases me to see the choice you've made, *Madame* Murray. But I regret to inform you that if you do not enter my shop forthwith, all will be lost."

She blinked. "All will be lost? What do you mean?" She had to raise her voice to be heard over a ruckus inside the inn. It sounded like a brawl had broken out. *Oh, no. Wilhelm!*

She rushed toward the door of the inn.

"But no! If you wish to help him, you must come to me. Now!"

She froze in place, torn. Should she trust the shopkeeper who seemed to have some kind of finger on the pulse of the supernatural or should she go inside the inn to see what the commotion was about? If Wilhelm was in trouble, she needed to be there for him. But the shopkeeper's entreaty resonated with her at a gut level.

Before she could make up her mind, the door to the inn burst open. She was so close she had to jump back or get hit.

Back plastered against the outer wall, heart hammering, she watched a dozen shouting men spill out of the inn. In the center, they carried a man by his arms and legs. Wilhelm!

His helm and armor were gone, and his face was bruised. He'd been disarmed. With a grunt, he twisted to put his eyes on the horses, where he had left her. Not finding her, his eyes widened. He began looking all around, gaze stuttering over the shopkeeper before moving on.

While he searched, he renewed his struggles only to be clouted over the head with a club-like weapon.

She clapped her hands over her mouth to stop herself from screaming.

His eyes fluttered. Weakly struggling, he looked barely conscious.

Please, don't hit him again.

A short, rotund man barked out commands. "Bind him. Quickly. Not so fierce now, are you, Murray? Without your pea-brained cousin to start your fires and fight by your side?"

She recognized that self-satisfied tone. Ruthven.

"Imagine my delight when I intercepted the message to your sire. Saved me a great deal of time by spelling out precisely where you intended to go." He stalked in a circle around his captive, and his weasel-like face split with a grin from ear to ear. "Where's your witch, Murray? Or did you use her and discard her? Do you have more sense than your daft sire, I wonder, or did you try to marry the wretched she-spy?"

That vile man was taunting her husband. He was talking about *her*.

She flattened herself to the wall, hoping to blend in with the shadows and not draw notice. *What do I do? How do I fix this?*

"Hurry." The shopkeeper's voice entered her ear as if he stood beside her.

Her gaze jumped to his shop.

He stretched out a hand to her. The voice had been his, but nothing but magic could explain her hearing it the way she just had.

The doorframe wavered the way a mirage does when it begins to fade.

"It is now or never, *Madame*." She heard the voice again even though his mouth didn't move.

Every inch of her being longed to run to Wilhelm, but what could she do to help him? He was severely outnumbered. If she threw herself into the fray, she'd be captured too. What good would she be to him then?

But she would have to run past the mob of men to reach the shopkeeper.

"Have faith," whispered the voice in her ear.

Man and shop faded more. Behind them, she saw the stone of the row houses as if no doorway would exist there in a few seconds.

She didn't think. She ran. Fast as she could. Her feet pounded the cobble stones step after step until she squeezed past the shopkeeper.

"No Lass!" Wilhelm's roar filled her ears as the door slammed shut behind her. He hadn't looked strong enough to shout so loudly. Had the sight of her running away given him a second wind?

Immediately, she regretted her decision. She turned to reassure Wilhelm, to reassure herself he was still fighting, still alive, but where the door had been a moment ago was a solid wall. She slapped her palms against it.

"Let me go back!" She beat on the wall until her hands throbbed, then she beat some more. "Let me go! I need to help him!" She strained to listen for Wilhelm's voice again, but no sound from the courtyard penetrated into the shop.

"You *are* helping him."

"How? How is this helping? That bastard Ruthven has him. How will I contact his clan? What are they going to do to him?" She wheeled on the shopkeeper.

He appeared unruffled. "Come, *Madame,* I have a fresh pot of tea."

"To hell with tea. I'll drink tea when Wilhelm is safe."

"I do not believe I have introduced myself. Bastien Gravois at your service." He pronounced it in the French way, *Bas-tay-ON Grahv-Wah.* After a brief bow at the waist, he leaned an elbow on a glass curio case, looking utterly at ease.

She wanted to shake him until he understood the seriousness of this situation.

Never mind. She would find a way out of here without his help.

The shop was wider than it had appeared from the street. Tall shelving made three aisles along the length and glass cases set off one section of the room. A seemingly unrelated collection of objects hung on the walls, like a gilt mirror, a feathered ceremonial mask, various creatures frozen in display cubes, and—heavens, was that a birdcage filled with shrunken heads?

Amidst the oddities, she looked for doors or windows. Besides a handful of Oriental wall hangings that could potentially conceal points of egress, she saw no way out.

Making a beeline for the nearest tapestry, she said, "How can you be so calm? Did you see what just happened? That evil jerk has my husband, and I don't believe for a second he has a fair trial in mind." Yanking up the corner of the tapestry, she saw nothing but bare wall.

"You'll find when my shop is closed, time is of no consequence. *That* is how I can be calm."

She was already looking under the next tapestry, taking care not to topple the stuffed, behorned lynx on a pedestal in front of it. Gravois's words stopped her. *Time is of no consequence.*

"I take it I won't find any windows or doors, then. Not until your shop is open again?"

His mouth twitched in a satisfied smile.

Though she got the sense that he had been around innumerable years, his face was smooth with youth. Even the slight crinkles at the corners of his eyes disappeared when his pleased expression faded.

"*Très bien,* my dear. I have not had a chance to offer you my congratulations, as yet. Allow me to treat you to a celebratory tea." He lifted one elegant arm and made a twirling motion with one finger, indicating she should turn around.

Puzzled, she looked at the tapestry again, but in its place hung a beaded curtain. Curiosity got the best of her and made her part the strings with one hand. Through the opening was a spacious room draped in silks and littered with floor pillows. A knee-height table in the center held a silver tea service complete with a five-tiered tray of sandwiches and petit fours.

She raised an eyebrow at Gravois. "Impressive. I'll be more impressed if you happen to have a plan for getting Wilhelm out of this mess with Ruthven."

"I may have a trick or two up my sleeve." He breezed past her with a delicate clatter of beads. Presiding over the table, he spread his arms in invitation. *"S'il vous plaît,* sit. Enjoy this bounty with me and we shall discuss this 'plan' you mention."

Worry for Wilhelm had her stomach in knots, but she picked a pillow and curled her legs beneath her. "All right, Gravois. I'll play. What do I have to do?"

He *tsked* her as he folded himself into a sitting position across from her. "First, we eat. One must replenish the soul beginning with the meeting of physical needs." He took his time pouring tea into two china cups with matching saucers.

A wave of frustration made her see red. Rather than let it get the best of her, she squeezed her eyes shut and took a deep breath. She could have tea. She could be polite. Apparently, rushing Gravois was an exercise in futility.

"Thank you." She took a sip from her cup. The tea was bright and citrusy with a nutty aftertaste. She used to take tea with her mother back in Chicago on special occasions. The flavor and aroma of this tea reminded her of one of her favorites.

"You approve, I take it." Gravois's onyx eyes took on the warmth of brotherly affection.

Despite her frustrations, she couldn't resist his charm. She found herself relaxing as the tea warmed her from the inside out. "This wouldn't happen to be Golden Monkey, would it?"

"I couldn't resist pampering you a bit, my dear. I have taken a liking to you."

He munched a sandwich then dabbed at the corner of his mouth with a napkin. Tall and slender and with features that brought to mind Mediterranean beaches and fast cars, there was no disputing his handsomeness. But her attraction was for one man. And Gravois gave off no vibes that he was anything more than a friend to her.

She allowed him to lead her in small talk, mostly about the culinary delights on the table, many of which were new to her, some of which she'd had dozens of times with her mother. The meal brought back soothing memories, but no amount of nostalgia could take her mind off what might be happening to Wilhelm at this very moment.

She took a chance on bringing the conversation around to her predicament. "You mentioned time is of no consequence when your shop is closed. What does that mean, exactly? Are we—I don't know—outside of time, somehow?"

He inclined his head, a gesture of approval. "That is one way to view it." She waited for him to elaborate, but he didn't.

"So we could have tea for an hour and then you could make a door and let me out and it could be only seconds after I came inside?"

His gaze unwavering, he said, "Perhaps, if time was amenable." He popped a lemon-yellow square in his mouth and moaned as he chewed. "Très bon. Have you tried the citrus squares?"

She frowned. He made time seem sentient. And he made those petit fours look amazing.

She snatched one up and nibbled it while she thought out loud. "Amenable. So, you wouldn't know whether or not you could open your shop at a specific time unless you tried? What if you tried to open a door for me so I enter the courtyard a minute before Wilhelm and I arrive? I could warn him not to go in the inn. I could tell him Ruthven is in there with a small army. You could try it, right? And if it doesn't work, no harm, no foul?"

She held her breath. Could the solution be simple as giving her and Wilhelm a chance to evade Ruthven? Could Wilhelm's capture be undone?

Gravois reclined on an elbow, a pastry held loosely in his fingers. "Even I, who have the ability to tinker, do not presume to understand the Great Agent or Agents of the world. Perhaps I serve their purposes. Perhaps," he added with a wink, "I annoy them. But until they see fit to remove my power, I shall do what pleases me, and that, my dear, is to complete broken circles. What you propose does not serve that purpose."

Her frustration rose again. He was speaking in riddles.

"Broken circles," she stated, giving him the opening he seemed to crave.

"*Oui.* You and your warrior. Two souls meant to create a unified whole, but time held you apart. I sensed the jagged edges of your hearts and I simply brought you together."

"I thought Leslie's wish brought us together."

He shrugged one shoulder. "However it happened, the edges are now joined."

He made the details of the magic seem unimportant. But to her, they meant everything. How could she free Wilhelm without understanding what her place here was, what her limitations were? Clearly, just by being in Gravois's shop, she was outside the normal workings of things.

"But the edges aren't joined. I mean, Wilhelm and I found each other, but now he's been arrested, and I have no idea how to free him. If Ruthven got his hands on that letter he sent to Dornoch, that means this Kenrick he's told me about isn't coming. No one knows Wilhelm is in trouble. I have nobody here to help me."

"Do you not?"

"Oh, of course I have you." If it wasn't for Gravois, she would have been captured along with Wilhelm. At least she was free at the moment and could potentially find a way to help him. "But you're a foreigner like I am. Don't tell me you have in that head of yours a grasp of Scottish law."

Actually, she wouldn't be surprised if he did. He seemed to possess no end of useful knowledge, but she sensed his method of helping, if he chose to do so, would be more indirect and mysterious. Gravois was a meddler who liked to work behind the scenes. Maybe she needed to put more trust in him. He seemed to have her best interest at heart, after all.

"I'm sorry. I didn't mean any offense. I'm truly grateful for your help. It's just—I can't lose him so soon after finding him. I need him, and so does Scotland."

He waved away her apology. "No offense taken. You are correct. Scotland does need your husband. And it needs you."

"Me?"

"But of course. Did you not think you might serve a purpose as the wife and confidante of a respected leader and lawmaker?"

Wilhelm wasn't a leader or lawmaker yet. Gravois spoke as though his eventual graduation to these roles was a foregone conclusion. Did that mean he would escape Ruthven?

"You are thinking too hard, my dear." He chortled and reached across the table to touch the crease between her brows. "When I suggested you had an ally here, it was not myself I had in mind, but another. One with the power to alter the current."

"Who? Terran? Anselm? Ewan?" She listed everyone she'd met who might have the ability to come to her aid. "How can I reach them to tell them what's happened?" Being from another time put her at a disadvantage. When Wilhelm was with her, it didn't seem to matter, but without him, she lacked the most basic knowledge. She didn't even know how to send a message.

"Your answer lies beyond that door." He nodded toward the wall where the original door had been.

The purple door looked like it had been there all along, complete with painted frame and a bell above to announce the entrance of patrons.

"You do know that's unnerving, right?"

His lips twitched. "One becomes accustomed to it."

"I'll bet." She approached the door. "All right, Gravois. I'll trust you."

The door opened by itself.

She'd expected to see the cobblestone courtyard outside, but a narrow brick road lined with row houses stared back at her, as if the shop had been picked up and put down in a completely different spot.

"Curiouser and curiouser," she said with a glance at Gravois, who merely shrugged one shoulder in response. "Well, where do I go? One of these houses?"

"Number seventeen. But wait one moment. I believe…" He trailed off as he looked down the road. "Ah, yes. Here we are."

A faint pattering sound drew her gaze to a spot of movement. Was that a—? "It's a monkey," she blurted. After the hour she'd spent with Gravois, she wouldn't have thought it possible to be shocked, but as a monkey in red overalls scampered toward her, she found herself laughing with surprise.

"Have you retrieved it, *mon petit ami?*" Gravois asked the monkey, who responded with a toothy smile as it displayed its prize: her backpack. "Well, what are you waiting for? Give it to her."

The little creature lifted the bag, which was almost as big as it was.

"Um, thank you," she said, taking the offering.

The monkey smiled broadly then leapt onto Gravois's shoulder as the man stooped to receive him.

Shaking her head, she said to Gravois, "You are full of surprises."

She could have predicted his response: a nonchalant shrug.

Hitching the backpack onto her shoulder, she said, "Number seventeen, huh? Will someone be expecting me?"

"Suffice it to say your appearance will create quite the stir."

"That's all you're going to give me, isn't it?"

"It is enough. Take care, Madame."

She recognized the dismissal. Bracing herself to 'create a stir,' she stepped out of the shop onto a street that had recently seen rain. The soft echo of her steps on the bricks told her there was no building directly behind her.

Imagining Gravois's twinkling eyes, she peeked over her shoulder. Sure enough, there was no shop and no mysterious Frenchman with a monkey on his shoulder. Only a grassy lawn sloping down to black water that might have been the River Ness, though a different stretch of it than she'd seen with Wilhelm.

A long glance in each direction showed no familiar landmarks, no tower marking the citadel and the courtyard where Wilhelm had been captured. Apparently, Gravois's shop could let a person out wherever it wanted—or wherever he wanted—and then vanish into thin air.

A sense of desolation swept over her along with the damp chill of the night. Her only ally, unusual as he was, was now out of reach. Rescuing Wilhelm was up to her...and whoever was behind door number seventeen.

The block of well-kept row houses appeared much longer than a traditional city block. As she walked, she noticed most of the houses were dark. Here and there a window gave off a little light, likely from candles or lanterns, but there were no bright, electric lights to be seen. No streetlamps, either. Medieval city dwellers probably didn't roam the streets after dark. At this hour, they'd be safe in their homes, getting ready for bed if they weren't in bed already.

Eventually, she came to number seventeen. One of the ground level windows emitted faint light, as if someone was active at the back of the house. An upstairs window glowed too. While she watched, the upstairs light went out.

At least she wouldn't be waking anybody since it seemed they were just now turning in.

Stepping up to the door, she grasped the knocker that looked like a roaring lion. There was no turning back now. Wilhelm depended on her.

Thud, thud, thud. Brass met plate with her firm knocks.

Gravois, you better be right about this.

After a minute the door opened. A balding man in a dark suit jacket stood in the opening. He held himself with formal bearing: shoulders back, chin high. "Rather late for callers," he said, but he stopped short. His skin turned ashen before her eyes. "M—M—Mistress Tarra."

His eyes rolled back in his head and he fainted.

Chapter 27

STARTLED, CONNIE STEPPED back. Why had this man lost consciousness at seeing her? Except for the backpack, which was mostly behind her, she was in period dress. She shouldn't appear shocking for any reason.

He'd called her Tarra. Maybe he'd mistaken her for someone else.

But that didn't matter at the moment. She couldn't leave the poor man like this. He might have hurt himself. Stooping to check for a pulse, she called into the house.

"Um, hello? Hello? Help, please!" Hopefully someone else was around since she wasn't sure how to tend to someone who'd just passed out. She pressed at several places under his jaw with no luck—she'd never actually checked another person for a pulse before. The warmth of his skin reassured her as she looked past him into the house.

A wood plank, wainscoted foyer opened before her. Above hung an unlit candle chandelier. Narrow stairs led the way from the foyer to the upper floor. Warm light came from a room behind the stairs. A silhouette momentarily blocked the light before a gray-haired woman in an apron came hustling from that direction.

The woman drew up short at seeing the man on the ground. "Lord Turstan! Chester's fainted at the door!"

Turstan? How strange. The man of the manor shared her last name, or almost. The pronunciation the woman had used reminded her of the way Ewan had written her name on her marriage contract.

Not sparing more than the briefest glance Connie's way, the woman bent at the waist to feel Chester's forehead. "Oh, dear, oh, dear."

Heavy, irregular footfalls on the stairs preceded the appearance of a tall bearded man in a dressing robe. Though he didn't appear older than mid-fifties, he leaned heavily on a cane.

"Here, here, what's this about?" said the man who must be Lord Turstan. When he spotted Connie patting the fainted man's cheek, he put his hand over his heart and gaped at her. He looked like he'd seen a ghost.

The woman glanced at Lord Turstan and then turned her attention to Connie. She made a surprised squeak.

"I'm not Tarra," Connie said, remembering the name the other man had called her before dropping like a stone. "My name is Constance Murray. I didn't mean any harm. Is there a bed or sofa he can be moved to?"

"Murray." The man studied her intently then blinked, seeming to collect himself. "Do you mean—" He broke off, looking down at the fallen man as if just remembering he was there. "Christ, lass, of course there's a bed. Chester. Chester, wake up, man." He knelt with a grunt of discomfort and grasped the other man's shoulders. "Mrs. Felts, get a cool cloth, will you?"

"Yes, milord." Before the woman left, she cast another look at Connie, as if she couldn't believe her eyes.

"I'm afraid I'm not fit to carry him. Old knee injury's acting up this winter." He drummed his fingers on his right leg. "We'll have to wake him first. You said your name is Con-*stance?*" Oddly, he placed the emphasis on the second syllable.

Before she could respond, a faint feminine voice came from upstairs. "Robert?"

"'Tis all right, love. Doona trouble yourself."

"What the blazes?" This came from the fallen Chester who blinked owl-like up at the ceiling.

The gray-haired woman returned with a towel. When Chester tried to sit up, she held him down and put the compress on his forehead.

"Just rest there for a moment, Chester," Turstan said. "You've had a shock."

"Thought I saw your girl," the man on the floor said. "Must have been sleepwalking on the job. It willna happen again, sir."

"You're not seeing things, dear," the woman said to Chester, her voice wavering. "We have a caller who could be the spitting image of the poor mistress. All except her hair."

Chester rolled his head her way and blinked a few times.

"Hello," she said. "I'm not who you think. Sorry to have startled you."

For the next few minutes, the three of them worked together to help Chester to his feet and then onto a couch in the parlor. Connie learned that Chester and the gray-haired woman, Mathilda, were both servants to Lord Turstan.

"Leave me be, woman," Chester grumbled. He waved his hand at Mathilda, who dithered over him, fluffing pillows and patting his body as if looking for injuries.

"I'll no' have you kicking off because ye think to return to work after such a fright," Mathilda said. "Tell him, milord. Tell him he's to turn in for the night and rest."

"No' until I ken who *she* is and what she supposes she's up to going about looking like the mistress." Chester eyed her suspiciously from his reclined position. He kept straining to sit up, and Mathilda kept pushing him back down. Connie wondered if the two might be married.

"A fine question," Lord Turstan said. He and Mathilda looked at her expectantly.

"Er, I—um." She pulled her shoulders back and gathered herself.

Apparently, she looked like someone they knew. No wonder they were so shocked by her appearance. Awkward as this introduction would be, she owed it to Wilhelm to make the best impression possible.

Donning the bearing of a well-bred woman like a character role, she said, "My name is Constance Emmaline Thurston Murray. I've been travelling the Highlands with my husband, but he's been arrested on false charges. My family is…far away. I have no one to call on for assistance and was told you might be able to do something about this unfortunate situation. I do apologize if I've caused anyone distress this evening."

"Did you say Constance *Murray*?" Lord Turstan said, this time putting the emphasis on her married name.

"*Turstan*-Murray," Mathilda corrected, sounding intrigued.

"No," said Chester. "She said it different." Dodging Mathilda's hands, he managed to sit up.

"She's sayin' it the English way, I suspect," Mathilda said. "Is there any doubt she's kin to the earl?"

"Silence," Turstan said. The other two snapped their mouths shut. "Mrs. Felts, bring us some ale, if you will. Chester, go on up to your bed. When the doctor arrives, I'll send him to you."

That struck her as an odd thing to say since she hadn't seen anyone send for a doctor. Maybe Turstan had sent for one before coming downstairs.

Chester's gaze dropped to the floorboards.

Mrs. Felts paled. "The doctor doesna ken she's—she's—" She broke off with a sob and hurried out of the parlor.

Connie felt like she'd missed something.

"I'm certain I doona need a doctor, sir," Chester said. His feisty mood had dropped with his gaze. "No need to keep the doc when he arrives." He sniffled, and Connie realized he was holding back tears. "But I'll go on up to bed if it pleases you." Bracing his hands on his knees, he stood up. Meeting Connie's eyes, he said, "Looks just like the mistress," and shook his head.

She looked between him and Turstan, unsure to whom he was speaking.

Turstan watched Chester go then said, "Have a seat, my dear." He went to the hearth and knelt, again with the grunt. With his back turned to her, he fiddled with something. When the fire caught, she realized he'd been using a flintbox.

He got to his feet again. His face drooped with weariness. Heavens, she felt awful for keeping him from his bed.

"I'm so sorry for disrupting your evening." She couldn't bring herself to sit as he'd asked. She felt like she was imposing. Why on Earth had Gravois sent her here? Did it have something to do with the similarity of their names?

Turstan studied her with furrowed brow, offering her no reassurance that she wasn't imposing. But his expression wasn't angry or put out. Rather, he reminded her of her father when he'd been up all night studying a difficult portfolio. She had an urge to offer the man a word of support. Odd, since they were near strangers.

"Forgive me," he said, wiping a long-fingered hand down his face. "Today has been—" He pressed his lips together and turned from her. He was a handsome man with age-appropriate lines on his face and a full head of graying hair, but something was off. He grabbed a high-backed chair from near the hearth and set it near the couch. "My daughter passed away this morning," he said, fingers gripping the chair.

That's what was off. He was grieving. It was deep sadness she saw on his face.

"I'm so sorry." Mentally, she cursed Gravois. Of all the places he could have sent her he chose a grieving family? "I'll go. I'll come back another time."

The offer came automatically even though she had nowhere to go. She couldn't go to the inn. Ruthven's men could still be there. Besides, she had no money.

Maybe if she left, Gravois's shop would appear again. He could put her up while she figured out some other way to help Wilhelm. Or maybe she could find her way back to Ewan's place. It was a full-day's ride away, but she remembered many of the landmarks they'd passed.

"Nonsense," Turstan said, lowering himself into the chair. With his cane, he tapped a leg of the couch. "Sit. Tell me where ye come from. What's an English lass doing in Inverness, and how did ye become the wife of the one man I'd hoped to see my own daughter wed to?"

She started to sit but froze mid-motion. He'd wanted to marry his daughter to Wilhelm?

Wilhelm had mentioned his parents setting him up before but that none of those matches had suited him. Had Lord Turstan's daughter been one of those noblewomen Wilhelm had met and decided not to pursue?

"Your own daughter—you mean—" Shoot. She'd dropped her accent. Recovering it, she obeyed and sat primly, as he'd asked her to twice now. "You know Wilhelm Murray? How?"

His eyes narrowed. He'd caught the slip.

She bit her lip. *Gravois, what am I supposed to do?*

She had an urge to tell this man everything. He felt like family, somehow, but that had to be her vulnerable position talking—and the fact they had similar surnames.

Mrs. Felts returned with two steins of foamy liquid.

"My thanks," Turstan said. "Go on upstairs and check on Chester, will you? And tell Mary we have a caller, but doona tell her the lass is the spitting image of Tarra."

"Too late for that, dear." A soft voice came from the parlor's entrance. A mature woman in a linen shift and silk robe stood hugging herself and staring at Connie.

She wanted to shrink to the size of an ant and crawl away.

"Oh, my," Mathilda said. "You shouldna be out of bed, milady. I'll help ye back upstairs."

The woman—Mary, Connie gathered—waved off Mathilda's help. "No, I believe I'll stay." She came toward the couch and sat beside Connie, never taking her gaze off her. Her lower lip trembled. She appeared thinner than was healthy.

"I'm so sorry for your loss," Connie said. Why couldn't she have Gravois's ability to disappear on a whim? How awful must it be for this woman to face a visitor who looked like the daughter she'd just lost—Tarra?

"Thank you, love. 'Twas a shock to us all when the pains struck her yesterday. We sent for the doctor, but he couldna be found until yester eve, and then the pains became worse, and—" She lifted a lacy handkerchief to stifle her sob.

Oh, so the doctor they'd referred to earlier was the one they'd summoned when Tarra became sick. And he still hadn't come? How tragic!

"Mary," Turstan said gently. He leaned forward in his chair to hold her hands. "Go back to bed."

"I'm fine. I'm fine."

Turstan emitted a resigned sigh. Glancing at Mathilda, who hovered with a worried expression, he motioned for her to leave them.

Still holding his wife's hands, Turstan said to Connie, "The pains grew worse and then the lass fell asleep. We took turns watching over her, but by morning, she'd gone terribly ashen and, well, she stopped breathing shortly after dawn."

"The doctor still hasna come," Mary said, dabbing at her eyes. "He sent a message that he'd be by after dark, but it's been dark for hours now, and still—" She pressed her lips together and shook her head, eyes wide and wounded. "Must be that rash of fevers we heard of to the north, do you think, Robert? Winter always brings the fevers and the ague, but she never felt fevered until near the end. What did ye say your name was?" Mary asked her.

"Constance," she answered, remembering her British accent.

She couldn't get over the heartbreaking situation this family was in the middle of. It sounded like Tarra had had an appendicitis attack or something like it. Intense pains, followed hours later by death. It reminded her that she was in a time when ambulances didn't come within minutes of a call.

Would the doctor have been able to do anything for the woman even if he'd made it in time? Would he have performed surgery on her here in this house? Was the woman's body still here? Why did she have a grisly urge to see this person she was supposed to look like?

Tears came to her eyes as she felt so sorry for this family and as she longed for Wilhelm's comforting embrace. She had let him become her point of reference, and now he was gone. She felt so lost.

"There, there, love." Mary wrapped an arm around her like her own mother would have.

Sadness and fear for Wilhelm swept over her and she found herself embracing the woman and burying her face in her neck. Mary wore her graying hair in a braided bun low on her neck, and she smelled like lavender and maternal affection.

Connie lost track of time. She didn't know how long she sobbed in the arms of the poor, grieving mother when a knock sounded at the front door.

"That'll be the doctor!" Chester's voice came from upstairs.

"Mrs. Felts!" Mary called.

Mathilda answered the door, and Connie remained on the couch while the Turstans spoke with the doctor and followed him upstairs. Sitting all alone on the couch, wrung out from crying, she hugged her backpack and drank her cup of warm ale.

Why am I here? She asked herself for what felt like the hundredth time. Images of Wilhelm battered and chained in a dungeon filled her head as she drifted to sleep on the Turstans' couch.

§

SOMEONE SHOOK CONNIE awake.

She started and sat up straight. She'd been slumped over on the couch in the Turstans' parlor, fast asleep. Lord Turstan eased himself into the nearby chair. He looked as weary as ever. It felt like the middle of the night.

"Doctor's gone," he said. "Forgive me for leaving you. 'Tis no way to treat a guest."

"Goodness, there's no apology needed. Honestly." She hugged herself, feeling chilly. Turstan must have added peat to the fire before waking her, because the flames leapt happily in the grate. She suspected the cold she felt ran deeper than the temperature of the room. It was a cold brought on from an atmosphere of grief and worry.

"Here," he said. "Move over to the fire. The lower floor is terribly drafty this time of year." He stood and moved his chair back to where it had been, next to a matching chair that he motioned to.

She joined him, glad for the warmth as she sat down. But her insides chilled even more when she saw her passport and the travel guide spread out on the hearth. Beside them, her backpack lay open and divested of its contents.

"I recognize you now," Turstan said, staring into the fire. "You're the supposed witch that maggot Ruthven intended to execute."

"I'm not a witch." The words came out shaky. Her heart pounded. Would Turstan try to hurt her? How stupid she'd been to fall asleep with her backpack right there for anyone to go through!

"I remember that night." He seemed not to have heard her. His gaze was still on the fire, trancelike. "I hadn't planned on attending his gathering. My wife's health has been poor. But I'd heard the Murray's son might be there. Mary and I had hoped for a match between Wilhelm and Contarra—Tarra, our daughter. I'd never met him, but I ken his da and have always admired the man.

"After Ruthven's dinner, I left the keep hoping to find the Murray lad and meet him, see if I liked him enough to suggest a meeting between him and Tarra. Then that debacle began." He curled his lip in disgust. "I noticed ye were naked and I looked away. It occurred to me ye looked like my girl, but her hair is darker, and I knew she was safe with her mother here at home. I couldna bring myself to remain and watch. I was taking my leave when I heard the commotion.

"At first, I didna ken who 'twas that mounted the dais, but I heard someone whisper his name. I respected his courage, but I figured he was a dead man taking on so many singlehandedly." He shook his head. "I didna have faith he would succeed, even though I'd heard tales of his strength in battle. I didna wish to see him cut down, so I continued my leave. 'Twas a disappointing night on many counts. I ken now, I underestimated him. You are proof that he survived. I should have done somat."

"I don't know what you could have done. If it had been me, I would have left as well."

He looked down his nose at her. "Cease this farce, lass. You're no' English."

"No. I'm not." She dropped the accent with a rush of embarrassment.

It was all or nothing now. She had to tell him everything and pray he took pity on her. He seemed to have respect for Wilhelm.

That was something. But she hated piling another problem on his plate after he'd just lost his daughter. If there was any other way, she would leave this family in peace.

I'm trusting you, Gravois.

"As you might have guessed, I'm not from any place you've ever heard of."

He glanced at her documents and nodded, looking too wrung out to register any more shocks. He was a man at the limit of what a person could handle.

She continued with a gentle voice. "Explorers are just now beginning to map the North American continent that will eventually become the United States of America and Canada." She plucked her driver's license from the hearth. "This—" She pointed to the numerals denoted by *DOB*. "Is the date of my birth. The eleventh month—November—on the seventh day in the year nineteen fifty-three. I'm from a state in the center of the continent. Illinois. The city I live in—lived in—is called Chicago."

She let Turstan take the little laminated card. He ran a finger over the date. For several minutes, he studied her license in silence. She had to remind herself to breathe.

"Is this why Ruthven accused you of witchcraft? These records?" He handed her license back and leaned forward, fingers steepled.

"I think so. And the fact I'd been wearing a piece of jewelry Ruthven called a hag stone. My sister—my twin sister, Leslie—the necklace was hers, but she put it on me and—you're going to think I'm completely nuts, but she made a wish. For my happiness and for me to find love. We were at Druid's Temple, and it had been the morning of the summer solstice. Nineteen eighty-one. Next thing I knew, I was here in the past—" She huffed with wry humor. "In the middle of a winter's night wearing a summer ensemble appropriate for my time. The men who found me— Ruthven's men, I assume—thought I was half-dressed."

The corner of Turstan's mouth turned up, and for an instant he reminded her of her father.

"I admit it had to have been magic to bring me here, but I'm not a witch. Neither is my sister or Aifric, the other woman Ruthven tried to burn."

"What's her story? The lass with child. Did she survive?"

She nodded and told Turstan what Ruthven had done to Aifric and how Wilhelm's cousin had married her after she delivered Anice.

"Thank the Lord she's alive. And her bairn." He leaned back again, deep in thought.

Could it be he actually believed her? Despite his commanding presence, he struck her as compassionate. Maybe Gravois had been onto something sending her here.

"So, the lad rescued you then decided that of all the candidates for marriage he's no doubt been presented in his twenty-five years, *you* would be the best partner for him?"

She bristled at the implication she might not be good marriage material because she wasn't of noble blood. Or was Turstan pointing out that she was literally nobody in this place and time?

"I believe in this day, you call it a love match," she said, lifting her chin. "Wilhelm's friend Ewan MacPherson drew up the contract just last night. I was concerned about having no legitimacy in this time, but Wilhelm insisted his clan would accept me. I wouldn't have agreed to his proposal if I thought I would hurt his reputation in any way. That's the last thing I want to do. He has brilliant ideas, and he's a good man. Scotland needs him, and I intend to support him in his political ambitions."

Turstan scrutinized her the way her father had the day she told him she wanted to be a mechanical engineer, with a mixture of incredulity and pride. "You've a spine of steel, my dear. And quite the astute mind. Good communicator." He sounded like he was ticking off checkmarks on a list.

She could see this man arguing for laws in parliament sessions. Might Wilhelm find a mentor in him? Would Wilhelm survive this mess to live his dream of serving his country with Turstan and his peers?

"This MacPherson." Turstan broke into her thoughts. "Did he send the marriage contract to Edinburgh as yet?"

"I'm not sure. I don't know how often he leaves his tower."

"Ah. He's a signalman?"

"Yes. His peel tower is a day's ride from here. It's where Wilhelm and I spent last night."

Turstan grinned. Years melted off his face as his eyes sparked with some idea he'd just had. "The sun will be up in a few hours. Between now and then, we've much to do. You may begin by tossing each of these items into the fire." He nodded at her documents and modern possessions—her travel guide, her Walkman, an emergency tampon, lip balm, her travel-sized first-aid kit.

"I can't! They're all I have of home."

"No. They're not." He leaned forward and tapped her temple. "You've got all you'll ever need from home up here. These—" He motioned at the papers scattered across the hearth. "Can only bring you harm. They serve no purpose here. Understand?"

She bit her lip. Goodness. He was right. In the wrong hands, her modern paraphernalia would condemn her, and Wilhelm by association.

"I'll leave you to it. I've messages to send." He leaned on his cane to rise and limped from the room.

Knowing what she had to do, she knelt in front of the fire. It was time to say goodbye to her past and commit herself fully to Wilhelm.

Maybe, like ripping off a Band-Aid, she should do it fast, dump everything into the fire without looking. But she couldn't. Turstan was right that she had her memories, but these things had become sentimental to her in the past week. Especially the Walkman.

Her throat tightened with sadness as she put on the headphones. During the ride, she and Wilhelm had listened to *52nd Street* three times. Afterward, she'd popped in the mix tape Leslie had given her upon her arrival in Inverness. She'd chosen it for its eclectic collection of songs, including hits from Kool and the Gang, The Pretenders, and Joan Jett. Connie had wanted to show Wilhelm the variety of music available in her time, but listening to Leslie's mix tape had served the dual purpose of filling Connie's mind with memories of her sister. It had been a bittersweet hour.

The mix tape was still in the Walk-man, and it was precisely what Connie wanted to listen to as she threw the remnants of her former life into the fire. Hitting rewind, she sent the tape back to the beginning of the side. When she hit play, she expected the familiar driving beat of Blondie's "Call Me," but instead she heard a male voice begin mid-sentence.

"…Canna believe my luck. That monk rode directly into our hands with a letter for the Murray from his pitiful excuse of a noble son."

Connie recognized that gloating, self-satisfied voice. It belonged to Ruthven. A wave of nausea gripped her stomach as the voice of the very man who'd arrested her husband filled her ears. She had an urge to rip off the headphones, but she resisted. Instinct told her to keep listening.

How his voice ended up on Leslie's mix tape, Connie couldn't imagine, but it had to have happened since Wilhelm's arrest. She and Wilhelm certainly would have noticed if Ruthven's voice had been on the tape when they'd listened to it during their ride.

Ruthven must have found Honesty and Justice outside the inn after arresting Wilhelm. Their cargo—and her backpack—would have been completely unprotected.

Heavens, she hoped the horses were all right.

Anger made her neck hot. How dare he take her and Wilhelm's horses and bags? What had he done with them? That little monkey must have slipped away with her backpack. Thank heaven! If Ruthven still had it, he would no doubt use it to strengthen his case against Wilhelm.

"Last thing Scotia needs.... Likes of him.... Stumbling blocks to justice at every opportunity." It sounded as if Ruthven didn't realize his words were being captured. The recording quality was poor, as if other items in her bag might have blocked the embedded microphone on the Walkman. Rustling noises swallowed up a word here and there, as if he was pawing through her bag and causing items to shift while he gloated.

Could he have accidentally pressed the play and record buttons while searching through her things? Or was this coincidence assisted by a meddling shopkeeper...or his little sidekick?

But never mind how it had happened. She focused on what Ruthven was saying. A tickling feeling in her stomach made her think this tape could be important.

"What we need is men of action.... Arena afraid to try crimes...iron fist.... Make men think twice about their thieving, raping ways."

Another man snorted and said something she couldn't make out.

Ruthven laughed. "Aye, well that's one o' the privileges of being a baron, is it not? That and serving justice as I see fit." His voice sank to depths of cruelty that caused a shiver to pass over her. "Make no mistake, I will find that witch. And when I do, ...suffer more than a simple burning. No one humiliates Jacob Ruthven and gets off...."

The other man spoke again. She made out the words, "Murray" and "woman," but otherwise, the speech was too distant to be understood.

Ruthven said, "She can't have gone far. Likely abandoned the Murray shite...went into the inn and... our waiting hands. Another bit of luck, I'd say."

There was a pause during which the other man said a word or two.

"I knew that witch's hag stone would bring me luck. At this rate, I doubt I shall ever take it off. Mayhap if I continue to wear it, I'll soon be commanding the Murray's holdings as my own."

Connie gasped. Ruthven wanted control of Dornoch. And he'd stolen Leslie's necklace. He'd condemned her to die in large part because she'd been found wearing that "hag stone". Now *he* wore it, claiming it brought him luck. What a dirty, rotten hypocrite!

Someone grabbed her shoulders from behind, making her scream.

She tore the headphones off.

"Lass, Lass? What fashes you?" It was only Turstan.

She willed her thumping heart to slow. "I think you need to hear this." She held out the headphones. "It might come in handy."

Chapter 28

SHE WAS GONE.

Ruthven's men had beaten Wilhelm until he could hardly breathe past the pain. They'd chained him in a pitch black dungeon without so much as a blanket for warmth. He'd been in and out of consciousness since they'd taken him off guard at the inn, their numbers so great he'd had no chance. Likely, he was on his way to the executioner's block. Mayhap, if Ruthven was feeling like nodding to the law, he would arrange a farce of a trial with this Bishop of Perthshire, but the outcome would be the same. Wilhelm's death.

And all he could think was: *She's gone.*

Earlier in the day—or had it been yesterday? He'd lost track of time—Constance told him of the shopkeeper her sister had met, the one who'd encouraged the wish responsible for sending her to him. Only hours later, while Ruthven's men carried him from the tavern below the inn, he watched Constance flee into a shop that had disappeared the moment the shopkeeper had closed the door behind her. At first, he thought he'd imagined it, but no. He knew what he'd seen: his Constant Rose returning to her time.

As he lay on his side taking shallow breaths, he wished he'd had a chance to bid her farewell. He wished he could turn back time to before entering the inn. He should have checked that no one inside might recognize him. He should have remained another day at Ewan's loving his wife and making certain she remembered him well.

So many regrets.

Constance would miss him. He wished he could take that pain for her. But at least she would be home, where her sister could comfort her. She wouldn't have to see him executed. 'Twas a blessing, even if watching her leave had hurt worse than the blows he'd received from Ruthven's men.

'Twas better this way. She would be safe in her own time. She would go on with her life as she'd fully intended to before he'd courted her.

His side was on fire from receiving the kicks of booted men, but worse was the unbearable ache of his heart at the thought of his wife going through life without him to care for her. His independent lady wouldn't appreciate that sentiment—she would insist she could care for herself in her own time. That strength of spirit was one of the thousands of things he loved about her.

He'd had less than a full day to prove his vows. Would she remember him a year from now, a decade, in her old age?

She is gone. And she's taken the best of me with her.

Including all his dreams for a Dornoch keep filled with their children.

Likely, now that he was captured, Ruthven would search in earnest for Terran. Thank the saints his cousin and his new family were safe with Anselm. At least Wilhelm could go to the guillotine kenning Dornoch was not without an heir.

A scraping sound at the door indicated someone was lifting the bar. One of Ruthven's men come to inflict more injury? Ruthven himself, come to taunt him? Certainly, no one would bring him food or drink, and he doubted Ruthven would hasten the execution. He would want Wilhelm to suffer a while first.

The cell had no window, making it impossible to tell whether he should count the passing of time in minutes or hours. Surely it could not have been days, unless he'd been unconscious more than he'd been awake. Considering the blows he'd taken to his head, he shouldn't rule out the possibility.

The scraping stopped and the door opened slowly, the creaking minimal. Why would Ruthven's men be stealing into his cell? He'd learned that Ruthven had been given charge over this wing of the citadel, which meant the baron had more than a bishop at his command. He'd known the man was dangerous. Here was the proof. He had allies in every corner of Scotia, including Inverness, the one place Wilhelm had hoped to find an impartial magistrate to clear his name.

"Will? You in here?" A whisper came from the blackness. The open door had let in the scantest amount of light. Not enough to see more than a dark shape. But Wilhelm didn't need light to ken that whisper.

"Terran?" He coughed and pain racked him. He'd wanted to ask what his cousin was doing here, but he couldn't muster the breath.

Terran rushed to him. "Easy, Will. Let's get you out of here." Terran's hands ran over him, looking for the chains.

"You. Shouldna. Be. Here." He coughed the words out, the pain making him see spots.

Terran shushed him. "Quiet. I only had to kill two men to get in here, but I suspect there's more."

Saints above. "No killing." It came out a growl. "Already. Enough. Trouble."

Terran found the chains. "Stay still. I donna wish to hack off your hands."

Terran used his axe to break the chains. The sound would bring Ruthven's other men, and Wilhelm was in no shape to fight.

"We must hurry. Dawn is coming. We must be clear of the citadel while it's still dark."

"Noooo." He moaned. This was all wrong. "More men," he forced out. "Least a dozen."

"What? I saw only three guards. One I knocked out, the others I had to fight."

"Ye must go. Dornoch. Canna spare. Us both."

"What's going on down there?" A voice echoed in the corridor.

Terran roughened his voice. "Giving the prisoner a fresh beating, that's all."

"Well, get your arse out here. There's been a breach."

The light was increasing as dawn approached. Wilhelm could make out Terran's wink.

Saints above. There would be no stopping his cousin. Soon they'd both be in custody. At least Wilhelm knew Constance would be all right. That gave him an idea. He ground his teeth against the pain as he said, "What will become of Aifric?"

Terran froze.

He took full advantage of his cousin's moment of doubt. "Go. Steal out. Find Kenrick."

If Terran insisted on saving Wilhelm, their best chance was to bring Kenrick in before Wilhelm went to the executioner's block."

"You imbecile!" A furious second voice sounded in the corridor. "There are no guards down there. Both men on watch are dead."

"Shite." Another voice. "Come on. Someone must be attempting a rescue." Footsteps approached.

Terran tensed. "I can take two," he said.

There was a scuffle in the corridor. "Doona be a fool," the first man said. "The baron says we keep a full guard against the Murray. He's a berserker." The last part was whispered with reverence.

So that's why Ruthven had lain in wait at the inn with so many men. He feared Wilhelm's strength as a warrior. Leave it to a worm who had never trained to credit a fine warrior with supernatural ability. He would have scoffed if he'd had the breath for it.

"Go rouse the others," the first guard said. "Hurry."

Wilhelm closed his eyes and prayed for a miracle.

§

"TWO FOR THE price of one. My thanks, lads, for making my work easy. If only you'd been so kind as to deliver the devil's whores to me as well. No matter. I shall find them and finish what I started."

Wilhelm had a perfect view of Ruthven's doeskin shoes as the baron stalked a circle around him and Terran, gloating, despite having done nothing to aid his men in their capture.

Though it had been ten to one in the citadel, Terran had put up a good fight. Unfortunately, Ruthven's men had subdued him within minutes. There was only so much one man could do against such a number, even if he outclassed each one man-to-man.

Now the twin blades of Dornoch lay trussed on a platform erected on the citadel's lawn. Wrists and ankles bound behind his back, Wilhelm felt like a fowl prepared for the spit even though 'twas the guillotine awaiting him and Terran.

Wanting an audience, Ruthven had called for the tower bells to be rung. As the morning dawned moist and cold, curious men, women, and children crowded onto the lawn. Would that one of them were Kenrick, but Kenrick wasn't coming. Nor was his father. His clan might not hear of their deaths for days to come. They would grieve bitterly, especially his mother and aunt.

Worst of all, his family would never meet his wife. Would they hear of the marriage? Besides himself, the only others with knowledge of it were Ewan, who had performed the rites, and Terran, with whom he'd had the chance to speak quietly while Ruthven commanded his men. Mayhap when Ewan heard of Wilhelm's death, he would send a message to his parents.

"At least you got to consummate your marriage, man," Terran whispered. He lay on his belly beside Wilhelm, surprisingly

299

unruffled considering the circumstances. "Would have been weeks before Aifric healed enough for bedsport. My biggest regret is not kenning her in a Biblical sense." His grin fell. "My wife. Christ, Will. Pray for her, will you, that she'll be all right. And bonny Anice."

"I shall, brother. I shall." He wished he could comfort his cousin more, but at that moment a robed man mounted the platform.

"Bishop of Perthshire, do ye suppose?" Terran said.

"No doubt."

Their supposition was confirmed when Ruthven introduced the bishop with far more flattery than was required.

The bishop read the charges against them, attempted murder of a clergyman and two counts of obstructing necessary purging by the church.

Bile rose in Wilhelm's throat. This, like the attempted burning of his wife and Aifric, was a perversion of justice. These all-too-common atrocities were what he'd wanted to fight against. Who would take up this mantle if not him?

"Is there anyone present with evidence to the contrary?" The bishop presented the crowd with an opportunity to protest the charges, somat Ruthven had failed to do at his gathering.

The question was more commonly asked at the trial rather than the execution, but Wilhelm supposed he should be glad for the concession to procedure. Of course, he wasn't well known in Inverness, so no one would speak up, but there was no reason Wilhelm couldn't speak on his own behalf. He did not expect to win over the bishop, especially since he could barely speak for the searing agony in his ribs, but he would be a worthless blight if he didn't make the attempt.

"I protest," he called out, his voice weaker than he wished.

Terran spoke up as well. "As do I. We doona deny instigating a skirmish, but we never touched Rat-bum's priest. And the women we saved from that bastard's pyres were innocent as wee lambs. I'd start a thousand fires to protect innocent wo—" He broke off with a grunt when Ruthven kicked him.

This got the crowd murmuring.

Wilhelm took a great breath, nearly blinding himself with pain, and prepared to demand a fair trial, but a voice ringing with authority came from the gathered onlookers.

"Release these men. Now."

He strained to see who the newcomer was, but the bishop's robes blocked his view.

"Who demands this?" asked the bishop.

"Magistrate Robert Turstan, that's who."

Och, Lord Turstan was the parliamentarian Wilhelm had wished to speak with at Ruthven's gathering. He'd been present on the night in question and would ken the truth: that Wilhelm and Terran had acted justly in defense of the women.

"This business doesna concern the Earl of Inverness," Ruthven said. "These men carried out their crimes in Perthshire. The bishop and I have it well in hand."

"It most certainly does concern me since you've chosen to carry out your execution in *my* city and since one of the accused is *my* son."

What?

He and Terran were in no way related to Lord Turstan. Could he mean—was Aifric his daughter? Did he mean Terran was his son by marriage? No. That couldn't be. Aifric had been from Perth and had told them her parents were poor cottars.

Still, his truth sense detected partial truth in Turstan's assertion.

Ruthven scoffed. "Nonsense. I ken this man's father." He kicked Wilhelm in the ribs. Pain like lightning crashed over him. "Who also happens to be this man's uncle—" A grunt from Terran filled the pause. "And I take as much umbrage to him as to these poor excuses for noble stock. I say again, this business doesna concern you."

"Leave them alone!" A feminine voice he knew well shouted the command. Constance!

Ignoring the discomfort, he craned his neck to lay eyes on her. There!

She wore a velvet gown the color of amethyst and a gray cloak lined with rabbit fur. Her hair was tied back from her face, but he could see it had been darkened somehow. Lord Turstan, a tall man with a cane, held her back from mounting the platform. Her eyes of every color were locked on Wilhelm. They flashed with anger and worry. The urge to comfort her was a living thing in his chest.

How was this possible? He'd seen her go with the shopkeeper. She'd disappeared like magic before his eyes.

Besides, she was not the daughter of a magistrate. She'd told him of her parents, who lived in a future time. He'd heard the truth in her words. He'd seen her documents.

"Easy, daughter," Turstan said, leading her by the elbow onto the platform. For the benefit of those gathered, he said, "Wilhelm Murray is the husband of my daughter, Contarra Turstan. He is my son by marriage."

"Lies!" Ruthven pointed a shaking finger, he said, "That woman isna his daughter. That's the witch! I recognize her! Seize her!"

Wilhelm's heart pounded. Apparently, Constance had found an ally in Lord Turstan. But what did she hope to accomplish by showing her face here?

"Turstan speaks true!" An aging gentleman came forward from the onlookers. "That's the earl's lass."

Wilhelm recognized the lie.

"I've known Tarra since she was a wee ane," a woman said.

Truth.

"That's her," the woman insisted, but Wilhelm sensed the lie. "You ought to be ashamed accusing an upstanding lass of witchcraft. Take your falsehoods back to Perth!"

Murmurs rose from the crowd.

Wilhelm's head was spinning as he tried to work out what was happening. Had Constance or Turstan somehow arranged for some of the onlookers to help them?

Och, all he wanted was to see his wife safe, but she was here in front of his enemy. She'd put herself directly in the path of danger. He was helpless to rescue her if the bishop called for her arrest. He'd been more at peace when he'd thought she returned to her familiar time.

"Any citizen here would vouch for the earl." Ruthven made a face like he'd tasted somat bitter. "This is Inverness, after all. Your Holiness, you must order her arrest. I doona ken Lord Turstan's purpose, but he's clearly protecting a charge of the devil.

"That woman is a witch and a spy. I witnessed the proof with my own eyes. Why, she attempted to control my men with a hag stone! Everyone kens that to wear such a stone is to align oneself with the devil. How shall our great Scotia remain pure if we fail to deal harshly with such evil?"

The onlookers shouted mixed messages. "Burn the witch!" "Go back to Perth, baron!"

'Twas difficult to determine whether the majority were for or against Ruthven, but it seemed every soul had an opinion. The lawn of the citadel buzzed like a riled hornet's nest. Even the children cheered, though for what they probably didn't even ken.

Turstan appealed to the crowd. "Lord Ruthven speaks true." He motioned to the baron as the crowd quieted. He'd gotten their attention by agreeing with his enemy. "He speaks true. Evil must be dealt with harshly, no?"

Several of those gathered shouted their agreements. The man had a talent for arguing before many. Would that Wilhelm could have met him under different circumstances. Perhaps he might have been a mentor.

"What's Turstan doing?" Terran asked. "What's your wife doing with him?"

He shook his head, wishing he knew the answer.

Turstan spoke into the weighty silence. "Those who embrace evil should be dealt with harshly," he repeated. "Especially those who put their faith in objects of demonic power. Do you nay agree, Your Holiness?"

"Say what you mean," the bishop growled.

"If you would be so kind, gentlemen—" Turstan motioned forward a pair of guards in plaids, who strode toward Ruthven.

The baron edged behind the bishop. "What's this about, Turstan?"

"I have it on good authority the very man who accuses women of witchcraft for wearing hag stones himself wears one. Men, inspect the baron for implements of demonism."

"Preposterous!" Ruthven sputtered, backing away.

When he trod close to where Wilhelm lay, he was sorely tempted to trip the man. But he refrained. He rather enjoyed seeing Ruthven retreating with panic in his eyes.

"Your Holiness, ye canna allow this! I refuse to be manhandled!"

"Yield to them," the bishop ordered.

Turstan's guards cornered Ruthven, each grabbing an arm. The bishop himself plucked at Ruthven's collar, treating the linen none too gently. He froze.

Wilhelm couldn't see the bishop's face, but Ruthven paled. "'Tis no' mine. This is the hag stone *that* witch was wearing." He jabbed a finger in Constance's direction. "I was keeping it out of the hands of those who would abuse its power."

The bishop tore somat from Ruthven's neck and tossed it away. The object skittered along the planks like a dead snake. When it came to rest, Wilhelm saw 'twas a stone the size of a doe's tail with a woven leather cord making it into a necklace. It landed at Constance's feet.

Wilhelm did not miss how her eyes lit with recognition when she saw it. *Och,* he prayed no one else had noticed.

But the moment was fleeting. She quickly returned her gaze to him. Their eyes locked, and the connection between them went taut as a bowstring. How he loved her! Dare he hope Turstan would succeed in whatever plot he and Constance had hatched? Dare he believe he might hold her again? Kiss her? Have a life with her?

"Furthermore, Your Holiness," Turstan continued as if denials weren't still falling from Ruthven's lips. "With all due respect, your area of oversight is Perthshire and her surrounding counties. As magistrate of Inverness-shire, I have full authority to carry out or stay executions within the county's borders."

Addressing the onlookers, he said, "It is my ruling that these two men are guilty of instigating, but with fair cause. The beatings they've received shall suffice as due punishment. They are to be released at once. It is also my pleasure to place Lord Jacob Ruthven, Baron of Perthshire, under arrest for failure to follow the laws proscribed by the crown regarding the administration of justice *and* for dealing in witchcraft. Officers, if you will."

Turstan's guards still held Ruthven by his arms. Though he struggled against them, they had little difficulty leading him away.

The bishop curled his lip, looking furious to have been dragged to Inverness for this. With a sweep of his robes, he stormed off the platform and disappeared into the crowd. Good riddance.

Constance broke free from Turstan and rushed toward Wilhelm and Terran, knife in hand. As sobs feathered from between her trembling lips, she sawed through his ropes first and then Terran's.

"Honestly, boys," she said in her English way, now touched with a bit of Scots. "I canna take you anywhere without you causing trouble."

When the ropes fell free, Wilhelm's joints screamed, but he ignored the pain and dragged his wife into his arms. Breathing in her scent, he assured himself she was truly his Constant Rose and not some illusion. When he ran his hands over her hair, his palms came away blackened.

"Saddle polish," she whispered in his ear. At his questioning look, she said, "'Tis a long story."

Terran picked her up and swirled her around, no worse for wear after the beating he'd taken. "I look forward to hearing it, lass. I knew ye were a loyal one. Didna I say to you, Will, that lass of yours is loyal?"

Wilhelm chuckled, but pain stole his breath.

Constance was there, supporting him as he sat on the platform.

While the spots cleared from his vision, he thought he saw, out of the corner of his eye, a wee monkey in trews leaping onto the platform and running off with the hag stone necklace. He blinked, wondering if he was seeing things, but when he glanced at Constance, he found her smiling and following the monkey with her eyes as it disappeared into the crowd.

"Let's get you back to my house, son." Lord Turstan stood over him, offering a hand.

Wilhelm clasped it. "My thanks, my lord."

"You'll call me Robert. I hear ye have a judicial act you're seeking support for. I'd like to hear about it while we break our fast."

With Terran under one arm, helping him walk, and Constance under the other, they followed Turstan to a waiting pony cart. All the aches of his beating couldna keep the grin from his face as he said to his wife, "You are my miracle, lass."

"I don't know if I believe in miracles," she replied, her natural speech low so only he could hear. "But I'm beginning to believe in magic."

Chapter 29

"WHAT ARE YE doing out here, lass?" Robert Turstan's voice came from a window above as Connie stood on the narrow ledge separating the backs of the row houses from a branch of the River Ness. "'Tis no place for a lady. Come inside. Mrs. Felt's got supper ready."

While Wilhelm and Terran slept the day away, beginning their recovery from Ruthven's cruel treatment, she'd ventured outdoors to inspect the sewage handling systems of these late medieval homes. Robert and Mary's home had a latrine on the second floor, a room with a shelf where a person could sit and relieve themselves into a pot.

Twice a day, Chester would pull a cord to empty the pot into a chute that would carry the waste directly into the river. The chute was like a chimney, constructed of mortared stone. She'd asked Chester what happened if it got clogged, and he'd said, "I capture some rats and send them down. They always find a way to come out the bottom."

Surprisingly, the river didn't smell of sewage. It ran north to south, and the Turstans lived in what she suspected was one of the nicer parts of the city in the north end. Neighborhoods farther south would see more pollution. She would have to ask Chester to take her tomorrow so she could see for herself how the less privileged residents of Inverness handled waste removal.

But for now, dusk was coming. She'd learned a great deal today, and she had more questions, but discovering answers would have to wait until morning light. "I'm coming," she called up to Robert, who smiled fondly at her before closing the shutters.

Sometimes, the earl looked utterly lost, as she would expect after losing his daughter only the day before. Other times, she would catch him smiling to himself. Remembering Tarra? Thinking about how he'd given Ruthven a very public taste of his own medicine? Once she had walked by Mary's bedroom on her way to check on Wilhelm and Terran, and heard Robert in there talking quietly with his wife.

He'd had an emotional couple of days, and she wasn't sure he'd slept much. Her worry for him was more than what she should feel for a stranger. He and Mary felt oddly like family. Might they be distant relatives?

Considering the possibility, she entered the dining room and stopped short at the sight of Mary. Usually too sick to be out of bed for long, she was currently sitting in a chair at one end of the table. Robert sat beside her, holding her hand.

He motioned to the seat across from him. "Sit," he said. The creases at his eyes made her feel welcome when she was tempted to feel like a burden.

This couple had no reason to be kind to her, but they'd done absolutely everything in their power to help her and Wilhelm. She owed them—and Gravois—heaps of thanks.

She went around the table to sit. The dining room was narrow and paneled with wood for an intimate feel. The simple sturdy furniture belied the wealth she'd learned the Turstans had. This home in Inverness was just one of Robert's holdings. He also had an estate outside the city and a row house similar to this one in Edinburgh.

"How are you feeling?" she asked Mary. She couldn't begin to guess what ailed the woman, but weakness and pain were evident in the lines on her face and her stiff movements.

"As well as God sees fit to make me," she said with a brave upturn of her lips.

Mathilda and another older woman in an apron served the first course, an oniony, creamy soup garnished with carrot shavings. Ale was served, and a pitcher of milk was set on the table. Robert poured milk for Mary, who didn't take any ale.

Connie drank the ale. It had been a crazy week. Alcohol was most welcome. Robert had seen her fed generously at lunch time, so she wasn't as ravenous as she had been, but she did start shoveling in the soup at a rate that was probably less than ladylike.

"How's your young man?" Mary asked.

"In pain," Connie answered. "But I think the only broken bones are his ribs." She'd learned from Chester, who had experience tending minor injuries, that as awful as Wilhelm looked, bruised and even bloodied in places, he wasn't bad off enough to need a doctor.

"Broken ribs will heal with tight binding," he'd told her, and he'd proceeded to wrap a folded sheet around Wilhelm until her husband had protested he could hardly breathe. *"That's the point,"* Chester had said. *"Got to keep those bones still so they can heal. Breathe from below."*

Wilhelm had obeyed and found that the bindings helped his pain quite a bit. Not to mention Mathilda had brought him wine spiked with henbane and rue, which Connie had learned helped with pain and preventing fevers. Wilhelm had gulped down the generous cup and fallen into a deep sleep soon after. Terran was in better shape and hadn't required any dressings, but he'd availed himself of the medicated wine and was sleeping as soundly as Wilhelm in another room.

"Difficult to see our loved ones hurting," Mary said, her eyes watery.

Connie gave her a sympathetic smile and said for what must have been the hundredth time, "I'm so sorry for your loss." The phrase was so inadequate, but all she had to offer.

The frail woman pulled herself up in her chair. "Robert and I will never forget Tarra, but we believe you were sent to us at this most difficult time for a reason. We both consider you our daughter, now, and—well, Robert, would you like to tell her?"

Robert set down his spoon. "We had a dowry set aside for Tarra. She willna be needing it where she is now."

"Bless her," Mary interrupted, crossing herself. "My grieving is lighter because I ken I'll be with her soon. But poor Robert..." She held out her hand, and her husband took it. Tears had sprung to Connie's eyes at the tenderness flowing between them.

Robert cleared his throat. "As I said, she willna need it. But you *do* have need of a dowry."

Connie had begun to protest, but he cut her off.

"Your husband is heir to a barony. Your lineage will be scrutinized as with any noble match. If no one kens where ye hail from, that'll reflect poorly on the lad."

She'd given some thought to her lack of legitimacy, but she hadn't considered it might hurt Wilhelm since he'd assured her his parents would approve a love match.

"'Twas not a decision we arrived at lightly," Robert had said. "But Mary and I have decided to give you Tarra's dowry and her place in our family. Only those in this household ken Tarra's gone—"

"And the doctor," Mary interrupted. "But he can be convinced not to file the death certificate with a bit of currency, I suspect. He's an auld friend of Robert's and kens better than to ask questions."

Connie balked, but Robert waved away her concern.

"Tarra was a loving lass," he said. "Generous of spirit and highly affectionate. She would want this."

"She would have liked you," Mary said.

"If you refuse, you'll insult me greatly," Robert said, and he picked up his spoon again and dug into his soup. The action had a feeling of finality about it.

She stared at him then at Mary, torn between objecting to this undeserved kindness and feeling deep relief. "I don't know what to say."

"I believe 'My thanks' would be appropriate." Robert quirked a grin at her, reminding her not for the first time of her father.

"My thanks," she said.

"You'll come down to visit us often," Mary said.

"And I'll be paying a visit or two to Dornoch. Doona think I have forgotten the contents of your 'travel guide.'"

She'd almost forgotten he'd been through her things—her now nonexistent things, since she'd taken Robert's advice and thrown it all, piece by piece, into the fire. She frowned, unsure what, specifically, he referred to. The page on Dornoch had been brief and hadn't shown any pictures, but it had mentioned a few points of interest that she'd been looking forward to talking with Wilhelm about, including a castle that would one day be owned by Andrew Carnegie. She couldn't remember anything that held obvious value to helping free Wilhelm.

"The marble mines," Robert said.

"What about them?" Connie had read a short two sentences about the ongoing mining of a greenish-yellow marble found in Dornoch and nowhere else in all of Europe. She'd assumed this unique marble was the reason Wilhelm's family seemed well-to-do and had been eager to see the workings of a late-medieval mine.

"They doona exist as yet."

She blinked in surprise.

"Dornoch is within the borders of Inverness-shire." Robert gestured with his spoon as he spoke. "I've visited once before and met Wilhelm's father. 'Twas years past. Your husband was at university at the time. Farm land, they have aplenty, and the land produces well enough to support the Murray as a clan and the seat of a barony. But they are nay a wealthy clan. At least not at the moment. They will become quite wealthy indeed once the mineral veins are discovered, which I have a feeling will be soon." He winked and helped himself to more soup.

§

CONNIE AWOKE TO the sensation of butterfly wings tickling her cheek. Opening her eyes, she found Wilhelm over her, caressing her face.

"I'll never tire of looking at your eyes, *mo luaidh.* They are like rocks of gold in a pool of spring water." Bruises covered his jaw, and his nose was broken. Both eyelids were swollen, one with a cut through his brow that Chester had stitched closed, but he was still the most beautiful thing she'd ever laid eyes on.

A burst of happiness puffed from her lungs. She had him back, not just from Ruthven but from the deep sleep that had claimed him for nearly two days while his body healed.

Wrapping her arms around his neck, she kissed him soundly. His chin bristled with stubble, and his lips were chapped. She didn't care. This was the first kiss they'd shared since before he'd entered the inn. It felt like a lifetime ago.

Goodness, it *was* a lifetime ago. She was another person now, at least as far as Scottish population records were concerned. She still felt strange about stepping into the role of the Turstans' deceased daughter, but that didn't stop her from being deeply grateful.

During these last days with Mary, she'd learned so much about Tarra she felt like she'd known her. In fact, the young woman reminded her of Leslie. Being Tarra helped her feel closer to the twin she would never see again.

She would never be able to thank the Turstans enough for all they'd done for her and Wilhelm.

"I thought I'd lost you, lass," Wilhelm said. "I thought you'd gone back to your time. I saw the shopkeeper, and then you disappeared. What happened? How did you come to be with Turstan?"

She sat up in bed and pressed him back into the covers, assaulting him with a new kiss, one that she took to heights of intimacy she wasn't sure his mending body could handle. A rising presence beneath the blankets suggested her fears were unfounded.

"I would never leave you," she asserted. "I *will* never leave you."

"Lass," he growled, bringing her in for more. She felt his love in every caress of his hand and nip of his lips.

The only thing that stopped her from tearing the blankets off him and giving him a bit of pleasure to take his mind off the pain was the growling of his stomach.

When she climbed out of bed, her body missed his. He was so hard and warm. Even wounded, he made her feel safe and protected, cherished in a way she'd never felt before. Wilhelm made her feel like a soft, beautiful woman. She would make him feel like the big, strapping man he was, but first, he needed some nutrition.

Wilhelm grabbed her wrist, tugging her back to him. "Where are ye going, lass? I'm only just beginning with you." He kissed the underside of her wrist, then her palm. Then he pulled her index finger into his mouth and sucked.

Her body responded to him instantly. "Let me bring you some breakfast," she said breathlessly. "I'll catch you up on the shopkeeper and Robert while you eat."

"And after?"

"After, darling, I'm going to make you forget each and every bruise on this magnificent body."

He hummed his approval as she left for the kitchen.

Mathilda had already fed Terran, who was up and about and eager to ride to Dornoch. He planned to tell Wilhelm's father about all that had happened and bring a few men back to the abbey to help transport Aifric and Anice safely home. When Connie invited him up to hear her story, he jumped at the chance. No longer did he act reserved with her. Instead, he was all smiles and jokes. Apparently saving his life had won him over.

"That answers all my questions, lass, except for one," Wilhelm said as he finished his marmalade-covered bread and ham with eggs. "How did you and Turstan ken Ruthven wore a hag stone?"

"You remember my Walkman?"

Wilhelm nodded, lips quirking in a smile.

"Wish I'd had a chance to listen to music from the future," Terran said. "Will says it pounds and screams and makes a body want to move."

During their captivity, Wilhelm had told Terran about Connie's history. He'd apologized for sharing her secret, but Connie insisted there was nothing to apologize for. She trusted Terran, but even more, she would never condemn Wilhelm for things he told his cousin when he'd assumed they were both about to die.

"Someday, I'll show you some moves," she promised Terran. "It turns out, the device can be useful for more than just entertainment. I'm not sure how it happened, and it might have involved a very intelligent little monkey, but somehow, the play and record buttons got pressed at the precise time Ruthven was crowing to his men about your capture. The tape recorded his voice right over my sister's mix.

"Apparently, after Ruthven arrested you, he found our horses and went through our things. He gloated about his extraordinary luck in finding the messenger you'd sent to Dornoch from the abbey, and how that luck led to his finding you at the inn. He told his men he'd stolen a hag stone from a witch, and his good luck was a result of wearing the stone. Then he wondered out loud if the stone would help him one day control your clan's holdings."

Wilhelm growled, and Terran cursed the baron, referring to him as Rat-bum.

She laughed. "Well, that's not going to happen now, stone or no stone, since the Walkman got it all. I never would have known if Robert hadn't encouraged me to throw all my possessions into the fire. He didn't want anyone to find them and accuse me of being a witch or a spy or anything else. I did it, but I had to listen to Leslie's tape one more time."

Wilhelm wrapped an arm around her. "I am sorry, lass. I ken that must have been difficult. But how fortunate that ye captured a confession of sorts."

"Wish you'd given me the Walkman," Terran said. "Would like to have listened to it with Aifric."

Connie smiled at the thought. "Well, it was on its last leg anyway. Last round of batteries, that is. With another hour of play, it would have been useless. But it lasted long enough for me to play the incriminating portion for Robert. You should have seen his face when he heard Ruthven's voice played back. The poor man has had more shocks in the last few days than anyone deserves. But he quickly rallied and realized the information could help you."

"And it did," Wilhelm said. "When I saw you at the citadel, I thought—" He huffed a chuckle. "I thought you'd either gone wode or you were a thespian of the most talented sort. You played the part of Turstan's daughter perfectly."

She sat taller on the bed. How unexpectedly nice it felt to be praised for her acting ability. Good thing she could pull off the part, because from now on, she would be considered a daughter of an earl, married off to the son of a baron, thus creating a partnership between their clans. It was like something out of a historical romance novel.

Her life had turned into a love story. She could practically hear Leslie's amused laughter ringing through the universe.

"The only part I'm interested in playing at the moment is that of your nurse," she said to Wilhelm. "I believe it's time for my patient's sponge bath."

"That'll be my cue to leave," Terran said. "See you at home, brother—and sister," he added with a crooked grin.

When they were alone, Wilhelm pulled her on top of him.

"Your ribs!"

"They're bound. I wish to hold you, lass."

She relaxed on him, feeling his lower abdomen move as he breathed with his diaphragm. He smelled of herbs, clean sweat, and her Wilhelm. His hands roamed over her back and head as if he needed to reassure himself they were really together again.

"I used to think love would hinder me," he said. "I doona ken why I thought this. My father is a better man for having my mother at his side. Mayhap, 'twas safer to suppose I had no room in my future for a bride rather than wonder at my lack of interest in the women I'd been presented."

She understood. There had probably been nothing wrong with those women. They'd most likely been beautiful and well matched to Wilhelm's position as an heir to a barony. Like Milt, they'd probably looked like perfect candidates on paper. But the heart didn't care about checklists and sensible choices. It seemed she wasn't the only one to have learned this lesson of late.

Wilhelm buried his nose in her hair and breathed her in. "I ken now why none of the others drew my eye, let alone my heart. My soul was waiting for you."

The sweetness of his words washed over her like the silkiest, most fragrant bath water.

Leslie used the term *soul mates* to describe two people perfectly suited to one another. Connie had learned to dismiss the notion since Leslie had bestowed the designation upon dozens of boys and men since their pre-teen years. Every one of them had broken her sister's heart. Connie had never understood the logic behind opening one's heart to another if doing so primed the heart for breaking.

She understood now.

Choosing to love wasn't a simple matter of weighing the potential benefits of a relationship against the possible risks. That was how she'd approached things with Milt. Rather, love—real, soul-deep love, looked outward.

Since coming to the past, she'd begun to understand that no amount of risk would stop her from loving Wilhelm. No matter what difficulties would come their way, she would do her best to support him. His goals held a higher place on her priority list than hers. His happiness meant the world to her even though she'd never much coveted happiness for herself.

Not even the possibility of a broken heart in the future would stop her from giving her all to him in the present.

Their present.

Her choice. Her Highlander.

She placed her hand over his heart. "You're my soul mate, too," she said without embarrassment or hesitation. "And my miracle."

Chapter 30

CONNIE STORMED DOWN the stairs and into the dining room of the Murray keep. "Where is my husband?" she demanded of Selia, one of the kitchen servants, who was cleaning up after breakfast.

"Good morn', milady," Selia said. "I saved you a wee bit." She hurried across the room to a covered platter. When she removed the cover to reveal a mound of scrambled eggs, several hunks of fish, and a half-loaf of bread with marmalade, Connie went weak in the knees. She nearly forgot her frustration that Wilhelm had let her sleep in. Again.

"Oh, bless you, Selia," she said grabbing the spoon and taking a scrumptious bite of creamy, parsley-garnished eggs. "Please accept my apology for greeting you with such an outburst." The English accent had become automatic. Often, she kept it up when she was alone with Wilhelm simply because she forgot she was doing it.

"Of course, milady." Selia grinned at Connie's abdomen. "I prefer your ire in the morn' to hearing you retching upstairs. Those days are past now, aye? Not much longer an' there'll be a new heir in the keep."

Connie took a long sip of tea before responding. "I'm half-way through and finally beginning to feel human again. Your excellent breakfasts help immensely."

Selia blushed. "'Tis a team effort," she said with a wink.

Connie had inadvertently introduced some modern lingo into the keep, and many of the staff enjoyed using her "queer phrases."

They tended to refrain around Wilhelm since any hint of her history made him uneasy, but after Connie's tea with Gravois, she suspected it would take more than a slip of the tongue to undo all that fate had orchestrated for them.

For the first time in her life, she had ambition and purpose and happiness. Leslie had known this was possible. She'd had faith that success in life could occur alongside joy and vast amounts of love.

"If you're looking for Wilhelm, he'll be out in the west pasture with Terran," Selia said. "What the two of them are on about, I've no idea, but they've a gentleman with them who stayed in one of the cottages yester eve. Seems to me they're making a course for some games." She brightened at this prospect.

Connie had quickly learned Wilhelm's parents were every bit as social as her parents had been. Parties, dinners, bonfires, horse races, and games were common occurrences in Dornoch. Connie's experience helping her mother plan fundraisers in Chicago had helped her feel like she had a place and a purpose in this new life. Not to mention Alpin and Gormlaith Murray were two of the warmest, most welcoming people she'd ever met.

Hunger sated, she trekked out of the keep to look for her husband. The scents of loam, freshly cut grass, and early-harvest apples made her chest swell with contentment. She'd loved living in the city, but no place around Chicago could hold a candle to her new home—Dornoch.

Arriving at the western pasture, she found Wilhelm unrolling a length of string between two pegs stuck in the earth. The stretch he was working on formed one section of a large network of squares made from the string. The entire grid approximated the size of a field hockey pitch.

Terran spotted her first and waved from where he stood with an unfamiliar man. They both seemed to be inspecting the grid.

She returned the wave, wondering how he was faring with Anice's teething. He looked rested enough. She would have to visit

Aifric later to make sure Terran was taking his share of midnight shifts with the precious six-month-old.

She'd been prepared to give Wilhelm a dressing down since he'd neglected to wake her when he rose at his characteristic pre-dawn time—again. But the sight of him in his great kilt with his sleeves rolled up to show off his muscular forearms spiked her lust and softened her annoyance.

There might be something to this berserker theory, because she'd never heard of anyone healing from broken ribs as quickly as Wilhelm had. Within two weeks of his arrest, he'd been back in the training yard with Terran. Now he was as fit and strong as ever, as evidenced by his stunning appearance and his mind blowing stamina in the bedroom.

Trying and failing to wipe the smile from her face, she went to Wilhelm. "You know, you're not the only one with things to do in the morning." He held out his arms to her, and she went into them without hesitation.

He stole her breath and nearly made her lose her train of thought when he surrounded her with his warrior's body and kissed her hard and long. He only stopped when Terran began catcalling.

"If she wasna already with child, that kiss might have done the job! Take it to the stables, like a respectable couple!"

"Aye," Wilhelm told her, ignoring his cousin. "You've verra important things to do, like resting and dining on a fine morning meal. Like dreaming about holding our bairn in your arms."

"It's impossible to stay mad at you." He was so darn romantic. They'd been married five months, and he still looked at her like he couldn't believe his luck in securing her love. She still got flutters in her stomach whenever he entered the room.

This is what Leslie had wanted for her. This was worth starting over in a new time, making new friends, adopting a new family.

"'Tis near impossible to leave you in bed in the morn' and not wake you in the brashest of ways." His smile conveyed naughty thoughts and tenderness all at once.

She didn't need truth sense to know he meant those words since he often *did* wake her with intimate caresses. On more than one occasion, they'd wound up staying in bed until midday. As a consequence, they would have to stay up late to get their various chores and duties done. Connie would never complain on those late nights. Wilhelm didn't seem to mind either, especially when the dark, quiet keep provided ample opportunities for lovemaking in interesting places.

She put her hands on her hips and looked over the grid to hide the blush that must have been evident from the heat in her cheeks. "Well, are you going to tell me about this mistress you left our bed for this morning?" She waved her arm over the grid.

Wilhelm had been sneaking around with Terran for months. From the excitement shining in his eyes, she suspected she was about to find out the reason.

"When we were in Inverness, Turstan told me about the book from your possessions. He'd read a passage about Dornoch."

"I remember."

"Close your eyes," Wilhelm said.

He must have a surprise for her. She'd learned that giving Wilhelm his way when he had that mischievous gleam in his eye always resulted in ample rewards. She obeyed, feeling utterly safe and cherished.

Something cool and smooth stroked down her cheek and across her lips.

"Can ye guess what this is?" her husband purred.

He stood so close their abdomens pressed together. She loved standing like this, aligned with him not just in purpose but also in body. Being near him felt so *right.*

"It's hard enough to be something quite unmentionable outside of our bedroom," she said, her cheeks growing even warmer.

Wilhelm groaned.

"But it's much too cool for that." She tapped a finger on her jaw." It's too smooth to be your work-roughened hand. Hmmm. Is it a polished stone of some kind?"

"My clever beauty. Open your eyes."

She did. And she gasped. On the palm of his hand, he held a brooch in the shape of a letter *C*. It was made of the most remarkable marble. It was a golden-greenish color with veins of sienna and rose. She'd never seen anything like it.

Wilhelm gathered her cloak-like shawl into a pleat just below the hollow of her throat and used the brooch to pin it in place. "The shape is for your name. The roses here and here—" He touched the two ends of the C where silver roses adorned the bracket, attaching the marble to the pin. "Are because you are my Constant Rose. The knotwork in the center represents life and love in perfect harmony. 'Tis a symbol of blessing." He kissed her forehead, the gesture itself feeling like he was bestowing a blessing on her.

Her eyes fluttered closed. She felt obscenely warm and loved. "It's beautiful. Thank you." He'd given her many gifts, but she'd never seen one made from a material like this. "Tell me about the marble." She bit her lip, suspecting he'd gotten the material from close by.

"We finally found it," he said, and she knew he was talking about the mineral vein Turstan had told Wilhelm ran beneath Dornoch. "Turstan was right. Your 'travel guide' was right." He lit up with happiness. "This will change everything. Consider it. A mine here in Dornoch. 'Twill bring my father clout he's never had before. Our judicial act will gain the attention it needs. And we shall become incredibly wealthy," he added with a disbelieving grin.

She remembered Gravois's assertion that Scotland needed Wilhelm. And her. She couldn't help feeling that this moment was the beginning of something big for them and for Wilhelm's clan. It made her feel proud to be a part of it.

"Congratulations," she said, fingering the precious gift he'd just given her. "I have a feeling this mine is going to be good not just for Dornoch but for all of Scotland. But, darling, what does a mine have to do with this?" She nodded at the grid.

"The keep is a fine structure. She has served our family well for generations. But we're short on rooms, lass, and our family is growing. I thought I might build you a castle in which to raise our children." He shrugged as if this was no big deal. "My father agreed. He and my mother will remain at the keep, but this will be our home and will one day become the seat of the barony."

Wilhelm was going to build Skibo Castle. Her travel guide had devoted a long paragraph to the structure that would one day house the wealthiest man in the world. It would be rebuilt and added onto over the years, but according to the guide, the site and some of the original structure would date back to late-medieval times. She'd wondered when the original castle would be built. How fascinating she'd get to *watch* it happen. She'd get to live in it.

History was unfolding before her eyes. How extraordinary! Especially since she had never discussed with Wilhelm the travel guide's mention of a castle in Dornoch.

Leslie, I wish you could see this. I wish you were here with me.

"That man with Terran is the master mason. We've been drawing plans for weeks and are finally ready to break ground. " Wilhelm nodded in the direction of Terran and the unfamiliar man. "The construction will take years and draw skilled workers and their families to Dornoch." His smile reached his eyes as he gazed down at her. "Our wee village is about to grow."

"Thanks to you," she said, overwhelmed with pride in her man and excitement for this enormous project. "I would love to see the plans—" She broke off, remembering that women in this time most likely didn't inspect castle plans. For Wilhelm's sake, she didn't want to do anything that might attract undue attention, no matter how badly she missed working with blueprints and plumbing designs. "I mean, I'm sure the castle will be amazing. I should probably get back to the keep. I'm helping your mother in the garden today."

She stepped away, but Wilhelm drew her back into his arms.

"I happen to ken of a woman who has vast experience with 'systems' for heating and handling water," he said. "I was hoping she might provide some guidance to help make our home one of the most modern and comfortable castles in Scotia. Do you suppose this woman would be amenable to inclusion on the 'design team'?"

Since Wilhelm had brought her home and introduced her to his family, she'd thrown herself into learning everything she could from Wilhelm's mother on how to be a productive woman in the fifteenth-century Highlands. From gardening and housekeeping practices to learning how to nurse hotheaded warriors to writing letters and documents using phrasings and spellings and penmanship of the time, there had been no end of work and education for Connie to apply herself to. But she missed engineering. There had been precious little problem solving for her to undertake, leaving a small snag in her happiness.

Wilhelm had just presented her an opportunity to become useful in a new and even more fulfilling way. This man knew her so well. He'd known she needed this.

"I think she would be honored," she said, holding back tears of joy.

Epilogue

WILHELM'S HAND SHOOK and he reached to take the bundle from his wife.

"Support his head—yes, just like that." Her bonny smile erased his worry over the agony he'd witnessed her suffer the last several hours.

No amount of weariness from being awake all night and helping her through the birth could temper his joy as his arms took the weight of his newborn son. Blue eyes blinked up at him from a perfect pink face, and he knew a different kind of love.

How many ways had he learned to love since his Constant Rose had come into his life? Thousands, it seemed. Yet here was one more. This kind hit him deep in the gut. It pulled on the connection he felt with his wife as if the three of them were now joined where there had previously been only two.

"He's heavier than I imagined," he said. "Sturdier."

"I'm sure he'll be a fine warrior like his father," Constance said. She smiled at him from her still-reddened face.

She looked completely drained of vigor but completely happy as well. Her beauty came in as many forms as did his love for her. After what she'd gone through to deliver their son, he had a new depth of respect for her strength and determination. This woman never ceased to amaze him.

"You can cuddle him, you know," she said. "He won't break."

"*Och,* I should ken as much." He'd held Anice many times, but there was somat different about holding his own child.

Feeling like the most blessed man in the world, he tightened his grip, bringing his son to his chest. It seemed natural to brush kisses over his smooth forehead. He smelled of the heather-scented powder he'd been covered in to protect his fragile skin against the wool blanket the midwife had wrapped him in.

Fine whitish hair dusted his skin, an interesting contrast to the dark hair on his head. He would take after his mother with her auburn locks, he guessed. The precious boy fit in his arms like the most welcome of burdens. 'Twas the sort of weight that brought balance and steadiness to a man, like a well-made axe.

"I love him already," he said. "I think I've loved him since the moment we realized he was inside you." Sitting on the bed, he leaned in to kiss his wife. This put their bairn safe between them.

He had a family. And in a year's time, they would have rooms fit for dwelling in the castle being constructed. The mines had brought wealth to their clan that had staggered Wilhelm. He'd not been prepared for the riches that had flowed into his father's coffers as demand for their rare marble soared. Even King James had ordered the stuff, enough to construct an entire hearth for a royal fireplace at Stirling.

All the wondrous changes in his life had come about because of his Constant Rose.

"I love him too," she said. "And I love you. Always, my darling."

"Always."

How incredible to ken his 'always' began in a future time he could scarcely imagine.

"I think we should name him Wilhelm," she said, making his chest swell with fatherly pride.

"Wilhelm Leslie," he said.

"Wilhelm Leslie," she repeated, her smile trembling. "Are you sure?"

"Aye, lass. We shall never forget where you came from. And all you sacrificed to be here with me." He positioned himself on the bed so they could recline together on the pillows, all three of them. "Come, love. Rest with me. When we wake, I'll fetch my parents. They'll want to meet their first grandson."

"*First* one?"

"Of course, lass. We'll have a castle to fill up."

"Wilhelm Murray, you're going to have to learn to take one thing at a time."

"Says the lass who had to be forced to her birthing bed because she had so many projects to finish before the bairn came."

"All right. Maybe we both have some things to learn."

"We'll learn our whole lives." He settled wee Wilhelm in the crook of his shoulder, where his mama could bury her nose against his soft cheek. "We'll do it together."

"We're going to have a lovely life together," she said, blinking up at him with drowsy eyes. "We're going to be successful. But more importantly, we're going to be happy."

His truth sense shivered within him. No truer words had ever been spoken.

A note from the author

Thanks so much for reading *Choosing the Highlander*. I hope you enjoyed it. This novel is the third in my Highland Wishes series, which begins with *Wishing for a Highlander*.

Whether positive or negative, reviews help an author immensely. Please consider leaving an honest review at Goodreads and/or your favorite retailer.

About Jessi Gage

USA Today Bestselling Author Jessi Gage is addicted to happy-ever-after endings. She counts herself blessed because she gets to live her own HEA with her husband and children in the Seattle area.

Jessi has the attention span of a gnat...unless there is a romance novel in her hands. In that case, you might need a bullhorn to get her to notice you. She writes what she loves to read: stories about love.

Do use the contact page on jessigage.com and drop her a line. There is no better motivation to finish her latest writing project than a note from a happy reader! While you're visiting her website, sign up for Jessi's newsletter so you never miss a new release.

Find Jessi at the following online haunts:

Website http://jessigage.com/
Blog http://jessigage.wordpress.com/
Facebook https://www.facebook.com/jessigageromance
Twitter https://twitter.com/jessigage

Made in the USA
Lexington, KY
05 June 2018